THE DAY THAT NEVER COMES

Book 2 of The Dublin Trilogy

CAIMH MCDONNELL

McFori Ink

Caimh McDonnell

Visit my website at WhiteHairedIrishman.com

First Printing: January 2017

ISBN: 978-0-9955075-2-4

OBEDIENTIA CIVIUM URBIS FELICITAS
"The obedience of the citizens produces a happy city"
The official motto of Dublin City

PROLOGUE

Detective Wilson took a long, deep breath and tried to steady himself. Even before his brain had begun to process the stench, his stomach had started to physically react and no amount of stiff upper lip was going to put the genie back in the bottle. His full Irish breakfast was being released back into the wild whether he liked it or not. He turned away and placed his right hand to his lips, his tongue already starting to spasm as his mouth filled with the warning wash of saliva. Now the 'what' of what was going to happen had been determined, the 'where' was everything. He tried to affect a determined but steady pace to exit the room the way he'd entered, like he was leaving to take an important call.

The body – what was left of it – was seated in the large open-plan lounge. The house had once featured in a six-page spread in a glossy magazine, back before its owner had become an embarrassment to the elite who produce, feature in and consume such publications. Much had been made of the marble fireplace that dominated the room. At obscene expense, it had been shipped over all in one piece from a villa in Tuscany. Its owner, himself a property developer, had

1

joked that it would have been cheaper just to move his whole house to Italy. It wasn't a terribly good joke but then the house's owner had enjoyed the kind of wealth that meant people laughed at your jokes regardless. He was now tied to a chair in front of that fireplace, his face twisted into a gruesome death-mask that, from a certain angle, could look like he was laughing, if all the other evidence had not so grimly excluded the possibility.

The headline in this morning's paper had been about twenty bus drivers winning the lottery. It had been a fun story. Tomorrow's wouldn't be.

As Wilson fled the room with as much casual haste as he could muster, he bumped into the shoulder of one of the incoming Technical Bureau geeks, and then pinballed against the wall. He raised his left hand in half-hearted apology and continued on, not daring to risk speech. Nowhere inside. It couldn't happen inside. He had to make it to the fresh air. Find somewhere discreet. It had been eight months since the incident in the Phoenix Park and three weeks since he'd last heard the nickname 'Chucker'; he was really hoping it had died a death. The next thirty seconds would almost certainly determine whether it had, or if he was to be lumbered with it for the rest of his Garda career.

In his own defence, he was hardly the only one affected. The poor cleaning lady who discovered the body had been damn near incoherent. Control had immediately dispatched a squad car and requested an ambulance with person-in-distress assistance training. The assumption had been that the woman would require sectioning under the Mental Health Act. All that could be made out from her screaming was the word 'Szatan' repeated over and over again. A translator brought in later on to listen to her 999 call in the hope it might provide a meaningful clue, would subsequently explain that it was the Polish word for Satan.

As Wilson exited the front door, he passed the familiar figure of Doctor Denise Devane, the state pathologist. She'd been called away from a more mundane 'seatbelts are for suckers' autopsy as a matter of urgency. Death had been her daily business for over seventeen years and if you'd have asked her yesterday, she'd have said that she had become able to view it from a clinical distance. Still, late tomorrow evening, when she finds herself alone in her office detailing the long list of physical abuses that had been visited upon the victim, she will close the blinds, sit in the visitor's chair and shed a silent tear at the base brutality of mankind. Nobody deserved all of that, not even him. She gave Wilson a concerned look as he passed because, while she was necessarily cold by nature, she knew enough to recognise trauma in the living as well as the dead.

Wilson spotted one of the distinctive Technical Bureau vans pulled up on the lawn to the left and made an instant decision. It was his best chance of cover amidst the hubbub. He made a beeline for it, ignoring the calls from Detective Sergeant Hickey trying to attract his attention. Like a sprinter leaning for the tape, he lunged the last few feet to get himself behind the van just in the nick of time. The contents of his stomach spewed forth. He'd made it.

Almost.

Detective Superintendent Susan Burns certainly knew how to make an impression. A striking woman, who even at forty-two – a remarkably young age to have reached such a senior rank – had an irrefutable air of authority. This, coupled with a spectacular success rate in dealing with gang violence in Limerick and the press's unerring knack of finding out about it, had led to her elevation to the role of head of the National Bureau of Criminal Investigation, a position she had so far held for all of one and a half days. She had the kind of piercing blue eyes that left a person with the unnerving feeling that she was focusing on a point three inches inside them, possibly where the soul was located. She was tall, with a rower's slender figure. Such women often avoided wearing heels so as not to make men feel uncomfortable. She wore them for precisely that reason. Also, clichéd as it may be, she had something of a weakness for shoes. They were her one indulgence in an otherwise strictly regimented existence. This last fact was of particular relevance to Detective Donnacha Wilson, or 'Chucker' as he would now be definitely known for the rest of his life. Two days ago Detective

3

Superintendent Susan Burns had bought a pair of Louboutins as a treat to herself on starting her new job. Two seconds ago Detective Wilson had thrown up on them.

The look on her face would stay with Wilson forever. It would, however, not be the memory that would cause him to wake up in a clinging cold sweat in the middle of the night. No. That would be another face; one frozen in unimaginable agony as its lidless eyes stared at the words scrawled on the wall above an obscenely expensive Tuscan fireplace. Tests would later confirm they had been written in the victim's own blood, almost certainly while he watched.

The words were simple.

This is the day that never comes.

CHAPTER ONE

THE PREVIOUS MONDAY – 4 JULY 2016

Paul slammed the office door, or at least he tried to. Due to its sagging hinges, it stuck on the worn carpet. He had to lift it up by the handle and then shoulder it into place to get it to close at all. When the lock finally clicked shut, he gave the bottom of the door a kick. This gave him a sore toe and none of the satisfaction that a slam would have provided.

He was in a foul mood. It'd been a disastrous morning at the end of a bad week that was putting the finishing touches to the worst month of his life. Eight months ago several people had tried to kill him; he was beginning to think it had been a terrible mistake not to have let them.

He'd just come back from a meeting with the Private Security Authority that had been nothing short of humiliating. Mr Bradshaw, the only human being left on the planet who still unironically wore a dickie bow, had been blessed with the most patronising manner imaginable. "So let me get this straight, Mr Mulchrone, you wish to set up a private investigation agency with your two partners, one of whom you've not spoken to in over a month and the other of whom you cannot currently locate?" Paul had gone for the 'honesty is the best policy' approach, thinking that his frankness would be appreciated. He had been dead wrong. He couldn't remember the last time he had been right about anything.

He'd tried ringing Brigit for about the thousandth time last night. Her phone had made a funny noise; he was 95% sure she had blocked his number. She'd not spoken to him in the forty-two days since 'the incident', although she had screamed at him a few times, just to make clear her position vis-à-vis him being the lowest scum on God's green earth. The fact that Paul entirely agreed with her assessment was now the only thing they had in common. Well that, and the fact that their names were both on the application forms they had submitted to the PSA back in their pre-incident happier days.

Bunny was a different story. Paul had left him about fifteen messages over the last three days, none of which he'd responded to in any way. The last time he'd seen him, Paul had gone to great lengths to impress upon Bunny the importance of the PSA meeting. Of the three of them, retired Detective Sergeant Bunny McGarry was the only one who had the required five years of relevant experience needed to qualify for a Private Investigator's Licence. He may not have been everyone's idea of what a Garda officer should be, and his superiors may have thrown a parade when they finally persuaded him to take early retirement, but nobody could deny that Bunny McGarry had been a copper and, in his own hyper-belligerent way, a very effective one.

Paul was vaguely aware that Bunny may have been struggling with the loss of the job that so defined him, but he was far too busy self-basting in his own misery to pay attention to someone else's. Besides, it wasn't like they had a particularly touchy-feely relationship. Prior to eight months ago they'd not spoken for fifteen years, until Bunny had decided to intervene in the whole 'people trying to kill him' situation. Whatever residual gratitude Paul felt about that had evaporated when Bunny had not shown up that morning and left him sitting there in the PSA's reception in his funeral suit, looking like an idiot.

The last time Paul had worn the suit was just over two months ago, when Brigit's granny had died and he'd accompanied her to the funeral over in Leitrim. She had introduced him to people as her boyfriend. He'd liked it. He'd never been a boyfriend before. The week after, when Paul had finally lost the use of his great-aunt Fidelma's house, he'd moved in with Brigit. Life had been good. As he sat in the PSA's foyer that morning, he'd found a sausage roll in the suit's inside pocket. He must have slipped it in there at the funeral buffet for the drive back to Dublin and then promptly forgotten all about it. In a fit of food-safety-standards-defying sentimentality, he'd eaten it, then sat there alone, with a broken heart and stomach cramps.

All of this was why he'd rolled into the offices of MCM Investigations in a particularly foul mood. Situated above the Oriental Palace Chinese restaurant, what their offices lacked in space, they made up for in dinginess. He thought of it as 'their' offices, but Bunny hardly ever put in an appearance and Brigit had never even been there. In his head, Paul had thought it might be funny to carry her across the threshold when they moved in. That thought now slapped him in the face every time he opened the door.

He had been sleeping there ever since Brigit had kicked him out. He couldn't afford to rent anywhere else. He was broke. This agency had been Brigit's big idea to solve all of their problems – Paul's lack of a job, Bunny's lack of a purpose and her own lack of a desire to change one more bedpan, nursing having lost its appeal. Besides, he didn't want to find somewhere else to stay. Although he didn't deserve it and he had no logical reason to believe it would happen, he was hoping against hope that she might take him back.

None of which was to say he was there alone. For the last two weeks he'd had company – Maggie. As he walked in, she was sitting in his chair behind his desk, calmly regarding him with those unreadable brown eyes. The room's only furniture was a bank of three desks pushed together, each with a chair behind it. She only sat on that chair because she knew it was his. She was constantly trying to assert her dominance in their relationship. When they went out, she dragged him from pillar to post, pointedly never going where he wanted to go. She was forever trying to engage him in a staring competition. Most of all, she did not like being left alone. This morning, she had elected to make that very clear by the most direct means available to her. She had shat in the middle of his desk.

"Ah for fuck's sake!" said Paul.

He had awoken two weeks ago in the middle of the night, to find Bunny McGarry standing over him, playing with his phone. "What the hell are you doing?"

"Setting your alarm," said Bunny, "you've got to get up to walk the dog."

"What – agh!"

Paul had turned to find Maggie's face inches from his, giving him a canine version of the bouncer stare. "What the hell is that?"

"Sweet mooning Mother Theresa, Paulie, you're a detective now. Four legs, waggly tail – work the clues. It's a dog, a German Shepherd to be exact."

"What's it doing here?"

"I got her for you."

"But — how am I going to take care of a dog? I don't know if you've noticed but I'm barely taking care of me."

"Exactly. You sit here alone all day looking like a eunuch at an orgy, it's not healthy. Bit of companionship will do you the world of good. She's ex-police too. Sure, she'll be an asset to the agency and all that."

Paul should have been suspicious as soon as Bunny had tried to justify his actions. Bunny never justified his actions. Along with the lazy eye, the ever-present sheepskin coat and the core belief that all of life's problems can be solved by walloping the right gobshite around the earhole, never justifying his actions was one of Bunny McGarry's defining characteristics.

Paul had leant across to pet Maggie and been greeted by a warning growl.

"Yeah, she's not big on being touched."

And with that, Bunny had belched a waft of whiskey, tossed Paul his phone back and left them alone in the office. Paul stared at Maggie. Maggie stared at Paul. Since that moment, their relationship had been a never-ending battle of wills. A battle that had now ended. She had taken the nuclear option.

"Right, that is it! That is absolutely it!" said Paul, pointing to the offending excrement presented in a surprisingly neat pile on his desk. "I know I said you eating my socks was it, but this, this right here – this – is absolutely definitely it. I don't care what Bunny says, you're out of here ye mad bitch—"

Paul was interrupted by the sound of a polite knock on the door. Both he and Maggie stared at the office door in silence, disbelieving their own ears. Paul quickly ran through the options in his head. It could be Mrs Wu, who owned the Oriental Palace restaurant below but she wasn't the polite knocking sort. She was the charge in, scream and then charge out again sort. It could of course be Bunny, but he had never politely knocked on anything in his life. Brigit – could it be Brigit? Paul's heart raced at the prospect but even as it did so, a voice of harsh reality sniggered at him from the back of his mind. Yeah, the woman you cheated on in a night of drunken stupidity is politely knocking on your door asking if you will come back to her. She's probably naked save for a decorative bow and a bottle of champers too. Idiot.

All of which left Paul inclined to dismiss as fanciful the concept of anyone having knocked on the office door at all, when someone knocked on the office door again. This time they followed it up with a 'hello?' too. It was in a soft, breathy, female voice. Paul and Maggie looked at each other, then at the door, then at the deposit she had left on his desk.

"Ehm, just a second," he said to the closed door.

Maggie disappeared under the table. She seemed to understand that she shouldn't be there and if Mrs Wu or anyone else found out, she might be forced to leave. Paul had a sneaking suspicion that the dog was way smarter than he was. That still left him the issue of her dirty protest to deal with. The bags he used when he took Maggie for a walk were in the pocket of his anorak, at the bottom of the stairs, at the far side of the breathy female voice. Leaving it on the table and trying to pass it off as an unusual office toy didn't seem practical. He couldn't see anything that he could use to cover it up – that left disposal as the only option. He moved over and, with difficulty, opened the window. The old wood of the frame was warped and screeched a tiny protest as he forced it up.

"Can I come in?" said the voice behind the door.

"Just a minute," responded Paul, looking around the room for something – anything – he could use to move the poo from point A to point anywhere that wasn't in the office. "I'm just finishing up a phone call."

"Yes," said the voice, "with the woman who ate your socks."

"Ehm... yeah." Paul's eyes fell onto the only book in the room. It was an omnibus collection of the stories of Philip Marlowe, Raymond Chandler's famous detective. Brigit had bought it for him as a present. She had called it his training manual in the art of being a private eye. Paul hadn't finished it, but he was pretty sure that at no point had Philip Marlowe had to get a poo out of his office. No, Marlowe had stuff happen like leggy blondes sashaying in to ask him to clear their name of murder. Paul picked the book up and then put it down again. He couldn't face using it as a pooper-scooper. Instead, he went to the waste paper basket and fished out the lad's mag he had bought himself in a moment of weakness. Using an Oriental Palace menu, he was then able to slide the turd onto the magazine. He was relieved to see it had a firm enough texture to all come in one piece. Clearly Maggie had enough fibre in her diet; she'd possibly obtained it from his socks.

"Are you still on the phone?" asked the voice.

"Yep," said Paul, as he made his way across the room with the slow deliberation normally only seen from members of the bomb disposal unit.

"Only you don't appear to be talking any more."

"I'm listening. She has a lot to say."

"About why she ate your socks?"

"Yeah, I mean... obviously, that was a metaphor."

"Obviously."

Paul had reached the open window. He looked down at the small car park behind the Oriental Palace where their delivery bikes sat. Two of the delivery guys were enjoying a cheeky fag before starting work. Dropping his payload there would be asking for trouble.

"Will this be much longer?"

"No."

Paul pulled back and gave the magazine his best forehand return of service. He watched in satisfaction as the doggie doodie sailed off into the distance, over the wall and into the alleyway full of storage garages beyond.

"What fucking spanner is throwing shite about?!"

Paul quickly ducked back inside and dropped the magazine and menu into the wastepaper basket. He surveyed the office. It looked like crap but at least it no longer contained any.

"Just a second."

He moved across to the door and opened it with a flourish. At least, he would have done but for those sagging hinges. Instead, it opened in a three-stage process, the third stage of which involved him walloping himself in the face with it. He rubbed his forehead and looked around the door. Standing on the far side was a leggy blonde. A smirk that sat somewhere between bemused and amused played across her full red lips.

"Don't mind if I do," she said, as she walked past him into the office.

Paul was a thoroughly modern man with thoroughly modern sensibilities. However, it was also a small office with only so many places to look. He couldn't help but notice some pertinent facts as she walked by. The red dress she wore was figure-hugging in a way that could be described as 'leaving little to the imagination', and yet Paul was pretty sure it was designed to dominate the imagination of any heterosexual male who came into contact with it for weeks after. He admonished himself on that outdated thought. It would, of course, do the same to lesbians. In fact, it might even push a few women who'd always been curious into signing up for full-time membership of that particular club. It was the kind of dress that could dramatically change lifestyles.

Paul tried to pull himself together as he struggled to close the door. "Please take a seat," he said, as he shoulder-charged it into submission. He turned to see that she already had. She was sitting behind the desk opposite his, and impatiently brushing non-existent dust off her perfectly-formed knee. Paul looked nervously around the office.

"Please forgive the mess; our cleaning lady is late."

She looked around her. "In the permanent sense?"

Paul smiled in lieu of an answer and sat down behind his desk. He tried to ignore the soft, warning growl that issued from beneath it. He'd forgotten that Maggie was there. He casually leaned back in his chair in an attempt to put as much air as possible between her and his nether region.

"So, Miss..." He left a gap that she did not fill. "What can I do for you?"

"I'd like to hire you."

"Really?" It dawned on Paul, as soon as he'd said it, that he probably shouldn't have sounded so utterly shocked by the concept. They did, after all, need to have some clients for the long-term viability of the business.

"Yes. You are the Rapunzel people, are you not?"

Indeed they were. That had been the case that had brought Brigit, Bunny and Paul together to work as an unlikely team. They had solved it, as far as Paul was concerned, almost as an accidental by-product of him trying to stay alive.

"That's us alright."

She leaned forward and lowered her voice slightly. "Can I ask, did your partner really throw his boss out of a window?"

Paul smiled nervously. "The press made an awful lot of stuff up about that case." They had, but not that bit. Bunny had indeed thrown the second highest ranked Garda in the country off a balcony. In Bunny's defence, he had been corrupt. It was also one of the many reasons why the Gardaí had been so keen for Bunny to consider other career options. It may have got results, but it set a dangerous precedent in terms of industrial relations.

"I should point out, we haven't technically got our private investigation licence yet so we can't technically take on any cases."

Why did he say that? The other problem with Bunny's disappearing act was that he was also supposed to stump up the money for the licence. Paul had eight days to find three grand or the PSA would automatically reject their licence application and MCM Investigations would be officially dead before it had even started. Paul looked across the desk. Could this be a sting operation by the PSA? He dismissed the notion. Their coffee had tasted recycled; they didn't have the kind of budget to run to that dress.

The woman in the red dress leaned back and smiled. "I'm not worried about technically. Lots of things are technically illegal in this country." It would dawn on Paul later that she didn't have a discernable accent. She spoke in a kind of purring, breathy voice that didn't exist in nature. It felt more like a crack team of female scientists had developed it to take advantage of the fact that all men are idiots.

"Where are your associates, by the way?"

"Mr McGarry is currently unavailable." It felt odd to refer to Bunny like that. He was only ever referred to as Bunny, DS McGarry or a vast array of other considerably less complimentary monikers. Never 'mister' though.

"And Miss... Conroy is it?"

"I cheated on her in a drunken one-night stand that has ruined my life and destroyed our relationship. Her position with regards to the agency is currently up in the air."

The room went silent after he said it. Paul had been dimly aware that he really wanted to talk about this with somebody. He had no idea how badly until he'd just blurted it out embarrassingly to a total stranger. Clearly his subconscious wasn't anywhere near done punishing him.

"Right," she said, hardly missing a beat. "Well, good luck with that. You should probably ask me about the case."

"What's the case?"

"I'd like you to follow a man called Jerome Hartigan."

Paul laughed. "That's the same name as that developer from the Skylark Three who are up in the High Court."

She looked back at him. She wasn't laughing.

"Is this a wind-up?"

The woman opened her handbag and casually dropped a wad of money onto the table. "I've got a thousand euros that says it isn't."

"But—"

"He's having an affair."

"Ah," said Paul, finally getting a grip on proceedings. "And you are the wronged woman?"

"No. I'm the woman who is doing wrong. He is having the affair with me."

Paul opened his mouth and then closed it again.

"Current legal proceedings notwithstanding, Jerome is a very wealthy man. I have put a lot of time and... let's call it 'effort' – into making sure I am in a position to acquire some of that. There has been a hiccup in that plan. I am concerned that he has betrayed me and started sleeping with his wife."

Paul left his mouth open this time.

She picked up the Philip Marlowe book from where it sat on the desk in front of her, and held it up. "As Raymond Chandler understood all too well, Mr Mulchrone, it's a dog-eat-dog world. Speaking of which; it seems to be my allotted role in this exchange to ask – is that a dog between your legs, or..."

Paul looked down. Maggie had apparently got bored and stuck her head out. He moved back and she silently exited from under the table. She hopped up onto the free chair and sat calmly staring at their guest. The woman looked back at her, for the first time looking as if she wasn't in total control of the situation.

"Does your dog bite?"

"She's not my dog."

"That's reassuring."

"So..."

"I want you to follow Jerome Hartigan for a week and tell me if he meets his wife, or any other woman."

"Because you're having an affair with him?"

"Yes." She gave him a mirthless smile. "Feel free to judge me all you want, but remind me; where is Miss Conroy again?"

"Touché."

"I'm an intelligent woman, Mr Mulchrone. Maybe I saw which way the odds were stacked and decided that, rather than spending my early twenties studying chemical engineering, I could use a little biology to my advantage instead. It's a man's world – I'm just playing the cards I've been dealt." She spread her arms out and gestured at herself, acknowledging her strong suit. "I just want you to find out if my opponent has somehow got the upper hand."

She stood and picked up the roll of notes from the table.

"One thousand euros now, another four if you find any evidence."

"But what if he is not having an affair?"

"Then I've paid you one thousand euros for a week's work, not too bad. This way, I'll know you really are trying your best."

"You don't have much faith in people, do you?"

"No, I've met them. Now, do you want the job or not?"

Paul took a deep breath. Like he had choices. "Yes."

"Good. I'll see you here in one week, at 8 pm, for your report. Please put the dog on a lead."

She tossed him the money and began walking towards the door. She grabbed the handle, kicked the door and opened it in one fluid motion, in a way that Paul would spend the rest of the night unsuccessfully trying to replicate.

"Wait!" said Paul.

She looked back over her shoulder at him.

"You've not told me your name."

She smiled. "No. No I haven't."

CHAPTER TWO

"All I'm saying," said Phil Nellis, "is we can't get into any car chases."

Paul took a deep breath and counted to five in his head. He was trying not to get annoyed; Phil was doing him a favour after all. He had started the journey by counting to ten but that had given Phil way too much time to say something even more annoying.

Four... five. "Don't worry, Phil. Like I said, we're not going to get into any car chases. We're just going to be following somebody. That's all."

"Because I told Auntie Lynn I was going for a drive in the country, and you know how she gets about her car."

Paul had a sneaking suspicion that Auntie Lynn would have let Phil go ram-raiding if it got him out of the house for a few hours. They weren't getting on very well at the minute. Phil Nellis was Paul's oldest friend, although that wasn't really saying much. They'd both been in foster homes together until Lynn and her dear departed husband had taken Phil in. He wasn't actually her nephew as he was a second cousin, but that was just a technicality. What was a reality was that Lynn's 'nephew' was now thirty and living in her spare room. What was it they said about no good deed going unpunished?

Paul spotted a parking space. "There's one!"

Phil slowed the car down even further than the 14 mph it was averaging, and gave the space a sceptical look. He shook his head. "Too small."

It was large enough to fit them comfortably, even if they had been towing a caravan, and they weren't. They'd been driving up and down the Phoenix Park inspecting perfectly good parking spaces for twenty minutes now. A car behind them understandably honked.

Paul heard a growling noise from the back seat. He turned to see Maggie with her head out the window, looking back in the direction of the honker.

"What's that bloody dog up to?" said Phil.

"She's fine. You just worry about finding a space."

"I don't even know why you brought her."

"Because," said Paul, "she has made her feelings on being left alone in the office very clear."

"Well, if she does anything to this car—"

"Relax," said Paul. "She's not going to do anything." He had absolutely no confidence that this wasn't an out-and-out lie. Maggie had spent the journey from the office with her head out the window, but not in the normal 'dog-loving-life' way. She had instead been staring at passers-by, giving the steely-eyed look you'd normally only get from a new inmate on a maximum security wing. It was like she was looking for the hardest nut to take down to establish her dominance of life. This had led to at least one cyclist at a traffic light nearly ruining his Lycra shorts.

The plan had been simple enough. Paul had quickly realised yesterday, as soon as 'the client' had left his office, that he had absolutely no idea how to follow somebody. More importantly, he had no idea how to first find somebody to then try and figure out how to follow them. Then he realised that his target, Jerome Hartigan, was going to be in the Central Criminal Court all day; the papers were full of little else. All Paul had to do was follow him from there. How hard could that be? On a pushbike, he reasoned, pretty hard. He had asked Phil to be his driver for the day, fifty euros, no questions asked. It wasn't that confidentiality was massively important, he just really didn't want to go through the ordeal of answering Phil's questions.

Phil possessed an odd kind of relentlessly logical stupidity. For example, he knew his Auntie Lynn really didn't like it when he repositioned the mirrors in her car. His solution to this was to move nothing, and instead try to squeeze himself into a driver's seat that was set up for a petite woman of five foot two. Phil was six foot seven, almost all of it made up of impractically long limbs. His knees were currently at near head height, and he kept inadvertently turning the windscreen wipers on.

A bus that had been dropping off a load of schoolkids on a trip to Dublin Zoo indicated to pull out. Even Phil could squeeze it in there.

"Woah, woah, woah," said the barman as soon as they entered. "No dogs allowed. There's a sign."

Paul stopped and looked down at Maggie. "The sign says 'except for guide dogs'. She's a guide dog."

"Oh yeah, and which one of you two is supposed to be blind?"

"Neither of us," said Phil, "but the sign says guide dogs are welcome. It doesn't say they have to be with a blind person."

"What?" A look of angry confusion spread across the barman's rotund face, "but... but a guide dog without a blind person is just a dog."

"Oh really?" said Phil, "then why would you put a sign up saying that guide dogs are welcome if, by your definition, a guide dog isn't a guide dog unless it has someone with them who is physically unable to read the sign? The sign should just say 'No Dogs'.'"

Paul looked at Phil, impressed despite himself. The barman wore the exasperated expression common to anyone who has just come into contact with the Nellis logic. "Two pints of Guinness and a pint of water please," said Paul, trying to press home their advantage before the barman could work out a counter-argument on the back of a beer mat.

Paul paid for the drinks and then brought them over to the table by the window. Phil sat there, nervously looking down at Maggie. She panted up at him cheerfully. It would appear that Maggie liked Phil, which was odd, as Paul was all too well aware that nobody liked Phil straight away. He was an acquired taste, like sado-masochistic sex or jazz.

Their seats provided them with an excellent view of the front of the Central Criminal Courts just down from the Phoenix Park gates. It was a fairly new building shaped like a cake tin, all shiny metal and lots and lots of glass. A window cleaner's dream come true.

"I thought you were off the booze?" asked Phil.

"I am," said Paul. He hadn't drunk a drop since 'the incident' – partly because he blamed it for its part in his downfall, and partly because it was just one of the ways he was punishing himself.

"So what are ye..." Phil looked horrified as Paul glanced around before surreptitiously placing one of the pints of stout under the table. "Ah no..."

"Believe me, just getting her one is better for everybody." Paul had discovered this on their only other trip to the pub. It had resulted in him getting banned from the four pubs nearest the office. Word had got around fast.

Phil shook his head as enthusiastic lapping noises came from under the table. "That cannot be hygienic," he said.

"You should have seen what happened when I didn't get her a pint," said Paul, "that really was unhygienic." Paul had originally thought Maggie would be like Hooch, the dog from the Tom Hanks classic, *Turner and Hooch*. He was coming to terms with the fact she was a lot more like Begbie from *Trainspotting*.

Phil lifted his pint and gave Paul a knowing look over it. "So, how are things with Brigit?"

"Oh tremendous, thanks for asking. I mean, she won't talk to me or anything but the last time she actually answered the phone, her choice of swear words was noticeably warmer."

Phil took a sip of his pint and shook his head sadly. "Ahh, the course of young love never runs smooth."

Paul braced himself because he knew what was coming.

"I've been discussing it with Da Xin," said Phil, "and she reckons you should try a big romantic gesture."

Four... five...

"Does she?" said Paul, using every ounce of his self-restraint not to sound sarcastic. Da Xin was Phil's imaginary former girlfriend, now imaginary fiancée. They had 'met' nine months ago while playing some online game and one thing had led to another, at least as far as Phil was concerned. As far as Paul was concerned, one thing couldn't lead anywhere until they'd actually been in the same room. They'd been 'engaged' for almost two months now. It had been his 'stag do' that Paul had been on when what happened, happened. True, you normally only had a stag do when you'd set a date but then, you normally had a stag do when your fiancée wasn't so clearly a con too. The so-called stag do had actually been just the two of them, an idea concocted by Phil's Auntie Lynn. She had been understandably horrified that Phil had now expanded his gullibility to encompass whole other continents. Paul had been supposed to talk him out of it. It had not gone well on any level.

"Yeah," said Phil. "Da Xin knows a lot about stuff like that."

Phil had a defiant look that Paul knew all too well. Like he was daring Paul to doubt her existence. It was heartbreaking to look at.

They'd not spoken over Skype or anything like that as the Chinese government blocked it in the region Da Xin was from. Her father was a dissident politician; the whole family was under house arrest. They were very wealthy but their assets were temporarily frozen, which was why Phil had to get them plane tickets. In short, Phil was doing the romantic version of helping a Nigerian prince by temporarily allowing him to put money in his account. It was like watching a painfully slow car crash and nothing could be done to convince Phil to step on the brakes. Paul decided to change the subject. The last thing he needed was Phil storming off again.

"So," said Phil, "how come Bunny isn't helping you with this?"

"Ah that drunken bumpkin has disappeared off the face of the planet. Hasn't answered his phone in days."

"Do you think he's alright?"

"Course he's alright. He's Bunny. He's just drunk in a ditch somewhere, having a whale of a time. Leaving me to do all the bleedin' work." Paul had become used to this behaviour from Bunny. For the last two months Bunny had appeared and disappeared, seemingly at random. At one point, three weeks ago, the dial tone when he rang Bunny's phone had indicated he was out of the country. Paul still didn't know where he'd been. When he'd asked, Bunny had just responded that he'd been topping up his tan.

Paul looked out the window. "There's a lot of press over there, isn't there?" He indicated the court steps across the street, where several photographers and two film crews were sitting around, looking bored.

"Yeah," said Phil. "So who is this guy you're supposed to be following?"

Paul lowered his voice. "He's one of the Skylark Three." He had hoped not to have to go into this, but if the alternative was comparing love lives, all bets were off.

"Are they like a band or something?" asked Phil.

Paul shouldn't have been surprised that Phil wasn't keeping up-to-date with current affairs, but he was. The Skylark trial was everywhere, dominating every front page and leading every news report. He would have assumed it was impossible to avoid.

Skylark had been the biggest development project in the history of the state. Paschal Maloney, Craig Blake and Jerome Hartigan, the three biggest stars in the crowded firmament of Irish developers had partnered up. A brown field site, formerly the old Gettigan's printing factory and warehouses, was going to be transformed. The three amigos had been on the chat shows, laughing it up; 'Awh shucks, no need to be calling us the dream team. We're putting our personal rivalries aside, just trying to do what we can for the country.' Property developers as rock stars. A whopping 524 high-spec two- and three-bedroom apartments, perfect for the first time buyer looking to start a family; a retirement village with another 186 homes offering unsurpassed assistance for the elderly; 88 luxury apartments at the very top end; not to mention the multiplex, supermarket, restaurants and so on and so on. It was going to be the be-all and end-all; the jewel in the Celtic Tiger's crown. Celebs were queuing up to put a deposit down on the fancy pads and there had been fist fights, actual fist fights, when the first tranche of as-yet-unbuilt apartments for the plebs had become available to buy.

Then the arse had fallen out of the economy. Skylark was fine though; people had put in so much money up front, how could it fail? Investors were reassured, bank loans renegotiated, politicians stepping in to make sure 'sanity prevailed'. Then, the first batch of happy buyers had begun moving in to Skylark 1 to discover a property with more than a few flaws. 'Teething problems' the spokesman had said, the three amigos having become a little camera-shy by this point. Nothing to worry about though, all in hand. Sure, nothing worked on the first day at Disneyland either! The other thing that they had in common was the massive part a mouse would play in their future.

The fire would eventually be traced back to wiring that had been incorrectly sealed, allowing a mouse to nibble through it. It was a miracle nobody had died. By sheer chance, a firefighter had lived next door to the apartment where the blaze had started and she had managed to contain it long enough for the building to be evacuated. Initially, the flat's owners had been accused of disabling the fire alarm but once the fire inspectors started looking, they were shocked by what they found. They discovered that less than half of the fire alarms in the whole complex had been installed correctly. Under the rather handy self-certifying system that some 'developer-friendly' politicians had put in place, nobody double-checked anybody else's work. Skylark 1 was designated as being unsafe and all the residents forced to move out. Questions were asked in the Dáil. Inspections were carried out, then more inspections, then some arguments, then a whole lot of arguments. Along with the wiring, the 'state-of-the-art' insulation was discovered to have been banned in Sweden, for very good reasons. Then, after six months, somebody noticed the subsidence. The building was condemned for being cheaper to rebuild than fix. Everybody blamed everybody else, but the three amigos assured all parties that they would not rest until everyone received the dream home they had been promised.

They said that in a statement released on a Tuesday morning. They'd filed for bankruptcy by Wednesday lunchtime. All three amigos had tried to file separately for bankruptcy in Britain where the rules were a lot more lenient but by this point, the authorities had copped on to that one. Meanwhile, most of the vast Skylark complex remained half-built and abandoned; an already crumbling monument to excess. The massive billboard you could still see from the motorway had been altered to read 'If you lived here, you'd be fucked by now'.

Amazingly, up until this point in the proceedings, nobody had done anything actually illegal. Some building codes hadn't been followed, but that was merely a slap on the wrist with a fine. It was only when the receivers moved in that the real fun started. That was when the great big black hole in the middle of the Skylark accounts had been found; 148 million euros, according to most reports. The three amigos were horrified, the investors were horrified, the banks were horrified, the government were horrified. The Skylark financial controller unhelpfully threw himself off a bridge while out walking the dog. The dog was, reportedly, horrified.

People had demanded answers, and politicians, keen to distance themselves from the development they suddenly always knew was a disaster waiting to happen, were mad keen that somebody else give them. The Director of Public Prosecutions duly announced that the three amigos were to face criminal charges for fraud. Finally, said the people of Ireland, somebody would pay for the suffering they'd caused.

Four... five... "No, Phil," said Paul, "the Skylark Three are not a band. Do you not read any news?"

"I do," said Phil, looking hurt, "but I've mainly been focusing on the news in the Xinjiang province, as if there's a change in leadership that might mean—"

"Uh-huh" said Paul, not listening. "Something is wrong."

"Well, the oppression of the—"

"Not that," said Paul, "this!" He pointed out of the window where the photographers and camera crews had suddenly been whipped into a frenzy of activity. "I looked it up. They expected the trial to go on until 4 pm today. It only started forty-five minutes ago. Shit, get the car."

Phil looked horrified. "But I've not finished my pint."

"Go! Now!"

"All right! Keep your hair on."

Phil knocked his chair over and stumbled into another table on his way out of the door.

"Watch where you're going, ye lanky string of piss!" said the barman, who was probably not in the running for a golden service award. Paul grabbed Maggie's lead and headed for the door. Luckily, she had finished her pint.

"What's going on?"

The photographer pushed Paul aside roughly and ignored the question. Uniformed police were now trying to belatedly put a cordon in place to hold back the crowds. More and more journalists and photographers appeared to be arriving all the time. An RTÉ van had just pulled up and disgorged a rather flustered-looking whats-her-name who used to do the news in Irish. Along with all of the press, members of the public were now crowding around. In Dublin, nothing draws a crowd like a crowd.

A couple of young guys in suits shrugged at Paul's questioning. "Dunno, fella, but it must be something though, hey?"

Paul kept making his way through the crowd who were all jostling each other for position, Maggie nimbly weaving around behind him. They pushed past punters with mobile phones at the ready, not knowing what was about to happen but hoping to capture it in case it could become a YouTube sensation.

Then Paul hit a strange air pocket of space and silence amidst the chaos, and he stopped. He turned to look behind him. The man's name was Dessie O'Connell. His picture had been in all the papers at some point. He'd even been on the chat shows, telling his story. Telling the world about the woman he'd loved. He was in his seventies. When anyone met him, it was the vivid brightness of the old man's green eyes that stood out amidst the creases and worry lines of his weather-beaten face. It was like an unexpected flash of colour in a black and white photograph. He held a framed picture of his wife in his hands, smiling back at the world from a happier time.

They had sunk all of their savings into Skylark, on the promise of a safe and cared-for future in that state-of-the-art retirement village. He had some problems with rheumatism, or so Paul thought he remembered. Yes, you could see it in the awkward way he gripped the picture frame to his chest. His wife had suffered from MS. When Skylark had fallen apart, so had she.

Paul had seen Dessie O'Connell read the note out on television. How she was sorry to leave him, but she was terrified about the future. How she didn't want to be a burden. How maybe there'd be enough money if it was just him. He had cried softly as he read it. Then the host had asked him in a voice barely above a whisper, why he stood outside the court every day holding up her picture? To remember, he'd said. What struck Paul as he'd watched wasn't the anger; the man didn't seem to have any in him. He knew nothing would happen, he said. There would be no justice. He just had to remember her every day, and if he did, he wanted them to have to as well. As Paul met his eyes, he wished he could recall her name.

"That's a nice dog you've got there," said the old man, bending down to pat Maggie on the head. He stood up straight again with a small wince of pain. "It's a mistrial," he said, without emotion. "One of the nice girls who brings me tea and sandwiches came out and told me."

"Oh," said Paul.

"They're not supposed to help me out, but they do. They've been very kind. They even snuck me in to use the toilet a couple of times. People are very good in their way, mostly."

Paul nodded.

"They won't have to do that any more, I guess. Now it's over." He looked down at the ground, as if this thought was just occurring to him for the first time. Like the rest of his life was a long empty road that had just opened before him, and he was too tired to walk any further.

"If there's a mistrial, they'll probably start again, won't they?" said Paul.

Dessie O'Connell laughed a soft humourless laugh. "Ah, what would be the point? They said something about how they'd discovered that one of the jurors was related to somebody who'd lost all their money in Skylark. Sure, you'd be hard pressed to find a dozen people who didn't know somebody."

He nodded over at the folding chair, golf umbrella and blanket that indicated where his station had been for the last few months. They were well over to the left of the main entrance, down by the railings. "There were a lot more of us in the first couple of weeks," he said. "Protesters and that, I mean. There was a nice family with two kids and a lot of other people, but they all gradually disappeared. Most people have lives to be getting on with, I suppose."

Then, any further conversation was swept away in a torrent of camera flashes and shouted questions. Hartigan, Blake and Maloney had appeared at the top of the steps, surrounded by lawyers and a couple of heavies in suits. Craig Blake wore a finely-tailored charcoal suit. His face was round and chinless, with one of those slightly upturned noses that hinted at both breeding and inbreeding. His expression was one of distaste, as if all of this was a great inconvenience, distracting him from something far more important. Hartigan, on the other hand, while about the same age as Blake, was all chiselled features and natural grace. He wore the white shirt and tieless black suit combination that Paul realised he'd seen him wearing in every picture. His hair was brushed back and slightly tousled, with the suggestion of a widow's peak that hinted at a no-expense-spared battle against male pattern baldness; one he was winning. In contrast to the other two, Maloney looked rumpled and edgy in a suit that seemed slightly too big for him, the sun bouncing off his irredeemably bald pate. His small eyes peered out apprehensively from round, frameless glasses as his hands clasped at each other nervously. He reminded Paul of Penfold from *Danger Mouse*, minus the cuddliness. He looked the type to stand in the background, cheering the big boys on while they stole your lunch money.

Hartigan strode down the steps confidently, and raised his hands for silence. He left a few seconds to let the undignified scrum of journalists holding out mics and digital recorders settle down.

"Thank you for coming. My colleagues and I are greatly relieved that this politically-motivated show trial has finally come to an end. We would like to thank Judge Green for ensuring that justice has indeed been served. As much as anyone, we are bitterly disappointed with what the dream that was Skylark has become. We will not rest until justice, real justice, is served for the good of all those involved, but looking for easy scapegoats is not the answer. Trying to punish those who fell victim to an economic downturn of an unprecedented scale helps no one. This country was built by those who took chances, punishing those who do so sets a dangerous precedent for future generations. Rest assured, we remain committed to getting to the bottom of what has gone on here, and we will do everything in our power to make it right. As always, we thank you for your support."

And with that, Hartigan turned and headed back up the stairs, his entourage in tow, a barrage of shouted questions plus a few catcalls following in their wake. As the glass doors swished closed behind them, Paul could see Hartigan putting his arm around Maloney's shoulder genially. Blake, in conversation with one of the lawyers, barked out a laugh.

Paul turned to go. He needed to find Phil and the car fast. As he hurried away, he glanced back to see Dessie O'Connell standing silently amongst the throng, wordlessly holding up the picture of his dead wife whose name Paul couldn't remember.

CHAPTER THREE

Brigit took a long drag on her cigarette and looked at the trees. She'd miss them. Hospital grounds always had such nice trees. There was something very comforting about watching them sway in the soft summer breeze.

It was not like she had actually liked nursing, she told herself. She hadn't actively disliked it either, though. It was supposed to have just been a means to an end. Train as a nurse, they'd told her, and you can see the world. People will always need their arses wiped – that'd been the half-joking sales-pitch they'd given each other in training. Nurses did a lot more than that, of course, and up to a certain point she had enjoyed that side of things. Helping someone get better, or at least feel better about what life they had left. That wasn't nothing. No, she didn't hate the job, she had just always felt like she was supposed to do something more with her life. She was going to have to now, she was about to get booted out on her arse.

The fire door banged open and Dr Luke Mullins stepped out. His hawkish nose, combined with the garish waistcoats he had a misjudged affection for, made him appear older than his forty-or-so years. He always looked like he was about ten pounds too heavy to comfortably fit into his suit, like he wasn't so much dressing for the job he wanted as for the body he hoped to attain. His standoffish manner made him one of the less popular doctors amongst the nursing staff, but Brigit had never minded him much. He was all business but he treated everyone the same, being just as happy to launch a rocket up another doctor's arse as he was a nurse's.

This unofficial smoking area, really just a shallow alcove between buildings, was normally the exclusive habitat of the nursing staff. They shy away from the officially sanctioned areas as the public tend to get hypocritically judgemental if they find themselves puffing away beside a medical professional.

Dr Mullins looked around awkwardly, like he'd forgotten what it was he had come out for.

"Don't worry," she said, "I'll be out of your way in a minute." She held up her half-finished cigarette. "I know you're not supposed to fraternise with the condemned."

"Relax," he said. "I'm not here. I also don't smoke."

Brigit gawped at him for a couple of seconds before she picked up on the hint. She opened the pack of ten she was holding and extended it. The thought briefly flickered across her mind to not offer him one but it seemed mean-spirited. After all, it wasn't his fault she was here.

Dr Mullins took the cigarette and bent to cup his hands around her proffered lighter. He awkwardly puffed it into life. She guessed he was only an occasional smoker, which was probably a good thing in a heart specialist. They stood beside each other and looked out across the lawn.

"So," he said, "unhappy romance?"

Brigit gave him a sideways look. "No thanks, I've already had one."

Dr Mullins nodded. "That's what I thought."

"Two in fact, now that you mention it. What's that got to do with anything?"

"I was just wondering."

Brigit looked across at his calm face and felt herself bristle. "Oh really? Trying to explain the irrational woman's crazy actions, are we?"

Dr Mullins held his hands up in placation. "Relax, Nurse Conroy, I come in peace. I've been sitting in that room for three hours being lied to, and I was just curious is all."

"Well," she said, turning and flicking her nearly finished cigarette towards the drain, "now you know."

"And for what it is worth," he said, "it was hilarious."

Brigit paused, slightly taken aback. "Thanks. I don't suppose you could take that into consideration?"

"No. We are sadly here to determine whether your actions constituted gross misconduct, not if they were highly amusing."

"Just my luck," she said.

"They were also, unfortunately, very stupid."

Brigit turned to fully face him. "You're going to stand there, smoking my cigarette and call me stupid? Really?"

Mullins remained steadfastly staring off into the middle-distance.

"Yes I am," he said. "Dr Lynch is a Grade A arsehole and we both know it. We also both know that you are actually a good nurse."

"There are lots of good nurses."

"Not really. There's plenty of serviceable ones, but I don't apply the word 'good' lightly. Don't get me wrong, there's not many good doctors either, although Lynch might well be the worst."

"Certainly the worst behaved," added Brigit.

Dr Lynch, or Letch as he was more commonly referred to, was exactly that; a lecherous piece of pond scum holding up a stethoscope. If he really did have healing hands, half of the nurses in the Health Service would have damn near immortal arses by now. He was careful of course, very careful. It was like he'd attended a seminar on how to not technically commit sexual harassment in the workplace, or at least how not to get caught.

Dr Mullins took an awkward drag on his cigarette. "Here's the problem, his version of events is crap, but so is yours, and in that scenario..."

"They're going to go with the doctor every time," she finished.

He nodded.

"They," she said, "being you and the other two people on the committee who currently hold my fate in your hands."

"Yes. The committee you just repeatedly lied to."

"I didn't—"

"Oh come come now, Nurse Conroy. Say what you want in there, but let's not pretend we're both morons out here."

Dr Mullins tossed his half-smoked cigarette into the gutter and finally turned to face Brigit.

"Here's what I think happened; Dr Lynch, being the classy piece of work he is, was undoubtedly hitting on one of the younger nurses, using his own inimitable style of flirtatious intimidation."

Dr Mullins cut Brigit off with a wave of his hand before she could speak. "Yes, I don't believe your story that he was hitting on you, and not because you're not attractive and blah blah blah, but let's be frank – you're not exactly the young and naïve 'doe lost in the forest' that a predator like Lynch is after, are you? Even an idiot like him would surely know that."

Brigit shrugged but remained silent.

"So," Dr Mullins continued, "old Letch is working his sleazy magic on one of the younger nurses, whose name I'm guessing you wouldn't give me on pain of death. She is understandably upset by this. You could have reported this to a senior member of staff of course—"

"Because that's always proven effective," interjected Brigit.

"But you didn't," he continued, "because she probably didn't want to make a fuss and, let's be honest, you were angry."

"At sexual harassment in the workplace?"

"Yes, and life in general, men in particular. I'm guessing Dr Letch couldn't believe his luck when he received a note from Nurse X telling him to meet her in examination room three, which I believe the staff have already unofficially renamed the Lynch Suite in commemoration." Dr Mullins gave a tight smile. "Long story short, he turns up because he is a horny little cretin. He is even dumb enough to remove all of his clothing, either through keenness to follow instructions or just being genuinely that stupid." Mullins left a long gap. "Really? Not going to give me that fun little titbit of information?"

Brigit remained motionless.

"Regardless, he is 'al fresco in flagrante'. When you rush in and — where did you get the handcuffs, by the way?"

"The Gardaí bring suspects into A&E all the time," said Brigit, "we've got a drawer-full."

"I see. Good to know. So Dr Letch is found ten hours later, handcuffed to a bed with masking tape over his mouth, naked save for the message 'This cock is married' written on his chest with an arrow pointing to, well... How close am I?"

Brigit shrugged her shoulders non-committedly. She'd got the idea from a rather memorable scene in *The Girl With the Dragon Tattoo*. Sadly, she hadn't had access to real tattooing equipment.

"You can't tell the truth," continued Dr Mullins, "because you're protecting your colleague, which means that his story about you attacking him unprovoked while he got changed to – and I can't believe the tubby little prick went with this – 'go for a jog', has enough credibility to pass muster. Especially seeing as the Lynch family have a long and glorious history in Irish medicine, stretching back generations."

"If the rest are anything like him," added Brigit, "they'll have killed more people than the Black Death."

"Indeed. Still, he's got powerful friends. Two of them are on that committee."

"Well that seems very fair," said Brigit.

Dr Mullins pushed his hands into his trouser pockets and leaned carefully against the wall. He gave Brigit an assessing look. "No, no it isn't. But here's the thing – you don't really care do you?"

Brigit gave a mirthless laugh. "Branching out into psychiatry now, are you Doc?"

"Seeing as even I couldn't fail to notice the crime novels you perpetually have somewhere about your person, Nurse Conroy, I assume you are familiar with the phrase 'death by cop'?"

Brigit shrugged. "It's when somebody gets themselves shot by the police in lieu of committing suicide."

"And this disciplinary committee is your trigger-happy cop, isn't it?"

Brigit looked down at her feet and said nothing.

"Didn't I hear you were leaving to set up – of all things – a private investigation firm?"

Brigit didn't like the way he said it. It was like how her brothers had said it. Like it was a daft idea and she was a silly wee girl for having it.

"Yes but not any more, thanks to the aforementioned unhappy romance."

"Ahhh, I see," said Dr Mullins, "how bad are we talking?"

"He cheated on me at a stag do..."

"Oh dear, how tacky."

"...and then texted me the pictures."

She didn't like to talk about it but something made her want to shock Mullins out of his air of smug certainty.

"Good Christ Almighty," he said, "why did he do that?"

"Damned if I know. Booze meets Catholic guilt, or just being a horrible human being. Does it matter?"

"I guess not. Weren't you two engaged?"

"No, that was the previous prince, who also cheated on me."

Brigit turned away to light another cigarette. She was annoyed to feel tears pricking at her eyes. Not here, not now and not in front of him.

In all honesty, the first time didn't hurt so much anymore. At least not since Duncan, the prince in question, had accidentally ended up in possession of her mobile phone during last year's 'bit of excitement', as Bunny had referred to it. This had led to Duncan almost getting killed by an assassin's bullet meant for Brigit, and having his ever-wandering wang temporarily damaged by the woman who had been entertaining it at the time. Ain't karma a bitch with sharp teeth?

"No offence," she said, "but all men are arseholes."

"You don't have to convince me."

It was the way he said it that made her pause. She looked at him and saw an embarrassed smile skate briefly across his face.

"Oh I'm sorry, is your gaydar malfunctioning? To be fair, I do fly quite close to the ground. I can't fix your make-up, redesign your house or teach you how to ballroom dance. I'm not one of those ones. I do, however, like a bit of cock."

Maybe it was the tension or just the element of surprise; either way, Brigit snorted so ferociously that she spat out the cigarette she had just lit. It hissed softly in the drain beneath her as she laughed.

She pulled a tissue from her pocket and dabbed at the corners of her eyes.

"God, I needed that."

"First time I've heard that from a woman."

Brigit briefly considered giving him a playful push, but looked at him and decided against it. It was still Dr Mullins, and the stone-like bearing to his visage was grinding back into place.

"If it is any consolation," he said, "my last prince broke up with me on the day the nation voted to legalise gay marriage."

"Jesus!"

"Yes. It appears he'd been banking on a homophobic refusal of reform as a way out of making a long-term commitment."

"Wow."

"So don't go thinking you breeders have cornered the market in two-faced little shits." Mullins looked at his watch. "I do feel we've rather wandered off the point though, that being you throwing away your career as vengeance against the wrong – though not undeserving – idiot. Seeing as you won't involve your colleague in proceedings, did you not consider going for the 'joke gone wrong' defence?"

"That's a defence?" asked Brigit.

"It can be. Did you ever hear that urban myth about the three medical students, who in a university rag week decided to take their assigned surgical cadaver out for a walkies? Dressed the body up and brought him on a pub crawl."

Brigit nodded, "Yeah, everybody has heard that one."

"My favourite version is the one where they bring him into a city centre pub, get him a pint—"

"And then," continued Brigit, " a woman walks in and screams. Having just met her dead husband out on the beer."

"Actually nephew and uncle but yes, that tale."

"Wife and husband is better," said Brigit, "from a dramatic standpoint."

"Indeed," said Dr Mullins. "Did you not notice how it doesn't end with the students getting kicked out of university, or indeed arrested? The medical establishment has a long history of forgiving pranks gone wrong."

"Yeah," said Brigit, "but only those carried out by doctors or doctors-to-be. Have you not noticed – there's never any nurses in those stories?"

Dr Mullins rubbed his chin as he considered this. "Do you know, I've never thought of that. Have you ever met Dr Lynch's long-suffering wife by the way?"

Brigit gave Mullins a suspicious look, thrown by the swift change of direction. "No, why?"

"She was a bridesmaid at my sister's wedding. Nice girl, albeit one with a truly appalling taste in men. Something you share, come to think of it. She's got two kids and a third on the way."

"And a massive arse for a husband."

"A situation she is finally remedying. It isn't common knowledge, but she has just filed for divorce, this sordid affair having been the final straw."

Brigit shuffled her feet nervously. "Well, I mean... that's..."

"Oh," said Mullins, "Nobody is blaming you. Here's the thing though, she could do without her private embarrassment being put out there for public consumption. As you can imagine, she isn't in the best of places right now. If this proceeds further, it is going to inevitably catch the attention of the press. That is why we're having this little chat."

Suddenly Brigit felt stupid. Like she'd said all the wrong things to the wrong person. Big mouth strikes again.

"What you need," continued Dr Mullins, "is a holiday. Maybe nine months to a year? Then you come back, and you will still be able to return to nursing if you so choose."

"And 'Letchy' Lynch will still be able to—"

"Oh that will be dealt with. Rest assured. Not the public flogging you'd no doubt prefer, but it's an imperfect world."

Brigit eyed him suspiciously. "Even if I was willing to disappear for a bit like you suggest, the rest of your little execution committee will never go for it. I don't know if you remember the last three hours, but it did not go well in there."

"No, it really didn't, did it? I'm about to tell the committee we have no choice. That you are in possession of some very damning and embarrassing information, and we have to make a deal for everyone's sake."

"And what piece of information might that be?"

Dr Mullins didn't answer. Instead, he looked down and gave his waistcoat a tug to reposition it, before pulling the fire door partially open.

"Dr Mullins?" Brigit repeated.

"You, Nurse Conroy, happen to know that one of the three medical students in that funny little urban myth, was called Lynch."

She looked at Dr Mullins's impassive face. He would be one hell of a poker player. "Shit the bed."

Mullins wrinkled his nose in disapproval. "What a colourful vocabulary you have."

"Wait," she said, "How could I possibly prove that?"

"You've got a picture," he said, patting the inside pocket of his jacket.

Brigit put her hand out and Dr Mullins laughed.

"Oh no. I'm not going to actually give it to you."

"Why not?"

"Nurse Conroy, I am disappointed. Aren't you supposed to be the detective?"

He pulled the door open and stepped back inside. She quickly moved after him and put her hand on his arm to stop him.

"You're in it, aren't you?"

Dr Mullins gave that tight little smile again. "Nurse Conroy, I've absolutely no idea what you are talking about."

And with that, he turned sharply on his heels and strode quickly down the hall.

CHAPTER FOUR

Gerry: Caller, you're on the air.
Caller 1: Yeah Gerry, I think it's a disgrace that this shower of—
Gerry: Sorry, caller, you've been cut off. Please, folks I know that Skylark is
an emotional issue but do watch your language. Remember you are live on
the radio. We have a seven-second delay for just this reason. Now, I believe
we've got Sarah on line two. Hello Sarah...
Sarah: Hello? Am I on?
Gerry: Yes, Sarah, you're live on the air.
Sarah: I'd like to hear the new song by Adele, please.
Gerry: I'm afraid we don't do requests on this show. Now, what's your point
about Skylark?
Sarah: Skylark? Oh that bunch of—
Gerry: And she has been cut off too. Again – please – watch the swearing!
Let's take a song. Ah for... really? All right, by sheer coincidence, here's the
new one from Adele.

Paul had received the call from a Sergeant Sinead Geraghty from
Howth Garda Station at about 10 pm the night before. He had been

taking Maggie for about her fifteenth walk of the day at the time. The sergeant had explained the situation to him, and then he agreed to meet her out in Howth the next morning. He didn't mention it to Phil when he got back to the car. He would have had questions. Phil always had questions. Paul hadn't known what to think, so he'd decided to try and not think about it at all until the next morning.

Earlier that day, more through luck than anything else, they'd managed to spot Hartigan being chauffeured out of the back of the Criminal Courts building in a dark green Rolls Royce. It said something of the man's attitude that he'd travel to a court where he was charged with embezzlement and fraud in that kind of motor. Typical Dublin traffic meant that, even on a Tuesday, it hadn't been hard for Phil to keep the car in sight. They'd followed the Roller all the way back to a bungalow in Seapoint out by the coast, where it had dropped him off. 'Bungalow' didn't do it justice; it was a big spread, worth a couple of million easily. High bushes mostly blocked it from view from the road, and a long lawn at the back stretched nearly down to the sea. Despite having grown up only a few miles away, Paul felt out of his element. Anyone from where he came from who ended up inside one of these houses was either cleaning it up or cleaning it out.

There was a silver Merc in the drive and, as far as Paul could see through the windows, there was nobody else at home besides Hartigan. At least, as Paul had sauntered casually by, the only person in view had been the man himself, leaning against an ornate marble fireplace in the front room, his phone held to his ear. Not that Paul had been able to watch for too long. There was only so long you could spend pretending your dog was taking a dump without it looking like there was something wrong with at least one of you.

When Paul had got back to the car, he had been disconcerted to find Phil using his initiative. He'd Googled Jerome Hartigan on his phone, and was reading all about him. "It says here that his strange wife lives out in another massive pad out in Dalkey."

'Estranged', Paul had silently corrected in his head. He really hoped they could sort out their marriage; he had four grand riding on it.

They'd parked in the car park of a pub called Casey's, a hundred yards away from the top of Hartigan's cul-de-sac. Initially they'd stationed themselves just opposite Hartigan's house, but they'd quickly noticed that – despite what films led you to believe – two men sitting in a stationary car are very noticeable. Admittedly, the German Shepherd with the penetrating stare probably hadn't helped. After the second neighbour had given them the evil eye, Paul figured they should move before someone called the Gardaí for fear of their property value lowering.

The cul-de-sac only contained five or six houses, so there'd not been much to-ing and fro-ing to keep track of. Every time any new vehicle had gone down the road, they'd taken turns bringing Maggie on a walk-by. Hartigan had thankfully stayed home, and his only visitor had been a takeaway delivery man at about 7:30 pm who he hadn't even tried to have sex with. They'd then seen him settling down to watch *Benjamin Button* on TV. Paul had seen it; he'd found it dull, but nowhere near as boring as sitting in a pub car park. Phil had passed the time telling Paul the conspiracy theories about 9/11 that'd he read about on the Internet. Paul had passed it quietly contemplating the various ways he could kill Phil.

By midnight they'd had enough and called it a night. If Hartigan was going to be getting or receiving any booty calls later than that, he was going to get away with it. Well, thought Paul, he'd got away with a lot more that day.

It had taken a pay rise to eighty euros per day to convince Phil to pick him up at half-seven the next morning. Their luck had held out, and they had reached Hartigan's just in time to see him loading golf clubs into the boot of the silver Merc. Hartigan driving himself had been a much trickier prospect to follow than the chauffeured Roller had been. He was a boorishly aggressive driver, who seemed to think that laying on the horn for long enough would make the morning rush hour just disappear. Through a combination of luck and following the honking, they'd managed to track him to Malahide Golf

Club. They'd sat in the club's car park for fifteen minutes, long enough to see Hartigan appear on the first tee with a man Paul recognised as one of the lawyer-types he'd seen him with the day before on the courthouse steps. They were both chomping on big cigars. Paul didn't know much about golf except that it took a long time, which suited him fine. Unless Hartigan had planned a secret dalliance in a bunker, that meant he had a few hours. He told Phil they had some business to take care of in Howth.

It was 9:45 am by the time they got there for the 9:30 am appointment. Traffic had been dreadful, but they still would've made it if Phil hadn't insisted on stopping the car for twenty minutes to let Maggie go poopie. Paul had considered this an undignified phrase for a grown man to use, but he let it slide.

They climbed the steep, narrow road that led up towards Howth Head. Sergeant Geraghty was already in the car park when they arrived, looking none too impressed with having had to wait. She was a short woman, with severely spiked red hair and an unusually muscular build. Paul guessed she was either big into her sport, or just mad keen to kick the crap out of somebody.

"Holy shite," said Phil as they pulled up to park, seeing the vehicle parked on the far side of the Garda car. "Is that Bunny's?"

"Yep."

"1980s Porsche 928S," they both said together. It wasn't that either of them were big petrol heads. It was just that every kid who had been trained by Bunny McGarry at St Jude's Hurling Club could recite the make and model of that car from memory. Bunny had taken great delight in showing it to every one of them, on the strict understanding that they never came within three feet of it. The story went that the car had belonged to a gangster and had been virtually totalled in a car chase with the Gardaí, a chase Bunny himself had been involved in. Paul didn't know if he believed that story or not, as Bunny was prone to exaggeration. He'd once told them that he had figured out who Jack the Ripper was, but the fecking English were too stupid to listen to him when he'd rung Scotland Yard.

What Paul did believe was that Bunny had bought the car off the insurance company, who were otherwise going to scrap it, and had then lovingly restored it. This meant harassing every garage in Dublin until they did it for him, no doubt at very 'Garda-friendly' rates. Regardless, it had been Bunny's life's ambition to own a Porsche, and now he did. Paul had never seen the attraction himself. It was just a car. It was admittedly a rather distinctive car, with its matte black paint and red leather seats. The name "Porsche" sounded a lot more impressive than the car actually looked. It wasn't one of the 'classic' Porsches. It was like one of those old footballers from the Sixties with the long hair and sideburns; the type who'd have a pint and a tab at half time. It may have been all right in its day, but when put beside its sleek, athletic descendants, it looked horribly out-of-date. Still, Bunny loved the thing. Despite often looking like he himself had been dragged arseways through a hedge, his car was never less than immaculate. Everyone knew that, should any harm befall this car or, God forbid, if somebody was monumentally stupid enough to steal it, the sentence would be a fate worse than death – the one hundred percent undivided attention of Bunny McGarry.

Paul got out of the car and walked over to Sergeant Geraghty. He would have preferred it if Phil hadn't followed him, but he couldn't think of a good reason to tell him not to.

"Mr Mulchrone?"

"Yes. And you must be Sergeant Geraghty. Sorry I'm late."

Paul extended his hand and they shook.

"That's quite all right," she said, in a way that made it clear that it definitely wasn't. She had a strong northern accent. "Can you confirm that this is Mr McGarry's car?"

Paul nodded. "How long has it been here?"

"It was first noticed on Saturday morning. Normally, it would have been clamped but..." Sergeant Geraghty looked annoyed about something.

"But?" asked Paul.

"Normally it would have been clamped but, apparently, this car is somehow exempt." Sergeant Geraghty failed to keep the sour expression from her face as she said it. "No clamping company will touch it. I also attempted to get it impounded, but that has also proven impossible."

"Ah, right," said Paul, "Bunny is a little particular about his car."

"I don't understand how one man can be exempt from the law."

"Have you been stationed in Dublin long?" asked Paul, as innocently as he could. The expression on her face indicated she didn't appreciate the question.

"I transferred down from Donegal six months ago."

"Ah right," said Paul again. "Well, I'm sure he's probably got a good reason for leaving it here."

"Yes," said Sergeant Geraghty and then she took out her notepad and pen. "When was the last time you actually saw Mr McGarry?"

"Last Tuesday."

"And have you spoken to him since then?"

"No, I've been trying to reach him," said Paul, "but he's not been answering the phone."

"I see. Has he been acting strangely recently?" asked Sergeant Geraghty. Paul watched her eyes dart to the left, glaring in the direction of Phil's giggle.

"Not for him, no."

"Would you say he is prone to emotional outbursts?"

Phil actually laughed at this.

"Phil, shut up!" said Paul.

"Sorry, sorry," said Phil, "but that's a gas one. 'Is Bunny prone to outbursts?' Wait until I tell Auntie Lynn that one."

"This is a serious matter," said Sergeant Geraghty, "we need to determine if Mr McGarry may have..."

She let it hang in the air. Paul knew where it was going, but didn't want to say it either.

"What?" said Phil, who knew as much about subtle hints as a sea lion does about astrophysics.

Sergeant Geraghty lowered her voice. "...may have... hurt himself. It's not something we like to advertise, but up on the cliffs there is, unfortunately, a popular spot with people who choose to take their own lives."

"What?" said Phil, the humour disappearing from his voice. "Suicide?! Are ye mad? Bunny?"

Paul turned, and saw the confusion on Phil's face. "Just let me handle this."

"Yeah, Paul, you just tell her it's bollocks. No offence, Guard, but it is. It's bollocks."

"Who is this gentleman?" said Sergeant Geraghty, clearly not enjoying Phil's assessment of the situation.

Paul put his hands out in a placating gesture. "Sorry, Sergeant. He's going to shut up now. This is all a big misunderstanding. I'm sure Bunny has probably just gone somewhere for a few days..." like 'on a massive drunken bender', Paul added in his mind, "...but I am confident he will turn up soon enough. There's no need to panic."

"Well," she replied, "I hope you're right. In the meantime, I believe you are a named driver on the insurance for this vehicle?"

"No, God no," said Paul.

Sergeant Geraghty flipped a page in her notebook. "You are Paul Mulchrone, are you not?"

Paul nodded.

"Well then, you are on the insurance for this vehicle."

Paul and Phil exchanged a shocked look. To their knowledge, Bunny had only ever allowed two people to even sit in that car. The idea that he would allow Paul to drive it was mind-boggling.

"Oh," said Paul," right, well... I'm sure Bunny will be back to take it away soon enough."

"I'm afraid we need it moved now. It can't stay here any longer."

"I appreciate that," said Paul, "but I've not got the keys for it, or—"

He stopped talking when she held up the keys. "Sorry, did I not say? The vehicle was found unlocked, with the keys in the ignition."

Paul looked at the keys, then at the car and then, despite himself, he looked at the path that led up to the cliffs.

"Now," continued Sergeant Geraghty, "has he ever gone missing before?"

CHAPTER FIVE

SIXTEEN YEARS PREVIOUSLY

FRIDAY 4TH FEBRUARY 2000

Tara Flynn looked up as the pub doors rattled violently. The way today was heading, stubbing her toe on the nightstand this morning might prove to be its highlight. Yesterday she'd put their cleaner on maternity leave. Seeing as Ralinka was working, wink wink, 'cash in hand', what she'd effectively done is give a woman a couple of hundred quid to stop turning up for work. Tara was the assistant bar manager of O'Hagan's public house, which sounded fancy until you realised there were only two other members of staff, and they were also assistant bar managers. O'Hagans was all chiefs and no Indians; literally in one case, as Dickie was chief assistant bar manager and Ricardo was head assistant bar manager. Nobody was clear on which of them that meant was actually in charge. Mrs Fionnuala O'Hagan, the widow of the titular Martin O'Hagan, was a genius in the field of human resources. She assumed that giving people a title meant they'd go to otherwise undreamt of lengths for you. Tara looked down at the mop she'd been enthusiastically shoving about the place for an hour; apparently the mad old bitch was right.

Tara had only started working there herself two months ago, after flaming out spectacularly from a degree in sociology. She didn't have the authority to put Ralinka on maternity leave, but she also didn't have the kind of conscience that would allow her to stand there watching a heavily pregnant woman mop a floor any longer. She had visions of the poor girl's waters breaking, and her mopping it up herself before politely getting on the bus to the hospital. So now, Tara was the unpaid cleaner as well as everything else. It didn't matter, she was only working there temporarily until she had enough money for Australia.

The doors rattled even more violently as the limited patience of the Mongol horde outside began to run thin.

"Just a second," said Tara, taking her pinny off, shoving the bucket into the corner and leaning the mop beside it. She knew who was outside. She'd called her. That didn't mean she wasn't dreading her arrival. As she walked towards the door, she could make out the ominous shape through the frosted glass. Five-foot-nothing, wrapped in seething anger and a shocking pink PVC coat.

"What the feck is taking so long?" came the voice from the other side.

"Just a second," repeated Tara, releasing the bolts at the top and bottom of the doors.

She'd not even opened the door fully before Mavis Chambers was through it. She was in her late sixties and was supposedly retired, having run a fish stall on Moore Street for most of her life, knocking out ten kids and killing three husbands in the process. Not actual murder as far as Tara knew, but she'd guess by the end at least a couple of them may have welcomed death. She was comfortably the most terrifying person Tara had ever met. She wore an eye-watering amount of perfume, presumably a habit left over from those six days a week surrounded by fish.

Mavis inhaled the entire second half of her cigarette, and then rasped through the resultant cloud. "Where is he?"

feckin' wish it was Hell by the time I'm finished with ye. You're a disgrace!"

"You're in O'Hagan's, Bunny."

"What'm I doin' here for feck's sake?"

"What's he doing here, he says!"

Tara redoubled her grip as Mavis tried to surge back at Bunny again.

"Mavis! Attacking him isn't going to help."

"This prick is past helping."

"I think I'm going to puke."

Tara kicked the bucket across the floor at him from where Mavis had dropped it. "Not on my floor please." She'd more than enough cleaning to be doing as it was.

Bunny gingerly picked it up and hugged it to his stomach.

"Ye pathetic creature. Would ye look at him!"

"Ara what business is it of yours?" snapped Bunny.

"I'll tell ye, shall I?" said Mavis. "D'ye remember St Jude's, the hurling team you set up? The one I sweated blood to help ye with? All them jerseys I washed, money I raised..."

Bunny nodded. "Course I—"

"Well it's gone, isn't it? Feckin' gone! Them bastard property developers with their bastard flats. You were supposed to stop the council selling off the field, weren't ye? You were supposed to sort it out!"

"I'm going to. The vote isn't until Thursday."

Even if Tara hadn't relaxed her grip slightly, she doubted she could have held Mavis back this time. She rushed over and started raining blows down around Bunny's head again.

"What the?!"

"It's Friday ye stupid, drunken bastard. FRIDAY!!!"

Tara got Mavis in a bear hug, pinning her arms down by her sides. The pensioner then attempted to throw a kick into Bunny instead.

He looked up at them with wide eyes and a wounded, lost expression, his lazy left eye only adding to the air of despair. "I don't... how can... I'll fix this."

Tara felt Mavis relax in her arms again. Her anger turning to despair. "And how're ye going to do that? We waited for ye last night. Kept believing you'd turn up. That you'd sort it. How could you..."

Her voice trailed off.

Bunny stared at the ground.

"I'm... sorry." He spoke it in a whisper to the cold concrete floor.

"I'd have never believed..." said Mavis. "After all we went through. All them kids, where are they going to go now? All this time. You made 'em believe in you and then you... 'tis cruel."

Tara released Mavis, and the older woman started to straighten her clothing.

"I'll..." said Bunny.

"You'll what?" asked Mavis.

Tara had never seen a man look so pathetic. Truth be told, she'd not known Bunny McGarry that long, but for the two months she'd been working at O'Hagan's he'd been a regular fixture. Larger than life, big, bold, uncouth – yet touched with a kind of ferocious, wild-eyed charm. All gone now. He looked truly lost, staring into an empty distance.

When Mavis spoke, it was almost in a whisper. "The vote, there was hardly anybody on our side. Even the ones who'd promised, who'd... they all screwed us."

"You could get a lawyer?" said Tara.

"What's that gonna do?" said Mavis. "They've got twenty and we couldn't afford the one."

"How much did you lose by?"

Mavis looked at Tara, a couple of expressions flickering across her face.

"We didn't."

Bunny looked up at them, watery eyes full of hope.

Mavis glanced into her handbag as she spoke, feigning obliviousness to the two pairs of eyes now fixed on her. "As it happens, the fire alarm in City Hall went off before the vote could be completed. The building had to be evacuated."

"You set off a fire alarm?"

"No," said Mavis. "There really was a fire. By the way, someone..." she looked pointedly at Bunny before continuing, "will need to give our Janet's Darren a proper scare when this is done about playing with matches. He's been sent some of them whatcha-me-call-its... mixed signals."

"Ah, Mavis," said Bunny. "I could kiss you."

Bunny made to get up.

"You stay the fuck away from me with that sewer of a mouth of yours, Bunny McGarry. All I did was delay the inevitable. Every one of those bastards was voting against us, and they will do on Monday night at the rescheduled vote, I'm sure."

"I'll sort this."

Tara heard a crash in the bar outside.

"Boys!" roared Mavis. Tara and Bunny winced, albeit for different reasons. "You've got three days, Bunny. Our Lord came back from the dead in that time; pull out a miracle or so help me, you're going the other way."

Bunny beamed up at them with a disconcerting smile.

"Not a problem. Tara love, could you get me my trousers, please?"

"Ehm..." said Tara, "You weren't wearing any when you came in, Bunny."

"Right. Could you get me someone else's trousers then, please?"

CHAPTER SIX

Two tubs of ice cream: Chunky Monkey and Cookie Dough – check
Two bottles of wine: one red, one rosé – check
Two massive brick-sized bars of chocolate – check
One box of donuts – check
One bottle of vodka, silly flavour optional – check
Phone locked in cupboard to prevent drunk dialling – check
Sweat pants – check
Saw Doctors T-shirt, two sizes too big – check
Six episodes of 'Don't Tell The Bride' recorded – check
One curry ordered, offensively hot – check

God, she loved a list – she really did! The trick, thought Brigit, to a proper pity party was planning. You couldn't totally mess up your life and then just improvise a full-on splurge of misery, you had to think it through beforehand. Yes, she had no job, no man, no future – but she did really know how to let herself go. She took pride in that.

She'd walked straight out of that disciplinary committee and made a list. Well, actually, she had said goodbye to a couple of the girls with the joyously demented air of a lottery winner, keyed Letch's BMW in the car park and then had a bit of a cry on the bus home. But after that, she had made a list. As she looked at it now, four hours later, she was still bloody proud of it. Fucking good list.

Everything was going according to plan. She'd polished off the bottle of red wine, one of the ice creams and all of the donuts, save for the one she had thrown at an episode of *Don't Tell the Bride*. She had done a lot of shouting at that show. It was perfect for her purposes. Watching men plan a wedding by completely ignoring their wife-to-be's every wish, and instead giving their nuptials a Formula One/zombie/reggae theme was a wonderful reminder of what a waste of oxygen they were. Admittedly, there had been a bit of a hiccup when she hadn't realised that an episode had ended, and she'd spent quite a while shouting 'Leave the bastard!' at what turned out to be a *Panorama* special on prison reform. To be fair, while it was an odd theme for a wedding, it was by no means the worst.

Brigit belched, which gave her a handy reminder that she must have eaten one of the bricks of chocolate at some point too. She was also halfway through the bottle of rosé. She was very drunk, and having a bloody wonderful time chasing highly-calorific oblivion. Phase Two – where she would inevitably throw up, followed by her Indian food being delivered – was bang on schedule. The rookie mistake in this situation was to have your Indian food first, then get stuck into the "death by chocolate" portion of the evening.

"No, no, no," she said, and then realised she wasn't talking to anyone. Mind you, the bloke on telly had just told the bridesmaids that they had to buy their own dresses, because he'd rented a fucking paintball arena.

"Prick!" she shouted.

This was the Conroy system; you had your Indian food after your drunken chunder (number one) because ice cream left a decent aftertaste, whereas recycled tandoori left the kind of sour reminder that could wreck a good drunken buzz. This was the upside of repeatedly getting screwed over by people you trusted, you really learned how to bring your A-game to the post-apocalyptic pile-on.

The doorbell rang. The Indian food was early, or late, or... the clock was being unhelpfully vague.

Brigit dragged herself to her feet. Right – bit early – but OK. She'd take the food, pay the nice man and then go talk to Huey on the big white telephone. Having stood up, she realised it was about that time. She hung onto the wall for a bit, until gravity stopped pissing about.

OK, good. She had planned ahead for this bit too, drunken genius that she was. The thirty euros was sitting beside the door. The food had come to a lot less than that but she factored in a big tip, as she was inevitably going to make a drunkenly suggestive remark to the terrified delivery guy. That was fine, but this time – she was not going to do the accent. That had been a real low point the last time. OK, good. She could do this. She adjusted her boobs a bit, then felt something funny. There was a moment of terror when she found what appeared to be a lump, but it was soon replaced with the joy of finding a chunk of chocolate that had somehow made its way into her bra. She scoffed it then patted herself down.

The doorbell rang again.

"I'm coming, ye prick!" OK, easy now. The delivery guy had done nothing wrong. Well, assuming he was a bloke, he almost certainly had... but not to her.

She moved forward with more speed than she had intended, and fell into the coat-stand a bit. She steadied herself, picked up the money and opened the door.

Standing in the hallway was Paul.

"Jesus!" she screamed, before hurling the money at him and slamming the door closed.

On many an early-morning commute to the job she now no longer had, Brigit had planned in exquisite detail what it would be like the next time she saw the cheating scumbag. She would be:

1. Sixteen pounds lighter;
2. Fabulous, and;
3. On the arm of a ridiculously muscular but highly sensitive beast of a man. On a particularly weak morning, she had

looked through the pictures of the Leinster rugby squad and narrowed it down to three.

In none of those situations had she taken Our Lord's name in vain, thrown money at Paul and then slammed the door. There had briefly been a different version of a plan for tonight that had involved something like that happening, but then she had sensibly crossed 'order male stripper' off her list. She planned to stay classy, at least as far as anyone else knew.

She risked a sideways glance at the mirror beside the door and then quickly stared back at the floor. It was as bad as she had feared. Her mind started unhelpfully assembling another list: red wine mouth – check; inevitable ice cream on face – check; donut dust and chocolate stains on T-shirt – check; hair a mess – check; and... oh God, she really fucking hated lists!

Brigit started softly banging her head against the door.

Wait – maybe she'd imagined it? Drunk people hallucinate things all the time. That was definitely a thing that happened.

"Brigit, are you OK?" said a familiar voice from behind the door.

Oh fuckity fuck fuck fuck.

"Yeah," said Brigit, with all the confidence she didn't feel, "I'm fine, and I don't need you ye... ye... prick! So piss off!"

"I can't leave," said Paul through the door.

Brigit took a look around her. Oh God, she hadn't...

No. This was definitely her apartment. For one horrible second she thought she had gone looking for him. That would have been pathetic.

"You and... your prick... ye prick... can prick off." C'mon, thought Brigit, you know way better swear words than that. Pull it together, girl!

"Bunny is missing," said Paul.

"Missing what?"

"No, missing. As in missing, as in nobody can find him."

"Like hide 'n' seek?"

"He has disappeared."

"So?" said Brigit, thinking to herself, why don't you go find him Paul? Oh yeah, because you've no idea how to be a detective. Oh, she should have said that out loud. That would have been a good one.

"So," said Paul, "I've no idea how to find him. I don't know how to be a detective."

Damn it!

"I need your help," he continued. "Look, can you open the door so we can talk about this?"

"No!" said Brigit, stamping her foot for emphasis. "I'm never, ever opening this door or anything else to you ever again, ye... prick!" Seriously – she knew hundreds of swear words. She had three older brothers. "Me and my friends are having a party and then later, a man is going to deliver some Indian food and... and, I'm going to have sex with him!"

"OK," said Paul. "The delivery guy is actually here with your food. He's standing right beside me."

"Right, good. Tell him I will be with him presently."

"Ehm... he's gone again."

"Not him," said Brigit. "A different guy. He plays rugby for Leinster."

"And he delivers Indian food?"

"Shut up!" said Brigit, "shut the hell up! You don't get to break my heart and then come around here and make me feel stupid. I feel stupid enough when you're not here ye... ye... oh for... what's another word like prick?"

"Arsehole?" said Paul.

"Thank you," said Brigit. "Arsehole!"

"I know all that Brigit, and I'm sorry, I really am, more than I can ever say... but Bunny is missing and I've no idea how to find him. The Gardaí don't care and I'm scared, all right? I've not got the first clue what to do. You're way smarter than me, and you understand this stuff."

"You're damn right," she said, punching the door with her fist. "I'm a... a... bloody good detective, probably... maybe. Never really had the chance. But I would have been!"

"So please," said Paul, "help me find Bunny."

"No!" she said. Even drunk as she was, she could hear how petulant her own voice sounded. "Not helping you do anything. I will find Bunny. You can... shut the hell up!"

Brigit nodded her head at the closed door. She may have started badly, but she was rallying. "I will do it. Me. On my own."

"OK" said Paul.

"You..." said Brigit, "I need you for absolutely nothing! Nothing! Although, write down the stuff about the... y'know and push it through the letterbox. Details and things."

"You don't have a letterbox."

"Are you giving me cheek?!"

"No Brigit. Sorry Brigit."

"Write it down, and I will deal with it tomorrow."

"OK."

"Now piss off you... you..."

"Arsehole?" said Paul.

"Yeah. That!"

"OK."

Brigit stood there and quietly listened to the soft rustling sounds from outside in the hall. Then she watched as a folded A4 piece of paper was slipped under the door. Then she listened for a couple of more minutes as Paul stood out in the hall. Then she heard him head down the stairs and out the main door.

And then she went and threw up.

CHAPTER SEVEN

"Hoi, sleepy bollocks!"

Paul awoke to the unpleasant sensation of a hurling stick jabbing him in the ribs. His eyelids flickered open to catch a brief snatch of perfect azure sky, before Bunny McGarry's bulbous face loomed into view and eclipsed everything else. Even by his high standards for incandescent fury, Bunny seemed angry.

"Bunny?" said Paul.

"Feck me, there's no end to the master detective's powers of deduction. Yes, ye skinny-arsed soap-dodger, Daddy's home. And what the fuck is this bullshit?"

Bunny stepped back and Paul looked around him. He was on a beach, surrounded by a perfect summer's day. He was sitting in one of those old-school deckchairs that were really nothing more than a length of cloth dangling from a basic frame; the ones that offered nothing in the way of lumbar support. Bunny McGarry was standing in front of him holding a hurling stick in one hand, which was no great surprise, while wearing a figure-hugging red dress, which was. It didn't look good on him. While the garment was supposed to cling, in Bunny's case it appeared to be doing so for dear life. His beer belly protruded unflatteringly over the waistline. He appeared to be one good sneeze away from Incredible Hulking the whole thing to shreds. The red also clashed with his face. Anybody who had ever been a member of the St Jude's under-12s hurling team had learned a sample colour chart of the shades of Bunny McGarry as a matter of survival. His face was currently a 'run for your life' deep burgundy.

"Ehm," said Paul, "I think this is a dream."

Bunny threw his hands out in exaggerated frustration. "Of course it's a fecking dream, ye shandy-drinking shite-sipper, are you suggesting I'd wear this by choice?"

"It's ..."

Paul glanced to the left. His mysterious, unnamed client – the woman he was refusing to refer to as the lady in red – was now sitting there, sipping on a cocktail and showing little interest in proceedings. She was wearing the same dress. The Devil in the Red Dress; those words stuck in his head, like a half-remembered song.

"See," said Paul, "it's a reminder of her."

"Great," said Bunny. "I've done a Lord Lucan and you're trying to get your hole off some low-end Kim Basinger wannabe."

Paul tried to stand up but found he couldn't.

"No, it's just... I got..."

"Ara – stop whining. At least you've got someone who knows her arse from her elbow looking for me now."

Paul glanced to his left again. Brigit was now sitting beside his client, in an identical deckchair and an identical dress. When he saw her, an icy bolt of shame and regret shot through his chest. Not that she wouldn't have looked good anyway, but he wondered if his subconscious was photoshopping the image a little, to maximise his rightly deserved pain. Brigit gave the other woman a disparaging sideways glance before focusing on the phone she held in her hand. Paul didn't need to see the screen to know what she was looking at. She was flicking through *those* pictures again. Every time she swiped forward, she shot him a look of pure hatred that felt like a punch in the solar plexus.

Bunny pointed the hurl at Brigit. "That's assuming, of course, she is willing to temporarily put aside her anger at you and your wandering penis."

"Brigit," said Paul, "I'm so sorry. I don't know how... I don't remember. I didn't..."

"Oh for feck's sake," exclaimed Bunny loudly, "I'm the one who has disappeared, and you're all 'me me me, wah wah wah' – grow a pair, would ye?"

"Alright," said Paul, "what do you want from me, Bunny?"

Bunny lowered his voice. "I need you to go on a spiritual journey; to forego all material excess and become one with the universe. Only then will you find your spirit guide, an animal that'll show you the path to enlightenment."

"Really?"

Bunny barked a laugh. "Yeah – I'm all about that dead-guy-in-a-bathtub Jim Morrison Wankanory bollocks. What you need to do is pull your head out of your arse."

That did sound more like him. "But I've no idea how to find you."

"No kidding. That's why you need Miss Leitrim over there. Getting her involved is the only thing you've got right so far. Let her get on with it. She ain't gonna let you in until she is good and ready; she made that very fecking clear."

"So, what do I do in the meantime?"

"Your actual fecking job. You've got a client and the rather urgent need to get the moolah to set up the agency, which is a key step in your awful plan to get the woman you love back and have something approaching a life. What did I always tell you, back in your hurling days?"

"If the ref doesn't see it, it didn't happen?"

"No."

"Whack it and hope for the best?"

"No!"

Paul looked up at Bunny who was pouting down at him, his lips pressed together in an ominously familiar, tight seal; like he was doing all in his power to hold back the inevitable wave of sweary invectives. It was ingrained in Paul's psyche that if you gave Bunny the wrong answer on the first two attempts, then keep quiet. Three was never the charm.

Bunny spoke slowly and deliberately. "There's no I in team."

"I have literally never heard you say that."

Paul winced and raised his arms as Bunny made to swing the hurl at him.

"This is your dream, ye scuttering gobshite. You know as well as I do, all of this is just your subconscious trying to work shit out, so stop pissing about. Now, how's the whole detective game working out for you?"

"Terribly," said Paul. There was no point in lying to himself.

After his trip out to Howth on Wednesday morning, Paul had returned to Malahide Golf Club to await Hartigan finishing his round of golf. He had now got Bunny's car, which was unsettling for obvious reasons, and helpful for different, but equally obvious reasons. He'd been able to allow Phil to take his auntie's car back. She had wanted to get her hair done. Again, that probably never happened to Phillip Marlowe either.

Paul had scooched down in the front seat and watched Hartigan shaking hands with his opponent on the 18th green before heading back into the clubhouse. He reckoned from the body language that Hartigan had won, although that may have been because Jerome Hartigan wore the air of a man who always won. Allowing fifteen minutes minimum for a shower, Paul reckoned he had enough time to take Maggie out for a quick walk around the car park. He was nervous enough about letting a dog into Bunny's car in the first place; the possibility of her using it for a toilet was too horrific to contemplate. They'd both stopped to watch a golfer tee off on the 10th hole. To Paul's credit, he'd realised just how bad an idea that was as the club had been on its downswing. Maggie had instantly hurtled off after the golf ball. Paul had dropped the lead; if he hadn't, his arm might have come clean off. He gave chase, but every time he thought he'd almost got hold of her, somebody else in her eyeline would take a shot and Maggie would be off again like a slobbering heat-seeking missile. One guy had made the mistake of throwing a club at her and had then been forced to climb a tree to avoid having a permanent reminder of why that was a bad idea. An old lady had taken the wiser choice of blaming Paul. She'd chased after him in a golf cart for two holes. He'd only lost her when she'd got stuck in a bunker on the 14th. By the time Paul had corralled Maggie and got her back to the car he was exhausted, dishevelled and sporting multiple bruises. He was also missing something; Hartigan's silver Merc was gone.

Without any other option, Paul had gone back to Hartigan's house. There had been no sign of him. Paul had parked up in the car park of Casey's pub and sat there seething, while Maggie had dozed happily in the back seat. He'd coughed loudly a couple of times in an effort to wake her up, but to no avail. He'd considered poking her but had thought better of it. Hartigan had eventually turned up four hours later; four hours of prime 'getting his end away' time. Paul had grimly calculated how many times Hartigan could have had sex in that time. He'd arrived at six, by crediting Hartigan with near-superhuman powers of recovery and a very limited interest in foreplay. At that point, Paul had rung Phil and asked him to take over the stakeout. Then he'd gone to do the only sensible thing he could think of regarding the Bunny situation. He'd gone to Brigit to beg for help.

While he'd been away, Hartigan had gone out again. Phil had followed him all the way over to Castleknock. He'd phoned Paul while in 'hot pursuit', although seeing as Phil liked to stay at least 10 mph below the speed limit, the pursuit would've actually been only tepid at best. They managed to converge on a pub called Myos just as the realisation had been dawning on Phil that Hartigan's wasn't the only silver Merc in Dublin. At some point in proceedings, he'd started following the wrong one. This one contained a middle-aged woman with a full-on eighties perm of blonde hair, big enough to ruin a trip to the cinema for someone two rows back. There had followed a full and frank exchange of views, during which Paul had fired Phil, while Maggie had dry-humped a nearby potted plant for reasons nobody wanted to think about. In short, Wednesday had been a less than a total success.

"So," said Bunny, "You've no idea what you're doing."

"That would be correct."

"Get the Nellis gobshite back for a start."

"But he's crap—" protested Paul.

"So are you, but at least that lanky rasher would take a bullet for you."

"And then what?"

"Figure it out," said Bunny. "This ain't one of those bullshit dreams where someone gives you all the answers. You were always a devious little sod, did you lose your bollocks somewhere along the way?"

"Well no, I—"

"If memory serves, you had a promising future as a scumbag conman before you went in another direction. Maybe you're thinking about this all wrong? In the meantime, that dog takes a dump in my car and I'll haunt you for all eternity."

Paul lowered his eyes for a second, trying to find a way of expressing the inexpressible thing he'd been avoiding.

"Bunny, are you..." He left it hanging in the air.

"How the fuck should I know? I'm just in your head, remember? Let's look at the facts though. I've disappeared, nobody has seen me for days and my beloved car was found out beside the seaside, where every Tom, Dick and Harriet heaves themselves into the great beyond. I've also been down in the mouth recently, not that you've bothered to notice, ye navel-gazing langer."

Paul nodded silently. By definition, all of these facts were things he already knew, unpalatable as they were.

"On the other hand," said Bunny, his tone suddenly brightening, "I don't really grab me as the dying sort."

Then Bunny bent down and licked the side of Paul's face.

Paul awoke with a start to find Maggie's tongue slobbering in his left ear. "Ah, get off me, ye mad bitch."

As he furiously scrubbed the saliva off his cheek, reality came back to him. They were parked just up from Hartigan's house on the cul-de-sac. Last night, Paul had decided to risk moving a lot closer, nosey neighbours be damned. Now that it was just him, he'd reasoned that he couldn't risk losing the target again.

A glance around told Paul that the world had lumbered into a grey, wet morning in his absence. The clock on the dash told him it was 8:07. He reached down with his right hand to locate the lever to return the driver's seat to an upright position. Just then, the distinctive green Rolls Royce that had brought Hartigan home from court two days ago, drove past and out of the cul-de-sac. Paul had stupidly parked with the front of the car facing away from the top of the road, so he'd have to pull a U-turn.

"Ah for—"

Thursday had barely started and he was fucking up again.

CHAPTER EIGHT

Gerry: And we're back. If you're just joining us, we're discussing the fallout from the mistrial of the Skylark Three. Will there be another trial? Do you think it is worth the effort? We've got Mick from Clonee, Mick – you're on the air.

Mick: Yeah, Gerry, d'ye know what? I don't see the point myself. I mean, people like that shower, they never face justice. We never lock up the people really responsible for stuff like this.

Gerry: You say that Mick, but Ireland did imprison a couple of bankers and a former government minister on corruption charges. That's more than Britain or America have managed to do.

Mick: Well, doesn't that just sum this country up? Even our crooks are rubbish!

Brigit rang the doorbell again. Nothing happened, just like the last five times. She tried to peer in through the tiny gaps in the closed Venetian blinds on the front window, but she couldn't see anything. At the sound of a squeaky wheel, she turned to see a large man on a mobility scooter cruising slowly by on the pavement, eyeing her suspiciously. Brigit gave him what she hoped was her most winning of smiles. His eyes remained fixed on her as he moved on down the pavement before eventually accelerating around the corner.

Brigit put her hand to her pounding head and sighed. In truth, the hangover was not as bad as it really should be. After Paul had left last night, try as she might, she couldn't get herself back into pity party mode. Instead, she'd gone to bed in that unhelpful stage of drunkenness where thought wasn't just possible, but inevitable. She'd spent hours tossing and turning, and running it all through again and again in her mind, before finally finding sleep, only to spend it in a fitful dream that re-ran it all yet again.

That morning she'd woken up and, to avoid thinking about the night before, she'd thrown herself into 'the Bunny problem'. Unfortunately, that had meant texting Paul, once she had unblocked his number. His note had said that he'd not heard from Bunny since Tuesday, that his car had been found apparently abandoned in Howth on Saturday, and he'd no idea what Bunny had been working on. She'd requested he text through Bunny's address from the documents they'd filled out for their private investigator's licence, and Paul duly had. She had to start somewhere, and here was the only place she could think of.

She also felt slightly guilty. Bunny had tried to ring her on Friday night, and she'd ignored it. He'd left a drunken voicemail where he'd sounded pissed as a fart, but happy. Of course, that was the thing with Bunny, his moods were a little like Russian roulette. 'Howeryanow, the Leitrim lovely. 'Tis Bunny. All your troubles are over. He's a good lad. Give me a ring and your Uncle Bernard will explain all. You'll be happier than a horny hound at a one-legged leper convention.'

She'd dismissed it as the ramblings of a drunk. It wouldn't have been the first time. He'd called a few weeks before and drunkenly given what she imagined his version of a pep talk must be. It'd been cringe-inducingly awkward, being heavily based on the concept of 'sure, have a chat and it'll be grand'. The last thing she had wanted was more romantic advice from Bunny McGarry. And now he'd disappeared, and she was standing outside his house pretending that she had the first idea how to find a missing person.

The house Brigit was currently standing in front of was a two-up, two-down mid-terrace residence in Cabra. There appeared to be nobody at home. To be honest, if there had been, that would have been a spectacularly disappointing – if successful – investigation. It occurred to her that she knew precious little about Bunny McGarry. He wasn't married and never had been as far as she knew, but she couldn't even be certain of that. He'd come into her life like a drunken whirlwind of violence and near-incomprehensible swearing, and she'd never really questioned what lay behind the bluster.

She fished her phone out of her pocket and rang Phil Nellis. Although she'd met him on the same day as she'd met Bunny, Phil she knew quite a lot about. He was a master of the overshare. For example, she knew that he was the nephew of a man called Paddy Nellis, who had apparently been Dublin's premier burglar back in the day. While she didn't approve, she was hoping to take advantage of any skills Phil may have picked up.

"Hello?"

"Hi Phil, it's Brigit. I was wondering if you wouldn't mind helping me with something?"

"Yeah sure. What is it?"

Now that it came to it, actually saying the next bit seemed a bit rude. Ah well, in for a penny...

"I need you to break into a house for me."

"What?" The outrage was coming through crystal clear.

"Only it's not really doing that. I'm just checking somebody is OK. It's like... a humanitarian mission."

"Like Mother Theresa and that?"

"Yeah, kind of. It's not even really illegal." That was a shaky guess at best, outright lie at worst.

"Have you tried the doorbell?"

"Yes."

"Right. And whose house is it?"

"Ehm... Bunny's."

Brigit heard a yelp, followed by a thud of the phone dropping.

"Are you bleedin' mental?" The question sounded like it was being shouted at the phone from a long distance away.

"Phil. Listen to me, Phil. It's OK. I work with Bunny, it's not a crime."

"Breaking into Bunny McGarry's house? You're right, it's a suicide bid."

"Phil, please pick up the phone. Phil?"

She could hear it being picked up, then dropped, then picked up again.

"What did you say?"

"I said, pick up the phone."

"Oh, right."

"He might be in trouble, Phil."

"If Bunny is in trouble, then I feel sorry for trouble."

"Please, Phil?"

"Stall the ball," he said, a tone of exasperation in his voice. "I'll bell you back in a second."

Then the phone went dead. As she looked at it, a video call came through from Phil. What the hell was the point of this?

"Hello?"

"It's Phil." He was holding a phone at such an angle that she had an exciting view up his long nostrils.

"Yes, Phil, I can actually see that."

"Show me the house."

"What?"

"Do you want my help or not?"

Brigit glanced around and then stepped back, wafting the phone about.

"Right, yeah, yeah, yeah," said Phil. "I can spot four possible points of vulnerability there."

Brigit turned the phone back around and whispered into it. "Wow, really?"

"Yeah. The front door, the two upstairs windows and the downstairs window."

"Oh." He had correctly identified everything that wasn't brick. Brigit was beginning to think that this phone call was not her best idea ever.

"See that plant pot?"

There was a large white plastic planter, dirty and dented, sitting beside the front door, its contents long since dead.

"Yeah."

"Look under it."

Surely not? Brigit held the phone to her ear with her shoulder and moved the plant pot.

"Ah for... " A set of keys were sitting on the ground. She felt suitably embarrassed. "Who leaves keys under a plant pot in this day and age?"

"Bunny, because nobody would be insane enough to try and rob him."

"Thanks for your help, Phil."

"I was never here."

"Ehm... you actually were never here."

"Exactly. Nellis out." Then the picture disappeared.

Brigit looked at the keys in her hand. It was a less than auspicious start to her investigating career.

Only as she entered did the thought occur to her that there might be an alarm. From the lack of insistent beeping noises, she guessed there wasn't. She supposed if you were blasé enough about home security to put keys under a plant pot, you were unlikely to have a highly sophisticated alarm system installed. She picked up the four pieces of post on the floor and put them on the side table, where two more already sat. As she stood uninvited in the hall of someone else's home, several sensations ran through Brigit. She felt uneasy, nervous and undeniably excited. There was a guilty thrill in being inside someone else's private space. It was why certain magazines sold so well.

She moved through the downstairs. Surprisingly for a man who, in person, gave the impression that he might have slept in a skip, the whole place was very neat and tidy, if a tad stuffy. The front room had been knocked into the kitchen. A large wide-screen TV dominated the area; in front of it sat a well-worn armchair and a near-untouched sofa in matching green upholstery. The wallpaper looked older than she was. A shelf full of videocassettes took up an entire wall. Brigit hadn't even seen one of those for years. Bunny appeared to have a fairly comprehensive collection of hurling matches, including every All Ireland final since the eighties, judging by the years scrawled on the sides. There were no photos, no overtly personal mementos. The fridge contained nothing but two bottles of tomato sauce and another of brown sauce. No cooking utensils were out, and three Tupperware containers were piled neatly beside the microwave. The place had a barely-lived-in feel.

She moved upstairs. To the right was a bathroom, again surprisingly neat. She wondered if he had a cleaner? A glance through the cabinet produced nothing unusual. Some of the medication she recognised as being for high blood pressure. That wasn't a great surprise. Bunny's face was an alarming shade of red at the best of times. A single toothbrush sat in the holder on the sink, dry to the touch. Some basic shampoo and shower gel. It looked like one person lived there and they hadn't moved out, or if they had, they'd done it in enough of a hurry to not bother grabbing the basics.

She moved into the next room. It was clearly a spare; a single bed sat beside one wall, piled high with various pieces of hurling kit. Maybe that should be her next stop? One of the few things she knew about Bunny was his absolute dedication to the youth hurling club he'd set up. The opposite wall emphasised this, dominated as it was by team photographs. Every St Jude's under-12s team stretching back for what looked like twenty years. The one common factor was Bunny, standing to the left in each photo looking imposing and in charge, as generation upon generation of bright-eyed young fellas beamed cheeky grins at the camera. Despite herself, Brigit honed in on the one she knew – the 2000 team. In the back row, Phil Nellis towering above all, looking slightly to the left of the camera. And in the front, wincing slightly at heaven knows what, a pre-teen Paul. Loss, pain and anger tugged at Brigit's heartstrings, and she turned away.

In the front bedroom sat an old wooden wardrobe, reasonably full of men's clothes, confirming the impression that it was just Bunny who lived here. One neatly-pressed suit alongside a series of more work-a-day ones, in various stages of wear and tear. There were also two overcoats, meaning he did actually have options outside of the damp-smelling sheepskin coat he seemed to perpetually exist in.

On the cabinet beside the bed was a framed picture, in pride of place and yet facing away towards the wall; like it was both important and painful. In it, a much younger-looking Bunny had his arm around a stunning black lady. He looked so different. Brigit realised it was the first time she'd properly seen him smile. Again, she'd never even thought of it but, in the right light, he wasn't an unattractive man, once you got past the wonky eye and the air of demented glee.

On the dressing table sat another picture; this one she recognised. It was of her, Bunny and Paul at a tapas restaurant up off the Quays, the night they'd agreed to start their own private investigation firm. MCM Investigations. Her big idea and her dream come true. It had all been sorted out before the food had even arrived. The look of joy in her own eyes burned into Brigit as it beamed out at her from the photograph. She'd had three copies of it printed out, one for each of them. It had been one of the happiest moments of her life. Paul on one side of her, Bunny on the other. It was lucky she'd got the waiter to take it when she had. Bunny being Bunny, had loudly proclaimed that tapas wasn't a meal, it was like a bunch of trailers for a meal. Then he'd drunkenly flamenco danced, briefly joined a child's birthday party and disappeared before the dessert had shown up. Brigit had burned her copy of it weeks ago, along with everything else that showed Paul's cheating face. She dropped it back on the table, turned to leave and then stopped. Bunny was a missing person. She'd need a current picture of him. Without looking at it again, she slipped the picture into her coat pocket.

Having completed the sweep of the house, she went downstairs and looked at the post. Everything looked like bills. She passed them back and forth through her hands. It felt like a step too far, messing with somebody else's post. Wasn't that technically treason or something? Maybe that was only in Britain. Apparently people messing with the post and swans were the two things Big Lizzy Windsor took very seriously. Ah, screw her and whoever else minded. If Brigit was doing this, she was doing it all the way. She started opening.

Bunny was paying too much for his electricity. He'd donated money to Africa, but apparently that hadn't sorted the problem and they needed a bit more. His bank wanted to lend him money; presumably seeing him as a safer bet than Africa had proven to be. Somebody else wanted to give him a new credit card and the GAA were having a couple of meetings that Brigit guessed, deep down, they didn't really want Bunny to attend. She'd bet good money that he could raise the mother of all points of order and batter your agenda sideways.

She opened the last letter and punched the air with delight. It was Bunny's mobile phone bill, and itemised no less. Thank God for him resisting the pleas to go online. He didn't strike her as the online sort. He also had no concept of how mobile phones worked, as he was on a shocking tariff. Still, she now had a list of every call he'd made and text he'd sent up until last Friday. The feeling of triumph was tempered by the last entry on the list. His last call before he'd disappeared off the face of the Earth had been to her.

CHAPTER NINE

Councillor James Kennedy stretched out on the massage table, popped his earphones in and squeezed his head into the hole that allowed him a view of the beige shag carpet below. He'd been doing this for months now. One of the lads down at the golf club had recommended it; said it had changed his life. Nothing better for stress, or so the man said. He'd been sceptical. Initially it had been weird, lying there while a stranger had put their hands on him, covering him in oil and kneading him like dough. Soon though, he got used to it. The headphones were a stroke of genius; they meant he neither had to listen to their new age plinky plonk music, nor feel obliged to try and chat with some butch bird whose name had too many syllables in it. He'd found the chatting excruciating. Kennedy didn't care what anyone said, there was no such thing as small talk when one of you is naked and paying the other one to be there.

He now did this religiously every Friday afternoon. It was his reward for getting through the morning clinic with his hapless constituents. Three hours of it felt like a month. Missing cats, whining about bills, the bins – not being picked up, being picked up too early, too late, being dropped back too loudly. And oh God, the speed bumps. Always with the speed bumps. As far as he could see, it had been a spectacular mistake to ever build a flat bit of road anywhere in Dublin. Here was the thing – not every little ankle biter was supposed to make it. When he was a lad, if you ran out into traffic, you learnt a valuable lesson – or else you became a valuable lesson for all the other kids on the street. It was natural selection in action. Nowadays people just wanted to wrap kids in cotton wool and it was producing a generation of soft-arsed cry-babies. Of course, he couldn't say that. He had his eyes on bigger prizes than his current seat on Dublin City Council, and you didn't get there by telling people the truth. Uncle Brendan, the revered political warhorse, would eventually die or retire from the Dáil and then he could step up to the big show – name recognition, healthy majority, junior minister gig – yes, please.

Kennedy heard the door behind him open, and pressed play on his minidisc player. The Corrs filled his ears. He spoke over the music. "I've got a lot of tension around the shoulders, so you can focus there... and don't be afraid to go deep."

With that, he closed his eyes and let his mind wander.

He felt hands on his back. Jesus, this one would want to get herself a serious manicure or something. Felt like she had big farmer's mitts on her.

Then the air was expelled from his lungs in one heave as a heavy weight landed on his lower back. His hands scrabbled around and he could feel thick, trousered legs either side of the table. Someone was straddling him; some man. He tried to turn around, but a large, meaty hand pushed his head back into the face hole. Breathe, he couldn't breathe! He struggled to get air into his lungs as a hand pulled his earphones out.

"Afternoon, Councillor," said the voice. Male, from Cork, and sounding like its owner was really enjoying himself.

"What the f—" Kennedy gasped, with what little air he could spare.

"Now now, relax, Jimmy. You're tenser than a cow that's not had her tits squeezed for a fortnight."

It wasn't the most – literally – pressing concern right now, but Kennedy hated being referred to as Jimmy. "Get off me!" He tried to pull a big breath in, to shout for help.

He felt the man shift his weight, and what little air he'd managed to inhale was once again expelled from his lungs. Then the voice, stinking of booze and onions, whispered disconcertingly close to his ear. "It's story time, Jimmy boy, so you just relax. Once upon a time, there was a Garda HQ... and in that Garda HQ there was a room that doesn't exist, with a filing cabinet that wasn't there, full of things that never happened."

Kennedy heard a rustle behind him, and then a creased sheet of paper appeared in his field of vision. He couldn't see it clearly, but he could make out the Garda crest and his own name.

"Like in 1997, Jimmy, when you were a naughty boy. Hit a parked car and blew a high enough score on the breathalyser that your breath was basically flammable. It's funny though – the whole thing went away, didn't it? Swept under the rug."

Kennedy's brain was trying to catch up, his adrenalin pumping. What was this?

"Well, I've had a look under that rug. Yourself, Councillor Burke, Councillors Walsh and West. We've enough of you to hold a drunken Dinky Derby, in fact. Councillor Marsh, meanwhile, she was stone cold sober when she attempted to break the land speed record in her BMW on the M50 last year. To be fair to you, I get why you and the lads are so keen on driving yourselves home, after Councillor Munroe got into that altercation with the taxi driver a couple of years ago. Nasty stuff, that. All of it hushed up. Even you-know-who from Clontarf has had his troubles, what with his daughter being a little too enterprising in the supply of a smidgeon of Class A to her uni friends. My point is, sure – we all make mistakes don't we?"

Kennedy said nothing. He could faintly hear the tinny noise from his headphones as The Corrs explained how they had never loved him anyway.

"Like, for example," continued the voice, "voting for the only playing field available to a bunch of scrappy inner-city youths to be gift-wrapped for some developer buddies of yours. Luckily, you've got a chance to correct that mistake. If you – and all your six bosom buddies here named – have a dramatic change of heart, then the things that never happened, stay that way. Otherwise..."

Kennedy felt the man's weight shift, and he was once again able to draw breath. "It won't work."

He felt the weight increase on his back and the air begin to be squeezed from him once again.

"Just... even without us, they've got the votes. We're a drop in the ocean, there's sixty-three members of the council. They've got Snow White. He'll never—"

"Ah, bless. You let me worry about that councillor. You just worry about voting with your conscience, then all these unfortunate incidents might just get swept back under that rug, understood?"

The weight shifted and then lifted entirely off his back, but the large hand remained in place, pushing his head down.

The voice reappeared at his right ear.

"Are we clear?"

Kennedy tried to nod but was unable to do so. "Yes. Yes. We're clear."

"Ah, tremendous. I don't know about you, but seeing democracy in action like this, it gets me harder than trigonometry, so it does. Hopefully this whole affair will have itself a happy ending." The voice drew even closer to Kennedy's ear, so much so that he thought he could feel lips brush against it. "Speaking of which, I'm going to toddle off now, and you're going to stay staring at that nice bit of carpet, as if I see you move, I'm going to come back here and give you the kind of happy ending that you won't ever forget."

Kennedy didn't move.

He stayed not moving for a long time.

Eventually, he felt female hands touch his back. Only then did he scream.

CHAPTER TEN

"Have you got any books on how to follow somebody?"

The woman behind the counter pulled a face like Paul had just shat in her hand and asked her to clap. She had a couple of facial piercings, and her dyed red hair looked like three different hairdressers had fought it out to an unhappy stalemate on her head.

"Who wants to know?" she said.

"Ehm, I do," said Paul. He would have thought that was obvious.

"Did Maureen send you? She accuses me of harassment and then she sends someone to my work? That is fucking typical!"

"No, no I—"

The girl leaned forward on her high stool, and jabbed at the wooden counter-top with her finger.

"You tell Maureen that I've as much right to go to an exhibition on the depiction of the female form in African culture as she does. It's not my fault that her and that... thing, were there."

"Right. I've not been sent by anybody, I promise. I just really need a book on how to follow somebody."

"Really?" she eyed him suspiciously.

"This is a book shop, isn't it?"

She looked around, as if confirming that his story was indeed correct. Paul looked around too, just to double-check that he really had walked into a three-storey building filled with books that were available for purchase. The assistant's level of aggression would have been nearly justifiable if he'd mistakenly gone into a delicatessen. Perhaps she didn't work there at all. Maybe she'd just wandered in and thought the stool behind the register was a good place to read her graphic novel.

"Is everything OK, Lianne?"

The question had come from a tall, bespectacled man that had been rearranging a stack of Dan Brown books in the large display window with the enthusiasm of a vegetarian working in an abattoir. His facial expression carried clearly legible overtones of 'what now?' Lianne waved back nervously. "Yeah, fine, Gerald. I'm just helping this gentleman with something." She lowered her voice. "C'mon."

She led Paul around the corner into the children's section.

"And you're sure you're not here about Maureen?"

"I don't know anything about your ex-girlfriend."

"Woah, how did you know Maureen was my ex-girlfriend?"

"I'm a private detective," said Paul, feeling slightly smug about it.

"And you don't know how to follow somebody?"

"It's my first day."

It wasn't. It was now his fourth day, although on each of the last three mornings, he had convinced himself that today was a fresh start, and this time he would get it right. To be fair, this morning had gone slightly better, after a dreadful beginning.

Paul hadn't been able to catch up with the green Rolls Royce after it had driven by him and out of the cul-de-sac, so he'd lost Hartigan yet again. He'd pulled over, swallowed his pride and phoned Phil. After some begging and the promise of a pay-rise to one hundred euros a day, Paul was now back to being the second worst detective on the payroll. He was aware that all of this was eating into the initial grand he'd got from the Devil in the Red Dress, but something about Hartigan convinced Paul that betting on him being a philandering scumbag was a risk worth taking. Then, following on from advice he'd received from his own subconscious in a dream, Paul started using the things he was good at. In particular, he'd always had a gift for 'social engineering', which was a phrase people who were good at lying had invented, to make it sound like a skill and not a character flaw. A Google later and he'd found numbers for six firms that provided chauffeur-driven cars in Dublin. A quick scan soon found the only one with a distinctive green Rolls Royce in their fleet.

"Hello, Prestige Cars, how may I help you?" The woman at the other end of the line had spoken in one of those posh voices that only existed for working class people to use when answering the phone.

"One of your drivers nearly killed me!"

"I'm sorry, what?"

"A green Rolls Royce. He's driving like a maniac on the Naas dual carriageway. I'm on to the Gardaí. I've got a dashboard camera. I'm suing, you see if I don't!"

"Sorry I... Tony is a very good driver, I'm sure there's some—"

"Good driver? Good driver?! This is going viral, love, I've over seventy-eight followers on Twitter!"

"But he's... could you hold on for just a moment please?"

Paul had sat there listening to some famous classical tune. It was either from an ad for aftershave or one for beer; he couldn't remember which. When the woman returned, there was an unmistakable tinge of vindication in her voice.

"I've checked, sir, and Tony is currently parked up on Stephen's Green, so whoever you—"

Paul had hung up and started driving immediately. Twenty minutes later he had eyes on the Roller, parked illegally on the south side of Stephen's Green. Hartigan wasn't there, but at least they had a lead. Paul wasn't sure, but he assumed that you hired chauffeur-driven rides by the day. Clearly Hartigan hadn't fancied the hassle of city centre parking. Paul could sympathise. With no other option that had allowed him to keep the Roller in view, he had parked in one of two free disabled spaces with the Porsche's hazard lights on. He doubted the 'Maggie is a guide dog' explanation would work in this situation. Forty-five minutes later he'd been joined by Phil. As it happened, he'd come into town on the bus first thing that morning. He'd been attempting to sell his collection of old 2000AD comics in an effort to raise money to bring his bride-to-be over from China. Paul couldn't decide which was sadder; Phil falling so completely for the con that he would give up his most prized possession, or his depression at realising that, judging by the price he'd been quoted, those comic books meant a lot more to him than they did to anybody else.

"Ye don't know any bus drivers, do you?" asked Phil.

"No," replied Paul. "Why?"

"Twenty of the lucky sods won the lottery last night. They'd be able to lend me a few bob."

Luckily, Paul had been rescued from another doomed attempt to make Phil see sense and the inevitable argument that would follow, by the Roller pulling out. They'd managed to follow it around the Green's confusing counter-clockwise contraflow system and there had been Hartigan, shopping bags in hand, just up from the Stephen's Green Shopping Centre. He'd caught them off-guard when he'd just dumped his bags in the car and headed off down Grafton Street. Paul had opened the car door and run across the street to follow, leaving a protesting Phil and honking traffic in his wake.

He'd managed to follow Hartigan down Grafton Street and left onto Wicklow Street, onto Exchequer Street before pulling another left onto Drury Street. Luckily, town had been busy so remaining unnoticed had been easy; the only trick was making sure he'd not lost sight of the target. At one point, Paul caught his own reflection in a window and realised how ludicrously excited he looked. He needed to calm down and hang back, or he risked blowing the whole thing. Hartigan had walked into an expensive-looking tailors. A quick fly-by had been enough to assure Paul that there was nobody inside that could be giving his target an unconventional, if thorough, inside-leg measurement. Then, he'd finally answered one of the calls from Phil. It'd been the fifteenth one in six minutes. He calmed Phil down, promised him that he had been added to the insurance on Bunny's car earlier that morning (which he definitely hadn't) and instructed him to just park up anywhere that allowed him to keep an eye on the Roller.

Thirty minutes later, Hartigan had walked over to Dawson Street for an early lunch. The restaurant was so posh it didn't have a name; there was just a funny-looking symbol over the door. It no doubt had some deep meaning, but to Paul, it looked like somebody was trying to crucify the letter P. He'd nipped in and asked about making a reservation, giving him just enough time to see Hartigan sit down with a man in his sixties. Ideally he'd have been playing tonsil hockey with his estranged wife or indeed anyone else but, while Paul's luck had improved, it hadn't improved that much. The maître d' had taken one look at Paul and informed him that they weren't taking bookings right now, his tone implying he'd be best to drop back when hell froze over.

In lieu of standing about outside looking dodgy, Paul had decided to nip up the road to Hodges Figgis. He reckoned he could use however long a posh lunch takes to find some kind of manual to aid his on-the-job training. In a bookshop of this size, there must be something.

Lianne stopped at the top of the stairs on the third floor and looked back at him.

"There's a section over there on mental health. We've got some very good books on coping with a broken heart."

"For the last time," said Paul, "I'm a private investigator. I am not romantically involved with the person I'm following. I've never even met him."

"Oh," she said, "it's a him. That's fine then."

Paul was tempted to point out how Jeffrey Dahmer had exclusively targeted male victims, but he couldn't see how that would be helpful. She took him over to military history and pointed at the shelf.

"There's some stuff there on general spying, lots of stuff about the

NSA, Big Data, that kind of thing. There's a few more 'how to' type books there, they might be useful. Little tip though... if you are already somewhere when the person arrives, then it's not legally stalking."

She tapped her nose after she said it. Paul reckoned that if you wanted a clear indicator of whether your life had gone to shit or not, ask yourself if you've felt the need to check the legal definition of stalking lately.

"Unfortunately, I'm following the guy. I've no idea where he's going or who he is going to see. That's kind of the point."

Lianne pulled an unhappy face. Perhaps he should've just taken her advice and moved on. He was on a schedule.

"Are you following this poor bloke about with one of those long-lens cameras? Invading his privacy?"

"Oh," said Paul, he'd not thought of that. "Is there anywhere around here that sells cameras?" He could use his phone but that'd be limited. Plus he could never figure out how to zoom in with the bloody thing.

"You make me sick," said Lianne.

"I get that a lot."

Just then his phone vibrated in his pocket. He was not in the least surprised to discover it was Phil. As he answered it, Lianne pulled a face that implied she didn't know the crucial difference between working in a bookshop and a library.

"Hey, Phil."

"You'd better get back here."

"But he's still having lunch," said Paul. "Look, just keep moving the car and— "

"No, no," interrupted Phil, "You don't understand. There's been a murder."

CHAPTER ELEVEN

Brigit looked up from the pint of Diet Coke she was nursing, wrenched from her thoughts by the sound of plastic hitting linoleum, followed by a muttered expletive. The barman of the Last Drop bent over to retrieve whatever he'd dropped. Brigit's seat gave her an unfettered view of his arsecrack, whether she wanted it or not, and nobody did. The man was carrying about 200 pounds of excess weight, at least when he wasn't leaning it against the bar. He'd also taken the unconventional approach of advertising the pub's food menu by wearing samples of it on his originally white shirt. When she'd entered the pub twenty minutes ago, he'd curtly informed her that lunch was no longer being served. From what she could see, it no longer being available was only one of the very many reasons you wouldn't want it. The carpet felt like flypaper, which was ironic given the number of flies in attendance. The lounge bar's only other occupants were two old dears playing Scrabble. One wore a big hat and a smile and the other wore thick-rimmed glasses and a grimace of concentration.

As the barman stood up, Brigit saw the TV remote he'd been pursuing. He pointed it at the TV on the far wall. The old dear with the hat glowered at him. He nodded his head towards the screen, "Newsflash."

Unmuted, the TV blared into life in time to give voice to Siobhan O'Sinard, or as she was more commonly known, the sexy, ginger one who used do the news in Irish.

"... survived by his two daughters and ex-wife. We can now go live to our reporter James Marshall who is at the scene."

The picture changed to a reporter standing on a leafy street of aged oaks and perfectly maintained hedgerows. The kind of greenery that screamed money. Two Gardaí in the background guarded an imposing front gate, while trying hard not to notice that they were live on national television. The reporter in the foreground wore his best solemn news-giving face, undermined by the dancing excitement in his eyes.

"Thank you, Siobhan. Exact details are sketchy at the moment, but here is what we do know. Prominent property developer Craig Blake, a member of the so-called 'Skylark Three' – whose prosecution for fraud controversially collapsed just two days ago in the Central Criminal Court – has been found dead at his home here in Blackrock. Unnamed senior Gardaí sources have confirmed that a murder investigation is underway and, given the exceptional circumstances, it has been put under the control of the National Bureau of Criminal Investigation."

Split-screen. Siobhan giving it her best steely-eyed serious news look.

"And do we know any more about those circumstances?"

"Well," said James, "we have heard that the scene has been described as 'horrific', and it is believed that an element of torture may have been involved. We expect the investigation team to hold a news conference later this evening."

Back full-screen to Siobhan in the studio.

"And we will bring you any updates on this story when we have them. To recap—"

And the bartender muted Siobhan once more.

"Serves the cunt right."

The three other heads in the bar turned to the woman in the hat.

"Janine!" her friend exclaimed, taken aback.

"Ah come on, Carol, the misery those three bastards caused. Hanging is too good for 'em."

"But there's no need for that kind of language!"

She wagged an unrepentant finger at the picture of Blake that was now filling the silent screen. "Scumbags like him are exactly why that kind of language was invented."

The barman nodded his approval and then went back to rummaging about in his ear with a finger.

Brigit looked at her phone. It was 3:25 pm. She was still five minutes early. Her phone was also down to 7% of its battery. She'd need to head home after this, she was always forgetting to charge the damn thing.

She had spent the afternoon ringing people she didn't know. Once she'd eliminated her own and Paul's numbers, that had left twenty-four unrecognised numbers on Bunny's phone bill that he'd either called or texted. She had received a surprising array of responses. One of the mobile numbers appeared to be dead, which was odd in itself; Bunny had had a four minute, thirteen second conversation with it only eight days ago. There'd been a pizza place, a curry house and his electricity supplier, all of which she'd filed under 'general admin'.

Nine of the calls to mobile numbers had gone to voicemail; five of them had just had the standard impersonal network message, which seemed odd. Who didn't even have their name on the message in this day and age?

Of the other four, one was to a lady called Sally Chambers, who sounded middle-aged and from central Dublin. The second was a woman who didn't give her name but did have a rather breathy sex-kitten message asking the caller to please leave a message. The third again had no name, but the oddly familiar voice of an older man from somewhere up north. He had formally asked the caller to leave their name, number and a brief message, and he would get back to them as soon as possible, God bless. As she'd listened to it, Brigit had made a mental note to ring her da.

The final voicemail had belonged to a guy called Johnny Canning, the man she was currently waiting for. He had sounded perhaps late-twenties on the phone. He'd been the only one to call her back so far. Their conversation had got off to a frosty start when she'd asked how he knew Bunny. This had struck Brigit as odd, seeing as he'd later revealed he assisted him with the coaching of St Jude's. Helping out a kids hurling team wasn't exactly controversial, even if they were considered the worst one in Dublin and quite probably beyond. Still, despite his initial wariness, he'd said he'd be more than happy to meet up and answer her questions. Of all the people she'd rung, he was also the one who seemed most concerned that Bunny had disappeared. He said he had a shift tonight, but he'd be able to squeeze her in this afternoon.

Of the others – as in those who had actually answered the phone – the response had been mixed, to say the least.

Six of the numbers were parents of kids who played for St Jude's. All she got from those was that he'd not been at the game on Sunday and that yes, that was unusual. They'd last heard from him the week before, which tallied with the bill. He'd been trying to get people to fundraise for a new clubhouse. Clearly he'd spent an evening doing a ring-round. This had made Brigit feel slightly guilty. She remembered the night the old clubhouse had been burnt down. She and Paul had found Bunny sitting in the ashes, drunk as a judge.

Another of the numbers was a bookies in Dalkey who said they'd no idea who he was, despite them appearing on the sheet five times over the month. When Brigit had pointed that out, they'd said that customer confidentiality was a core part of their business and hung up. Clearly drink wasn't Bunny's only vice.

Two of the other people who had answered had been women who'd both declined to give her a name, and said they didn't know any Bunny or Bernard McGarrys. They had been very keen to get off the phone too.

Another member of the uncooperative category had been the

man with the strong Belfast accent and a stammer, who clearly did know Bunny; his profanity-filled explanation of how he wished he'd never met him had made that very clear. She'd tried to get a word in edgeways but he'd hung up on her too, when he'd finally run out of breath and vitriol.

Then there'd been the last one. Brigit blushed as she remembered it. That had been awkward, and it did make her suspicious about some of the other ones. Bunny McGarry, it appeared, didn't just limit his vices to drinking and gambling.

She looked up from her phone when a man entered the bar. He looked at her, and she shot him a nervous wave. This couldn't be Johnny Canning, could it? As he strode across the lounge towards her, Brigit was busy tearing down whatever mental image she had constructed for the man she was there to meet. To say the least, he was not what she had been expecting. In fact, allowing for the fact that they were both Caucasian Irish males above the age of consent and below the age of infirmity, he was pretty much the polar opposite of Bunny McGarry. A snatch of a half-remembered song referring to 'magazine-quality men' flittered through her mind. Johnny Canning was what it had meant. His smile, downright un-Irish in its dazzlingness, sat amongst perfect features and flawless skin, beneath a tightly-groomed coif of sandy brown hair.

A man like this shouldn't be walking into a dump like the Last Drop. A man like this shouldn't be walking around full stop. It was unfair to other men – and in a way, women. 'Here's what you could've won, ladies.' An immaculately tailored casual jacket hung over a well-toned physique, wrapped in a tasteful shirt-and-slacks combo. His shoes were shined so perfectly you could probably see your face in them, and if you had his face, it'd be worth the effort. He was probably a little older than she'd figured too, maybe mid-thirties, but 'well-preserved' didn't cover it. He was a walking, talking work of art.

Brigit touched her hair self-consciously and felt her cheeks redden. Suddenly she hated her hungover self from six hours ago, the one who had thought throwing on whatever clothes were handy had been an acceptable course of action. Pull it together, girl, this isn't a blind date – you're here on business.

"Brigit, I presume?"

"And you must be Johnny."

They shook hands and he sat down on the stool opposite her.

"I am indeed. Thanks for meeting me here. It's handy..."

"I knew it must have something going for it."

Johnny smiled to acknowledge her joke. "It's so nice to finally meet you. I've heard a lot about you."

Brigit eyed him suspiciously. "Really?"

"Oh yes, Bunny talks about you all the time. Apologies, I didn't put two and two together until halfway through our chat earlier. When you said you worked with him, in my head I stupidly thought you were a cop."

"Ah, right."

"Not that I've any problem with the Gardaí, you understand. I run a nightclub and I'm the law-abiding proprietor of a clean-as-a-whistle establishment. Big friend to the Gardaí. No trouble here, Your Honour." He held his hands up in mock surrender.

"Ah," said Brigit. "That's where you're working later on?"

"Ehm, no," said Johnny, looking slightly bashful. "I volunteer one evening a week on a helpline. No big deal."

Oh fuck off! Outwardly Brigit smiled and nodded. He was getting annoying now. Nobody was this perfect.

"Which nightclub is it?" asked Brigit.

"The Fin, up off Leeson Street. Do you know it?"

"Only by reputation." Brigit wasn't a big fan of clubbing, but she knew the name. It was where the rich and famous went to party. The drinks cost more than her car was worth.

"Ignore what you've heard, we're honestly not that awful." He gave her a charming smile. "Rich idiots need to unwind too."

She was finding him difficult to dislike. He could have come across as arrogant, but somehow didn't. Just then the barman appeared beside him and carefully laid down a sparkling water

Johnny hadn't ordered. The glass it came in was the cleanest thing in the whole place. There was even a slice of lime in it.

"Cheers, Rory," said Johnny, before pointing at Brigit, "Do you want another?"

"Nope. I'm good thanks."

The barman scratched his belly and then departed silently.

Brigit was tempted to ask what on earth had just happened, but didn't get the chance. Johnny took a sip and then his face became a picture of concern. "So, what's the deal with Bunny?"

"Well," said Brigit, "that's what I'm trying to find out. The last time anyone heard from him was late Friday night." The memory of Bunny's number flashing unanswered on her phone popped unbidden into Brigit's mind again.

"Right," said Johnny. "The last time I heard from him was the previous Wednesday. I tried him a few times Saturday, and pretty much every couple of hours since he didn't show on Sunday. I even sent people over a couple of times to knock on his door."

"Is he always at the matches?" asked Brigit.

"Pretty much. That team means the world to him, as you know."

"Did you play for it growing up?"

Johnny pulled a face. "Christ, no. I'm not a fan of team sports and besides, I'm from Navan." He layered on the Meath accent for the last word. Brigit was taken aback.

"Wow, you keep that well hidden."

"Well, I don't go back much. At all. Ever. Anyway."

"Hang on," said Brigit. "How'd a Navan boy who hates sports become an assistant coach at St Jude's?"

Now it was Johnny's turn to look embarrassed. "Very grand title. I drive the bus, wash the kit, stop him over-terrifying the kids, that kind of thing. General dogsbody. Bunny asks, I do."

"Has he got compromising pictures of you or something?" Brigit's smile died on her face when she noticed it not being returned.

"No, it's just..." Johnny shifted uncomfortably. Brigit was about to attempt a hurried segue off the topic but he waved her concerned expression away. "I met Bunny at the lowest point of my life. He helped me when nobody else would. The least I can do is drag my sorry arse out of bed on a Sunday morning, even on four hours kip, and help him where I can. Let's be honest; he's not overly burdened with friends, is he?"

Brigit nodded. "Tell me about it. I tried to make a list of his enemies earlier."

Johnny gave a small laugh. "Christ, good luck with that."

"Did you and he talk much?"

"I guess. I mean, yes, we did. There was a lot of driving to and from matches and all that, and Lord knows we could never have agreed on a radio station." Johnny smiled sadly.

"How was he recently?"

Johnny took another sip of water and considered this. "Alright, I guess. I mean, he was mightily pissed off about getting pushed out of the Gardaí, no mistake about that. But he was looking forward to working with you."

"Really?" Brigit was genuinely surprised. She'd always thought even getting Bunny to agree to the idea had been a stretch.

"Oh yeah," said Johnny, lapsing into an alarmingly faultless impersonation of Bunny's Cork accent. "Oh, she's a cute whore that Leitrim lovely, and no mistake. Smart as a butcher's dog."

"Oh God."

"He meant 'whore' there in the positive sense."

Brigit gave an embarrassed smile. "Glad to hear it."

"He rates you though. I mean, you'd have to speak fluent Bunnyese to know it, but I am a world-renowned expert in the art." Johnny fished the slice of lime out of his drink and pushed it onto the rim of his glass. "He was very disappointed with how your little team broke up before it got a chance to get going."

Brigit coughed and then fidgeted nervously. "Well, y'know. Some things go a bit beyond 'forgive and forget'."

"I'm afraid you're telling the wrong guy." Johnny extended his hands. "You're having a drink with the poster boy for second chances."

Brigit doubted anyone was kicking Johnny out of bed for eating crisps. Or burning down an orphanage for that matter.

"I'm sure you didn't do anything as bad as—"

"No," interrupted Johnny, "I did a hell of a lot worse."

Brigit looked into his eyes to see sincerity staring back at her. "Ask yourself, how much does a man have to mess up in his life to be lucky to have Bunny McGarry for a friend? I may know nothing about hurling, but St Jude, patron saint of lost causes?" Johnny fished a medal of St Jude from under his shirt. "Three meetings a week, the helpline, spending my Monday nights washing kit. I've got all kinds of penance to serve." Johnny slipped the medal back under his shirt. "Anyway, sorry... you didn't ask me here to sermonise or pry. What are we going to do about Bunny?"

"Do you know if he was... I don't know, working on something recently?"

"Well," said Johnny, "as you know, he was off in France a few weeks ago."

"Was he?"

"Oh, ehm, yeah. Sorry. I'd thought he'd have said. All I know was he was over there for a few days. No idea what it was about."

"Right."

Brigit unlocked her phone and took that down in notes. It belatedly dawned on her that she should take notes; it was the kind of thing detectives were supposed to do.

"When I asked," said Johnny, "he did say the trip went fine, all sorted – whatever that means."

"OK. Anything else?"

Johnny puffed his cheeks out. "Nothing immediately jumps out. I mean, he was always sorting something for someone, and people were always wanting a quiet word, but he never spoke much about it. There have been countless things over the years, but nothing particular that springs to mind. I assume you know that, well... let's just say, any man who lays his hands on a woman between Croke Park and the Aviva Stadium, Bunny sees it as his personal mission to deal with that situation with what I believe you'd call 'extreme prejudice'."

Brigit nodded, but she hadn't known that. It was dawning on her that she really didn't know very much of anything about the man she was trying to find.

She looked at her notes and tried to think of the questions that would undoubtedly pop into her head five minutes after she left the pub. "Can you think of anyone else I should be talking to?"

"He drinks down at O'Hagan's quite a lot. I'd ask in there."

"OK," said Brigit, noting it down. "And where is that?"

"Baggot Street."

She noted that down too, then she remembered.

"Oh," she reached down and took the phone bill out of her handbag. "I've been going through his last phone bill, and I was wondering if you could help me identify some of the numbers."

"I'll try."

Brigit looked at the notes she'd scribbled on it. "Do you know a lady called Sally Chambers?"

"I do," said Johnny. "Her son is our fullback, when he turns up."

"OK. Her number appeared a few times. I thought they might be seeing each other or something."

Johnny scratched his lightly stubbled chin. "Christ, Bunny McGarry dating. There's a concept I'm going to spend the rest of the night trying to get my head around. But eh, no – not Sally anyway. I'd bet the house on that. I'd imagine those calls were about young Darren's inability to turn up. You've got to understand; we're less of a hurling team and more of an early intervention scheme for potential young offenders. Having said that, as far as I'm aware, there's no trouble at home. I mean, there's never been a dad in the picture that I know of."

"Right. OK. One last thing. The other thing is..." Christ, thought Brigit, just say it. This is an investigation. Investigate. "Going back to the subject of women. I was trying all these numbers and one of them is for an... escort agency."

Johnny's perfectly trimmed eyebrows made a concerted attempt to jump off his head. "Fuuuuuck."

"I take it that's not something that he'd—"

THE DAY THAT NEVER COMES

"Ehm, no," said Johnny.

It was a toss-up as to which of the two of them was the more embarrassed. She slurped a nervous sip of her Diet Coke and ploughed ahead, not making eye contact as she did so. "Do you know if he would've ever... ?"

She let that hang in the air filled with awkward silence. In the background, the barman noisily cleared a nostril.

"I don't know what you're asking," said Johnny.

"Neither do I," said Brigit.

"I guess, I mean, he could be lonely. Probably is, come to think of it. We just never... Bunny didn't ever talk about stuff like that." Johnny shifted a little in his seat. "To be entirely honest, last time I saw him, we had a bit of an argument. When I wasn't getting responses for a few days, I thought he just had the hump with me."

"What was it about?"

"Nothing really, I mean in hindsight." Johnny shrugged. "I thought he was maybe going a bit heavy on the booze. He didn't exactly appreciate the input. I'm a little... well, those twelve steps can lead to a high horse at times I guess."

This brought Brigit onto the other thing.

"I also wanted to ask you. They found his car out in Howth. You don't know any reason he'd be out there?"

Johnny shook his head.

"Only... it was in a car park near what I suppose you'd call a popular suicide spot."

"Oh," said Johnny.

"You don't think he'd..."

Johnny ran his right hand through his hair and sighed. "I don't know. I really don't know."

"I mean," said Brigit, "he doesn't exactly strike you as the type."

"Here's the thing," said Johnny, "and I speak as someone who is going to be manning a helpline in an hour. In the right circumstances, in the right moment of weakness... everybody is the type."

CHAPTER TWELVE

Detective Wilson took a deep breath and knocked on the door.

"Come in."

He entered. Detective Superintendent Burns was sitting behind her desk, putting on a pair of running shoes. Wilson blushed. His timing wasn't getting any better. He'd been terrified of coming in here, taking two nervous pees and a walk around the block to build up the courage. It had been three hours since he had introduced himself to his new boss by throwing up on her shoes after viewing the mutilated corpse of Craig Blake. Since then, he had considered resignation, suicide and briefly, throwing up on somebody else's shoes, in a desperate hope that he could turn it into a fun 'rite of passage' team bonding thing. Then he had remembered that they were a team of highly trained law enforcement officials, and sadly not a university rugby team.

"Superintendent sir, er... ma'am, have you got a second?"

"The news of the murder has just hit the media, so if this is about my shoes, then you've already apologised."

Wilson glanced down, and noticed the footwear in question sitting in the bin.

"No it's not, I mean... although, can I just say again... if you'd allow me to replace them..."

"Yes, you can buy me shoes, and then the other detectives can take turns taking me to dinner and getting me sexy lingerie. Forget it. Now, I've got a high profile corpse to deal with so unless there's anything else, or you'd like to pee in my handbag..."

"Yes," said Wilson, blushing again, before adding, "I mean on the 'something else' front. About the body... or, I mean, the words on the wall. 'This is the day that never comes.'"

"Yes, I was there too. What about them?"

"They rang a bell with me, and I double-checked."

Wilson took the laptop from under his arm and pointed towards the desk. Burns nodded and Wilson put the laptop down.

"There is a Metallica song of that name," said Wilson.

"Oh Christ, if you're going to pitch me some heavy metal killer cult angle Wilson—"

"Oh no, ma'am," interrupted Wilson, as he turned the laptop around to face her. "This is a speech delivered about six weeks ago by Father Daniel Franks."

"Oh Christ, no," said Burns. "I'll take the cult, please."

Father Franks was famous, or indeed infamous depending on whom you asked. Certainly everyone knew who he was. A short man, bald, save for wild tufts of hair that sprouted above his ears, with blazing green eyes that spoke of a forest fire in the middle-distance. He was from Armagh, but he'd been stationed down in Dublin for most of his stint in the collar, having only found his calling in his thirties. Until recently he'd been a mild-mannered parish priest in central Dublin, toiling away in obscurity; that was, until he went rogue. When a needle exchange had been closed down due to cutbacks, he'd gone off to a reporter from the evening paper. Drug use should be decriminalised, prostitution should be legalised. Rather than condemnation, the country should offer support and understanding to those that found themselves on the fringes of society. It'd all been said before, but the collar on the guy saying it had made it news. Still, it was only a one-day story except a canny TV producer had spotted it and put him on one of the political panel shows. Franks had torn a junior minister to shreds to such an extent that the poor lad had nearly been in tears by the end. The phrase he'd numbly repeated over and over again – 'We're establishing a working party' – had become a social media punchline. While the once-future Taoiseach had seen his dreams go up in smoke on national telly, his tormentor had only been getting warmed up. There was a hypocrisy at the heart of Irish society that needed to be addressed, said Franks. Corporations were beatified while ordinary people were sacrificed. The meek might well inherit the Earth, but what state would it be in when they did? He'd roared his frustration out into the world, and a lot of people had found it echoed in their front rooms. It wasn't a particularly new message; far from it. It'd been said many ways, many times before, but somehow Father Franks had found himself standing at the point where opportunity and circumstance collided. It could have been anyone, but it wasn't – it was him.

The opposition parties had been quick to try and latch onto him, only to receive their own smacks in the chops. If you'd been in power at any point in the last twenty years then you were part of the problem too. You also couldn't claim to be on the side of the common man while your former brothers-in-arms ran protection rackets and dealt drugs on street corners. Franks was unafraid, and he was knocking down walls.

It was powerful stuff, some old-school fire and brimstone. Suddenly his parish church in the Liberties went from a third-full on a Sunday to rammed to the rafters every morning. The Church was delighted. This was the new face of modern Catholicism, reconnecting with their lost congregation. Franks was all of that, right up until he started preaching that it was sinful how the Church and the religious orders owned billions of euros worth of property while so many slept homeless on the street. Then he questioned why the Bishop of Rome lived in a golden palace, while so many went hungry around the world. Why the life of a child was sacred right up until the point it was born. They'd tried to whisk him away for a time of prayer and reflection, bring him to Rome, send him on a mission to Africa, give him a wee sabbatical – anything. Still, the man the press had dubbed 'Ireland's turbulent priest' was not for moving. Instead, when they'd locked him out, he'd turned up to his own church and preached from the steps. The public flocked to him and, love him or hate him, he was must-see TV and a headline waiting to happen.

In short, anything linking him to her first big case as head of the National Bureau of Criminal Investigation was something Detective Superintendent Susan Burns needed about as much as another shoe full of Wilson's breakfast. She sighed. "Go on, play the thing."

It was the speech that Franks had delivered outside the GPO. He'd turned up with a mobile PA, and word had spread like wildfire on social media. Thousands had flocked there. The Gardaí had initially tried to shut him down, but had eventually closed off the street instead. The Commissioner had been left with a no-win call; allow an illegal gathering and receive all kinds of grief from government ministers, or wake up to a pile of Sunday newspaper front pages filled with pictures of her officers dragging a campaigning priest away. She had opted for the private grief, rather than being publicly lambasted as a leader of jackbooted thugs. Still, it hadn't helped that she'd been forced to officially reprimand two uniformed officers when they were filmed enthusiastically cheering along.

Wilson pressed play on the video. Franks was standing on top of an honest-to-God wooden crate for a stage. It was shaky mobile phone footage that wobbled about as its owner was jostled in the large crowd.

"They tell us, 'these are the days of austerity. These are the days when we all have to tighten our belts.'"

Boos from the crowd.

"But what of the corrupt corporations? The profiteers? The speculators? When will those who cut corners, who fiddled the deals – who defied the laws this country was built on, both legal and moral, to line their own pockets – when will they be made to justify what they have done?"

Cheers.

"When is the day that they will pay their fair share?"

Cheers.

"When is the day when those who brought this country to its knees will be made to stand and face the people's wrath for their wrongdoings?"

Cheers.

"When is that day? I tell you, my friends; that is the day that never comes."

Wilson clicked the mouse to stop the video.

DSI Burns looked up at the ceiling for a long moment. "Tremendous. Just what this case needs. Politics."

"I thought it might help with motive."

"Yes," said Burns, "it narrows it down to Father Franks, and anyone who heard him speak, read about it or has access to the Internet."

"Actually, it can't be Franks himself," said Wilson.

Burns looked at him for a couple of seconds before realisation hit. "Oh, of course – he's holed up in that bloody Ark thing isn't he?"

It had happened right after the GPO speech. Catching the Gardaí cold again, he'd marched his supporters down the Quays into the International Financial Services Centre and straight into the vacant Strander building, left conveniently open by a sympathetic security guard. Built for a Spanish bank at the Irish Government's expense, it had sat idle and empty since completion. Along the way it had been given to an Irish bank, then bought back when they too had gone into receivership. The government had now paid for it twice and nobody had used it. It was an embarrassment they were keen to shift. Franks had decided to take it off their hands. He'd moved in and opened it as Dublin's biggest and newest homeless shelter. The neighbours were less than pleased; it didn't quite fit in with the vibe the Financial Services Centre was going for. While the government had debated and dawdled, Frank's enthusiastic supporters had built barricades and settled in for the long haul. When the Gardaí had been instructed to stop food supplies being delivered, the public had hurled the supplies over the barriers. It was yet another lose-lose situation. The Gardaí had already been made to look bad. They'd arrested a 73-year-old woman when her erratic throwing motion had resulted in a guard getting a can of beans to the earhole. One of the newspapers had done a cartoon. It hadn't been funny, but then they never were.

"What a mess," said Burns. "Right, I'll have to take it upstairs. A murder like this: the torture, the showmanship, the message. This whack job isn't going to stop until he's caught. We need to warn the other two of those Skylark pricks that they might be in danger, for a start."

"Yes, ma'am."

"It might be nothing, but seeing as you found it, I want you to – carefully – start looking into the Franks angle. See if there's anyone around him who might have decided to put the good Father's words into action."

"Yes, ma'am."

"I'm not going to mention this just yet, in the team briefing or in the news conference. The frenzy is already going to be quite something. Craig Blake and his buddies weren't exactly popular. We've currently got four million suspects. Let's try and get that number down slightly."

"Yes, ma'am," repeated Wilson, as he turned to leave.

"Oh and Wilson... good work."

"Thank you, ma'am." He allowed himself a slight smile of relief.

"I want you to remember I said that, when you close that door and realise that your fly has been open this whole time."

"Yes, ma'am."

CHAPTER THIRTEEN

SATURDAY 5 FEBRUARY 2000 – MORNING

Councillor Veronica Smyth pulled the duvet tighter as her husband nudged her in the back.

"Not a chance, Niall, and you know why."

"No I... I think there's somebody outside."

She opened one eye, and looked at the closed curtains that thin beams of sunlight were beginning to sneak around. "It's morning; I'd imagine there's lots of people outside."

They'd been out late at a function the night before, and it'd been his turn to drive. She'd availed herself of the free bar, and then they'd replayed the argument greatest hits on the drive home.

"There's someone in the garden," he insisted.

"Ah, get up and look if it—"

She sat bolt upright as something very solid thumped hard against their window.

"What the?!"

Niall clambered out of bed and rushed over to the curtains, pulling the edge aside to peek out. Sunlight flooded in around him as he spoke.

"It's... kids."

Veronica lay her head back down on her pillow and turned over.

"Go and tell them to piss off."

"No I mean it's... it's lots and lots of kids."

Veronica Smyth, having hastily dressed, was standing at their patio doors with her husband Niall, looking out in disbelief. Their large back lawn was her pride and joy. She didn't do any of the work on it herself, mind you, but she gave the gardener extensive directions. It was the biggest on the road, and they'd gone to great lengths to achieve the perfect blend of perennials to ensure that it would be glorious in summer and a dark-hued delight in winter. Right at that moment, twenty or so pre-teen children were traipsing across it, wielding hurleys and inexpertly whacking balls to one another. Directly in front of her, one young boy was attempting to wallop a ball out of an arrangement of lilies which cost more than the average weekly wage.

Veronica heaved the door open. "What the hell is the meaning of this?"

Twenty young faces turned to look at her.

"Keep going, children."

Veronica turned to look at the source of the voice. Sitting in a deckchair under the shade of the house was a woman in her sixties, wearing a garish pink PVC raincoat.

Veronica marched towards her.

"Are you in charge here?"

"That's right love, I am."

"This is private property. You have no right to be here."

"Ah, well," said the woman, looking disconcertingly relaxed as she opened a flask of tea and began pouring it. "What you're looking at here, is the St Jude's hurling team who're about to lose their field. We heard how youse had a massive garden – lovely rhododendrons by the way – and we thought, 'sure let's go out and practice there.'"

"You can't... all complaints about issues involving planning permission can be raised through the proper channels."

"Yeah, yeah. We tried all that, now we're doin' this instead."

"You have two choices, madam; either you remove yourself and these children from my property instantly, or I will phone the police."

The woman noisily slurped at her tea, and then smacked her lips.

"I'll have option two, ta very much."

"Right, well then, so be it."

Veronica turned, walloping into Niall who was standing gormlessly behind her.

"Christ's sake, Niall..."

"Hello. Did someone call the Gardaí?"

Veronica turned back to see a large man in his mid-thirties, leaning over the side gate and holding up a Garda ID card. "Detective McGarry. We received a complaint."

"Yes," said Veronica, " I mean I was about to—"

"I called you," interrupted the older woman.

"You did?" said Niall.

"Yes. I wanted to complain about this criminal waste of wide-open green space. Shocking, so it is."

Veronica marched over to the man who had identified himself as Detective McGarry. "This is ludicrous! This woman and these children," she said it in such a way that it implied she'd just found them on the bottom of her shoe, "are trespassing on my private property, and I want them removed immediately."

The Guard looked down at the trespasser.

"Is this true, love?"

"Yes Bunny," she responded.

"Will you come peacefully?"

"I will not."

"I am then forced to arrest you."

"Ye can try."

"I'll have to use handcuffs on you."

She grinned up at him. "I'm not into the kinky stuff, officer. At least, not in front of the kids."

The woman took Detective McGarry's proffered hand and pulled herself up out of the deckchair.

"What the hell is going on here?" interjected Veronica. Detective McGarry ignored her as he pulled out a pair of handcuffs and, with practised efficiency, put them on the woman's meekly extended wrists.

"Are you the sole adult responsible for these children, madam?"

"I am," replied the woman.

"Right," said the Guard, only now returning his attention to Veronica. "I'm going to have to call Child Services. It's a Saturday, and they'll need one carer for every two children so it could take a while. Then we'll need to get separate cars to bring all the nippers home. There's very strict regulations on—"

He was interrupted by a camera flash going off. Veronica looked up to see a man in his twenties leaning over her fence. "Councillor Smyth, would you like to give a comment on the situation with the St Jude's club being re-developed out of existence?"

"Now look here," said Niall, "this guy is trespassing too."

"I'm afraid he's not, sir," responded the policeman. "He's on public land there. He'll have a good view of this pensioner and all these children being hauled out into police cars, I shouldn't wonder."

"Oh dear," said the woman, "I'm not an expert on these things but, would that be the kind of thing that'd look bad in the papers?"

Veronica and the woman locked eyes for the first time. Under the casual tone, she recognised in her the kind of resolve that she too prided herself on.

"We're only five minutes from RTÉ here too," said Detective McGarry, "I wouldn't be surprised if they send the van."

"Christ," said Niall, "he's right, Veronica. This won't—"

"Shut up, Niall," interrupted Veronica. She took a deep breath and slowly let it out. Rage was coursing through every fibre of her body but deep down, she was a deal-maker. Politics was all about only fighting the battles you could win. What was it that whiny country singer had said; you didn't need to be a weatherman to see which way the wind was blowing?

"What we have here," said the woman, "is one of them photo opportunities. How does the headline "Councillor throws her support behind inner city kids ' sound to you?"

The women locked eyes again, and exchanged smiles that had about as much warmth as a witch's tit.

"C'mon, children. Come and meet the nice lady who is gonna help save our field."

CHAPTER FOURTEEN

"The Minister for Justice, Padraig O'Donohue, gave a statement in the Dáil this evening saying that – regardless of the circumstances – vigilantism was never the answer. He added that he would ensure the National Bureau of Criminal Investigation had all the resources it required to get to the bottom of what he called 'a heinous crime'. Detective Superintendent Susan Burns of the NBCI said that initial investigations placed Mr Blake's time of death as late Tuesday evening, and she is appealing for any members of the public with information to ring the confidential tip line at 1800 666..."

Paul leaned forward and turned off the radio. While the media had spoken about nothing else since the shocking discovery of Craig Blake's body earlier that morning, they'd actually had very little information to impart. The man was dead, someone had killed him, and they'd apparently not been too genteel about it. There was a tone of ill-suppressed giddy excitement in the reports, like a child with a secret that it really wanted to tell; desperate to share the gory details. Paul had no doubt that at least one of the tabloids would spill the beans in the morning and then take the fine on the chin, knowing it would be paid for twice over in increased circulation.

So, in the big picture, Blake's murder made for a media feeding-frenzy, but it was the little picture that most concerned Paul. It was now Thursday evening; he had until Monday to find evidence of Hartigan having an affair – or indeed a happy marriage – or else four grand was going up in smoke. Paul had spent his day forlornly checking his phone for updates from Brigit or any word from Bunny, but neither had happened. In the meantime, he had to hope that the traumatic news about his best bud turning up dead might push Hartigan towards the comforting arms of a woman. Any woman.

Earlier, Paul had got back to the restaurant just in time to see his quarry making a hasty exit. His mobile held to his ear, Hartigan power-walked up Dawson Street where he was soon picked up by the green Roller. They had then followed him home. Actually, they hadn't; by the time Phil had negotiated Stephen's Green's traffic system, Hartigan had been long gone. What they'd done is drive back to Hartigan's house, and been relieved when they'd seen the green Roller pulling out of his cul-de-sac, having just dropped him off. After a quick drive-by to confirm it looked like Hartigan was indeed at home, Paul and Phil regrouped in the car park of Casey's pub. This had consisted of Paul speed-reading from a book, while Phil took Maggie for an overdue walk.

How to be a Private Investigator was written by James T Blando, who wore an honest-to-God fedora hat on the inside cover. Paul had found the picture really off-putting, but the potted CV said Blando had been a PI in Los Angeles for over thirty years. Paul had a sneaking suspicion he'd originally rocked up there hoping to break into movies. Certainly the dust jacket picture made it look like he was auditioning to be a detective in a Broadway musical. Even for a Yank he had too many teeth and too much enthusiasm for life. Still, Paul had bought his book. It was a choice of that, a tie-in to a TV show that only got one series, or a children's book entitled *The Complete Guide For The Junior Detective*. Paul had seriously considered the latter, but he couldn't bring himself to buy it under the withering gaze of Lianne, the shop assistant from hell. The Blando bible it was. He had got about fifty pages in by the time Phil had returned with Maggie.

"It says here that we should have surveillance kit for watching Hartigan," said Paul, "like cameras and binoculars and all that."

"I could get Uncle Paddy's bird-watching kit if you like?" Paddy Nellis hadn't watched a bird in his entire life, but Paul wasn't about to point that out. Phil could get a little funny about his dear departed uncle. Still, it stood to reason that if you wanted to pull the kind of high-end jobs that Paddy Nellis had, you needed the gear to scope the place first. Phil had duly been dispatched home, Paul's desperation forcing him to take another chunk out of his budget to splurge on a taxi for him.

He'd returned two hours later in another taxi, only he was driving this one.

"Oh God," said Paul, "please tell me you've not become a hijacker now?"

"No, smartarse. Uncle Abdul was over at our place again, helping Auntie Lynn move a wardrobe."

Paul made every effort to maintain a blank expression as he nodded. Abdul wasn't really Phil's uncle, or indeed related to him in any way. He was, however, quite clearly engaged in relations with his Auntie Lynn. She was still a woman in her prime, and he guessed she was done with the mourning. Paul had picked up that Abdul had previously 'stayed over' a couple of times as their house was nearer some unspecified location he had to be at early the next morning. He'd also dropped over to use their iron, take a look at their boiler and clean their chimney. You name it, he hadn't really done it. If Lynn didn't want to explain their relationship to Phil, Paul would be damned if he was going to. Still, with the merry widow's nephew coming back in the middle of the day unannounced, Paul was pretty sure Phil may have interrupted the wardrobe-moving process at a very key juncture. He tried not to think about the fact that he'd hired the most obtuse man in Dublin as his assistant detective.

"Yeah," said Phil, "Abdul said I could have a lend of his taxi for as long as I liked." Definitely a key juncture. "I reckoned it'd be good for the following stuff you were talking about. I mean, who pays attention to taxis? Be like hiding in plain sight."

That was the unnerving thing about Phil; he could go from incomprehensible stupidity to moments of sheer genius, often in the same breath. He was right, of course. Taxis drove like they owned the road and parked like nobody else existed. It was absolutely perfect. In stark contrast to Bunny's Porsche, which stood out like a sore thumb, nobody would pay a blind bit of notice to yet another taxi. That had been the first thing in the vehicular surveillance chapter of the Blando bible; drive something inconspicuous. In other words, everything Bunny's Porsche wasn't.

"So what've I missed?" said Phil.

"Not that much," said Paul. "That lawyer bloke we saw Hartigan play golf with yesterday went in just after you left, then two Laurel and Hardy-looking characters turned up about an hour ago. I'd bet my life on them being Garda detectives. They've all been in there since."

"There's not much chance of him knobbing any of them."

"Jaysus, Phil, you're a shocking loss to the greeting card business. Did you get your uncle's bird-watching gear?"

Phil went around to the boot of the taxi and came back with a large silver case. It turned out that Paddy Nellis, God rest his soul, must have been one of the most thorough birdwatchers in history.

The case contained a couple of cameras. One of them was one of those big, impressive-looking things with the massive lenses like those paparazzi types use. There were three additional lenses, but they didn't know how to change them and were too scared of breaking it to try. Besides, the one already attached had allowed them to zoom in close enough to see that somebody in a house way down the street was watching *Coronation Street*. That'd do the job nicely. The other camera had been a smaller, more discreet, digital one that seemed pretty good, and certainly a lot more inconspicuous. In addition to the cameras, the case contained a powerful pair of binoculars. Paul raised a prayer of thanks to the heavens, although it would be open to serious debate whether a career criminal like Paddy Nellis would be there to receive the message.

"And Lynn said we could use all of this?"

"Yeah. She said I could take whatever I want."

She must have been positively gagging to get that wardrobe shifted.

While Phil watched the top of the cul-de-sac to see if any of Hartigan's guests had made a move, Paul nipped into the pub for a quick field bath. Sitting alone in Bunny's car, he had begun to smell himself. For the last few weeks that he'd been sleeping in the office, he'd nipped into Digger Doyle's boxing gym down the road every couple of days for a shower. He was smelling well past due. On his way out, he'd bought four packets of cheese and onion to show willing. He was worried that the bar staff may have started to notice how he seemed to spend a lot of time in their car park and not much time in their pub.

Nearly two hours after they'd arrived, Paul saw the two Garda detectives pull out of the cul-de-sac in their nondescript blue Vauxhall Astra. Paul wondered how that interview had gone. 'To your knowledge, did the deceased have any enemies?' 'Yes, everyone.'

About half an hour later, the lanky lawyer fella finally left too.

"Right," said Paul, "look alive. Hartigan is alone and – please God – hungry for love."

"I dunno," said Phil. "Is he really going to be trying to get his hole? I mean, his friend has just died and that. Seems a bit disrespectful."

"True. On the other hand, he is a narcissistic monster who destroyed countless people for personal gain so, y'know..."

"He might be horny?"

"Precisely."

Paul pocketed the small camera and slipped the lead back on Maggie. Luckily, she seemed to have an infinite capacity for walkies.

He took her down to the cul-de-sac. Maggie inspected the same tree she always did, which granted Paul plenty of time to casually look in the general direction of the Hartigan residence. Lights were on in several windows and the silver Merc was in the drive, so he was definitely still at home. The green Roller was nowhere to be seen, so if he was going anywhere tonight, odds on he'd be driving himself.

Maggie finished her sniffing about and declined to pee on

anything. Paul was about to turn and head back when a blue BMW with tinted windows turned the corner and pulled up in front of Hartigan's house. Paul looked down at Maggie and whispered, "keep going, don't stop the music." Unnervingly, she then went back to sniffing enthusiastically around the base of the tree. Paul put his hand into his pocket and excitedly fingered the small camera. This could be it, finally. Please let this be a car full of hookers.

The driver's door opened, and a man of about forty with short-cropped salt-and-pepper hair and a boxer's physique stepped out. Paul vaguely recognised him as one of the security guys from the court. The man stopped and looked directly at Paul, giving him a peculiar smile. Paul felt himself redden under the man's gaze and covered by looking down at Maggie. "Come on, Chardonnay, hurry up." He had no idea why he'd decided to give Maggie a false name, and why he'd chosen the seventh most popular one for strippers. Paul was painfully aware that the man was still staring at them, and that Maggie had now started staring back. She emitted a low growl.

Luckily, the tension was broken as the far passenger door of the BMW flew open, and an ill-tempered whine emitted from it.

"Oh don't worry about me, I'll open my own fucking door then shall I?"

The driver rolled his eyes as the bald head of Paschal Maloney emerged from the back of the car, followed by his petulantly scowling face.

"What the fuck do I pay you for?"

Even in his peripheral vision, Paul couldn't help but notice the driver's wince of irritation. Maloney did a double-take when he noticed Paul and Maggie, as if a man walking a dog was an unprecedented occurrence. "Oh, hello." He recomposed his face and beamed a false smile across the car roof at Paul. "What a lovely dog."

Paul mumbled his thanks and started moving away down towards the bottom of the cul-de-sac. Maggie was resistant, and Paul had to tug on the lead to get her moving at all.

The driver moved around to the boot and opened it.

"Well come on then," said Maloney, as he started to walk down Hartigan's drive.

Luckily, Paul had been already pulling on the lead as otherwise Maggie's sudden snarling surge forward would have sent him flying. As it was, she nearly ripped his arm clean out of the socket as she hurled herself towards the car, barking furiously. Maloney let out a girlish scream and then scurried up the drive. In contrast, the driver stood calmly where he was, giving them a look of quizzical amusement. Paul stumbled forward, losing the tug of war. "Chardonnay! Sorry, she's... normally very friendly."

Thankfully, the tree Maggie had been inspecting moments before lay between them and Maloney. Paul was able to halt her progress by going to the other side of it and wrapping the lead around the trunk. It still took all of his strength to hold her in check. A car alarm beeped once and then Paul turned to see Maloney's driver walking up the drive, a black briefcase in his hand. His boss was now standing on the porch, joined by Hartigan; they were both looking back down the drive at the man with the insane dog. Paul quickly turned away and concentrated on trying to shove his body in front of Maggie to obstruct her view. "Will you stop, ye mad bitch!"

Eventually, Maggie's barking turned into a frustrated whine. Paul looked behind him, to see a now empty porch. He quickly unwrapped them from around the tree and dragged her down towards the bottom of the road.

"You stupid... I can not believe you! That is it. I know I said you taking a shit on my desk was it, but this – this – is really it! You've completely compromised the case. Hartigan has seen us now. I mean, what the hell is your problem?"

Maggie unsurprisingly didn't answer. Instead she just kept growling as she paced back and forth, like a boxer waiting to make their way to the ring.

"I've had enough of this. You're going to the dogs home tomorrow. Bunny has disappeared, Brigit won't speak to me and you have to go and balls up the one chance I have to try and make things right."

Maggie made defiant eye contact with Paul, raised her leg and peed against someone's garden wall.

"Unbelievable!"

Paul realised he wasn't just vibrating with rage, his coat pocket was also vibrating. He took his phone out and answered.

"A car went down, did you see?"

"Yes, Phil. It was what's his name – Maloney – the other member of the Skylark Three. Maggie," said Paul pointlessly pointing in her direction, "decided to try and attack the little fucker and blew our cover in the process."

Maggie sat down and looked haughtily off into the distance, as if unwilling to dignify that with a response.

"Jesus, what brought that on?"

"Hell if I know, but it's going to make following Hartigan a right ball ache now. He's seen me and her, and we were incredibly memorable!"

"Shit. What are they up to now?"

"I dunno. I'll have a quick squiz on my way past, assuming madam here doesn't go all Godzilla on me again. I'll be back at the car in five. We'd better stay sharp. Who knows, Maloney and Hartigan might head out on the town to commemorate their fallen brother-in-arms."

Paul hung up the phone and then bent down to Maggie. "Right, we're going back to the car. Can I trust you to keep the head as we go past you-know-where?"

Paul looked up and noticed an old lady standing in her front porch, regarding him with undisguised dismay. He gave an embarrassed wave and started walking quickly away.

As they passed Hartigan's house, Paul stopped and pulled Maggie back. Through the front window he could see Hartigan and Maloney and they were quite clearly arguing. Paul crouched behind one of the gate pillars. Hartigan was towering over the smaller man, pointing a finger angrily in his face. The double glazing must have been good, because there appeared to be shouting going on, and Hartigan was doing the lion's share of it.

Maloney said something and suddenly Hartigan knocked the

glass of whiskey out of the smaller man's hands and pushed him. Maloney stumbled backwards and fell onto the couch. Hartigan leapt on top of him. Paul watched in stunned disbelief as he could see Hartigan bearing down on the other man, his hands clearly wrapped around his business partner's throat.

"Holy shit."

Maloney's leg flailed wildly, knocking over a tall lamp. As Paul was considering what to do, a door flew open and Maloney's driver appeared. With the relaxed calm of a parent breaking up two rambunctious kids, he enveloped Hartigan in a bear hug and physically lifted him off of his boss and out of the room.

Maloney stood up a couple of seconds later, his face red and clearly gasping for air. Paul watched him drag in a few coughing, ragged breaths as he leaned against the mantelpiece, before picking up a cushion and petulantly starting to wallop the sofa with it. Then, as if suddenly aware of his surroundings, Maloney turned to look out the window. Paul pulled Maggie away, resisting the urge to glance back to see if their departure was being noticed

Only as he walked away did Paul think of the camera in his pocket and curse himself. He didn't know what it meant, but clearly, all was not well amongst the remaining members of the Skylark Three. As he hurried back towards the car, another thought struck him. Hartigan had a violent temper. They'd lost him on Tuesday night and so they had no idea where he'd been when Craig Blake had been murdered.

CHAPTER FIFTEEN

Detective Superintendent Susan Burns calmly closed the blinds to her new office, checked that this did in fact prevent any member of her team from seeing her, and then kicked the wall. The thinking behind this was twofold. Firstly, she'd read an article in the *New Scientist* that said distracting your brain with a pain stimulus was a good way of refocusing it, to take a fresh view of a problem that was proving unsolvable. There had been quotes from a neurologist, coloured diagrams of the brain and a detailed plan for further academic study of the hypothesis. The second reason she'd kicked the wall was that she really felt like kicking something.

On her desk sat two provisional reports, prepared with lightning speed by their respective departments. The call had gone out; her team were to be given every assistance. She had wasted a remarkable chunk of the last twenty-four hours on the phone, with the commissioner, two government ministers and the Taoiseach's right-hand man, having that made clear to her.

The first report had been prepared by Dr Denise Devane, the state pathologist. She was legendary for her thoroughness, and this was the thickest such report that Burns had ever seen. In it, she had listed in gut-wrenching detail the indignities that had been delivered unto Craig Blake. Amongst the highlights that would live too long in Burns's memory were that the subject had had his lips, ears, fingernails and eyelids removed, almost certainly antemortem. Toes had been broken, there was evidence of electrical trauma to the genitals and puncturing of the left eyeball. In short, somebody had gone to great lengths to inflict as much pain and suffering on Blake as was humanly possible. The cause of death was put down as a heart attack brought about by severe shock and loss of blood. Reading between the lines, death was the best thing that happened to Craig Blake that night. Dr Devane was also renowned for being frustratingly reluctant to speculate, yet this time she had been moved to. She believed, in her professional opinion, that anyone with the capability and knowhow to perform such acts had significant medical knowledge. Devane had also followed up the report with a less official late-night call. 'Susan, do you have any idea what kind of a mind it takes to be able to calmly stand there and do something like that to a living, breathing, human being?'

The second report had been from the Technical Bureau, compiled by Doakes – widely considered their very best – and signed off by his boss, DSI O'Brien. She could see how keen they were to show their workings-out too, and to emphasise how the report was only provisional. Fingerprints in the house had been minimal, once the victim's own had been eliminated. Along with his Polish cleaning lady's, there had been evidence of three others currently unaccounted for. While not directly saying it, the report made clear they weren't "likely lads". Two sets had been found upstairs and a third set in the kitchen area, away from the body. They'd chase them down, but they'd quite probably end up belonging to an electrician and a couple of dinner party guests. The blood splatter analysis also made grim reading, mainly for the lack of it. Brutal as this was, there was precious little evidence to indicate that any of it was done in a frenzy. To put it into the more common policing vernacular; they were looking for a Grade-A sick and twisted bastard who enjoyed his or her work.

Hollywood skewed the public's perception of such things but in reality, leaving aside organised crime, most murders were ill-considered acts of spontaneous passion. Those that weren't were mostly poorly executed plans, reality warping what the perpetrator expects from the act. Not in this case. Whoever had done this was cool, calm and knew exactly what they were doing. They'd left all kinds of twisted carnage, but precious little actual evidence. The Technical Bureau's assessment had also matched the one given by detectives at the scene; there was no evidence to suggest a break-in. Blake may have known his killer, or he just might have opened the door to find a gun pointing in his face.

There was a polite knock on Burns's office door. She moved back behind her desk and sat down.

"Come in."

The door opened and Superintendent Mark Gettigan, head of the Garda Press Relations office, stuck his head in.

"Susan, I have something for you."

"Is it good news?"

"I very much doubt it."

She waved him inside and he closed the door behind him.

"Do you know what a Púca is?"

"Some kind of fairy?"

"It is a spirit in Irish mythology. Considered to be bringers of both good and bad fortune. There are various versions of the myth, of course, it varies wildly."

"OK," said Burns, still not getting it.

He pulled an A4 sheet from the folder in his hand and slid it across the desk to her. "This is a copy of an e-mail the RTÉ news desk received just under an hour ago; 8:17 am to be precise. The *Irish Times* have confirmed they've got it too. I'll inform the Tech Bureau guys as per protocol, but odds are high it came from an untraceable darknet e-mail address."

"Christ," said Burns, not looking up from what she was reading. "Do we have any reason to believe it is genuine? Could be some keyboard warrior living out his fantasies in his ma's spare room?"

"I'm afraid there were attachments."

Gettigan took out two pictures and slid them across the desk too. One was of Craig Blake, tied to the chair, still alive. DSI Burns looked at it and felt her stomach churn. She was looking at a man who must have known he was about to die, and yet who was still attempting to smile for the camera. She remembered what one of her instructors had told her down at Templemore; never underestimate the human desire to stay alive, regardless of the circumstances. The other picture was of the bloody writing on the wall. 'This is the day that never comes.'

"Christ," said DSI Burns, "Can we stop all of this getting out?"

"Yes and no. Nobody legit is going to publish the first picture. I guess the sender knew that. It's just there for veracity's sake. With regards to the rest, RTÉ and the papers will grumble to varying degrees, but they'll play ball. I've got to return calls to the AP and *Fox News* when I get back upstairs though, and I'm guessing my call-sheet has got longer in the meantime. If this has gone to Internet news, *Al Jazeera*, the Russians..."

Burns leaned back in her chair and looked up at the ceiling.

"God help us all."

"I'm afraid so," said Gettigan. "This is out there. I strongly suggest we brief the press this morning and try and do whatever we can to manage it."

Burns gave a hollow laugh. "Good luck with that."

Gettigan gave her a smile that spoke of sympathy and more than a little relief that he wasn't sitting in her chair.

"OK Mark, set it up and draft a statement. I'll brief the team and liaise with the tech boys."

"Sure. I'll touch base in an hour."

He turned around and headed back out of her office.

Burns lowered her head and read through the e-mail again.

To whom it may concern,

We are the Púca. For too long the ordinary hard-working people of Ireland have had to suffer the consequences of crimes committed by the wealthy, privileged few. A country has been brought to its knees by the corrupt acts of an untouchable cabal, who have been allowed to walk away without facing the consequences of their actions. They sit amongst their ill-gotten wealth and watch the common man suffer. The politicians have given the Irish people no justice. The law has given the Irish people no justice. We are that justice. Craig Blake was the first to taste that justice, he will not be the last.

Nobody who has a clear conscience has anything to fear from us. Those that do not, this is your one and only warning. Confess your sins and make right your crimes. The day of judgement is at hand. Welcome to the new revolution.

We are the Púca, and this is the day that never comes.

CHAPTER SIXTEEN

Gerry: And we're back. We've Richard on the line who is completing his PhD in economics out in UCD. So, Richard, explain to me again this system you're proposing?

Richard: It's very simple, Gerry – we put a price on a human life.

Gerry: But ye can't do that, can ye?

Richard: Sure you can, we do it all the time. When they decide on the funding for the Health Service – we all know, the more money you put in, the more lives you save. When insurance companies pay out compensation, when a faulty car part leads to a loss of life, they effectively set a price. Why not just come out and put it out there? Call it a million euro. If you cost a life, that's the price.

Gerry: So, no prison?

Richard: For murder? Absolutely. But if you do it indirectly, then you pay the fine. So say, your... oh, I don't know, disastrous housing development costs lives, which it does. When you add up the effects of stress, financial hardship and so on, it costs lives. A judge looks at it, puts a number on it, then you have to pay that fine.

Gerry: And then the person who is responsible for the loss of all those lives walks away free?

Richard: Isn't that what they're doing now? At least this way, we get a few quid to chuck into the Health Service and save a few other lives.
Gerry: And what happens if you can't pay the fine?
Richard: Then... we kill you.

Brigit turned off the car's engine and sighed. She was tired, dog-tired. The rain was teeming down around her with such velocity that it made loud, plopping splashes as it collided with the windscreen. Typical Irish weather; when they finally got a bit of summer heat, it combined with the perpetual rain to unleash a thunderous downpour.

It had been a long and largely fruitless day. After her meeting with Johnny Canning yesterday, she'd gone home and come up with what looked like a comprehensive plan of attack for the Bunny investigation. She'd spent the day going through it step-by-step and getting nowhere fast.

She'd started by heading out to Howth in order to meet Sergeant Sinead Geraghty. The good sergeant had come across as wary and stand-offish from the get-go. Brigit got the impression that the word may have come down from on high that the Gardaí didn't want anything to do with Bunny McGarry, disappeared or otherwise. Brigit couldn't tell if Geraghty was angry about being questioned, angry with not being allowed to help or just angry at something entirely unrelated. The woman gave off the vibe of having so many chips on her shoulder that she could open her own shop. She'd tersely confirmed the basic facts about Bunny's car that Paul had left in his initial note and not much else. Brigit had been assured that Bunny McGarry was now listed as a missing person, and the Gardaí would do everything in their power to assist in his safe return. It was all said in a 'don't call us, we'll call you' kind of a way.

From there, Brigit had gone up to the car park near Howth Head where Bunny's car had been found. Then she'd taken the path up to the cliffs. On a sunny Friday morning, the place had been deserted save for the occasional sprightly pensioner out on a stroll, or a jogging yummy mummy. The tourist buses would be arriving soon enough, and the place would be crammed with unimpressed continental youth.

When she'd found herself alone on the cliff walk, Brigit had closed her eyes. She'd read this technique in a book once. She drew in a lungful of sea air and tasted salt on her lips as seagulls argued in the distance. I am Bunny McGarry. I'm a ham-fisted, bollock-booting, larger-than-life force of nature who seems to have little going on save for a consistently awful hurling team and a job. A job I love. A job they've taken away from me because I was willing to do whatever it took to see justice. I'm a drinker and – remembering that night when she had found him amongst the burnt ruins of the St Jude's clubhouse – I've got one of those melancholic Irish hearts, prone to bruised introspection, especially when inebriated. Then she remembered his younger, happier face in that picture by his bed, his arm around the beautiful woman and how that picture had been turned towards the wall. The look of pride in his eyes in each one of those team photographs in his spare room. And Johnny Canning saying that in his experience, given the right circumstance... everyone was the type.

Then she'd opened her eyes and tried to imagine Bunny McGarry, almost certainly drunk, taking a few steps back to allow a run-up before he hurled his immense body into the great beyond, to crash on the rocks below. She couldn't see it. She was aware that emotion was quite possibly getting in the way of logic but still; she couldn't imagine Bunny McGarry throwing himself off a cliff. Throwing somebody else off a cliff, now that was a different matter.

She'd left there and visited the four pubs and two takeaways that were on the Howth promenade, showing the staff at each place the picture of Bunny and each in turn had said they'd never seen him. She left her number with a few of the pubs, in case their usual Friday night staff remembered anything when they came in. It didn't seem likely, but you never knew. Bunny could be accused of a lot of things, but not being memorable wasn't one of them.

From there Brigit had headed into town and visited some of the parents of St Jude's players who had appeared on Bunny's phone bill. Here the picture had proven to be a different kind of help. Once they'd seen Bunny with his arm around her, people had opened up. It'd been educational but not much else. They all spoke of him with a mixture of reverence and fear. Everybody had a story of someone who he'd helped and somebody who had made the mistake of crossing him. There'd even been a couple of cases of both.

She'd caught Sally Chambers as she'd returned home in her lunch hour. She worked as an administrator at the Department of Public Works. She had that perpetually harried edge about her. She was a mother to four boys, whose father was in prison in England last she'd heard or rotting in hell; either was fine by her. She had explained this with an embarrassed smile as she'd scurried around the front room, picking up toys, clothes and TV remotes. Brigit had felt bad, but Sally had insisted a cup of tea on her and then furiously set about cleaning the house around her, apologising all the while.

As they'd made small talk, Brigit had heard a couple of thumps from upstairs. Sally had seemed to visibly sag at the sound and winced as an elderly, angry female voice had bounced down the stairs.

"Sally?"

"I'll be up in a minute, gran."

"Who's downstairs?"

"Just a visitor. Stay where you are."

"I'm coming down."

"There's no need."

"I'll be down."

Sally rolled her eyes then tried to play it off with a smile. "She's a bit of a handful."

Four boys and an elderly relative, thought Brigit, Sally might be in line for some kind of award.

"Bunny has been very good though, helping with my Darren. He plays fullback. He's a good boy but he can be a bit ... he's got that ADHD, so the school says. They gave us medication for a while but then it stopped because of the cutbacks. Didn't help that much, to be honest with you."

An elderly woman of what must be eighty appeared in the doorway, with her blue wig at a jaunty angle and a face like thunder. She gawped at Brigit through thick glasses. "Oh, I thought it'd be that Maguire scumbag, trying to squeeze his money."

"Gran!" said Sally, clearly keen to avoid that subject.

"Who're you?" she said to Brigit, ignoring her granddaughter entirely.

Brigit stood up and extended her hand. "My name is Brigit Conroy. I'm a friend of Bunny McGarry's."

"That bastard," she spat.

"Gran!" said Sally again, the outrage lending more urgency to her voice this time.

"He locked up our Cormac last year. Never done nothing wrong, the lad. Bloody fascist peelers."

Sally moved towards the door as Brigit stepped back and withdrew her unshaken hand.

"My lunch hour's nearly up, gran. Can you go into the kitchen and microwave the rest of last night's curry for me, please?"

The two women locked eyes and Brigit looked away in embarrassment as they held a silent conversation. Brigit stared at the family portrait of Sally and her four sons on the mantelpiece, four grinning bundles of energy and a mother's eyes full of pride, hope and worry.

She heard the old lady turn and shuffle down the short hall to the kitchen, mumbling beneath her breath as she did.

"Sorry about that," said Sally in a soft voice. "She's... well, the boys are all angels as far as she is concerned. Her and Bunny used to be great pals, back in the day."

Sally stood beside Brigit and pointed to the tallest of the boys in the picture. "That's Cormac, my eldest. He fell in with a bad crowd. You try your best and all but..." there was a crackle of emotion in her voice as she spoke. Brigit did her the courtesy of keeping her focus on the picture as Sally wiped a sleeve across her eyes. "Bunny did arrest him, but then he turned up at court and spoke on his behalf too. He's down in Mountjoy now. Bunny wrote him. Said when he gets out next June, he's got him an apprenticeship down with an electrician in Waterford if he wants it. Get him out of here for a few years. Stop him getting sucked back into..." Sally sniffled. "I'll miss him, but we can go down and visit. It's for the best."

With a sudden urgency Sally had squeezed Brigit's arm and leaned in. "He's a good man. I hope you find him."

Once she'd spoken to a couple of other parents, all polite and concerned dead ends, Brigit had gone onto O'Hagan's pub on Baggot Street. It was the place Johnny Canning had told her Bunny frequented. She'd been expecting an 'old fellas' pub, but O'Hagan's was all fresh paint and old-school charm, clearly aiming at the after-work crowd and the odd tourist. She'd met the owner, a nice lady called Tara, who'd been most helpful once Brigit had established her 'friend of Bunny' credentials.

"Oh yeah, he came in late last Friday night all right. Last time he was in."

"Is that unusual?" asked Brigit.

"Well," said Tara, "He's a regular but not regular, if you know what I mean. He could pop in at any time of the day really. Could see him three times in a day and then nothing for a week. You know Bunny, he's always got something on the go. He'd a bloody dog with him a couple of weeks ago."

"What was his mood like last Friday? Did he seem depressed?"

"Depressed? Jaysus, no. He was celebrating!"

This took Brigit aback.

"Really?"

"Oh yeah, he was on the good whiskey. He only has that on special occasions."

"Did he say why he was celebrating?"

"Not as such, no. He bought me one, not that I actually charged him for it, and we had a quick toast. I don't normally drink when I'm working but sure, you can't leave a man to celebrate alone. Wait...

now that I think about it, I remember him saying 'I got the bastard,' because I said 'You always do.' Yeah, that's right."

"Did he give any more details?"

Tara stared at the bar in concentration for a few seconds. "No, sorry. It was a Friday evening so y'know, busy."

"Is there anyone else he might have spoken to?"

"Not really. He wasn't actually in here that long. I think he just wanted a quick one for whatever had him in such a good mood."

"So did he leave here alone?"

Tara laughed and then raised her hand in apology. "Sorry, but Bunny didn't come here to pick up chicks, God help us if he did. Yeah, he left around midnight maybe. Hard to be sure. I think he used to park the car up on Fitzwilliam Square and the last thing he said to me was not to worry, he was getting a taxi home. I'm always on at him about that."

"He wasn't worried about leaving the car?"

Tara pulled a face. "Nobody would be stupid enough to touch Bunny's car."

"What would you say if I told you it was found out in Howth the next morning?"

Tara hadn't said much in response, but for really the first time in their conversation, she looked concerned. That wasn't uncommon. Amongst all the people she'd spoken to that day, Brigit had noticed a recurring theme. Though they'd not directly expressed it, they all seemed to have the impression that Bunny McGarry was invulnerable.

Brigit had thanked Tara for her help and left her number in case she thought of anything else.

And now here Brigit was, sitting in her car having fought her way home through the chaos of Friday night rush-hour traffic. She'd found out plenty, but nothing that seemed to help. She was going to order a pizza, open a bottle of wine and take a fresh run at trying to figure out where to go next. She was painfully aware that a week ago tonight, Bunny had tried to ring her and that'd been the last time anyone had any confirmed contact with him.

Brigit looked out the window at the rain that showed no sign of stopping. The door to her apartment building was only about fifty yards back across the street. On a normal night, this was a good parking spot. She often had to leave the car two streets over. In this kind of a downpour though, that was more than enough distance to ensure she'd be drenched to the bone by the time she got inside.

She took her keys out of her bag in preparation, and grabbed her raincoat from the passenger seat. She made a hasty exit from the car, and holding the coat over her head she made a dash for dry land. Her left foot splashed into a deep pothole, nearly sending her flying and cursing the gods as she squelchingly limped towards the door of her building. Amidst the downpour, she saw a figure running in the opposite direction on the side of the street she'd just left.

As Brigit fumbled with her keys a hand touched her upper arm and she screamed with shock.

Put it down to stress, jumpiness or perhaps an overly keen survival instinct, but three years of self-defence classes instantly kicked in. She reeled around and rammed the heel of her hand straight into her assailant's face.

He fell backwards, bounced off the car that always seemed to occupy the best parking space and then slumped to the pavement.

Brigit looked down into a face of wounded indignation as the rain instantly diluted the trickle of blood from his nose.

"Oh my God," said Brigit, "I'm so sorry."

Dr Sinha looked up at her, his tone unjustifiably apologetic. "That's quite all right, Nurse Conroy, entirely my fault."

CHAPTER SEVENTEEN

Paddy Nellis stretched his legs out, adjusted his sunglasses and breathed in deeply. It was in the nature of how he made a living that he preferred dark and enclosed spaces. He liked to see and not be seen. He was a thief and a damn good one; sitting in the middle of a park in broad daylight was about as unnatural an environment for him as it was possible to have. On the upside, Sunday morning seemed to be high time for ladies going for a jog. He was a very happily married man, but there was no harm in looking.

It was because of his beloved wife Lynn that he was here in the first place. Mavis Chambers had been on to her, and then she in turn had badgered him. He'd hated the idea from the get-go, even if it was of benefit to their nephew Phil. The kid was a goofy string-of-piss and no mistake, but since they'd taken him in, Paddy had grown to love him. The kid lived for that hurling team, despite the fact he had no discernible athletic ability of any kind. Still, there are some things you don't do. Paddy had said no. He'd put his foot down. Then Lynn had pulled out the big guns. She'd brought up how she'd waited for him while he'd been inside. It was never spoken but they both knew that he was away for their prime years. She'd wanted a child of her own and his actions had maybe, just maybe, denied her that. She'd never used it before, she'd only even implied it this time, but it had been enough. And here he was. The "here" in question was Bushy Park, way out on the leafy high-living south side of Dublin. It'd been a ball ache to get to, but anonymity was priceless in the circumstances.

"Paddy."

He jumped and then blushed as Bunny McGarry sat down on the bench beside him, seemingly appearing out of nowhere.

"Fuck's sake, Bunny, for a big culchie beast you don't half move quietly."

"'Tis the ballet training, Patrick. I'm light on my feet. You should see my *Swan Lake*, it'd make you shit a brick. You've a God-awful sense of direction, by the way. This is the south side of the park, not the north. Bad enough you dragging me out all this way, I've not got the time to play hide 'n' feckin' seek with you."

"My sense of direction is fine, and we're here because I don't want to be seen chatting with the Garda Síochána. That'd do my reputation a power of good."

"Well, I'm not mad keen on consorting with criminal scum, but sure, here we are."

Paddy bristled. "Fuck you, Bunny. This wasn't my idea."

"Wasn't mine either."

"Ah, I can't be bothered with your bullshit, I'm out of here."

Paddy stood up to leave.

"Ara calm down Paddy, alright? Let's just remember why we're doing this. Don't pay any attention to me, I've sweaty bollocks from running around a park for an hour."

Paddy looked down at Bunny, who was giving him what he probably thought was a smile. He imagined the look on the wonky-eyed muppet's face as he just walked off. Then he imagined the look on his wife's face when he told her what he'd done. He turned and sat back down again.

"If you could keep your sweaty bollocks out of the remainder of the conversation I'd appreciate it."

"I'll try to, but something might come up."

Paddy glanced sideways and noticed Bunny looking back at him. They both smirked and the tension eased.

"So," said Paddy, "do I need to ask about a wire?"

"Do I?"

Another long silence stretched out.

"Look," said Bunny, "I don't like this and I'm not supposed to, but needs must. These pricks have got us by the short and curlies. No wire, you can check me if you like."

Bunny stood up in front of him and Paddy looked him up and down before waving him back to the bench. "Tempting as it is to cavity search a big sweaty Cork boy, I'll pass."

Bunny sat back down.

"So?"

It hung there for a moment.

"Aren't we going to talk about what I get?" said Paddy.

"Course," said Bunny, "How does 'fuck-all' grab you?"

"No get out of jail free card?"

Bunny shifted uneasily. "That's not the deal."

Paddy gave him a steely-eyed stare before cracking a smile. "Still hanging onto the moral high ground there, Detective, how's that working out for you?"

Bunny leaned back and looked up at the sky. "Not the Mae West to be honest. Not in the current circumstances."

"Yeah," said Paddy, "I can imagine. How's about you and I do each other the favour of forgetting this ever happened?"

"Agreed. So, what are we forgetting?"

"Well, I'm forgetting your request to break into the highly secure offices of Phoenix Construction on just a day's notice."

Bunny looked around nervously. "There's no need to feckin' broadcast it."

"I'd never do such a thing. I'm a simple car mechanic, Bunny, I don't know what you've heard to say otherwise."

"Ah for—"

"What were you expecting? That I'd be able to tell you they've a safe with twenty grand in cash and a ledger, hand-written but in some kind of code."

"Something like that."

"Well I can't tell you that. I also can't tell you that said code, if it existed, is pretty good and it ain't going to give you the kind of leverage you need to sort your Monday evening problem. I mean, three months from now when you figure a couple of things out, maybe but—"

"Fuck it," said Bunny. "Was there anything else?"

Paddy stared at Bunny, who after a moment did the best attempt at rolling his eyes that the lazy one would allow. "Sorry, if you were to have hypothetically blah blah..."

Paddy lowered his voice. He'd not been looking forward to this, but nobody had their hands clean here. "There's a certain councillor, who you'd think would be on your side. He's not."

"Really?" said Bunny.

"There's... you'll see."

Paddy stood up.

"How will I see?"

"Look under the passenger seat in your car."

"When did—"

"I know the difference between north and south, ye daft culchie prick."

Paddy stood up to leave.

"Wait," said Bunny. "What about the money?"

Paddy Nellis just winked and walked away, whistling happily to himself.

CHAPTER EIGHTEEN

Detective Wilson tugged at the leg of his trousers, in an attempt to prevent the unpleasantly damp fabric from clinging to his lower leg. He watched a laughing couple spill out of the warm, inviting lights of the nearby Harbour Master pub, the man's tie wrapped jauntily around his companion's neck. They'd probably stayed there longer than intended, waiting for the truly biblical rain to stop. Wilson had only been able to close his umbrella five minutes ago and, despite having it, his shoes and the lower pant legs of his best suit were still soaked through. The happy couple clung to each other and headed off into the night, either to continue their Friday evening's drinking elsewhere or to swap a lot more than the tie. Wilson sighed to himself and shifted his feet again. In hindsight, of the many pros and cons of joining the Gardaí, he felt that everyone had criminally underplayed the effect it would have on your ability to get your end away. Here he was on a Friday night, a man very much in the prime of his oat-sowing years, standing around in soaking trousers like a dipshit who's been stood up on a blind date. Only a copper could fully appreciate how little justice there was in the world.

He checked his watch again; he'd been standing there for thirty-six minutes now and been pissed off for about thirty-four of them.

"Wilson."

Wilson jumped at the voice and instantly hated himself for it, not least because that was no doubt exactly the effect the voice's owner had been going for. He turned to see a man in a trench coat and a smug smile.

"Livingstone, I presume?"

Wilson's words were greeted by an eye roll and a grimace. "Wow, never heard that one before. Come on."

Livingstone brushed past him and walked off in the direction that Wilson had been expecting him to come from in the first place. He was forced to break into a skip to keep up.

"You're late," said Wilson.

"Yeah," said Livingstone without looking back, "it was raining."

Bloody Caspers, thought Wilson. In truth this was his first contact with the most reclusive branch of the Gardaí but their reputation preceded them. Caspers, as in *Casper the Friendly Ghost*, was the nickname for the NSU or National Surveillance Unit. The name was intended to be ironic, the Caspers being legendary for their unfriendly and sneering attitude towards the rest of the force. As Wilson's old boss, DI Jimmy Stewart, had once described them, 'busy little shits running about like they're the bloody Secret Service or something. In the land of the blind, the one-eyed men truly are king.'

Keeping an eye on stuff is what the NSU did. They were the Garda Síochána's covert surveillance specialists. They operated primarily out of the Phoenix Park headquarters, same as Wilson's NBCI team did, but they weren't exactly hanging out drinking in the same pubs. Mind you, if the NSU were any good, you'd not have known if they were.

It was now thirty-six hours since Craig Blake's tortured and mutilated body had been discovered, and about thirty-two hours since Wilson himself had found the admittedly tenuous link to Father Daniel Franks and his so-called Ark. As DSI Burns had pointed out, somebody simply quoting Franks by using the phrase 'This is the day that never comes' was the flimsiest of flimsy circumstantial evidence and yet, it was something and it couldn't be ignored. That was the problem. Officially linking the Blake killing with Franks would be like throwing napalm onto a roaring fire. The Ark and the trial of the Skylark Three had dominated the media over the last two months, linking them was a newspaper editor's wet dream. DSI Burns didn't want to drag her investigation into a political three-ring circus. And so, it'd taken time. They had been forced to go through unofficial channels.

There was, of course, the official, publicly-known Garda operation around the Ark. Since Franks and his supporters had moved in over two months ago now, there had been a police presence around the building. Initially, they'd been there to ensure public order but it had become political fast. There had been the government's attempt to stop supplies going in, which had met with public outcry before being struck down by the High Court as being unconstitutional. The Gardaí had been forced into the position of bad guys on that one and had hated every minute of it. Stopping food being delivered to hungry people wasn't what anyone had signed up for. Similarly, getting the water and electric turned off had been struck down by the courts. The case for saying that the electricity bill for the building was an excessive expense on the holding company that legally owned it, even though it itself was owned by the government, had looked promising until a generous anonymous donor had stepped in and paid it. All the smart money was on the donor being a backer of the opposition. They knew a potential administration-ending debacle when they saw it and they didn't want it ending any time soon.

Then there was the other Garda operation, the NSU's one. Anybody with half a brain who gave it more than fifteen seconds thought would have guessed that the NSU would have been carrying out surveillance on the Ark, but there was knowing and there was having it admitted. Burns had been forced to pull in favours. Wilson's unofficial meeting with a team carrying out an operation that didn't exist was what he'd been waiting around in the rain for.

Livingstone rounded a corner and the Ark itself came into view. A five storey building that had previously looked similar to pretty much every other shiny corporate office in the International Financial Services Centre. Any politician worthy of the name who had seen a bit of power in the preceding fifty years had tried to claim credit for the IFSC. It was an oasis of corporate prosperity on the banks of the River Liffey. A shining light that showed Ireland to be a dynamic, forward-thinking nation. You could see how everyone from the Taoiseach on down would be pissed off with one of its buildings being turned into a great big homeless shelter by some priest who had wandered off the reservation. It was now a big glistening reminder of a mishandled economic collapse, and those that the recovery had left behind. A rising tide might lift all boats but if you were without one, you drowned.

The Ark building did stand out now though, and not just because it'd been pictured so many times on the front of newspapers. Cardboard and improvised curtains blocked out many of the windows. Barriers also surrounded it. That had been the latest brainwave. The government realised that turning off the electricity or water might not pay, but they could damn sure stop anyone else getting in and detain those leaving. The deadline to leave without facing trespassing charges had passed two days ago. Some had come out, many more had stayed.

"How many people are in there now, do you reckon?"

Livingstone turned for the first time. "Say nothing until we get inside. If anyone asks, you're with Symonds Auditors Limited."

Wilson was really starting to dislike Livingstone. Like two ordinary Joes would walk by the most well-publicised building in Ireland and not be discussing it. Still, he dutifully stayed silent as Livingstone swiped them into a nondescript building across from the Ark, signed him in past a security guard who was doing little more than holding up a uniform, and then into a lift to take them up to the sixth floor.

It was only when they were in the lift that Wilson realised quite how bad Livingstone's breath was. It smelt of barbecue crisps, off milk, and tramps' feet. He also had a Jimmy Hill chin and a bit of a squint. He doubted that Livingstone's absence on a Friday night was being unduly mourned by the Dublin dating scene.

"The bank only let us have the space if we pretended we're from a German auditing company, just here to run some feasibility tests on moving part of their operation. No company wants to be seen as publicly against the Ark. Priority number one is maintaining our cover."

"Right," said Wilson. "Don't mention the War. I did it once, but I think I got away with it."

Livingstone threw a sarcastic smile onto his face which did nothing to improve its aesthetic appeal. The lift doors opened, bringing the small-talk section of the evening to a close.

Livingstone swiped them into an area of open-plan office that looked deserted, save for a sliver of light from under an office doorway at the far end. They walked towards it, Livingstone placing his hand on the handle and stopping to give Wilson a look. "Can I remind you, yet again, that the existence and nature of the operation you're about to see is considered highly confidential."

"Noted," said Wilson.

Livingstone opened the door and they entered a large corner office. It was occupied by a woman in her forties and a chubby man in his twenties, that Livingstone pointed to in turn. "Brady, Tonks... this is Detective Wilson from the NBCI. The DSI says we've to give him every assistance with his investigation, provided it doesn't impinge on ours."

Wilson raised his hand in salute. Brady barely looked up from what she was typing to nod, Tonks waved enthusiastically from behind his bank of monitors.

"Any updates?" said Livingstone.

"Nothing much," said Tonks, in an unexpectedly chirpy voice. "That Polish couple are at it again up on the fourth floor."

"Christ," said Livingstone, "they're like rabbits."

Wilson moved around to stand behind Tonks as he looked at the three large computer screens before him, each showing four different camera feeds. "We've got eight HECs," said Tonks, "that's hidden external cameras to you, and we eventually got feeds of the CCTV footage from the nearby buildings as well. That took a while. Banks get awful funny about giving anybody access to their security systems. Now, we've got the building pretty much covered from outside, bar the areas where they've boarded it up, which is quite a lot of it. Every time they get a box of supplies, the cardboard is used to block another window."

"Why're they doing that?" asked Wilson.

"Well, partly because these offices aren't designed with sleeping in mind. So in practical terms, the people inside need to block out the light to get a bit of shut eye. They also know we're watching though, and they don't like it," Tonks beamed again, "well, apart from that Polish couple, they seem to actively seek out windows. They properly seem to get their ya-yas off that. Last week—"

Livingstone looked up from reading various things Brady was showing him on her terminal and coughed pointedly. Tonks pulled an 'aw shucks' kind of face.

"How many people are in there?" asked Wilson.

"We reckon about two hundred, but it's hard to judge from infrared. Not designed to deal with those kind of numbers in close proximity. Sniper reckons—" and then he stopped talking suddenly and looked up at Livingstone.

"Sniper?" asked Wilson.

Livingstone glowered at Tonks. "Codename. We've a man on the inside, have had for three weeks now."

"Right," said Wilson, "would he not be able to do a headcount?"

Livingstone picked up a stress ball from the table and pointed at one of the office chairs for Wilson to take a seat. He tossed the ball from hand to hand as he waited for Wilson to assume his assigned position.

"What you've got to understand is, in there," he said, pointing out the window to the Ark, "is something we've not seen before. You've got a very disparate group of people. Firstly, you've got your ordinary, everyday rough sleepers. Let's call them group number one. People who'd most nights end up on the street if they can't get into a hostel.

Mostly male but some women, variety of ages, quite a lot of them young people. Within that group, all sorts of mental health issues, rap sheets for petty crime, drug addictions of various forms – basically your unhappy buffet of human existence. We've sat down and gone through them with the local forces; there's a few with violent tendencies, but most are just poor bastards who fell through the cracks. A lot of them are the types that don't go to the shelters because they don't want to be around drugs. The most shocking thing is how far some fell. There's an honest-to-God architect in there. They don't all fit the profile you'd expect. Not by a long shot."

Brady looked up from her screen and tapped Livingstone on the arm.

"Kids," she said.

"Oh yeah," continued Livingstone, "there's also a few families with kids. Four, we reckon. It seems that when some people become homeless, they're terrified to go to the Social for fear of the kids being taken into care, so they ended up in there too. Along with them, there's group two - the foreign nationals. Mostly people who came here looking for a decent life and found it hard to come by. Eastern European, Africans. Some have been here a while. Came in the boom years and when the arse fell out of the economy, they'd no safety net. Others came here pretty recently we reckon. That lot makes us nervous, because we don't know who most of them are."

He pointed to a corkboard behind him that featured long-range photographs of various people. Some had names, but many just had question marks beneath them.

"Then," continued Livingstone, "you've got your professional protester types; the kind that do actually have homes but the need to piss mummy and daddy off supersedes all others. Most of them we know. They've protested bypasses, water charges, pipelines, evictions. You name it, they've held a placard for it. They spend a whole lot of their time arguing with each other about stuff, but they're mostly harmless. Then there's group four..."

Livingstone turned to Brady and she handed him a folder.

"These are the ones that keep us up at night." Livingstone pulled out a picture and handed it to Wilson. It was of a man of about six foot two, with an extensively tattooed gym-body build, maybe mid-thirties. "Andy Watts, career militant. Born in Barnsley but lived all over since his dishonourable discharge from the British Navy where he was a Signals Engineer. Calls himself an environmental socialist these days, but he's basically spent his life looking for a fight. He's tried to join any organisation with the word 'militant' attached to it. Interpol have a long file on him. He's currently wanted for an assault in Germany. Nasty piece of work, but from what we've been told, not that bright."

Livingstone handed Wilson another photo, this one of a brunette woman in her late twenties, with a lot of piercings and tats. "Belinda Landers, Belgian national. The wild-arsed progeny of a famous Belgian family, would you believe. I didn't even know such a thing could exist. Grandad was a highly regarded left-wing politician, mother came second in Eurovision..."

"With the 'La La La' song," interrupted Tonks.

"Yeah," said Livingstone, seemingly irritated by the fact he'd failed to knock the enjoyment of life out of Tonks yet. "Point is, she went looking for trouble too, and found it with Watts. Been boyfriend and girlfriend for a couple of years, although it's one of those open relationships. Watts has a temper, Belinda seems to enjoy watching it blow. Between them, they've enough issues to keep a whole building's worth of shrinks in business."

Livingstone handed another picture across. This was of a thin man with long white hair who looked to be perhaps in his sixties but in good shape for it. "This one is Gearoid Lanagan; Irish and proud, but a real superstar of international naughtiness. Born in Offaly, he joined the INLA at an early age but, following a bit of a falling out, he took the show on the road. Went to Germany in the eighties and was linked to the Red Army Faction, the German terrorist group that came out of that Baader-Meinhof lot. The group was active for over twenty years; kidnapping, assassinating and the like. While Lanagan was pictured talking to people around the edges, they could never link him to anything. He then disappeared completely, showing up again in Colombia in the Nineties. They reckon he was helping FARC turn cocaine into guns but again, no proof. Then he was gone again, off the radar for five years. Interpol located him in 2006 in France, but they don't reckon he was there long. He was also pictured a couple of years ago hanging out with some of those 'good old boy' militias the Yanks have. He's smart and clearly morally flexible. He's also," said Livingstone, as he pointed out the window, "got a lot of influence in there."

"Really?" said Wilson, "I mean Franks is hardly the militant sort."

"Ah, but that's it. Lanagan is a smart cookie. They'd a couple of incidents, you see. Think about it. You get people with drug problems, mental health issues all crammed in one place with a bunch of ordinary citizens, stuff is going to happen. Couple of fights, bit of thievery, one guy getting way too friendly with the hands. Lanagan dealt with it all and made himself invaluable in the process. Became a sort of de facto head of security. Father Franks is all big picture and nice speeches, odds are he has no idea who Lanagan and his fellow travellers really are. We tried to open up lines of communication but Lanagan has fed the paranoia, so Franks doesn't trust us or the government boys at all. At the end of the day, Lanagan hasn't got any meaningful convictions and no outstanding warrants. All we've got is what Interpol reckons."

"Jesus," said Wilson, "he sounds like a scary fucker."

"That he is," said Livingstone, "and we can't really figure out what his angle is. Which brings us to our really fun joker in the pack."

Livingstone handed him a fourth picture and then put the empty folder down on the desk. This one was of a stockily built man of about five foot ten, with a shaven head, glowering directly down the lens of the camera. "He's calling himself Adam but we're pretty sure that isn't his real name. We have tried everything and neither us, nor Interpol, nor even the CIA have the first clue who this bloke is. He hardly speaks, and there are conflicting reports that he might be Irish, Scottish, American or even Canadian. All we know is he reeks of ex-military, but whose, we've no idea. Sure as shit, nobody is claiming him."

"Right," said Wilson, "so these four are around Franks and the good father doesn't realise quite who they are. Are they in communication with the outside world?"

"Oh yeah, all the time. They've got mobiles, and we can't get a trace because we can't narrow down to their numbers. There are dozens of phones in there and no judge is going to give us a licence to tap all of them."

"Can't you block them?"

"If only," said Livingstone.

Brady spoke up properly for the first time, in the kind of husky voice that sounded like forty-a-day. "Take a look around you, Detective. You're in the middle of a financial services centre. Have you any idea how much hassle we'd get if the mobile phone network went down?"

Wilson ran his hands through his hair. "I assume you've seen the news?"

"The Púca," said Tonks in a deep, ominous voice. "Yeah. Fun name."

"Christ," said Brady, "shut up and make some tea, would you Mark?"

Tonks stuck his tongue out and exited the room, clearly in a huff. Wilson imagined there'd be discussions about professional behaviour as soon as he left.

"Do you think Lanagan could be behind it?" asked Wilson.

Brady and Livingstone exchanged a look.

"We're not saying he is, and we're not saying he isn't," said Livingstone, in a deliberate way that gave the impression that he and Brady had agreed this beforehand. "What we can tell you is: one, I certainly wouldn't put it past him; and two, four nights ago Adam snuck out through a fire exit and managed to break through the ring of steel. Now, not only do we not know who he is, we don't know where he is."

Wilson looked at the pictures in his hands again. It looked like Detective Superintendent Burns wasn't going to be getting that quiet life any time soon.

CHAPTER NINETEEN

"I am so sorry," said Brigit, for what she was aware was at least the twentieth time. Apologising for something was supposed to make you feel better about it, but it hadn't helped so far.

Dr Sinha did not raise his head up from dangling forward over a teatowel to avoid getting blood on the sofa. "Honestly, it is fine. Don't mention it. I should not have startled you."

Brigit sensed that her apologies were now reaching the point of being potentially very irritating. She resisted the urge to apologise for that too.

"I'm really not a violent person."

"Of course not, Nurse Conroy," said Dr Sinha, without any trace of irony as he briefly held the wad of blood-soaked tissue away from his nose to examine it.

Brigit thought that she'd never been more embarrassed in her life, and then was horrified when the memory of answering the door to Paul two nights ago popped into her head. "I've just... it's been a very stressful few days."

"I can imagine. I heard you had taken a sabbatical after the incident involving Dr Lynch."

"Yes, well, that's one way of putting it. I didn't think you'd know about that."

"Nurse Conroy, you handcuffed a doctor naked to a bed for eight hours. That is the kind of thing that gets around."

"Oh God."

"Don't be embarrassed. I'd imagine you are a folk hero to every nurse in Ireland by now, and a few of the doctors as well. Dr Lynch does an impression of my accent. He finds it most amusing."

Brigit had known Dr Sinha for eight months, but it wasn't like they were friends. They had first met when he'd patched Paul up after he'd got stabbed in the shoulder by a homicidal octogenarian, although judging by what Paul had done since, that may have been pre-emptive karma. Since then, she'd met Dr Sinha occasionally through work. He'd always been cheerful, polite and really quite formal. All she knew about him was that he was from India, he'd moved over here a couple of years ago and the nurses considered him good, nurses being the only people who can really tell. They had never met socially. She had no idea what he was doing at her apartment. That would've been her first question if she'd not assaulted him.

Dr Sinha lifted his head up and gingerly felt his nose.

"The bleeding has stopped and no bones are broken," he diagnosed with a tentative smile.

"I'm really—"

Dr Sinha held his hand up to stop her. "There is absolutely no need, Nurse Conroy."

"OK, I'll make you a deal. I'll stop apologising if you stop calling me Nurse Conroy. I've known you for a while now, you're in my apartment and I've properly clocked you one. I reckon that puts us on a first name basis. It's Brigit."

"Alright, Brigit," he said, taking a foreigner's care to try and get the pronunciation right. "In that case, please call me Simon."

"Honestly, I'm really good with languages, I can use your real name."

He smiled and nodded again. "I appreciate that, but it really is

Simon. My parents are not terribly religious and my father is an enormous Paul Simon fan."

"Oh," said Brigit.

"Don't be embarrassed, it is a common assumption. You can only imagine how difficult life is for my sister Garfunkel."

Brigit laughed nervously at first, and then properly as her confidence grew that this was definitely a joke.

"OK, Simon, well, can I get you a cup of tea then?"

"Oh, no, thank you. I actually have to get moving. I have a... I am meeting a young lady for a drink tonight."

"Right," said Brigit. "In light of this new information, can I break the previous agreement and apologise yet again."

"Nonsense. My nose will be an excellent conversation piece and besides, what are the chances of getting punched in the face twice in one evening?"

"Fair enough," said Brigit.

"The reason I am here is... I believe you are looking for a friend of yours, a Mr Bunny McGarry?" Dr Sinha said the name in such a way that indicated that, while he was fairly certain he had the right words in the right order, he couldn't believe they were a name.

"Yes," said Brigit, "that's right. How did you know?"

"You have left a couple of phone messages for a friend of his. That friend would like to meet you."

"I see," said Brigit, who didn't see at all. "So, why are you here?"

"Ah," he said. "the problem is, who that friend is."

CHAPTER TWENTY

"What do you mean, you've got a flat tyre?" asked Phil.

Paul looked down at the flat tyre and then at the traffic hurtling by on the M50. He had to shout into the phone to be heard over it. "What words in that sentence are you having trouble understanding, Phil?"

"But... you can't have a flat tyre."

"And yet I do," said Paul.

"I'll tell you what this is – karma."

The 'karma' Phil was referring to related to Paul's destination. He had finally decided on a solution to the Maggie problem. The problem currently had its head out the back window of Bunny's car, and Paul could swear it was enjoying his discomfort immensely.

"Serves you right," says Phil, "for trying to kill that dog."

Paul sighed. He was on his way to an animal sanctuary in Rathfarnham owned by the Dublin Society for the Prevention of Cruelty to Animals. It had wide open spaces, lots of animals, it even had a pond. An actual pond. If the option was available, forget the dog, Paul would happily have put himself in there. Unfortunately, he had made the mistake of describing it to Phil as a lovely farm in the country.

"For the last time, I really am taking her to a nice farm in the country. An actual farm, they've got geese and shit."

"Yeah, right" said Phil. "That's what Auntie Lynn told me about Roger the tortoise and Veronica the parakeet and Wilbur the gerbil and Geri Halliwell the goldfish and Grandma Joan..."

Apparently, inspired by some TV programme, Phil had decided a couple of years ago to turn his aunt's rather large back garden into a vegetable plot. It was then that he had discovered the mass grave containing his childhood. Well, all of it apart from presumably Grandma Joan.

"Look, I'll take a picture as proof when we get there," said Paul, then he checked his watch and realised there was a very good chance he wasn't going to get there before closing. It probably wasn't like one of those charity shops where he could squeeze his donation through the letterbox.

"What am I supposed to do if Hartigan goes somewhere?" asked Phil.

"Follow him. That's what I'm paying you for."

"Speaking of which, you've not paid me for the last two—"

"You're breaking up," interrupted Paul, then hung up the phone before Phil could negotiate another pay rise.

Maggie looked at him. He looked back at her. He had no logical explanation of how, but on a fundamental level, he believed she was somehow responsible for this.

"I am fixing this tyre and then you..." he emphasised with a finger jab, "are going to an actual farm in the actual country. I'm not going to be beaten by a bloody dog."

Paul moved around to the boot. He'd never opened it before, and the car was old enough that a key was still required. After some waggling and pushing it popped open.

He looked down at its contents. It contained one item, lying there as if in a display case. Bunny's hurling stick. Thirty-seven inches of ash, with a metal band around the end. Bunny gave each new one a name, but Paul didn't know this one. The last one had been Mabel. Paul had broken that dealing with Gerry Fallon, the gangster that had been trying to kill him, Bunny and Brigit. Paul ran his fingers along the shaft of the hurl. Nobody had seen Bunny for a week, as far as Paul knew. He also knew he was unlikely to leave either his car or his hurl behind if he was going somewhere.

A juggernaut roared by and shook the car violently. Maggie barked in response.

"Alright, alright," said Paul, pushing the hurl back and lifting the faux carpet cover where he assumed the spare would be.

He did a double-take. On top of the spare tyre sat a handgun. Paul had seen more than enough films to know it was a revolver. It had a wooden handle and a long steel barrel. It was some straight-up Dirty Harry shit. He glanced around him nervously. Bunny would have had a gun in the Gardaí, but Paul was fairly sure this one wasn't legal. You couldn't just have a handgun in Ireland, could you? Even if you were an ex-copper. Until the Rapunzel affair, Paul had never been near a gun and even then, he'd not been the one holding it.

Paul reached down and touched the gun's barrel. The metal was surprisingly cold. There was a giddy attraction to the thing. You wanted to hold it and were afraid to at the same time. He picked it up tentatively by the handle and, careful to keep it out of view, he felt the heft of it in his hand. Only then, when he'd lifted it, had he noticed the yellow Post-It Note stuck to its underside. It had the name "Simone" and a mobile phone number on it.

Paul jumped with fright and dropped the gun as his mobile vibrated in his pocket.

"Jesus!"

He fished it out and looked at the display. It being Phil again was no great surprise, he was the only person who ever rang him these days.

"Hello?"

"Hello, Control," the voice on the other end was Phil's, only it wasn't. He appeared to be doing a funny accent.

"Why are you talking like that?"

"I'm just letting you know that I've picked up a fare." Phil was definitely doing an accent. Badly, but an accent nonetheless.

"What are you on about?"

"Yeah, that's right, out in Seapoint."

Paul closed his eyes and counted to five. "Please tell me that you didn't actually pick up the guy we are following?"

"That's a big ten-four, Control. I am on my way into Leeson Street now."

"You absolutely fucking... and why are you talking like that?"

Even as Paul asked the question, he knew the answer. The taxi was licensed to 'Uncle' Abdul. Paul had never met him, but he'd bet the farm that Phil was attempting an impression of whatever Abdul's accent was. In the world of Nellis logic, he'd be maintaining his cover.

"Never mind," continued Paul, "I'll get there as soon as I can. Just... don't talk to him."

"No problem, Control. Will use my initiative."

Paul felt a shiver run down his spine. As terrifying two-word combinations went, 'Phil's initiative' ranked right up there with 'performance poetry' and 'amateur surgery'.

"No, no. Do not—"

"No problem."

"Just don't lose him!"

"I can't believe you lost him."

Thirty minutes had passed.

"It wasn't my fault. We got stuck in heavy traffic. He said 'I'll hop out here' and then he just legged it. Nearly walloped a cyclist with the door."

Paul used the fingers of his non-phone-wielding hand to rub his temple. He could feel the mother of all headaches coming on. "Why didn't you follow him?"

"Because," said Phil, "I was stuck in heavy traffic."

"Which way did he go then?"

"That was the funny thing. He said Leeson Street, but I saw him wave down a cab going the other way and head back out of town."

Forget headache, massive migraine.

"I think," continued Phil, "he was trying to make sure he wasn't followed."

"Yeah," said Paul, "I think you're right. Why did you pick him up in the first place?"

"He walked over and just got in. I didn't even have the light on. I'll tell you what though, he gave a decent tip."

"Oh super," said Paul, "well, I'll be docking that from your pay. Seeing as you drove the getaway car for the bloke you were supposed to be following."

"Ye know," said Phil. "I know you don't mean it, but your tone can be very hurtful at times."

Paul counted to fifteen.

"Right, I need you to come out and find me on the M50." Paul looked down at the flat tyre, resisting the urge to further damage his foot by kicking it again. "It turns out Bunny's car has a spare wheel but no jack."

As he spoke, the third car in an hour slowed down to honk and wave at him. Who were these people? It was enough to make you lose your faith in mankind. The little demon on Paul's shoulder suggested the truly awful idea of waving the gun at the next idiot that cruised by for a gawp and a giggle.

"I'll only come out," said Phil, "on one condition."

Paul sighed. "Alright, fine; the dog can stay."

Maggie looked through the back window at Paul. He could have sworn she was smiling.

CHAPTER TWENTY-ONE

DSI Susan Burns leaned back in her chair and looked up at the ceiling. It wasn't how tired she was, it was the feeling of how tired she was going to be. She was forty-eight hours into a murder investigation, and every lead just seemed to drag them further and further into the mire. Today, she was supposed to have gone house hunting with her brother; that had obviously been shelved. In the last two days, what food she had eaten had been at her desk. Luckily, they had her in an apartment at the back of Garda HQ in the Phoenix Park that was normally used for visiting dignitaries. She'd only managed to grab three hours sleep on Thursday night and probably even less last night. This was not the quiet first week in the job she'd had planned.

She was just back from a semi-official briefing to a couple of senior civil servants at Government Buildings. She had given an update on the investigation's progress, or lack of it. Not that she'd phrased it like that. The new possible angle involving the Ark and Father Daniel Franks had been discussed at length. Unsurprisingly, the men in grey suits were very keen on that. It didn't take a genius to see that they were on the lookout for any reason that'd give them enough cover with the public to shut it down. They didn't have it, and it had been her job to make that clear. They got very excited to find out there was an outstanding German warrant on Andy Watts too. Finally they had a tenant of the Ark who they could give to the public as a bona fide bad guy. One wanted for assault in Germany no less, and if there was one golden rule of post-crash Irish economics, it was that everything possible must be done to keep the Germans happy. DSI Burns didn't much care. If they wanted to send teams in knocking down doors, it wouldn't be on her say-so. Right now, the only evidence linking the Ark or anyone in it to the murder of Craig Blake was flimsy and circumstantial at best.

She looked at the four pictures that she had placed on her office wall. The same pictures were on the evidence boards outside, but she liked having something just she could look at. Gearoid Lanagan and his merry band of lunatics were unnerving, all right, and were certainly of interest to the Gardaí in general, and her investigation in particular, but that didn't mean they were the 'Púca'.

And boy, hadn't that taken off. It was all the press could talk about. On the short drive from the Phoenix Park to Government House, she'd passed two walls and a billboard with the words 'We are the Púca' spray-painted across them. Somebody, somewhere, was undoubtedly working on a T-shirt.

There was a polite knock.

"Come in."

Detective Donnacha Wilson stepped inside and closed the door behind him. He looked as exhausted as she felt. She had him in at 7 am briefing her on the Ark situation, following his visit with the NSU boys late last night. Then they'd agreed on the shortened briefing he gave the rest of the team.

"I've got an update from the Caspers, ma'am," he said.

"Go on."

Wilson looked nervous, but that wasn't a surprise given how they'd met. She didn't want to make him feel better about his lot in life. In her experience, people on edge worked harder. She wasn't here to make friends.

"Adam," said Wilson, indicating the picture of the almost unknown man.

"We've found him?" said Burns.

"Sort of. He broke through the cordon around the Ark at about 4 am this morning. He's back inside."

"Oh for... you are kidding me! What the hell are the uniforms doing?"

"Apparently he timed it well and caught them cold. He gave one of them a right smack around the earhole when they tried to stop him."

"Great," said Burns. There's another fugitive from the law inside the building, the grey suits will be pleased. "Instruct NSU to send over any reports on the incident ASAP. Anything else?"

"Not really, ma'am. Remember I told you that Doctors Without Borders had agreed to send a doctor into the Ark today, as per their request?"

"Yes." She remembered it well. They'd specified an Asian doctor, and their logic had been embarrassingly obvious. How many Asian members did the Gardaí have?

"Our request to talk to him when he exits has been denied. No Garda access at all."

"Oh for—"

"UN have guaranteed it, would you believe? All stuff about doctors being free from—"

"Right," interrupted Burns, tossing her pen down onto the desk. "I got it. More bloody politics. I've got some demented shower of vigilantes slicing up punters and nobody seems to give that much of a shit about it. My dad was an award-winning dairy farmer, y'know Wilson? I could've taken over the farm. Farmers don't have to put up with this kind of crap. At least they can see the shit they've to deal with."

"Yes, ma'am."

"What does your dad do?"

Wilson shifted his feet nervously and gave a nervous smile. "Ehm... politician, ma'am."

"Fuck off, there's a good lad."

"Yes, ma'am."

CHAPTER TWENTY-TWO

Brigit looked at her phone. Three new messages, all from Paul.

'Any news on Bunny?'

'Did you get hold of that Simone woman?'

'Can I get an update? I'm worried about him.'

Brigit shoved her phone back in her pocket and looked up at the Ark. She was here because that male voice on a voicemail message that had sounded familiar belonged to Father Daniel Franks. She had no idea how he knew Bunny, but her supply of anything else resembling a lead had dwindled away to nearly nothing. Paul had texted her last night to say he'd found a number for a woman called Simone on a Post-It Note in Bunny's car. It was the one from his bill that Bunny had only texted once. Brigit had tried ringing it again last night, but got the same network-standard voicemail as the last three times. If, at the end of this, it turned out Bunny was just off getting his end away, she'd be annoyed but she'd definitely take it.

The fact that Father Franks wanted to talk to her hopefully meant he had something significant to say. Certainly, he'd gone to quite some trouble to say it. As Dr Sinha had described it to her, the chaplain from St Mary's Hospital had been the point of contact.

Apparently he and Franks went way back, having been in seminary together. He'd got the message out that he wanted to meet her. Brigit being a nurse had been a happy coincidence. The Ark had already requested a doctor, so all he'd needed to find was one that knew her, hence Dr Sinha's involvement.

Brigit glanced over at the good doctor, who was nervously bobbing up and down on his heels beside her.

"This is probably an odd time to ask, but why are you doing this?" Brigit asked.

Dr Sinha shot her a nervous smile. "Well Nurse Conroy—"

"Brigit."

"Brigit," he repeated. "Throughout my whole life I have been a good boy, a studious boy, a boy who has kept his head down and stayed out of trouble."

"OK."

"I thought it was about time I did something a little... how would you say it? Badass."

Brigit laughed. "You're like... Clint Eastwood meets Gandhi."

"Thank you," he said grinning, "that is precisely what I am going for."

"Oh, I never asked, how did your date go last night?"

"A gentlemen does not kiss and tell."

Brigit looked him up and down.

"Are you wearing the same clothes as yesterday?"

"Let us just say that ladies like a badass."

Brigit smiled and turned back to look at the Ark. It certainly was imposing. Technically, it wasn't any bigger, in fact, it was smaller than most of the surrounding buildings, but pictures of them hadn't been on the front of national newspapers.

Two hours ago, they'd reported to the on-site Garda command centre and there'd been all manner of faffing. Dr Sinha had explained Brigit's presence to Sergeant Paice, the on-site commander, as being required in case any of the women felt uncomfortable with a male doctor. Brigit hadn't mentioned how she was currently on sabbatical after taking a doctor hostage at her last job. It hadn't seemed relevant.

Sergeant Paice gave the impression of being a man who hadn't enjoyed anything since birth, and that he found Brigit's presence particularly irksome. Eventually, Sinha had made clear that he thoroughly understood his misgivings and would it be okay if they held their press conference on the steps outside? Yes, the one where they explained how the Gardaí were withholding medical attention from children. Suddenly, previously insurmountable problems had magically found solutions.

So there Brigit was, carrying a large bag full of medical supplies. They had drawn a small crowd of curious onlookers but it being a Saturday, the IFSC was a lot quieter than normal. Under the supervision of Sergeant Paice, the uniformed Gardaí created a gap in the circle of sturdy steel mesh fencing surrounded the Ark and waved Brigit and Dr Sinha forward.

"OK," said Dr Sinha, "Off we go."

They strode through the gap and towards the building's main door. Most of the windows had been blocked out with a mix of newspaper and cardboard with slogans written on them. 'Fight the Power' and 'We Shall Overcome' rubbing shoulders with 'People Not Profits' and an incongruous 'Happy Birthday Barry'.

As Brigit and Sinha stood outside the building's main doors, a muscular man with tight-cropped hair and tattoos aplenty was moving aside the furniture barricading the main entrance. A man of about sixty with a long mane of white hair watched from behind the glass as they approached. He looked like a short-arsed Gandalf. As they reached the door, he put his hand up to stop them advancing any further. When his colleague had moved most of the furniture, he made eye contact with Sergeant Paice and, smiling, placed his hands together. Brigit saw the Guard grimace and then order his men to put the steel fencing back in place, with them on the other side of it. Brigit guessed they'd been through this negotiated procedure before, and that Paice hadn't enjoyed it any more on the previous occasions.

Once the barrier had been restored, the man with the long white hair placed his hands together again and gave a half mocking bow of gratitude. Then he clicked his fingers, and the muscly guy bent down

155

to release the locks at the top and bottom of the glass doors. As they opened, Gandalf stretched his arm out expansively, ushering them in. "Welcome to the Ark."

The other man looked less pleased to see them, his face forming into a sneer as Brigit passed him before he immediately started re-locking the door. Brigit looked around the reception area. At one end there lay piles of rubbish, looking starkly out of place on the marble floor surrounded by the no doubt expensive 'bunch of coloured shapes' modern art on the wall. The lights were off, which meant that the whole area was only illuminated by a mixture of light diffusing through newspaper, and the occasional shaft that snuck through the gaps in the cardboard.

"And now the sofas please, Andrew," said the white-haired man. Brigit was finding his accent hard to place. He was Irish, but there seemed to be a little bit of everywhere in there.

"But they'll be out again in a couple of hours..."

"Sofas now, please," said the white-haired man, still smiling and never taking his eyes from Brigit and Dr Sinha. Muscles grumbled something beneath his breath, but he duly began pushing the large sofas back in front of the doors, their metal legs screeching on the marble floor. "We have to take security seriously, you understand."

"Of course," replied Dr Sinha. "I am Dr Sinha, and this is my colleague, Nurse Conroy."

He smiled at them both in turn. "Charmed to make your acquaintance. You can call me Ger."

As he spoke, a dark-haired woman emerged from a side door and strode across the reception towards them. She wore a scowl and enough metal in bits of her that it must take a month to get through airport security. She nodded curtly at Ger, and stood behind Brigit.

"And now, if you'll forgive the further imposition, I'm afraid we must search your person."

The search the female guard had given Brigit on the other side of the barricades had been a lot more civilised. The Girl with the Dragon Tattoo started patting her down with a lot more vigour than necessary.

"Easy!" said Brigit.

"Now Belinda, play nicely," said Ger, which resulted in a marginal improvement in the level of rough-housing. Brigit looked across to see Dr Sinha smiling patiently as he received a similarly thorough examination from Muscles. When it had finally finished, and the woman they called Belinda had technically got further with Brigit than any of her first three boyfriends, the searchers took a step back.

"And now," said Ger, holding out a Tupperware container, "your phones please."

"I'm afraid," said Dr Sinha, "we were told to keep them with us, in case of... circumstances."

Ger shook his head. "Not possible. They are too easily used as a listening device."

"But—"

"This is non-negotiable."

Ger's smile slipped down into a firm, straight line and he gave Dr Sinha a look of absolute steel. Sinha looked at Brigit, shrugged and then put his phone in the box. Begrudgingly, Brigit did the same.

"Thank you. You will, of course, get them back on your departure."

There then followed a thorough inspection of all the medical supplies, which were taken out of the two backpacks they were in and placed in carrier bags. The contents of Sinha's carefully packed doctor's bag then received the same treatment. Finally done, Ger led them up the stairs. "Apologies for the walk, but we don't use the lifts. Can't have someone getting trapped in there."

They reached the first floor, where a large open-plan office had once been. The desks had been mostly pushed against the windows, and this was now acting as some form of communal area. A couple of improvised washing lines were strung across the far end. Various people looked out at them from doorways. One group sat around a meeting table, playing an enthusiastic game of Monopoly. In one corner, a couple of women and a man were working in an improvised kitchen. Pots sat on camping stoves while they chopped various vegetables and perused a supply of cans. A few kids ran around the place and then hid behind desks, eyeing them with suspicious curiosity as they passed. The whole place had the feel of a music festival, without the music, that was being held in an office block.

Ger guided them into an empty meeting room that had its blinds drawn down. One desk was pushed up against the window, with another sitting in the middle of the room, two leather office chairs on either side of it. Muscles and the Girl with the Dragon Tattoo filed in behind them. "We have set aside this room for you to use as an office. The residents have agreed to visit you in a certain order to avoid queueing."

"Can I ask," said Brigit, "where is Father Franks?"

"He is upstairs working on something, but you will both meet him later on and he thanks you for coming. In the meantime, one of my two colleagues will stay with you, obviously depending on the gender of the patient."

"No." Dr Sinha said it with an air of calm, as if he'd just been asked if the number 39 bus had passed yet.

"I'm afraid" said Ger, "that in the interest of securit—"

"My interaction with any patient," said Dr Sinha, "occurs entirely under doctor-patient privilege, and it is not ethical to allow any observation of that."

Ger's charming smile slipped off his face. "Apologies, but this is also non-negotiable."

"I am sorry to hear that," said Dr Sinha, picking up his bag from where he had placed it on the desk, "please take us back outside. Do pass on my best wishes to Father Franks."

The two men stared at each other for a long moment, Dr Sinha keeping the smile fixed on his face while refusing to flinch.

"Very well," said Ger, before turning to the others, "you can wait outside."

With that, all three of them turned and left. Dr Sinha calmly began taking supplies from his bag and placing them on the desk nearest the window. Brigit joined him and started taking the supplies out of her bag. She nudged him with her hip and whispered, "badass."

. . .

They spent the next two hours dealing with a random series of maladies, ranging from the innocuous to the concerning: one older gent with high blood pressure had run out of meds, a couple of recovering addicts had the kind of problems you have for life once heroin has ravaged the human body, and two women and a man were experiencing remarkably similar STD-related issues. Brigit wondered if they each knew exactly how similar. There'd been one sprained wrist and one broken foot, both having been ably managed thanks to one Romanian lady's first aid training. Colds, bumps, bruises, itches, in they came and out they went. A couple of parents with limited English and wearing the same worried looks Brigit had seen on every parent's face in her time at A&E. The kids had been fine. The same couldn't be said for a middle-aged man with chronic bronchitis. As agreed, Sinha wrote prescriptions as required, keeping them to be given to the authorities to be filled and sent in.

The mood of the place wasn't quite as Brigit had expected it to be. There was an air of unspecified oppression. She noticed Muscles and The Girl with the Dragon Tattoo having a quiet word with everyone before they entered. Still, in the privacy of Sinha's makeshift surgery, nobody had seemed particularly keen to unburden themselves.

Their final call of the day had been the best. A couple in their early thirties, getting confirmation that she was in fact pregnant. The two of them holding hands and beaming at each other like idiots. As the happy couple left, Ger re-entered. "The Father will see you now."

They were taken up two further flights of stairs to a quieter floor of the building. Here the open-plan office area had no desks, and the offices and meeting rooms, now transformed into bedrooms, had blankets hung from the windows for privacy. Brigit guessed this was the 'executive floor' where Ger and his cronies had their digs. They brought them to a large corner office, and Ger held his hand up as they reached it.

"Please wait here," he said. He knocked quickly on the door then entered, closing it behind them. They stood looking awkwardly at each other – Brigit and Dr Sinha plus their escort of Muscles and The Girl with the Dragon Tattoo.

"So," said Dr Sinha, when the awkward silence clearly became too much for him, "you have plenty of room here. Seems very comfortable."

"More comfortable than our presence is making those fascists that are using economics to oppress the masses," said Dragon Tattoo. As Brigit watched her speak, she got the feeling like this was an almost knee-jerk response. Like 'God bless you' to a sneeze.

"Yes," said Sinha, "lots of room. How many floors is this building?"

"Enough," said Muscles, like that was a state secret too. They could just stand outside and count the windows.

The door opened and Ger stepped out. "He can see you now."

Dr Sinha moved forward and Brigit followed him. As they reached the door, Ger put his hand lightly on Sinha's chest. "Can I just remind you about patient confidentiality."

Sinha smiled. "I am delighted to see you have got so onboard with the concept."

They entered the large office. All of the blinds were down and covered with improvised curtains, save for one which the sun streamed through. In one corner, a large oak table with a lot of blankets on it was being used as a bed. In the other sat two large chairs. Father Daniel Franks sat nearest the window, cocooned in blankets so that only his bald head was visible. The tufts of hair over his ears were unkempt, framing a face that looked haggard and drawn. In the chair beside him sat a middle-aged woman, who held a cup of water and whose face showed an undisguised concern. Franks shone them a weak smile. "Doctor, thank you so much for coming." His voice was more of a raised whisper, robbed of the oratory skills that had captivated a nation. It still had that northern burr to it, but mixed with short inhalations that seemed to require effort each time they were drawn.

Dr Sinha and Brigit both looked at Ger, before moving across the room towards Franks. His formerly chubby face was now gaunt, and his skin carried an off-milky texture.

"Thank you, Gearoid," said Franks.

Ger looked at them, hesitated, and then left the room.

"Father Franks," said Dr Sinha, "you do not look well."

Franks patted the hand of the concerned woman beside him as he spoke. "No flies on you, Doc. I was diagnosed with stage four cancer six months ago now. I'm on a wee bit of borrowed time."

Franks looked at their faces. "About five people know what you now do. And yes... if you're doing the maths... you're right."

Brigit understood what he meant. Six months ago, that was when he'd first come to prominence.

"You want to really find out what's important in your life, know it is truly going to end. When your tomorrows start running out, you realise you can't wait for them any more. You want to do something important before you go."

Dr Sinha placed his hand on the man's brow and then moved his head to look into his eyes. "You should be in a hospital."

"Ah, Doc, it's all right. I've made my peace, so I have. Ye can relax."

"Would you stop doing your job if I asked you to, Father?"

Franks looked up at Dr Sinha. "Fair enough," he said with a weak smile, before making eye contact with Brigit for the first time. "He's a bit of a terrier this one, isn't he?"

Brigit tried to force a smile back at him.

He turned his head to the woman looking on with concern. "Bernie, love, would ye mind stepping out for a wee bit."

She nodded, touched his hand affectionately and then got up to leave. He watched her go. "She's an angel that one. So how're things downstairs? Everyone healthy and all that?"

Dr Sinha began gently pulling the blankets down that cocooned Franks. "I am happy to report no serious issues."

"Ah, great. They're good people. Thanks again for doing this."

"You're welcome." Dr Sinha put his stethoscope to Frank's chest. "Take a deep breath, please."

"It's been a while since I've done that."

Franks spent the next couple of minutes breathing in and out, while Dr Sinha listened to his chest, his face becoming a steadily more unhappy picture. Feeling suddenly useless, Brigit didn't know what to do with herself. Franks pointed to the empty seat beside him and smiled, before falling into a racking coughing fit. Brigit noticed a box of tissues beside her chair, grabbed one and held it out for him, which he took. Once his breathing had returned to normal, Dr Sinha began taking his pulse.

"I'd like to run some tests," said Dr Sinha.

Franks looked up at him and held his eyes for a moment. "We don't need to do that, Doctor, no disrespect. If I was just another patient in your hospital, they'd be calling for me, not you."

"I can at least give you a shot, and something for the pain."

"You're a good man."

Sinha moved away and started taking some supplies from their bags. Franks turned back to look at Brigit, giving her a soft smile. "Thank you for coming, Nurse Conroy, I know it was an odd request. I hope you appreciate why."

Brigit nodded.

"They don't want my phone up here. The government are monitoring our communications. If they were to find out about my condition... we don't want it being used as an excuse."

Brigit nodded again.

"Bernie told me about your message. I'm afraid I don't understand."

"Well," said Brigit, "Bunny McGarry has disappeared, last seen eight days ago now. I'm just trying to gather any information on where he might be from those who spoke to him last."

Franks gave her a quizzical look. "I've not spoken to Bunny in sixteen years."

Brigit had double-checked the bill last night after Sinha had told him whose number it was. "A couple of calls to you, and three or four texts, are on his bill."

"I dunno where you're getting that from, Miss Conroy, but we've not talked."

Brigit ran her hands through her hair and puffed her cheeks out.

THE DAY THAT NEVER COMES

"Ah, the lady... Bernie, could she have—" Brigit stopped as Franks shook his head emphatically.

"I'll not say why but just... rest assured, she wouldn't be communicating with McGarry, hand on heart. Not possible. When I say we haven't spoken, I mean we don't speak." He gave her a meaningful look. "Now, maybe he was trying to get hold of me, texts didn't arrive or..."

"According to his bill, you had a twenty four minute chat on Tuesday, a week ago." Brigit took the copy of the bill that she had shoved into her coat pocket that morning and showed it to Franks. He stared at it and then he looked back at Brigit.

"With God as my witness, that didn't happen."

Brigit looked again at the phone bill, not knowing what to think.

"Can I ask," said Franks, "what's your interest here?"

"I work with Bunny."

Franks gave her a confused look.

"Bunny has left the Gardaí."

"Ah," said Franks, "I see." Then Franks looked at her for a long moment. "Be careful."

A wheezing cough shuddered through his frail body again.

Brigit picked up his cup of water and placed the straw in his mouth. "Oh, I'm sure I'm not in any danger."

Franks let the straw fall away. "Thank you. I meant, be careful... of him."

Brigit looked at him and then dabbed at his mouth with the tissue.

"Bunny McGarry is a rare thing. A man truly capable of anything. The only compass he follows is his own. One day, you'll end up on the other side of something and, believe me, it will go badly for you. He'll lie, cheat, blackmail – whatever it takes. He's not a bad man. He's worse than that. He's a good man who'll do bad things for what he thinks is right."

Brigit looked at the window. An azure blue sky provided a backdrop for the building opposite, the sunlight gleaming off its silvered windows.

With the gap in conversation, Dr Sinha stepped forward, a needle in hand.

"Now," said Franks, "why don't we let the good doctor do what he must and then you two can be on your way." Franks closed his eyes. "This has been a very long day."

CHAPTER TWENTY-THREE

SUNDAY 6 FEBRUARY 2000 – AFTERNOON

Jarleth Court stared into his pint of lager, watching the bubbles fizzle to the surface and then disappear. Truth be told, he wasn't normally much of a drinker. Still, when his phone had rung at lunchtime on a sleepy Sunday, tearing his life down around him, drink had felt appropriate. It must be buried somewhere in his Irish DNA, the belief that alcohol can somehow help. In a way it had been a relief. The upside of the worst thing possible happening, was that it couldn't happen again. There would be a certain freedom in disgrace.

A woman he recognised from one of his constituency clinics walked by and shot a shy wave in his direction. He knew a lot of people in the pub and more of them knew him. He'd been a fixture in local politics for twenty years. Ten as a councillor, before moving up to four as an independent TD. Then they'd redrawn the boundary and split his hardcore support down the middle. It was decried in the press as dirty politics. The main parties played dumb and pretended it was all a quirk of geography. Still, last time out he'd given it a damn good shot anyway. His opponents had spent ten times as much and he'd still run them close. Then he'd gone back onto the Council and redoubled his efforts. If anything, the whole thing had made him even more popular – the working class hero who terrifies the establishment, that's what they'd called him. That'd change now.

A man whose name he couldn't recall patted his arm on his way back to the main bar from the loos, the roar of the Super Sunday football calling him home. The lounge was relatively quiet, blessed as it was with an absence of the big screens that seemed to be ubiquitous in pubs these days. There was a big football tournament in the summer though. Marla the landlady had proudly told him how they were getting a load more screens put in, and a little bit more silence would die.

People had mostly let him be for the last few hours. None of the usual polite chat before bringing up a little thing they needed help with. Maybe his body language was sending off the vibe that now was not the time. He'd sat there alone and steadily drank, still he was nowhere nearer the oblivion he sought.

The stool beside him squeaked softly as it was drawn back from the bar and a bulky form in a sheepskin coat plonked itself down. Court didn't look up, he didn't need to.

"Do you never take that bleedin' coat off Bunny? Ye'll not feel the benefit."

"It cuts down on ironing, Councillor."

"Does it now?" Court picked up his half empty pint and slurped at it. Bunny waved at Anto the barman, pulling him away from flirting with a couple of soccer widows at the other end of the bar.

"A pint of Arthur's," said Bunny, "and same again for himself."

"The condemned man ate a hearty last meal," said Court.

"There's no need to get all melodramatic about it."

Court barked a humourless laugh and went back to finishing his pint.

He drained it and then put his glass down on the counter harder than intended.

"Do you know how many people in this pub I've helped over the years Bunny?"

"Plenty, I'm sure."

"But do you know the actual number, I mean? I've been sat here counting. Seventeen, I reckon. I mean directly like, not counting the stuff that we all benefit from. I've not taken a holiday in eight years, d'ye know that?"

"You've done good work, Jarleth."

Court turned and faced Bunny for the first time, jabbing his finger into the big man's face. "Don't you... don't you use my fucking name. We're not friends, alright? If we were friends you'd not be here!"

"Cool your jets," said Bunny, nodding towards Anto as he brought their drinks over. The soccer widows at the end of the bar were surreptitiously glancing in their direction now too, attracted by Court's raised voice.

They sat in silence as Anto placed the drinks in front of them before retreating back to his station.

Court lifted up his pint and then put it down again untouched. "Back in the day, I helped you set St Jude's up, backed you all the way. I went down to Croke Park with you and all but battered them into throwing in some funding."

"You did," said Bunny. "You painted a couple of walls and shook more than a few buckets too. You even hosted that fecking table quiz to fix the roof."

"And I wrote the questions."

"And you wrote the questions."

"Yvonne Wild still brings up that fifth Beatle thing. She sent me a book with a quote from Paul McCartney saying it was Brian Epstein and not George Martin. The book is worth more than the prize money would've been! Cost me votes, that quiz."

Bunny shook his head and smiled. "Some people never forget."

Court ran his finger up the moist side of his pint glass. "You do."

"No, Councillor," he said, "I remember all you've done to help us. Then I remember that last Thursday you raised your hand to vote to tear it all down."

Court said nothing, he just lifted the pint he didn't feel like drinking and took a couple of gulps. When he spoke next, it was in a near whisper. "That tape... I've got two kids, Bunny."

"A couple of hundred kids go through that club every year."

Court leaned back on his stool and felt himself sway slightly. "It was... a mistake."

"Which part?" said Bunny.

Court stared down at his own feet as he spoke. "The tape. I... it was just after I'd lost my seat in the Dáil, and she was helping out in the office—"

"Don't," interrupted Bunny, "there's no point. All that matters is that they had it and I've got it now."

"Ha," said Court, reaching a hand forward and steadying himself. "Had? Like that was the only copy. They rang me, offered to drop one around, to reassure me they've got plenty. They've got me by one bollock and now, you've got me by the other. Doomed either way."

"So you might as well do what's right."

"For a blackmailer you're fierce fucking moral, Bunny." Anto and the two ladies glanced again in their direction. Court looked down and swept some invisible dust off the leg of his slacks. "They know what you're doing," said Court. "They think I can talk you out of it."

"We both know that isn't true."

"Yeah, yeah we do. The great Bunny McGarry, the unstoppable force."

Court grabbed at his pint, spilling a bit as he lifted it. Then he put it down again and turned to look Bunny in the eye, as much as it was possible. "You can't win this, d'ye know that? All of this is for nothing. They've got Snow White, and he brings nearly half that shower of wannabes on the council with him. They'll vote as a bloc and there's nothing you can do about it. You're going to have me vote against the tide for no reason and still get destroyed."

"And what about the next time?" said Bunny.

"What?"

"Don't kid yourself, Councillor, it won't just be this time. Now that they own it, they'll be renting your arse out all over town. Fuck's sake, tell me you don't honestly believe they'll let you off the hook after this? You'll be their feckin' lapdog from here on out. How many people will ye be helping then?"

"You ever made a mistake, Bunny?"

"Plenty. That's why I came here to look you in the eye and tell you. You do their bidding, I'll do exactly what ye think."

"Oh, I've no doubt."

"I won't enjoy it."

"You're a feckin' martyr."

Bunny stood up, dropped a tenner onto the counter beside his untouched pint and headed towards the door.

Court watched the big man opening the door to step out into the winter evening's fading light.

"Here, Bunny."

Bunny turned to look at him. Court could sense several pairs of eyes on him now but he no longer cared.

"Remind me, what's the difference between you and them?"

Bunny looked him dead in the eye, giving Court the wonky-eyed stare that had broken many the supposed hard nut.

"The difference, Councillor, is that I'm going to win."

CHAPTER TWENTY-FOUR

Gerry: And we're back. We're discussing the shocking death of Craig Blake, a member of the so called Skylark Three. What is this? Vigilante justice? Plain old murder? The switchboard is lighting up, so lets go for a blitz. Clare from Blanchardstown on line one, go!

Clare: Yes, Gerry, I think it's just awful. Nobody deserves that. You can't have people going around killing people, that's not right.

Gerry: OK, Phillip from Glasnevin on line two.

Phillip: This fella is dead but how many people are dead because of what he did? Cheating ordinary people out of their hard-earned money. Let it be a warning to the rest of 'em, I say.

Gerry: Sean from Balbriggan on line six.

Sean: Viva la revolution! We are the Púca! Fuc—

Gerry: Woah! The revolution will not be televised with that kind of language. Therese from Blackrock on line four.

Therese: People are angry, Gerry but you can't go about taking the law into your own hands, that'll lead to chaos.

Gerry: Maybe, Therese, but maybe we need a bit of chaos? Look where the status quo has gotten us? What do you think, Sarah from Balbriggin on line three?

Sarah: Gerry, I'd like to see them all strung up, and to hear the new one

from Adele.
Gerry: Ah for—

"I don't understand how you can eat that stuff," said Phil.

Paul placed his chopsticks back into his container of noodles and looked across the seat at him. "Well, it is a lot easier when you stop saying things like that. I offered to get pizza if you wanted some."

"I'm watching what I eat. I've got to fit into a wedding suit."

Paul avoided saying anything he'd regret by resuming shovelling noodles into his face. They were sitting in the front seat of Uncle Abdul's taxi, seeing as there was no way Paul was going to dare to eat in Bunny's car.

Phil looked into the back seat again. "She is still looking at you."

"She can look at me all she wants, she is not getting any."

"I Googled it – a small bit of Chinese food is all right for a dog."

"That's not why she isn't getting any. She is being punished." He looked back at her, "and she knows exactly why."

Phil shook his head in disapproval.

"The two of you need to work on your relationship."

"No, no we don't. I have no desire to have a relationship with the bloody dog. Far as I'm concerned, she is going to the pound at the first opportunity. End of story."

"So you can't forgive Maggie for basically just being a dog, and yet you expect Brigit to forgive you?"

"Really?" said Paul, throwing his container of noodles onto the dashboard and turning to face Phil, "you're seriously comparing those two things?"

"I'm just saying," said Phil.

"Well, stop."

Paul looked out the window at the occasional cars rolling by on the main road. This was his third day sitting in the car park of Casey's pub, and he was now thoroughly sick of the view. He picked up his noodles again. "She had that chicken earlier on, and she's had plenty of water."

The car fell silent, save for Phil's constant finger drumming on his knees and Maggie's panting in the back seat. Paul looked at the noodles. He was fast losing his appetite.

"It's not even real Chinese food."

Paul rolled his eyes. "This again?"

"Da Xin's never even heard of Orange Chicken! It's not a thing. Same as that Egg Foo Yung stuff, it doesn't exist."

"It does exist. What you mean is it isn't authentic. There's lots of fake things from China."

"What's that supposed to mean?"

"Hartigan!" said Paul, ducking down as low as possible in the passenger seat.

"Don't change the subject," said Phil, his anger rising.

"No," he nodded his head towards the road, "Hartigan."

Phil looked up just as Jerome Hartigan, dressed in black running gear, jogged by alone.

"Holy... who goes for a run this late?"

Paul popped his head up and looked at Hartigan jogging away from them.

"More importantly, who goes for a run with a rucksack on his back."

Paul opened the door and quickly slid out of the seat. He looked back to see Maggie diving into the space he'd just vacated to devour the dinner he'd left behind.

Following Hartigan proved surprisingly easy. Poser that he was, he of course looked the business in his sleek running gear but Paul guessed he'd not actually done that much running previously. Certainly his pace was nothing too taxing, and having the two cars meant even Paul and Phil could keep a visual on him. He jogged along the N31 for about a mile, heading in towards Blackrock, turning left to follow the main road around. All they'd had to do was take turns driving past, then parking up for a bit until he ran by. They were doing more or less what the Blando bible described as a "two car rotation", although Paul was now wishing he'd paid slightly more attention to the diagrams. Still, on a dark night beside a busy dual carriageway, one passing car looked pretty much like another.

Paul caught a break, being fifty yards behind Hartigan when he turned a corner off into a residential road. He took a right and drove quickly past Hartigan, shielding his face from view as he did so. The street was lined with big houses, mostly hidden behind imposing shrubbery and gates of wrought iron or thick wood. Further roads branched off to the left and right. Paul guessed this area alone could keep half of the landscape gardeners in Dublin busy.

Bunny's car was distinctive, but he'd have to bank on Hartigan being too focused on pounding pavement to notice it. Paul had his headphones plugged into his phone to keep his hands free for driving. "He's turned off, we're on..." Paul craned to see the road sign as he drove by it, "Rosemount Drive."

"Roger that," said Phil. "I've got to circle back but I've got bullseye on your twenty. ETA five minutes."

"Just talk normally, would ye?"

"Roger."

Paul glanced into his rear view mirror. Hartigan had run about halfway down the wide, tree-lined road before coming to a stop at a corner, hands or hips, sucking in air.

Paul parked up about a hundred yards further down, on the far side of the road. He killed the engine and watched in the side mirror. Hartigan seemed to be looking around him. Had he clocked them? He did a couple of stretches and then resumed jogging slowly. Paul ducked down low in his seat, feeling suddenly exposed, as Hartigan drew closer. He had seen Paul a couple of nights ago outside his house, if he caught sight of him here again the whole jig would be blown. After a long minute, Paul looked up to see Hartigan had passed him and was jogging away. Then he stopped suddenly again, forcing Paul to scrunch back down in his seat.

Phil's voice filled his ears, causing Paul to jump. "I'm on your six, over."

"What?"

"I'm on Rosemount Drive."

"Shit," said Paul. "He's stopped running. Don't pull over here, drive past, don't let him see you. And for the love of God, keep Maggie out of sight."

"Roger that, she's lying on the back seat. I don't think that Chinese food agreed with her."

Now did not seem the time for 'I told you so'.

Sitting just high enough to peer over the steering wheel, Paul watched as Hartigan started walking back towards him. Luckily, he seemed to not be looking in Paul's direction, instead taking a great interest in one of the houses he was passing. He was trying to peer through its high hedge before he came to a complete stop outside of its imposing wooden gates. Hartigan looked around and then stretched himself onto his tiptoes to catch a glimpse over the gate. Paul watched him flinch as a pair of headlights approached, bending down to tie his shoelace as Abdul's taxi cruised past.

"I am past the bogey."

"Loop around the estate, just try not to draw attention to yourself."

"Roger that."

As Paul watched Phil's taillights disappear around the corner at the end of the street, Hartigan stood up and resumed walking back towards him. This time he turned the corner, following the house's high wall around. Hartigan scanned his surroundings again. While Paul was nervous, he didn't appear to be the only one. Hartigan stood there for a minute stretching his arms above his head and then bending from side to side, glancing around as he did so. Then he placed his hands on the wall and began stretching his calf muscles out.

"What's he doing?" said Phil.

"Pretending to stretch. Maybe he's waiting for somebody or... HOLY SHIT!"

"What?"

"He's just hopped a wall."

Hartigan had indeed looked around him one last time, then in one surprisingly swift motion, reached up, caught the top of the wall and dragged himself over.

"Fuck it, this could be it. He might be finally getting his end away."

"D'ye think it's one of them weird fantasies where he pretends to be a burglar and—"

"Shut up Phil."

Paul sat there for a few minutes staring at the spot where Hartigan had disappeared. If he was doing what Paul expected then he'd be in there a while. If he was doing what Paul expected, this was a pretty weird way of doing it. What was wrong with going through the front gate, exactly? Assuming Phil's freaky fantasy idea wasn't worthy of more consideration than he'd given it. He is hardly shagging somebody's missus while the sap is upstairs asleep? Not even the great Jerome Hartigan could be that arrogant, could he? Well, whatever was happening, sitting here wasn't going to get him any evidence. Paul shoved his phone and headset into the pocket of his jeans and exited the car.

Hartigan had a few inches on him, which was why Paul had to take a run up to get a grip on the top of the wall. He pulled himself up, as quietly as he could and then looked over. He could see trees and not a lot else. He got his elbows onto the top of the wall and heaved himself up. Looking down and around there was no sign of Hartigan, although Paul's view was obstructed by the trees that lined the sides of the garden. As quietly as he could, he lowered himself down on the far side, his feet landing softly on the peaty ground. He crouched behind the trunk of a tree and looked around him, letting his eyes adjust to the near-darkness.

A grand lawn wrapped around a large, stylish house. Evergreen trees appeared to line it on every side, ensuring the owner's privacy from all but spy satellites. Paul could see what he guessed to be a tennis court at the back of it. The house itself had large windows, all of which were dark. The whole thing seemed eerily quiet. Not just sleeping, deserted.

To his right, about fifty yards down from where he was, Paul spotted movement at the treeline. He could see a crouching figure, quickly making its way across the lawn. Paul flinched as a penetrating floodlight burst into life. Hartigan stood in the centre of the lawn, looking around him like a terrified animal. He turned to hurry back the way he came then stopped after a few steps when the light cut back out. Automatic sensor. Hartigan moved towards the house again, this time keeping going as the light came on. He paused at the front door. Only then did Paul notice the yellow police tape stretched across it. "Holy shit," he whispered to himself.

As he watched, Hartigan slipped his rucksack off and started taking things out. He put on gloves before trying to quickly and carefully take the police tape off without breaking it. Paul retrieved his phone from his pocket and put his headphones back in. He quickly dialled Phil, who answered on the third ring.

"We're in big trouble," said Phil.

Panicked, Paul looked around him. "What?"

"The dog has only gone and thrown up in the back of Abdul's taxi."

"Oh for..." whispered Paul, "I'll get it valeted. I've just realised where this is."

Having finished removing the tape as best he could, Hartigan was now pulling other stuff out of his rucksack.

"What?"

"This house, I think it belonged to what's his face, Craig Blake."

"The dead fella?"

"Yes, the dead fella. There's police tape on the door."

Paul watched as Hartigan selected a key from a keyring and placed it in the lock. He opened the door and quickly entered. Seconds later, the floodlight turned off.

"He's breaking into his old partner's house," said Paul.

"Why the fuck is he doing that?"

"I dunno," said Paul, but his mind was racing. They had lost track of Hartigan on Tuesday night, which was when the Gardaí had said Blake had died. Paul had seen Hartigan's violent temper first-hand when he'd watched him attack Maloney. Was it possible he was returning to the scene of the crime? Paul watched as a flashlight bobbed back and forth around the house, before entering one of the upstairs bedrooms.

"Ah man, this is fucked up," said Paul. "I'm supposed to just be finding out who he's knobbing. This is—"

"Should we call the cops?"

Paul thought about it. Maybe they should? If they did though, bye bye four grand. He was fairly sure getting evidence of Hartigan having sex in prison was not what his client had had in mind. Plus there'd be the whole awkwardness of having to explain to the cops that he was working as an investigator without a licence. "Nah, let's just see what happens."

"This stinks," said Phil.

"I know, but we've no choice."

"What? No, I meant the spew your dog just heaved up on the back seat. Filthy shit. I bet real Chinese food doesn't smell like this."

Paul crouched there for another ten minutes, running it all through in his head again and again. By the time Hartigan re-emerged from the front door, he'd made a decision. Paul watched him carefully close the door behind him and then begin trying to put the police tape back as he'd found it. Paul fished the digital camera out of his pocket and fumbled for the switch to turn it on. Whatever this was, he probably needed some evidence of it.

He found the right button and zoomed in on Hartigan. Paul let out an involuntary yelp as the flash went off, unforgivingly bright in the otherwise near-pitch darkness. Hartigan looked around.

Paul took the wall in one swift jump and he didn't look back as he sprinted to the car.

"You all right? What're you doing?" said Phil in his ear.

"Getting the hell out of here," responded Paul.

CHAPTER TWENTY-FIVE

Verity Ward considered herself to be a very practical girl. No, scratch that, a very practical woman. She was nineteen now, and nearing the end of her first year as a university student. She had set herself the goal of no longer being a virgin by the end of it and time was running out. That had not been her only goal for the year, as that would be tediously tragic. In fact, she'd had six. She had already won a fresher's debate, read a book on Buddhism, drank shots, learned enough bass to join a rock band (truth be told, owning and being willing to play a bass had turned out to be the major qualification there) and lastly, made three proper friends. All she had to do was get number four off the list and it was a clean sweep. She had already revised her timetable slightly, having decided that the deadline should not be exam time but the start of her second year. Still, the clock was ticking.

Some people have very fluffy bullshit ideas about this kind of thing, Verity did not. She wasn't expecting earth movement and choirs of angels. The last thing she wanted to do was wait for someone special. She wanted to know exactly what she was doing when that someone showed up. She was a great believer in preparation.

That being said, she was of course not willing to let just anyone assist with the removal of her virginity. She rejected utterly the concept of some man 'taking it' – it gave them far too much control in the situation. Come to that, she wasn't losing it – she was carefully disposing of it. Loss implied carelessness.

This was why, following an appropriate three-date structure, she was allowing Matt Willis to assist her in this matter. He was nice. He was also, she felt reasonably sure, a virgin. Certainly, judging by the last fifteen minutes, he was not what you'd call experienced. He had spent a great deal of time locating things – the lever to put the seat back, an appropriate radio station, her vagina...

...and then there'd been the whole kerfuffle with the condom. Honestly, that bit there was no excuse for. Matt could have practised that beforehand, it did not require her presence. Fail to prepare, prepare to fail – that was Verity's motto – not that she said that out loud of course. University had so far been a very successful relaunch of the Verity brand. If asked, her supposed life motto would be 'eating is cheating' – patently ridiculous though it was.

Matt had been vigorously applying himself to the task in hand for some minutes now, and had been considerate to the point of fatigue in his constant querying of 'is that all right? Are you ok? How is that for you?'. He was a nice guy, his mother had raised him well. Verity was not surprised by this, the fact that Matt's mother owned a Smart car spoke very well of her character. Having said that, it was perhaps not the most appropriate vehicle for their current activity.

If she was to plan this again – which by definition she wouldn't be – she would have taken geography into account more. In particular, she would have selected a virginity-removal partner who came from down the country, or better yet, abroad. That way, they would have their own student digs. Matt, like herself, came from Dublin and hence lived at home. This meant the only venue open to them had been his mother's car. Even with that, there had been the extensive search for a quiet location. This was the third spot they'd tried, dog walkers having proven a shocking blight in the previous two. The night had been less romantic and more heavily logistic.

Verity was aware that soon she should begin vocalising some

enthusiasm. Matt had gone to a lot of trouble and fair was fair, she should give him the impression that female orgasm had been achieved. She'd done some research on this. As one blog had put it, 'the fact that he's so concerned to make sure it happens is why he deserves to think it has'. She groaned. This did indeed seem to raise Matt's spirits and consequently his tempo. Verity held him a bit closer while simultaneously carefully moving her long, black hair so it wouldn't get pinned under his elbow again.

She looked out the window. This location was ideal, a long way as it was from anywhere and shielded from view by two large billboards. They were near a large housing complex but as anyone who had seen a paper knew all too well, it was not occupied. As she groaned again, she looked over at the hulking outline of the Skylark complex. Some of the buildings were still cocooned in scaffolding. Such a waste.

She threw in an 'oh, yes...' to indicate to Matt her continued approval of proceedings and let her eyes wander. Just then the clouds parted, and a full moon threw illumination onto a previously overcast night.

Verity looked up at the back of the billboard and her mind froze. It tried to deny what it saw, reason against the likelihood. Someone was watching them. Then she'd looked again, looked lower, past the wide, staring eyes to see the body below it, tied to the billboard's supporting struts. Cables hung down from it, glistening in the moonlight. Her eyes followed their path, down to the ground and then back up to their source. They were emerging from the watcher's lower torso. Then the tiny voice, that had known all along that what she was looking at wasn't cables, had finally made itself heard.

Verity Ward screamed. For the first time in her life, a full-on proper scream of terror.

Due to Matt's inexperience in these matters, he crucially misinterpreted this as a scream of pleasure. This would lead to issues in later life.

CHAPTER TWENTY-SIX

Gerry: Caller, you're on the air.
*Caller: (Distorted) My name is Tyler Durden, and I am the official
spokesman for the Púca. This is the day that never comes. Prepare yourself
for the revolution.*
*Gerry: Right, well, Mr Durden, before we go any further with this
conversation, I should point out that we've a very sophisticated call logging
system here at the station that records the numbers of all calls we receive.*
Caller: (Distorted) Ehm... what?
*Gerry: And obviously we will be passing that information directly to the
Gardaí.*
Caller: (distorted) Ah Jaysus, don't do that, me ma will kill me!

Paul tossed Phil a can of beer. It said something of his mental state
that he'd somehow forgotten the legendary Phil Nellis reaction speed,
or rather lack thereof. The can walloped him on the right shoulder.

"What the fuck?" said Phil.

"Sorry, sorry man – my mistake."

Phil grumbled to himself as he bent down to retrieve the can from under the desk.

For the first time in several days, Paul was back in the offices of MCM Investigations. Phil sat behind the table opposite him. The chair behind the third table was occupied by Maggie, who was currently staring at him in that unnerving way she had.

"No," said Paul.

Maggie said nothing.

"You wanted that Chinese food earlier and look what happened there – you spewed all over the back of Abdul's taxi."

"That smell is going to take forever to shift," said Phil from beneath the table.

"See, Phil agrees with me."

Maggie said nothing.

"Leave me out of this," said Phil.

"You'll be ill again."

Maggie said nothing, pointedly.

Paul leant down and picked her bowl up and placed it on the table in front of her, then he cracked open a can and poured it in.

She watched impassively until he'd finished and then started lapping it up immediately.

"Pace yourself, ye mad bitch."

She managed to casually growl without looking up. Paul moved his chair further away to give her more room.

Phil sat back up in his seat, opened his can and promptly sprayed lager all over himself.

"Fuck's sake," he said.

"At least it'll cover the smell of dog vomit on ye."

"True enough."

They both took long glugs of their drinks in silence.

"Remember how I said I found that number for that Simone woman in Bunny's car?" asked Paul.

"Did she ring back?"

"No."

"Do you reckon Bunny is off getting his hole?"

"No," said Paul, "he's been gone a week for Christ sake."

"He'd be red raw by now. Oh God," said Phil, "can we talk about something else? I've had enough upsetting images tonight to last a lifetime."

Paul had tried to show Phil the picture he'd taken of Jerome Hartigan breaking into the house of his former colleague and current very dead guy, Craig Blake. When he'd looked in the memory of Phil's uncle Paddy's camera, he'd found a blurred picture that showed a bit of a tree and some grass - and no Hartigan. Ergo, no evidence. He'd then scrolled back through the camera in disbelief at his own ineptitude. That was when they'd come across the other pictures. The camera had not been used for a couple of years, since Phil's uncle Paddy had died of a heart attack. A quick scroll through the memory had revealed that the last time the camera had been used, Uncle Paddy and Auntie Lynn had been 'capturing a special moment' involving no clothing and a fair amount of 'implements'. Phil had seen things he couldn't unsee.

"I'm freaking out," said Paul.

"So am I," said Phil.

"I don't know what to think."

"Neither do I. How can I ever look her in the eye again?"

Paul rolled his eyes. "Oh for Christ's sake, not that. I've just seen the guy we're following break into a dead guy's house. He could be a murderer!"

"But," said Phil, "them Púca lot, they killed whats-his-name?"

"Craig Blake."

"Him. They killed him."

"But who are they? Nobody knows. Anyway, my point before was... when I found that Simone's number, it was stuck to a gun in Bunny's boot."

"Like a 'gun' gun?"

Paul pulled a face. "No, a water pistol, dumb arse. Yes, a gun."

"Can I've a go on it?"

"What? Don't be daft. My point is, I've seen a killer—"

"Possible."

"Alright, possible killer, breaking back into the scene of the crime."

"Possible."

"Shut up with the possible. Should I, like, have a gun for protection?"

"You know," said Phil, "all them Americans who have guns for protection?"

"Yeah."

"They end up shooting themselves."

"Yeah, but not deliberately."

"Shot is shot."

"Yeah," said Paul, "you're probably right. I took the bullets out. It freaked me the fuck out, to be honest with ye."

"So," said Phil, "are you going to the cops about Hartigan?"

"With what? We've no evidence and if we've to explain why we were following him, we'll be the ones getting arrested."

"Are you going to keep following him then?"

"I dunno. I do need the four grand."

Paul was sitting in the chair that the Devil in the Red Dress had been sitting in; he reckoned it still smelt faintly of her.

"I'll tell you what you need," said Phil. "You need to talk to somebody smart, who actually understands this kind of stuff."

"I'd love to," said Paul, "but she won't answer my calls."

CHAPTER TWENTY-SEVEN

"And this is definitely the last one?" said Dr Sinha.

"Absolutely," said Brigit, nodding emphatically. That was true, at least for today. There were still the three numbers she hadn't got a response from, including whoever this Simone woman was, but she didn't think the good doctor's patience would stretch to help her with them. It hadn't been the easiest sell in the first place, convincing him to spend his Sunday afternoon visiting prostitutes.

She'd had the idea after meeting Father Franks the day before. His exact words had stuck in her head, 'he'll lie, cheat, blackmail - do whatever it takes to get what he wants.' It put a whole new context on not just her view of Bunny McGarry, but of his phone bill. Perhaps the whole thing with the escorts he'd rung was something entirely different from what she had originally assumed. He may have been trying to blackmail somebody, and if he was, that person would have every reason in the world to have wanted Bunny to disappear, permanently.

And so she'd begged Dr Sinha to front for her and ring the numbers that had appeared on Bunny's bill. The idea being that he'd book an appointment, and then Brigit could go with him and ask the ladies of negotiable virtue what they knew about Bunny McGarry. In practice, it had proven a little bit more tricky than that.

They had arrived at the first one, at a rather nice apartment on the Quays, at 2 pm. They'd buzzed and been let up but then the woman had refused to let them in. 'I don't do couples' she had said through the closed door. Brigit looked at the peephole and cursed her own stupidity. Left with no choice, she'd explained that they were looking for their friend. The woman told her to go away. She had felt bad doing it, but it wasn't like she had much choice.

"OK, but do you mind if I knock on the rest of the doors on this floor? I just need to check if anyone saw my friend visiting the prostitute in Apartment 708."

The door had then opened as wide as the chain would allow and the girl had scowled out at her. She had long dark hair, mid-twenties, with a slight Belfast accent that got more pronounced when she was annoyed, which she now definitely was. "Fucking hell, there's no need to be such a bitch about it."

Brigit had apologised and then shown her the picture of Bunny. She'd squinted to look at it and then told them to wait. A minute later she returned, this time wearing glasses. She looked at the picture again, her eyes widening in recognition.

"Oh yeah, that big prick."

"He was here?" Brigit had asked.

"Aye, briefly. He walks in, takes one long look at me and then walks out again. Tells me I'm not what he's looking for."

"Is that unusual?" asked Brigit, only realising how bad that sounded after she'd said it. "Not that I mean... you're lovely for a... I mean, you're lovely."

The woman gave her a look that could freeze lava. "Occasionally, very occasionally... you'll get someone who is disappointed because, y'know, the pictures on the website don't show your face."

"Why not?" asked Dr Sinha.

The woman didn't even answer that. "So, is that everything?"

"And he didn't say anything else?" asked Brigit.

"Nope. Walked in, insulted me, then left. Real fucking charmer your friend, so he is."

"And when was this?"

"Christ," she said, looking up at the ceiling. "Thursday or Friday a week ago, I s'pose."

"Thank you very much, you've been very..." The door closed firmly in their faces, "...helpful."

And so it had gone. Following the earlier experience, Brigit now let Sinha knock on the door and make contact before she put in an appearance. The second woman had been an unnerving, chipper girl from Poland, who'd told much the same story. She'd opened the door, Bunny had looked at her, then he'd apologised and left. 'It was a shame, I like a big man,' she'd said. She had then explained to Brigit and Dr Sinha that she *did* do couples and they were already here so... They'd left, and then been unable to make eye contact for a good twenty minutes while having a remarkably detailed and enthusiastic discussion of the weather. It was unseasonably hot – record setting – though not as hot as it got in India. Still hot though, yes, very hot for Ireland.

The third girl had been French, and considerably more enterprising. It had taken fifty euros in cash to get her to talk. Brigit hadn't got it on her, but she'd sworn that she'd pay Dr Sinha back as soon as they passed a cash machine. He then explained in an embarrassingly loud voice that he was paying for information only, worried that this might be some form of a sting operation. The woman had taken the money, shoved it into the cleavage of the basque she wore under a silk robe and then explained how Bunny had turned up on Wednesday a week ago, said she was supposed to be a brunette and promptly left. The girl explained that she had recently dyed her hair blonde. Brigit and Dr Sinha had then assured her that it did look very nice, and really suited her. Brigit also noted to herself that the other two women were indeed brunettes.

The fourth girl, a brunette from Dublin, swore blind she'd never seen Bunny, although when Brigit had explained Bunny's rather distinctive accent, the girl's face had lit up. "He might've been the one

I had booked in a couple of Fridays ago. Never showed. Fucking time waster! He owes me two hundred euros." She'd looked at them expectantly. They'd thanked her and left.

The fifth one was the last on the list, bar the numbers like Simone's that hadn't answered or responded to Sinha's voicemail. This apartment was over in Drumcondra, in a very swanky building. Come to think of it, the crappiest apartment Brigit had been in today had been her own. She stood around the corner and then nodded at Sinha, who sighed and knocked on the apartment door.

"Just a second," came the shout from inside. Sinha stood there nervously for about a minute before the door opened.

"Hello, big boy," said a soft female voice. Then Brigit put her head around the corner and looked at the source of the voice.

Revelation hit her like a brick to the head.

She had seen this face before. It was burned into her memory.

The woman's look turned to one of confusion as Brigit strode towards her.

Then Brigit punched her right in the face.

CHAPTER TWENTY-EIGHT

DSI Susan Burns looked up at the body again. Whoever the sick individual or group behind the Púca were, she'd say this for them, they certainly knew how to make an impression. The body of Councillor John Baylor had been found crucified, thirty feet in the air on the back of a billboard with his intestines dangling down. The billboard in question had once advertised the Skylark complex to passing motorists on the M50. The sickos weren't exactly subtle in their messaging. If anyone was in any doubt, there had been a note in the victim's pocket, wrapped in a sandwich bag for safe-keeping, claiming the credit on the Púca's behalf. The wording had been identical to the last note. It was off in the lab being analysed, but Burns wasn't holding out much hope.

The crime scene itself was an absolute nightmare. It had been discovered by two teenagers the night before, who had no doubt been doing what teenagers had been doing on Saturday nights since caveman times. According to Dr Devane's initial report, her best guess was that Baylor had been killed elsewhere via strangulation and then his body had been brought here, mutilated and staged. Her initial tests put the time of death as sometime on Friday night, which meant the body had been up there for over a day. The local wildlife had certainly been taking advantage. The Gardaí were now bringing in a mobile hydraulic platform to take it down. It was awkward as all hell, but apparently it was the best way to ensure what Devane had called 'the integrity of the subject'. They'd been processing the scene since 2 am, and it was now 4 pm on a Sunday. Nobody who was anything in Irish law enforcement was having much of a weekend. Burns imagined an awkward meeting a couple of months from now about this overtime bill. That's assuming she was still in a job by then.

This thing had started out political, but now with body number two, it was hitting the stratosphere. The Taoiseach had been on personally. Baylor had been some kind of mentor to him, one of the great unseen forces of Dublin's political landscape, apparently. She had been left in no doubt, himself was taking a personal interest. The press were going to have a field day. Thankfully it had missed the Sunday papers, but the radio and TV crews had started massing over near the gates at first light. A provisional statement had kept them quiet for a couple of hours, but they'd need another news conference before long. It wasn't just the Irish press any more, every international news organisation was represented somehow. They were in no doubt over there now, jostling for position as they did sombre reports to camera, with the broken Skylark skyline in the background.

Burns had put uniforms patrolling the perimeter all morning, but the reality was that the site was wide open, and all you needed was a long lens. The pictures of the first crime scene released by the Púca were already available in the dingier corners of the Internet. They'd have no need to release the pictures this time, the public would undoubtedly do their work for them.

Burns turned to find Detective Garda Daly standing nervously behind her. She was a decent officer from all Burns had seen, but she had a lack of confidence that she'd need to get knocked out of her if she was ever going to move up the grades.

"How long have you been there?"

"Sorry, ma'am, I just thought you might be... y'know..."

Daly waved in the vague direction of the body, nervously.

"Daly, if you remember one thing about this job, it should be this. Instinct is invariably what some lazy prick will tell you they rely on, when they can't be bothered putting the work in to find out all the facts. This is not art, this is science."

"Yes, ma'am."

"Speaking of which..."

Daly looked back at her with a look of vacant terror. After a moment, Burns nodded down at the notebook that the younger woman held.

"Oh, right," said Daly, blushing as she opened it. "Councillor Baylor, sixty-nine years of age, was due to retire from public life next year. He was described as a pillar of the community, universally well-regarded by his constituents and his colleagues alike."

Burns pointed back over her shoulder. "Clearly not universally. Don't editorialise in your reports, Daly."

Daly nervously pushed her hair back behind her ear. "Yes, ma'am, sorry ma'am."

Burns felt like a bit of a bitch for being quite so nitpicky. It wasn't Daly's fault she was struggling to function on three hours sleep. "How come such a beloved individual disappeared for over a day, then, and nobody noticed?"

"Well," continued Daly, "his kids are grown up and off doing their own thing, and the wife is down in Waterford visiting family. She says he was planning a quiet weekend indulging in his love of making pottery."

"Throwing," said Burns.

Daly looked at her in confusion.

"Throwing," repeated Burns. "You 'throw' a pot. Technical term, doesn't matter." Even as she spoke, a voice inside her head was wondering if she was actively trying to promote the idea she was a pedantic cow.

"Right," said Daly. "I spoke to his private secretary who confirmed what the wife said."

Over Daly's shoulder, Burns watched an Astra pull up beside the line of Tech Bureau vans, and Detective Wilson emerged from it. He noticed Burns, and she pointed in the direction of the grandly-titled catering truck, which was basically a font of regrettable lukewarm beverages and the occasional sandwich that time forgot.

"Thanks, Daly. Get back to the secretary and tell her we want a detailed list of every appointment the councillor had in the last week, and specifically ask for the list of unhappy constituents that I guarantee they have kept. You can't be that long in politics without somebody bearing a grudge."

"Yes, ma'am."

"I'll see you back at the store for the meeting at 7 pm."

"Yes, ma'am."

Burns started walking towards the catering truck where Wilson was now standing. He looked no happier than when she had dispatched him three hours earlier. A large part of her job was using every resource available to her, whether that resource wanted to be used or not. Following their previous conversation, she had checked out his HR file. Wilson's grandfather was an Irish political institution, who had been Minister for Finance for a big chunk of the Seventies. His dad had made a stab at continuing the tradition until he'd been caught with his pants down. Burns was only guessing, but she figured Wilson joining the Gardaí might not have been the family's first choice. Certainly Wilson seemed extremely reluctant when sent to get her the insider's view on Baylor. Burns didn't care; she had two bodies, zero substantive suspects and no time for niceties. Wilson's awkward Christmas dinner was not her problem.

Burns nodded to the left of the truck and Wilson joined her.

"Well?" asked Burns.

"Councillor Baylor was a much loved—"

"I've already had the puff-piece report, Wilson."

"Yes, ma'am. In that case, unofficially – bent as a two bob note, but very smart. All the investigations, tribunals on planning back in the day, through all that – nothing could touch him. While he was considered the great mover and shaker in the planning permission game, he was incredibly cautious. Nobody ever directly asked him for anything, handed him money etc, etc."

"I see. Did he have anything to do with that?" said Burns, nodding her head in the direction of the Skylark complex that stood at the far end of the waste ground.

"I asked. Nothing specific but, put it this way, they said if he didn't have a dog in that particular fight, it'd be the first serious development in Dublin for thirty years that he didn't."

"Really?"

"You know how most councillors are waiting to move up to being a TD? Well, apparently the joke was that Baylor wouldn't as he'd not take the pay cut."

"So, had he any enemies that we should be looking at?"

"People that'd crossed him, or he crossed? Thousands, but..." Wilson looked over in the direction of the body, and Burns had to resist the urge to step back to protect her shoes, "nothing that would explain that."

"Any skeletons in his closet I should know about?"

"That's the other thing," said Wilson. "He was apparently the dullest man on the planet. No sneaky meetings, no late-night liaisons. The guy was a really holy Joe apparently. Didn't even drink. His nickname was Snow White."

"Well," said Burns. "He pissed somebody off. Whoever is behind this really loves their work, and I can't believe they started in the job a few days ago. Amateurs don't have this level of showmanship. We're going to be—"

Burns stopped talking as she felt her phone vibrate in her pocket. She took it out and recognised the number as being the Technical Bureau. "Hang on..." She answered it. "Doakes, what've you got for me?"

"Actually Susan, this is DSI O'Brien here, but Doakes is with me."

"Oh, hello Mark."

"The note you found on your victim, we've got a result on it. There was a partial print."

"Good." Burns noted how wary O'Brien sounded. The fact it was him calling was unusual in itself.

"We've triple-checked this, and I got one of my best to confirm. The print is on our elimination list..."

Burns felt like punching something. The elimination list contained coppers and techs. All there to make sure that if their prints showed up at a scene they'd attended, they could be eliminated from an investigation. Of course, if they'd done their job right in the first place, they shouldn't have been there to begin with. "Who the hell contaminated my crime scene?"

"Nobody," said O'Brien, "This isn't that. The print belongs to a recently-retired former detective. It's Bunny McGarry."

CHAPTER TWENTY-NINE

Gerry: ...And we're back. The Púca have been condemned by every Irish politician, the Church, even Bono has said he is not a fan, yet on my way in to the studio I've seen the graffiti on walls, on bus stops and everywhere else you look. Clearly, there is a minority out there who their actions speak to. Who do you think that minority are? Are you one of them? We're taking your calls. Niall from Maynooth.

Niall: Yeah, Gerry, now hear me out – how do we know the Púca are even Irish?

Gerry: I don't get you, Niall?

Niall: I'm saying, could be foreigners, couldn't it? Like your Al Qaeda, they're your ISIS now, maybe they've changed their names again, like?

Gerry: So your point is, maybe a bunch of Jihadi terrorists have renamed themselves to the Gaelic name for a creature from Irish mythology?

Niall: Well... there's no need to try and make me sound stupid, Gerry.

Gerry: I'm not Niall, that was all you.

Dr Simon Sinha had never been in a fight with a woman in his entire life. It wasn't something he was particularly proud of. He considered it the bare minimum of behaviour for a man who had been raised properly. Being proud of that would be like being proud of putting on clothes before leaving the house, certain standards were just expected. He considered himself a feminist, although equality did not extend to violence. Violence, in his opinion, was a measure of failure in a human being's character. This was why he was so disappointed to be in a fight with not one, but two women.

To be fair to himself, his role in the fight was that of being the person trying to stop it, but he had been singularly ineffective in that endeavour. The fight was between Nurse Brigit Conroy and the woman he was thinking of as Diane. That had been what she had called herself over the phone. Given her profession as a lady of negotiable virtue, he was not naïve enough to think that Diane was her real name, but he preferred it to thinking of her as 'the prostitute'. All of Dr Sinha's attempts to break up the fight had so far proven disastrous. Any time he'd dragged one of the participants away, the other had used it as opportunity to get a cheap shot in. He was fast realising that while women may look like the more refined gender, when that broke down they were whirling dervishes of jewellery, nails and heels.

The fight had started when Nurse Brigit Conroy had punched 'Diane' right in the face for no explicable reason. Dr Sinha liked Brigit and wanted to believe this behaviour was out of character for her, but this week alone she had punched him in the face and been suspended from work for taking a naked colleague hostage. A trend was beginning to develop.

Following the initial punch, there had been a great deal of hair pulling, screaming, biting and gouging as the two – he was struggling to still think of them as ladies – rolled around on the floor. The fight had mainly taken place in the apartment's entrance hall, but it would no doubt spill over to other areas if allowed to continue unabated. His last attempt to pull them apart had resulted in him rolling around on the floor with them. It sounded a great deal more appealing in theory than it was in reality. This had been a very big weekend for Dr Sinha, having lost his virginity on Friday night. Now, a woman had bitten him for the first time, he wasn't sure which one. He was going to require a tetanus shot.

"I'm gonna figgning 'ill you," said Brigit, her voice muffled by the presence of Diana's fingers in her mouth.

"Yer fucking mad bitch," replied Diane, in a succinct summary of proceedings.

Sinha managed to regain his footing and then grab hold of Brigit. He physically lifted her off the other woman, her arms swinging wildly, desperately trying to connect for another blow.

"Nurse Conroy, please!!"

He put her down facing the door and tried to place his body between her and her still prone opponent. Having finally been given a moment's respite, Diane's fingers were now in her own bloodied mouth, tentatively poking.

"You broke my fucking tooth!"

"Yeah? Well you broke my fucking heart!"

"OK," said Dr Sinha, "Why doesn't everyone take a moment and we can—"

Dr Sinha had been so preoccupied with keeping the two women physically away from each other that he hadn't noticed Brigit picking up the large vase that had been knocked off the hall table in the initial skirmish. He only noticed it when she lobbed it over him. Diane ducked just in time for it to narrowly miss her head on its way to shattering against the wall. She turned and scurried out of view into the front room on her hands and knees.

Dr Sinha turned to look at Brigit. "Nurse Conroy! What on earth is going on here?"

"She..." said Brigit with an accusatory point, "She's the one who..." tears welled up in her eyes. She took her phone out and started trying to put her code into it. "She... there was..." she was fighting to hold back sobbing gasps now. "She..."

Dr Sinha extended a placating hand and lowered his voice. "Whatever is the—"

Then, inexplicably, Brigit's anger seemed to get its second wind.

"I'm gonna..." she was past him with a nimble sidestep and heading towards the front room, "...fucking kill the..."

Dr Sinha turned to follow Brigit. He ran into the back of her when she unexpectedly stopped in the entrance to the living room, sending her sprawling onto the carpet in front of him.

"Sorry, I—"

Dr Sinha stopped. Bleeding from the mouth and with a black eye forming, Diane stood at the doorway to the bedroom holding a handgun. It didn't look very big, but size wasn't everything.

"Don't move," she said, the gun oscillating between pointing at him and then down at Brigit.

"OK," said Dr Sinha, "let's just calm down."

"Calm down? Calm down?! I don't know what kind of sick shit you two are into, but I will blow a new hole in the next one of you that moves."

"All right, I understand your anger," said Dr Sinha, who'd seen more than enough violent disagreements in his career as an A&E doctor to know something about dispute resolution. He put his hands out in a placating gesture. "Let's all just..."

He stopped and looked away.

Diane gave him a confused look. "What?"

Dr Sinha, still averting his gaze, pointed in her general direction. "Your, ehem, your..." Diane looked down to realise that her négligée had ripped in the fracas, causing her left breast to pop out.

"Oh, big fucking deal!"

Actually it was. While he had, of course, seen all parts of the human anatomy numerous times through the course of his work, he was trained to think of them as work. Problems to be solved, issues to be managed. Discounting those breasts, this one was only the third he had seen 'in the wild'. He had lost his virginity in the company of the other two, only a couple of nights previously. He was very much hoping to continue his acquaintance with the first two boobs and their delightful owner as soon as possible. This was just one of the many reasons why he didn't want the owner of boob number three to shoot him.

"Yeah," said Brigit, "she doesn't care. In fact, why don't you ask to see the flower she has tattooed on her arse?"

Diane looked down at her in confusion. "How did you—"

Brigit held her phone up and waved it at her, sneering.

"I've got a picture of it on my phone. One of the many also featuring my former boyfriend."

Diane stared at Brigit for a moment and then turned her eyes to heaven. "Oh for fuck's... I wish I'd never taken that job. It's more hassle than it was worth."

"Worth? You ruined my—" Brigit hurled her phone at Diane, which, with a sickening crunch, struck her full-force on the bridge of her nose. As she reeled backwards and distractedly clutched at her face, Dr Sinha rushed forward and snatched the gun. Brigit was now hurtling towards Diane again.

"Enough!" said Dr Sinha, pointing the gun in Diane's general direction while at the same time putting his body between her and Brigit. "Somebody must please explain this to me now, right this instant, immediately! I have no desire to be arrested in a prostitute's apartment." He turned to Diane, whose hands were now cupped around her bloodied nose. "No offence."

She did not respond.

A moment of unexpected – though welcome – silence descended. Dr Sinha took a handkerchief from his pocket and handed it to Diane, while still keeping the gun pointed just to the right of her. She took it and placed it beneath the steady stream of blood running from her nose.

"I was told it was a joke," said Diane. "When the guy approached me. He said it was a prank on his friend."

Dr Sinha looked at Brigit who looked, if anything, more confused than he was.

"What?" she asked.

"The guy, when he approached me. Said it was a joke for the guy's stag do. He offered two grand just to do a few pictures. It seemed harmless enough when he explained it but... when I turned up at his place, the guy was out cold and there were these two other fellas with the first guy but, y'know..." she paused and looked at the handkerchief, moving it around to a still clean bit, "it wasn't a stag do was it? It was something else. The two goons were some kind of hired help. I was... you just do it and get out. It was—"

"Oh Christ," said Brigit, slumping down onto the sofa. "He was out cold."

Sinha lowered the gun and looked between the two women. "I'm sorry. I am entirely lost here."

Brigit looked at him, her eyes filled with a cold fury. "Somebody drugged Paul then paid her to take compromising photographs with him."

Shocked, Dr Sinha looked at Diane. "Is this true?"

Diane nodded. "Look, it's not something I would've... I mean if I'd known, but... I tried to forget about it ... then the big culchie turned up asking questions."

Dr Sinha took the picture of Bunny McGarry out of his pocket and showed it to her.

"Yeah. Him."

Brigit leaned back on the sofa. "For Christ's sake," she said softly. "Bunny must've reckoned Paul would never... I just assumed he had, whereas Bunny gave him the benefit of the doubt. Went looking for an explanation that didn't involve him being..."

"I didn't tell," said Diane, pointed at the picture, "him, anything. He asked a load of questions that I wouldn't answer then he left. I rang the guy straight away, said I was freaking out. He offered me five grand to keep quiet."

"Yeah," said Brigit, "I bet he did."

"And," said Sinha, "you never saw our large country friend again?"

"No," said Diane.

"He wasn't blackmailing anybody," said Brigit to nobody in particular, looking at the floor. "Bunny was proving Paul's innocence."

Brigit stood up, Dr Sinha braced himself but she didn't seem inclined to resume hostilities. "When did all this happen?"

Diane waved her free hand in the air," I dunno, I—"

"Think," said Brigit.

"Alright," said Diane, "your friend came around Thursday week ago... yeah, Thursday."

"And I bet you met this guy who hired you to get your payoff on the Friday, didn't you?" said Brigit.

She nodded. "Yeah, out in a pub in Dalkey. I wanted a public place—"

"Fun fact for you, sweetheart," said Brigit, real venom in her voice. "The man in the photo – former guard. He's been missing since that Friday."

What blood that hadn't flowed out of her nose already, drained from Diane's face. "I don't know anything about—"

"If I was you," said Brigit, "and I didn't want to be looking at a charge of accessory to murder, I'd start remembering stuff fast. Like this guy's name?"

"I don't," stammered Diane, "He paid in cash but I have his number somewhere. I might even have an address or—"

"What did he look like?" asked Brigit.

"Pretty short," said Diane, "posh, south-sider accent. And his hair was..."

Diane waved a hand around her forehead area.

"Jesus!" said Brigit, "Artificial turf?"

"Do you know him?" asked Diane.

"You could say that," said Brigit. "I almost married the prick."

CHAPTER THIRTY

"I'm an accessory to murder!" said Phil.

Paul didn't even lift his head off the desk. "No, you're not." Paul thought about this for a bit, he was 95% certain he had that right.

It was 7 pm on Sunday night, and neither of them had left the offices of MCM Investigations all day. They'd started drinking at 1 am and hadn't stopped. At least, they hadn't stopped consciously, not until they'd lost consciousness. Paul remembered watching the sunrise out the window. He was officially off the wagon. In fact, he felt like the wagon had run him over. He had even found the bottle of stuff he had bought from a guy in the Broken Rod pub ages ago and forgotten about. He couldn't pronounce the name, but it had a lot of weird-looking accents and dots liberally scattered around it. The guy had sworn that it was the greatest drink that Albania had ever produced. He had also been blind in one eye and called everyone Diego. Before he passed out, Paul remembered doing a lot of crying about the state of his love life, then planning a trip to South America, while Phil had read a poem he'd written to his non-existent girlfriend and Maggie, having consumed a heroic quantity of the unpronounceable beer, had spent twenty minutes attacking the filing cabinet while they'd both cowered under a desk. She'd then trotted over, licked Phil's hand and collapsed in the corner, the constant snoring and farting assuring them she was at least still alive.

Mind you, with the horrendous hangover he was now lumbered with, he would have welcomed his own death as a blessed relief.

Phil had taken his phone out to check for messages from Da Xin, that was when he'd noticed the report. He'd read it out slowly. "The Gardaí have said that the body of Mr Baylor was discovered last night, but provisional reports put the time of death as some time on Friday night. Gardaí are appealing for anyone who may have seen Councillor Baylor to please come forward with any information they may have. While police sources have refused to confirm it, it is strongly believed that this murder is being linked to the so-called 'Púca' who claimed responsibility for the murder of prominent property developer Craig Blake earlier in the week." Phil had stopped reading and they'd looked at each other. "Friday night."

"We don't know where Hartigan was then," said Paul.

"No."

Then they'd both sat around in silent contemplation for a bit, while unpleasant facts, suspicions and vicious hangovers battled it out for headspace.

At one point, Phil had got up to open the window as Maggie's arse was giving the full twenty-one gun salute.

They'd then spent most of the day going over and over the same ground, as the same basic report was repeated every fifteen minutes on the radio.

They didn't actually know much, bar the fact that Hartigan had broken into Craig Blake's house – a fact they'd obtained while illegally following him, and while Paul himself was trespassing in Blake's garden. Best case scenario, it was going to be a very awkward chat with the Guards that might well destroy what little chance Paul had left of getting MCM Investigations an actual licence to investigate.

That thought had brought him back to Bunny. The urge to ring Brigit was immense, but he had to resist it.

"Seriously, though," said Phil, "I drove him on Friday. I could be an accessory to murder."

Paul looked up at him. "For the last time, you're not. You didn't know where he was going, if he was going anywhere. Just relax, will ye? You're doing my head in."

They were thankfully interrupted by Paul's phone ringing. He looked at the display. Brigit. He almost dropped it in his rush to answer.

"Hello?"

"We need to talk."

CHAPTER THIRTY-ONE

As the titles rolled on the main screen in front of her, Helen Cantwell took a deep breath. No matter how many times she did this – and she'd done it plenty – she still got nervous. Tonight wasn't just any show, though. Tonight was the night where the whole country would be watching. It had been trailed at the top and tail of every ad break for twenty-four hours. An exclusive juicy enough that other channels had begrudgingly reported it as news. If they got this right, they'd be the joke show no more. She would be able to remember telling her old boss to go screw himself with fondness instead of the current lead-stomached dread. She'd no longer cry herself to sleep regretting not taking the Sky News offer and moving to England.

"OK, good show everybody."

She looked at the monitor to her right. Ciaran Hearn was a picture of newsman gravitas. You'd have never guessed from looking at him that, when the confirmation of this interview had come through, he'd danced about like a giddy schoolgirl. Half the country was about to realise that he hadn't died on the day he'd taken a commercial contract and departed from the screens of the national broadcaster.

"OK Ciaran, with you in five...four..."

As the rest of the count played out silently on the monitor to her left, she quickly blessed herself as always, maybe giving it just a little more juice this time.

Titles end.

"Full on Ciaran, Camera One."

"Good evening, and welcome to the Sunday roundup in what, I think it is fair to say, has been one of the most extraordinary weeks in recent Irish history. On Tuesday the trial of the three men behind the Skylark development collapsed in controversial circumstances. On Thursday, one of those developers was found dead after being brutally tortured, with a previously unknown organisation calling themselves 'the Púca' claiming responsibility. Then, this morning, we received news that a well-known politician had been similarly murdered, with the so-called Púca again being linked to the crime. Tonight we ask, is the rule of law in this country breaking down? Who are the Púca, and who do they truly represent? Later in the show we'll talk to former Garda Superintendent David Dunne about how the police investigation is proceeding, but before that we will have an exclusive interview with Jerome Hartigan and Paschal Maloney..."

"Camera Two..."

The two men, sitting in armchairs, filled the screen. Hartigan was a picture of composed stillness, Maloney a fidgety mess.

"...the two surviving members of the so-called Skylark Three. But first, we sent roving reporter Zoe Barnes out on the street to get your take on the Skylark mistrial and the Púca."

"...And roll package one."

The voxpop video started.

"And we're clear."

Ciaran moved over to the main set and took his seat across from the guests. They had discussed this. He would always need to get into position anyway, but Helen had briefed him to chat to the guests to cover over the voxpop video. They had debated what they should and shouldn't put in the VT long into the previous night. The old woman with her hair in rollers saying that hanging was too good for them was great TV, but Helen didn't want them seeing it for fear they'd bolt before they got them on camera. Their lawyers hadn't been keen on them going on TV in the first place, the last thing she needed was Ciaran Hearn talking to two empty chairs. That really would be the end of her career.

Hartigan, chisel-jawed in an understated – if no doubt obscenely expensive – tailored jacket, looked like a slightly older *Baywatch*-era David Hasselhoff. Maloney looked like the hapless victim he had saved from drowning in his own flop sweat. Helen opened channel three on comms.

"Lindy, do what you can with that, will you."

"I'm on it."

Helen cut the channel off as she could hear her make-up artist mumbling under her breath. A second later she appeared on the monitor, Maloney looking irritated as she tried to – once again – take the gleam of sweat off his bald pate.

Beside him, Hartigan was steadfastly ignoring Ciaran's attempts at small talk, and his eyes remained fixed on the monitor as the voxpops played out. In the interest of journalistic balance, they did have a couple in there talking about psychopaths running around claiming to represent the people, and an old dear discussing about how murder is murder and you can't take the law into your own hands. The final clip was the one they'd agonised over. The guy was seventy if he was a day and spoke in a thick Dublin accent, but the way he'd phrased it still rang out like poetry. How to sum up psychos killing robber barons.

"Ah well, y'know, two wrongs don't make a right, sure enough, but if one of them wrongs kills off the other, then that leaves ye with one wrong plus a bleedin' good warning for the next wrong that tries to come along and rip off hard working folks."

"...And back to Ciaran."

"Jerome Hartigan and Paschal Maloney, thank you for joining us."

Having been clearly outraged by the last remark, Maloney's mouth opened and closed in rapid succession, as if starting and stopping saying several things.

Hartigan looked calmly towards Ciaran. "Thank you for having us, Ciaran, but before we go any further, I'd like to point out something that I feel is criminally missing from your reporting there." Then he looked straight down the camera. "Craig Blake, a man with two children and a wife that loved him, is dead. John Baylor – a father of four – is dead, leaving his poor wife Kathleen as another widow. I find it disgraceful that in all this, the very real cost in human lives seems to hardly be getting a mention. Children are without a father, wives are left widows, and all the catchy sloganeering in the world isn't going to change that."

As Maloney nodded vigorously beside Hartigan, Ciaran looked a little on the back foot. "OK, then, let's talk about that. Firstly, how did the death of your colleague Craig Blake make you feel?"

"Well," said Hartigan, "horrified, of course, as any right-thinking person should be. We weren't friends as much as business associates, but the shock of such news, and then the details of the horrific treatment he appears to have suffered, it was truly chilling."

"Yes," said Maloney, "absolutely appalling. It is a nightmare."

Hearn nodded thoughtfully. "And what do you make of the so-called 'Púca'?"

"They are terrorists," said Hartigan, "Pure and simple. This is just a bunch of psychopaths running around, claiming to be killing people on behalf of the Irish public. What is the difference between them and some serial killer who says he's killing because voices in his head are telling him to do it, or he has received messages through the TV? We are businessmen, that is all."

"Yes, yes," chimed Maloney, "businessmen who, as the courts have proven, have done nothing wrong."

"Ah," interrupted Ciaran, "that isn't technically true though, is it? A mistrial isn't a proof of innocence."

"And," said Hartigan, "accusation and innuendo are not proofs of guilt – at least they never used to be."

"But can you understand the sense of frustration that seems to exist amongst elements of the public, at what they see as people who have done wrong not receiving justice?"

"Justice?" said Maloney, "We are businessmen. We were part of a business deal that went wrong, which of course, has never happened to anybody else has it? Some Joe Bloggs can't make his mortgage payments and it's a tragedy, we can't make our budget on a building project and we're monsters. I've had to hire security to protect myself, and I believe the government should foot the bill for that."

Hartigan flashed a brief look of annoyance at Maloney.

"And is that what happened on Skylark? Was it simply a budgeting miscalculation?"

Hartigan spread his hands out open wide in classic nothing-to-hide body language. "Ciaran, I'd love to take you through exactly what we believe happened, at least as far as we know. However, as you're all too well aware, there may well be a retrial, which — to be clear — we would welcome. However, that does tie our hands on what we can say on TV. I will say – all business involves risk. In hindsight, would I do things differently? Absolutely. But fundamentally, our country was founded by people taking risks and following their dreams. By the nature of such endeavours those dreams are sometimes not realised, but if, as a society, we start trying to punish those that take risks, that strive for more, what message are we sending to future generations?"

"But," said Ciaran, "you understand that people are angry?"

"Yes," said Hartigan, "of course I do. Frankly, I'm angry too. I want to get to the bottom of what happened, but perversely, the Garda investigation – prematurely launched, in my view – has prevented me from doing so, due to all of our files being seized."

"Can I ask – John Baylor. What was your relationship with him?"

"Our relationship," said Hartigan, "was the exact same relationship as everyone who has been involved with development in the Greater Dublin area in the last twenty years. John Baylor," Hartigan blessed himself; nice touch, thought Helen, "was a senior member of Dublin County Council. As such, he had dealings with anyone in our business, all of whom will tell you that he was a tireless worker, and a very well-liked man. He is a big loss to Irish political life and should be mourned."

"And finally, can I ask, are you worried for your own personal safety?"

Maloney nodded so vigorously that it reminded Helen of one of those nodding doll toys that her Auntie Joan was so creepily enamoured with. "Absolutely," he said in a barely restrained whine. "The stress we are under is immense. The Gardaí seem to be doing nothing, and as I lay awake at night I'm thinking to myself," his arms flapped around in front of him, "the Púca are coming, the Púca are coming, the Púca are coming!"

If Helen was right – and she was – those last five seconds would be a meme on social media by the morning.

Hartigan looked directly at the camera again. "Am I worried about my own safety? Of course I am. But more importantly, I'm worried about this country. Who are we, as a nation, if we allow the devil to run amok?"

CHAPTER THIRTY-TWO

Gerry: We've Mairead from Castleknock on the line.
Mairead: Gerry, I'm in no way condoning the actions of the Púca but still,
doesn't it almost feel like it was coming? All this anger is in the Irish system
like an infection, it has to go somewhere... Ordinary people feel like they've
been taken for a ride, like those in power are playing us all for mugs, and
the choice at election time is the same again, or something even worse.
Gerry: It's a fair point. If this were France, there'd have been riots in the
streets years ago. They don't stand for stuff like this, why is it that we
Irish do?

DSI Burns entered her own office to find a woman sitting in the guest's chair, taking a phone call.

Burns looked down at her. She had black hair pulled back into a bun, and the kind of cream business suit you could wear when you didn't have to spend six hours at a crime scene in the middle of a muddy field. The woman smiled up at her and held up a finger to indicate 'one minute'. "Yes, Marcus, I'm afraid the minister feels very strongly on this point. We hate the visuals on the first batch."

Burns moved around to sit behind her own desk. She was aware that she was tired and irritable as all hell, so while the temptation to throw this woman out was large and growing, she should probably find out what this was about first.

The woman smiled at her again, as whoever Marcus was rabbited on in her ear. Burns did not smile back, instead she pointedly looked at her watch.

"I'll touch base on this later, Marcus, I've got to reroute now." And with that, she hung up. "Sorry about that—"

"Yes," said Burns, "this is a secure area. You should not be in this office unaccompanied."

"Sorry, your PA was away from her desk."

"She's gone to get sandwiches. We've a lot of hungry, over-worked people here. I'm one of them, and you are?"

The woman extended her hand across Burns's untidy desk. "Veronica Doyle. I work for Gary."

They shook hands briefly. "And what can I do for the Minister for Justice?"

"We believe there have been some developments in the investigation."

"I'm not at liberty to discuss that," said Burns. "We have agreed that I will give daily briefings to Margaret Armitage and Terry Flynn at the Ministry but, with all due respect, Ms Doyle, I don't know who you are. Are you an employee of the Ministry?"

Doyle beamed that smile again. "As I said, I work for Gary."

"That's not the same thing now, is it?"

"We understand," continued Doyle, "that evidence at the second scene has conclusively linked a former Garda officer to this affair."

Burns took a breath. "I have yet to brief anyone at the Ministry with regards to that development." She was going to rip the whole team a new one. Somebody, somewhere had decided it was their job to whisper into the ears of higher-ups.

Doyle put her hands out in a placating gesture. "We're all on the same side here."

Burns straightened a file on her desk. "I don't have a 'side', I have an investigation. Mr McGarry has become a person of interest, but at this point it is too early to speculate beyond that."

Doyle nodded, as if she were agreeing. "Exactly. And we further understand that the copy of McGarry's phone records you obtained under the Communications Act shows that he has been in contact with Father Daniel Franks, and—"

"All right," interrupted Burns. "I've known that for exactly forty-five minutes. I demand to know where you are getting your information from."

"We're just trying to manage the situation."

Burns slammed the cover of her laptop down and pointed across the table. "That is not your job. I am in charge of this investigation."

"Nobody is suggesting otherwise," said Doyle, that practised warm grin still plastered across her face. "We're just aware that you are new to this position, and you've a lot on your plate. Gary is keen to ensure you get all the help you need. We understand there are already wanted criminals in the Ark, and now that Father Franks has become linked to a prime suspect—"

"Sorry, but can we go back to the 'who the fuck are you?' question for a minute?" asked Burns, "because you're sitting in my office – that of the head of the National Bureau of Criminal Investigation by the way – telling me how to run an investigation, and I've not got the first idea who you are."

"Gary just wants you to know that he will fully support your decision, if you feel it necessary to enter the Ark."

"Super. If that situation arises, I will consult directly with the Minister."

"Clearly, there is now significant evidence that—"

"Whatever your job is, Ms Doyle, it is not the interpretation of evidence. Now if you don't mind, I'm a little busy here."

Veronica Doyle sat back in her chair and adjusted her suit jacket.

"Susan, I think we've got off on the wrong foot here."

"Do you?"

"I appreciate you are under a massive amount of stress. Gary just wants you to know—"

"Is the minister ordering me to take the Ark?"

"That's not something he could do, obviously."

"Oh, but it is. What you mean is, he won't order it. He wants me to. Well I'm afraid, I don't currently see a justification for that course of action."

"But don't you—"

"And if I do," continued Burns, "it will be a decision entirely justified by the probability of evidence. In the meantime, if the government requires the Ark to be dealt with, it will not be done so under the auspices of this investigation. We are the Gardaí. We are not anyone's private army."

"There's no need to be melodramatic Sus—"

"It's 'Detective Superintendent Burns', Ms Doyle. If the Minister wishes to discuss something with me he knows exactly how to do so, and this..." Burns waggled an accusatory finger between the two of them, "isn't it."

"Very well, DSI Burns," said Doyle, "if that is your attitude. We were only trying to—"

"I know exactly what you are trying to do."

Doyle leaned over the desk and lowered her voice. "When we selected you for this role, we believed you were considerably smarter than this. You should consider your career here. This will be remembered."

"I've no doubt. If I'm the jackbooted thug who sends Gardaí charging into peaceful protests, I'll be remembered for a very long time."

"Fine," said Doyle, and turned to leave. "Let's forget I was ever here."

Doyle exited the office. DSI Burns got up from her desk and followed her out.

In the open-plan office area outside, over twenty members of her investigation team were scattered around the desks.

"Everyone," said DSI Burns in her loudest, most commanding voice. The room stopped and looked at her as one. DSI Burns pointed at Veronica Doyle, who had stopped and was looking back at her open-mouthed. "This is Veronica Doyle, who works for the Minister for Justice in some unspecified capacity. Could you all please remember she was here."

Veronica Doyle stormed off towards the lifts.

DSI Burns re-entered her office, slamming the door behind her.

CHAPTER THIRTY-THREE

"... and that's what happened," said Brigit.

She'd spent the last ten minutes or so staring at the Formica table top as she spoke. Paul had sat opposite her in absolute silence. She hadn't looked up. She didn't want to see his reaction. She had, more than anything, just wanted to get through it all in one go.

They were sitting in a greasy spoon café just off Abbey Street. It was quiet, 10 am on a Monday being too late for all but the most tardy of breakfasters, and way too early for lunch. A busy Dublin morning proceeded on its way outside the window in the sunshine, oblivious to their little drama. On the drive in, Brigit had heard them say on the radio that it was expected to be the hottest day of the year.

Their only audience was a incongruous German Shepherd dog, that Paul had grudgingly introduced as 'Maggie'. The café owner had objected until Paul had ordered two breakfasts just for the dog. She'd long since devoured them, while Paul and Brigit's orders remained untouched before them. Brigit could feel the unnerving canine stare boring into the side of her head.

"So I didn't—" said Paul.

"No," replied Brigit.

"Right."

Brigit dared to look up, to find Paul staring at the Formica table top too.

"I'm going to kill him."

"No, you're not," replied Brigit. "*I'm* going to kill him."

He looked up, and for almost the first time since he'd walked in, they made eye contact. She shot him a small, nervous smile and looked away. She'd been thinking about it since the previous evening, and she still did not know what to think. The last couple of months, all that hurt and pain. Still, knowing what she now knew, there was an irrational pocket of anger there. 'How could Paul do this to me?' But he hadn't.

"That's..." said Paul, "I mean, he's broken all kinds of laws."

"Oh yeah, once we're done killing him twice, he is definitely going to prison."

Paul had only met Duncan McLoughlin, Brigit's ex-fiancé, once. It had been about eight months ago, and they'd been on the run at the time. Paul had dumped Brigit's mobile phone into a shopping bag belonging to Duncan's companion. His idea at the time had been to put the Gardaí off their scent; instead, it had resulted in McLoughlin and his companion having a near run-in with an assassin's bullet not meant for them. While the bullet had missed them, due to the activity that Duncan and his companion had been engaged in at the time, his "sensitive area" had received some... unfortunate damage. They'd been told he would make a full recovery at the time, but it appeared he still bore quite the grudge.

"The last thing I remember," said Paul, "of that night, I mean, was Phil storming off after I'd said... well, y'know."

"That his fake girlfriend was bullshit."

"Yeah. Then I went back into the bar to get my coat and finish my drink and..."

He couldn't think of the next thing to say. He'd prodded at his hazy memory of that night countless times, like the gap where a missing tooth should be.

"Thing is," said Brigit, "after all this, I'm not any closer to having the first idea where Bunny disappeared to."

"No," said Paul.

"The last contact was 11:34 pm on the Friday, when he rang me."

"What?" asked Paul, "Hang on, he rang you?"

"Yeah," Brigit looked down at the Formica table again. "I... let it go to voicemail. He was drunk, happy sounding. I'm guessing he'd figured out—"

"What'd really happened."

"Yeah. The..." she tried out a couple of options in her mind before deciding on "...woman, said she'd seen Duncan on the Friday afternoon, to get her hush money."

"She told you that?"

"Yes," Brigit's explanation of her investigation and the revelation about what had happened to Paul on that fateful night had rather glossed over the nature of the conversation she'd had with Diane. It had taken the careful application of some additional foundation to disguise the bruise on her right cheek and the scratch on her neck from the fight. She had still come out the better from it, as the experience had left the other woman with a broken nose and some dental damage. Brigit was cringingly embarrassed about that, even if she didn't actually regret it.

"So," said Paul, "Bunny finds this out, confronts Duncan and then he disappears?"

"Well, he drops into O'Hagan's pub where Tara, the owner, says he was in great form. Ties up with his message to me and then..."

"He disappears. Do you think Duncan has something to do with it?"

Brigit shook her head. "Honestly? I don't. I mean, he's sneaky pond scum who deserves everything he's got coming, but I can't see him taking down Bunny."

"Maybe he drugged him too?" said Paul.

"He could've done but again, Tara said Bunny was fine when he left. They'd have noticed him being carried out I'd imagine."

Paul drummed his fingers on the tabletop and looked out the window. "I suppose Duncan could have jumped him somehow? Caught him cold?"

"That little shit is scared of his own shadow. I can't see any version of the world where he goes up against Bunny McGarry—"

"And wins," added Paul. "I take your point. Still, does it seem any more likely than Bunny bunging himself off a cliff?"

"No," conceded Brigit.

"He's not the type," said Paul.

Then Johnny Canning's words came back to her. 'In the right circumstances, everybody is the type.'

CHAPTER THIRTY-FOUR

DSI Burns sat quietly in the corner of the Portakabin that was being used as the on-site Garda command post for the Ark. It smelled of stale feet and stewed tea, and there was a brown stain on the ceiling where the roof had leaked.

They'd been very careful how they'd phrased it, of course. Assistant Commissioner Sharpe had been brought in to 'assist with the investigation'. She had in no way been removed. That was the official version. The reality was that as soon as Sharpe had entered the incident room, the legs had been completely taken out from under her. He was in command and everybody knew it. Maybe they'd have liked her to resign but she wasn't about to – not in the middle of an investigation anyway. She had pleaded her case, for all the good it had done. She'd never met Bernard 'Bunny' McGarry, but how believable was it that any former police officer was going to leave his fingerprint on a note attached to a victim's body? That was amateur hour. Sharpe had dismissed her point. According to the Assistant Commissioner, McGarry was some kind of old-school lunatic with a history of violence. It was rather well known that he had dropped Sharpe's predecessor in the job out of a window. She'd have thought he'd have been more grateful for the promotion. They needed to find

McGarry as quickly as possible, that she agreed on. Although, seeing as he'd been reported missing ten days ago now and his car had been found at a well-known suicide spot, what were the odds of that?

The powers-that-be had put together a theory; McGarry was on a homicidal rampage that he didn't expect to live through. He was shuffling off the mortal coil and he wanted to go down in a blaze of vengeful glory. The fingerprint had been deliberately left at the crime scene as his signature. He had become the one-man suicide squad of Father Franks. Burns had noticed how that in-depth psychological profile had been drawn up on the back of a fag packet, to try and explain away any inconvenient facts. Never mind that at no point had Franks urged anything more than peaceful protest. He was now a person of interest, whose phone records proved that he had a relationship with McGarry and they needed to interview him. They could not request to do so, for fear of tipping their hand. They had rolled all this in with Andy Watts's outstanding warrant in Germany, and the assault on a police officer that the person unknown – codename Adam – had committed while regaining entry, and it had added up to what they needed. Enough justification to remove an annoying thorn from the government's side.

Sharpe was a tall, thin man with more than a touch of the Basil Fawlty about him. He had an unfortunate moustache, and a reputation for berating those below while fawning over those above. It did no credit to the system that this flaw hadn't stopped him rising to the position of second-highest Guard in the land. He clearly had ambitions on one further promotion though, as he had ordered the breach of the Ark within an hour of assuming control. Assistant Commissioner Michael Sharpe: every politician's go-to guy for the dirty work.

DSI Burns would rather have avoided being here for this, but she'd not been given an option. Ideally she would have been back at the office coordinating an actual investigation, instead of being here for whatever this willy-waving contest was going to achieve. Sharpe, along with the on-site commander Sergeant Paice, and Livingstone who was the ranking Casper, was standing looking at a map of the building and its environs. On the opposite side of the table stood Flannery, who was head of the Garda Armed Response Unit. Armed units had seemed like overkill, but it had been justified by the military record of Andy Watts. They had hypothesised that he might be armed, so the breach team had to be armed. Nobody had cared for Burns's opinion, which was why she was sitting in the corner, while the boys with their toys proceeded to fuck the whole thing up beyond all recognition.

Anyone with a TV knew storming a building in broad daylight wasn't considered good practice, but a delivery of food and medicine had been previously agreed to happen at 2 pm. The Caspers had stated that Watts and Belinda Landers had come out with a couple of the other residents to collect all previous deliveries. The plan was to isolate and detain them before storming the building proper. They'd have the element of surprise, in case the armed men against unarmed civilians wasn't enough of an advantage.

Flannery's walkie-talkie crackled into life, and a voice reported that Alpha was in position. Beta reported that they too were in position. Flannery looked at Sharpe, who paused for dramatic effect and then nodded sombrely, "you are go."

Honest to Christ, she reckoned it must have taken all his reserves of willpower not to orgasm as he said it. The other two looked envious that they'd not had a chance to tell the men with guns 'you are go' too. He should have really been made to pass the walkie-talkie around, so everyone could have a shot at it. Maybe he'd let them say 'roger' into it later on.

Burns stood up and headed towards the door of the Portakabin. Sharpe stared across at her. "Where are you going?"

"I'm stepping out, sir, to check in with the Incident Room, unless you require me for this?"

Sharpe shook his head like a disappointed parent. "No, that's fine."

Burns left and walked out to the Liffey's edge. Dublin did look great in the sunshine, although she supposed everywhere did. The temperature must have been nearly 30 degrees Celsius, nobody with

Irish skin could stay out in it for more than ten minutes unprotected without risking spontaneous combustion.

She sat on a shaded bench just down from the Famine Memorial, which looked even more incongruous than normal in the bright sunshine. People were walking back and forth, suit jackets off, grabbing what little slice of sunshine they could before being dragged back into the air-conditioned confines of their offices. The world was full of people going about their ordinary, everyday lives. The first they'd know of the armed raid happening only about 100 or so yards away would be when somebody caught the story on a news website. Burns took a moment to look up and feel a little sun on her face. A long, sweeping smear of cloud stretched out across the sky in a fat line; like the trail of an aeroplane, only five times too big. It had been years since she had been on a proper holiday. Now that her meteoric ascent had been fatally halted, when this was done, she was going to take one. She would need some time to think.

'Careerist' was a word that had been constantly thrown at her over the years. It was supposed to be an insult, but she'd never seen it as such. She saw herself as being focused on doing the best job possible, and the best way you could do that was to have as much power as possible. Ambition made sense if it was a means to the end of getting something done, improving the lot of law-abiding, ordinary people. People who worked hard, and just wanted to feel safe in their own homes and walking their own streets. Burns had used every scintilla of power she could get hold of to crush the gangs of Limerick, and it had worked. She'd combined politics with sound policing and had got the job done. She wasn't naïve; even now, new blood would be rushing to fill the gap she had created. Still, guns taken off the streets, drug supply lines severely disrupted – those things made a difference. Ambition and integrity had worked hand in hand, and they'd allowed her to get the job done.

Days into her stint in charge of the NBCI, and ambition and integrity had been facing in opposite directions. For what it was worth, she'd chosen integrity. She wouldn't have her investigation used for political ends, not when she couldn't justify it. Her instincts

– those things she didn't believe in – told her that the 'McGarry as Franks's vengeful angel' idea was so much wishful bullshit. Still, a refusal to play along had no doubt scuppered her career as soon as it had reached the capital. When you rise fast, those you passed will take particular delight in the fall. Maybe she should jump now? See if somebody in the private sector likes the idea of making the woman who slapped sense into the Limerick gangs their new head of something?

She pulled her phone out of her pocket and then looked to her right. The bronze figures of the Famine Memorial stood frozen, walking towards her, bundles in their hands. Five emaciated figures, with a stick-thin dog trailing in their wake. Some moron had left a half-eaten packet of crisps tucked into the crook of one of their arms.

She considered ringing the Incident Room for an update, but it was important to let people get on with the job. They had a team out going over McGarry's house, another retracing his last known steps in Howth where the car was found, and a third poring over his phone records, which she had already been informed contained the numbers of several escorts. She'd also received a report on at least some of the incidents that had been noted on McGarry's file. She could see why the force were nervous; there was an awful lot there that would be embarrassing to explain, for a multitude of reasons. She had also dispatched officers to re-interview everyone involved in the Rapunzel case, in light of the new information. Sharpe had, however, overruled her on calling Brigit Conroy and Paul Mulchrone in for questioning. He was working on the theory that McGarry's two 'known associates' might be assisting him in his current killing spree. He had also applied for taps on McGarry's phone, which they would get, and Conroy's and Mulchrone's, which they shouldn't get; but given the current hysteria, no doubt the right, swayable judge would assist.

Her brief moment of peace was interrupted by the sensation of her phone vibrating in her jacket pocket. She fished it out.

"DSI Burns speaking."

"Where the hell are you?" It was Sharpe.

"I'm just outside sir, I was about to—"

"I don't care," interrupted Sharpe, "get in here now."

"Yes, sir. Is everything all right?"

"No," said Sharpe, speaking as if through gritted teeth. "Nothing is all right, Franks is dead."

CHAPTER THIRTY-FIVE

Gerry: I tell you, folks, I've been sitting here listening for weeks, months, years in fact – and it does feel like something is changing. Maybe people have had enough. Maybe 100 years or so since the last one, the Irish people are due another revolution. A very different kind of revolution, one about social justice. Father Franks has his Ark at one extreme, and at the other there's the Púca – whose actions neither I nor the station are condoning – but it feels like... it feels like we've reached some kind of tipping point, doesn't it?

I'm in the mood for playing some Dylan, because it feels like the times, they are a changing. Unfortunately, it isn't on the playlist, so instead we've got... (sighs) Ronan Keating with 'When You Say Nothing at All'.

"OK," said Brigit, "I know it isn't going to be easy, but just try and stay calm."

Paul nodded solemnly, or at least as solemnly as it was possible to be while licking an ice lolly shaped like a grinning green frog. They were sitting on a bench in Herbert Park, waiting. The bench they had chosen sat beside a path in the shade of a large tree, partly because they didn't want to be seen, and partly because it was the hottest day of the year and neither he nor Brigit had sunblock. Catching a few rays had not been in either of their plans when they'd started the day. In the background, a bunch of teenagers were enjoying a languorous game of footie, where estimates of the score varied wildly.

"I mean," continued Brigit, "you've got every right to be furious, obviously, but let's focus on what's important here. Bunny."

Paul nodded again. She was absolutely correct. He did have every right to be livid. Duncan McLoughlin had made a strong effort at destroying Paul's life. He'd hired someone to drug him and then take very compromising pictures of him. A part of Paul really was angry, but that was only one of many voices currently shouting for attention. There was an overwhelming sense of relief. He'd spent the last forty-nine days buried under a crushing sense of guilt and self-loathing, for being a truly awful human being. Now, he had proof that he wasn't. The guilt was still there though, like the phantom feeling of an itchy big toe from a foot that had been amputated. He had repeatedly tried to remind himself over the last couple of hours that he wasn't an arsehole, but so far he'd not managed to talk himself into it.

Then there was the happiness. Brigit was talking to him again. They weren't exactly *them* again, but at least they were within ten feet of each other and nobody was shouting. Brigit had been somewhat distant, as if her phantom fury, like his guilt, hadn't entirely gone away. If anyone had a right to be angry it was him, but then, he couldn't really blame her for believing what had been presented to her. It had never occurred to him that it was a set-up either. There was the irony. The only person who'd believed Paul was better than that, had been Bunny McGarry. He felt a wave of affection towards the mad old bastard, then a wash of sadness. He had been missing now for ten days. The belief that he could just have gone off on the lash or for some romantic getaway was getting harder and harder to hold onto. This brought Paul right back to anger. Bunny was gone, and Duncan McLoughlin was probably one of the last people to see him alive.

Maggie strained at her lead as a woman in a breezy summer dress walked by with a Yorkshire Terrier yapping at her heels.

"Did we really need to bring her?"

"Trust me," said Paul, gently dragging Maggie back, "you do not want to leave her alone in your car."

After they had agreed that talking to Duncan was now priority number one, they'd headed over to the offices of the architects he worked for.

"And you're sure about this?" asked Paul, not for the first time.

"Yes," said Brigit, annoyance pulling at the corners of her voice, "The receptionist was very clear about it."

"When she'd said he was out of the country?"

"It was the way she said it. Like she wanted me to know that she'd been told to say that."

"Why didn't she just tell you he wasn't out of the country?"

"Because that would be unprofessional."

"But—"

"Clearly, she doesn't like Duncan because..." Brigit left that hanging and even Paul didn't need her to fill in the blanks. If Duncan was such a relentless hound dog with the ladies, he'd have undoubtedly pissed off the receptionists at his work. Receptionists were the canaries down the coal mine of the modern office; there was nothing worth knowing that they wouldn't know first.

"And then she'd said he'd be going there?" Paul pointed in the direction of Debonair Grooming, a shop whose signage proclaimed it was 'so much more than a barbers' in such an ostentatious tone that the newsagents next door had a hand-written sign stuck in the window that said 'just a newsagents'.

"No," Brigit sighed, "I asked if he still went once a fortnight to get a manicure at that male grooming place—"

"And she said yes?" Paul knew she hadn't, but some part of him was enjoying annoying Brigit.

"No, she said 'well, he didn't go last week.'"

"Oh well that makes perfect—"

Paul stopped talking, because although he'd only met him once, even he could recognise that the man who had just emerged from Debonair Grooming was Duncan McLoughlin. He wore expensive-looking sunglasses, over an expensive-looking suit and a pair of shoes that Paul guessed fitted in well with the overall theme of expense. On top of it all sat a fine head of hair, most of which was no longer with its original owner.

The plan – such as it was – had been simple. They needed to get him alone, so they could ask him some questions. They reckoned he'd either turn right and head back to work, or left and head home. What they hadn't expected was for him to cross the road into the park, heading straight for them.

"Shit, should we—"

Brigit put her hand on Paul's knee to stop him moving. While Duncan was walking towards them, he wasn't looking in their direction. Two female joggers were warming up in the sunlight, and Duncan was... distracted was the wrong word, that implied they'd temporarily drawn his attention. Duncan was locked onto them with such laser-like focus that you'd swear he'd just got out of prison, or was an alien from another planet where they had not yet invented the breast. Whatever subtlety sunglasses might offer anyone having a gander, it didn't work if you turned your head to look directly at the thing you weren't supposed to be looking at.

Brigit, Paul and Maggie moved onto the pavement, and stood there as Duncan walked right into the one woman, one man and his dog that had come to mow his meadow.

"Watch where you're—" The words automatically apportioning blame on someone else stalled in Duncan's throat, as he took in who was standing in front of him. He looked at Paul, then looked at Brigit, and realised exactly what them standing there together meant.

After a moment's reflection, he screamed and bolted between them, running down the path as fast as Italian leather could carry him. Before Brigit or Paul had time to react, Maggie had slipped the lead and was off in hot pursuit.

The shadows cast by the tall trees divided the path into near-even patches of light and shade. Paul was a little impressed that Duncan managed to make it all the way to the second patch of sunlight before Maggie caught up with him.

It was like a scene from a nature documentary, one where wolves hunted down besuited bastards of the wild frontier. Maggie leapt onto him, and bodily took Duncan to the ground. He fell messily, arms splaying out, glasses tumbling off – the grip offered by Italian leather shoes having never been their biggest selling point. He tried to turn his body around, better to fend off his attacker. Maggie clamped her jaws around his throat.

Absolute stillness. For a second nobody moved.

"Christ," said Paul.

"Holy—" said Brigit, "Get her off him!"

"I'll... I'll try..." said Paul.

He slowly moved up the pavement, stepping with the care of someone in the midst of a minefield. "OK, Maggie, just relax. Good dog. I'm just... picking up your lead now..."

Paul bent down towards the lead. A low growl issued from around Duncan's throat. Paul gently picked up the lead. "OK now, Maggie... let go."

Nobody was more surprised than Paul when she did so, sitting calmly back, while never taking her eyes off her opponent. She licked her chops extravagantly. It may have been purely for intimidation purposes, but Paul guessed that she was probably trying to get the taste of expensive aftershave out of her mouth.

Duncan made to move, and another ominous growl told him it was an inadvisable course of action.

Brigit looked down at him.

"Hi Duncan, how've you been?"

"I've, well, I... I can tell you're upset."

Brigit looked across at Paul. "He could always read me like a book."

"I... I don't... I'm really sorry—"

"Really sorry about what? That you tried to destroy my life? That you drugged Paul and— I can't even find the words for the next bit."

"I'll pay. Like I told your friend, I'll pay."

"Oh you'll pay, alright."

"Brigit," said Paul.

She looked at him and he nodded his head back down the path. Unsurprisingly, a man being taken down by a German Shepherd had garnered a bit of attention. Two mothers pushing prams were discussing them, and the game of football had ground to a halt for everyone bar the fat kid, who'd found himself inexplicably able to burst through from midfield and slot one home past a statue-like defence.

"Everything is fine," said Paul with a wave, "It's just a dog training exercise. All under control."

He delivered it with as much confidence as he could muster but one of the mothers still eyed him suspiciously before retrieving a mobile phone from inside her handbag.

Brigit looked down at Duncan again.

"Tell us about how you met our friend, exactly."

"That nut job?!"

Brigit nodded.

"I wake up, and the dude is standing over me. I mean, actually on my bed standing over me, poking me with a bloody hurley."

Well, thought Paul, at least they were all definitely talking about the same nut job.

"When was this?" asked Brigit.

Duncan stopped to think. Maggie leaned in slightly, close enough that her breath played across his face.

"Friday. Friday week ago."

"Time?"

"About ten. I was in bed. I'd an early tee time the next morning down at the K Club, those are really hard to get."

There was something almost admirable about the fact that Duncan had managed to use his current predicament as a bragging opportunity.

"What did he say to you?"

"I..." Duncan's eyes darted back and forth like a trapped animal. "Is he here?"

"No," said Brigit. "In fact, he's been missing since that night, and you're damn near the last person to see him alive. What did you do?"

Paul didn't think it would have been possible for Duncan to look more alarmed, but there it was. "I didn't do anything. I... I woke up and he was there! On top of me. Said he... said he knew all my sins. What I'd done and... to be honest, I thought maybe it'd all been a really vivid bad dream. Look, could you please take the dog away."

"I'm afraid," said Paul, "that the dog has a mind of her own, and it appears she doesn't like you."

Paul noticed Brigit's glance towards the two buggy mummies, one of them was on the phone now.

"Who did you tell?" said Brigit.

"Tell what?"

"Tell that he'd found out what you'd done?"

"Nothing, nobody. Who am I going to tell? He told me he'd found me. He showed me his doo-dah."

Paul and Brigit exchanged a quick look.

"Excuse me?" said Brigit.

"His doo-dah," said Duncan. "It was a small black box with a, a little green man on the side. Said he'd used it to find me. That's all I know. Please, call the dog off. It was a joke, it was all a joke."

"A joke?!"

Paul had seen that look in Brigit's eyes once before, the fact that it wasn't directed at him this time made it only marginally less terrifying. He looked at the buggy mummies again. The proactive one was off the phone now, and they were looking around like they were expecting somebody to arrive fairly soon.

"Brigit?"

"The only joke here is you, you pathetic, narcissistic, limp-dicked scumbag. I hope it drops off. In fact..."

Duncan reflexively clamped his hand around his nether regions as Brigit lifted her foot in a menacing manner.

"Brigit, don't," said Paul. She looked at him, a mixture of anger and confusion on her face. "You're better than that, don't sink to his level."

THE DAY THAT NEVER COMES

She gave him a look that Paul couldn't read, then lowered her foot.

Paul subtly dipped his head back in the direction of the buggy mummies. "I think our audience may've called the cops. Head up that way, I'll be with you in a sec."

Brigit nodded and with one last look down at Duncan, she started slowly walking away.

Paul bent down as if about to help Duncan up but not actually doing so.

"She's worth ten of you, ye pathetic little shit." Duncan's pained expression was less to do with the put-down, and more to do with the crunching noise of Paul's foot destroying some high-class eyewear.

"See ya."

Paul started to walk off, but was halted by a tension on Maggie's lead. He turned back to see her looking up at him, while simultaneously cocking her leg and relieving herself on Duncan's expensive suit. Its owner merely whimpered at the sheer injustice of it all.

Once done, Maggie calmly trotted off up the path towards Brigit.

After a few feet, Paul looked down.

"Really? I'd got that whole crushing the shades thing with the 'see ya' and all that, but oh no, you had to go and one-up me, didn't you?"

Maggie did not respond.

CHAPTER THIRTY-SIX

DSI Burns sat outside the room of the third floor of the Ark. Somebody had brought herself and Assistant Commissioner Sharpe a couple of chairs. They were sat there like grieving relatives. It had been four hours since the raid and, if it wasn't the worst four of Sharpe's life, Burns guessed it must be up there.

"It was, basically, when you think of it, just bad timing. Natural causes really." said Sharpe. He was a different man now, seeking assurance at every turn.

Burns nodded. Sharpe was right, of course. Franks having a heart attack wasn't the same as somebody shooting him, of course it wasn't. No doubt the Garda Ombudsman, who was in there right now with the medical examiner and an independent doctor, would clear the Gardaí of any responsibility for his death after a long and thorough investigation. All of this was true. All of it was also entirely irrelevant. They'd sent heavily armed men into a peaceful protest, and one of the most famous men in the country was now dead. Spin that how you liked, and best of luck for the future.

They could have all the training days they liked, but the reality was, when push came to shove, the higher-ups had no concept of how social media worked. They were trying to batten down the hatches and think everything through before commenting. All well and good, but as a near-tearful Gettigan from the Press Office had already tried to explain to Sharpe three times over the phone – truth is time dependent. Beyond a certain point, if you don't put it out there, the lies have taken up too much room. Twitter was already ablaze with the idea that Franks had been shot dead by a Garda hit squad. Rather than refute that and give nuance to the situation, Sharpe had been scrambling for political support that was suddenly nowhere to be found. The Taoiseach's office had already issued the boilerplate 'the government does not comment on ongoing police operations.' Right now, Assistant Commissioner Sharpe was all about Garda solidarity, but Burns had no doubt it would occur to him soon enough that Burns could be a handy solution to his perception problem. She also guessed he'd recheck his e-mails at that point. She had been very clear in lodging her objections to the current course of action. He was dangling off the side of the building, and she was watching from inside with a nice cuppa on the go.

Not that it was a cause to celebrate. Her investigation had still been blown all to shite, and the Púca were nowhere to be found. Who they weren't, were Gearoid Lanagan and his merry band. She'd just been down in the basement for a provisional briefing from the tech boys. The man they'd known as Adam had now been identified from papers as an Israeli national called Benjamin Lewington. He'd done the mandatory national service there, but he was only ex-military in the sense that most Israeli citizens were. His main claim to fame was his abilities as a hacker. They'd been trying to drill their way into fibre cabling that travelled below the building. Their goal had been a hardwire hack into the banking systems. They'd already tried to frame it as an attempt to destroy capitalism but Burns expected that, when the truth came out, it'd emerge that it was a good old-fashioned bank job. She guessed that when Franks and his sincere protesters had taken over the building for their innocently-stated motives, Lanagan had seen an opportunity.

All of the above was a little bit of good news for Sharpe; his operation had foiled an attempted robbery. That was the thing though, it really hadn't. 'Adam', who had apparently gone out last week to pick up some more equipment, had already started singing like the proverbial canary. Their whole plan was based on outdated ideas on how the communications worked. They got the idea of physically hacking into fibre cabling when somebody had tried it at a bank in Minnesota two years ago. Thing is, the whole banking industry had noticed that too. Burns hadn't understood most of the explanation that followed, but the bank security specialists they'd brought in had concurred fully with the Garda boffins; that lot would have had more luck pulling a gun on an ATM machine and demanding it hand over ten million euros.

Burns had checked in with her people chasing down leads on Bunny McGarry. Nothing so far. They were also yet to locate Conroy and Mulchrone, but Burns didn't hold out a great deal of hope there. If they did know where McGarry was, why go to all the fuss of lodging a missing person's report? McGarry was, by all accounts, unstable and comfortable with the use of violence, but it was still a long walk from there to psychopathic serial killer. Christ, that had just occurred to her. McGarry – if it was him – would be the first confirmed serial killer in the history of the Republic of Ireland. This week just kept getting better.

Added to all of this was Sharpe's inability to pass up a microphone. Burns could sympathise on this one. A lot of times, the determination to not look like you are hiding something while simultaneously not say anything can be your downfall. Sharpe had been accompanying the independent medical expert through the cordon, when James Marshall from RTÉ had nipped through and put a microphone in his face. They'd probably use the clip as a warning exercise for years to come on media training courses.

'Is Father Daniel Franks dead?'

'The Gardaí can neither confirm nor deny that at this time.'

Ouch! Because of course, the Gardaí normally refuse to confirm or deny whether suspects in custody are alive or not. That's a thing.

The noise outside had been steadily rising, and she could no longer ignore it. She moved across to the window and even she was taken aback. The crowd had doubled in size since she'd last looked. From above, she could see how thin the line of Gardaí holding it back was.

The situation was highly flammable. All it would take was one spark and the sky would burn.

CHAPTER THIRTY-SEVEN

JC blew into his hands and hugged himself close. It wasn't actually that cold, at least not for this time of year, but at night, in the Phoenix Park on higher ground, there was precious little shelter from the wind. Even on a summer's night it could cut through you. There was that, and then there were the shivers, goosebumps dancing across his skin. It'd been a day and a half since his last hit, and he was starting to feel the ache in his bones again.

He'd sworn the last time he was up here would be the last. Swore blind. He and Daz had done a couple of houses together. They'd found some jewellery in some old dear's bedside cabinet, reckoned it'd really be worth something. Daz had promised he knew a guy that'd take care of 'em, not rip them off like if they went to Fish with it. He'd promised. JC felt like an idiot. Who the fuck trusts a smackhead to stand by their word? He'd have taken the money and run too.

Car lights came up the hill, and he made an effort to put his hands down by his sides, look casual. He was a pretty boy last time he'd checked, though he avoided mirrors like a vampire these days.

238

Still, you get that junkie shuffle about you and the citizens don't want to know. Makes it all a bit too real. You'll have the odd one who doesn't care or seems to get off on it, but those boys are the ones to avoid. Not that he had much choice. He needed money, and he'd only got one thing to sell.

The lights passed and headed up the hill. Along the grassy verge, fading in and out of the trees, various figures stood. There'd been some hassle earlier; one body saying another body was standing way too close. It was always like this. Generally just bitching, though one bad night, before Christmas, Jar had cut some new lad who didn't know better and was too pigheaded by half. They'd all been pissed at that. Had to clear off, and there'd been cop cars driving by for the next couple of weeks after. Luckily, somebody had called an ambulance so the kid hadn't died. Wasn't no Florence Nightingale move that; everybody knew that if somebody died, the cops would be up there in force. They'd have to go find a new spot, and the citizens would be scared off.

The lights disappeared over the hill, not stopping. Fucking lookie-loos, 'just passing through, officer'. Yeah right! Is there something wrong with your car that it drives that slowly up a hill? Coward.

As the night went on, the number of passing cars increased. 11 pm was the sweet spot. That's when the citizens would be done with all their family obligations, and be looking for a bit of excitement to see them through the work-a-day grind of the week ahead. Lights going up and down; two, three, four cars stopped. No interest in JC. He tried to chill. The more "desperate junkie" he looked, the less likely the citizens would be. One passed three times. He tried to give him a reassuring smile, then the fucker picks up Bazzer up the hill. Fuck him.

Hang in there, cars are rolling by, plenty still. Hands in pockets, think James Dean. Finally, a live one pulls up. Black car, big executive job. JC casually strolls towards the window. As he looks in, he recognises him – it's the Whale. That's the name JC gave him. Big, fat guy. He'd had him before. Has a nasty way about him. Looks at you like you're trash, and seems to get off on it. A lot of the citizens are just guys who are living a lie and looking for a little truth. Some of 'em are always trying to be extra nice to you, wanting to think that everybody is getting something out of this. Happy, happy, happy. There's that fella who cries after, sometimes during. Off putting, truth be told.

The Whale wasn't that, though. He'd a sneery way about him. Never dropped you back neither, seemed to like making you walk. All part of his little kick.

Still, teeth and tits – JC smiled in through the window. The Whale waved him inside, and he opened the passenger door and slid in.

"Hey there, how's it going?"

The Whale didn't answer, just pulled away.

"There's a nice spot up—"

"I know where I'm going."

JC didn't try and engage him in any further conversation. He wasn't the chatting sort, and there wasn't any need to haggle. The Whale knew the score. Instead, JC focused on looking out of the window. The leather seats felt nice, but the urge to pick at his own skin was coursing through him. He was feeling twitchy as fuck, and trying not to show it. At one point, JC thought he saw a car on the road behind them as they turned a corner, but when he glanced back again he couldn't see any lights.

The Whale pulled over in a spot that was about half a mile further into the park than they'd needed to be. All part of his little power trip. He was going to have to walk back through the darkness. JC hated the dark.

"Right," said the Whale as he undid his seatbelt. "You'll do what I tell you, when I tell you."

JC nodded.

The Whale threw some money onto the dash. JC reached for it.

"No. Not until after."

The Whale gave him a smile that was pure nasty. Then he reached across and grabbed the back of JC's head and...

The back door suddenly opened, and a big man slipped in.

"Evening, Councillor."

The smile crashed from the Whale's face.

"What is the meaning of—"

The big guy in the back seat was cheery as he spoke in a lilting Cork accent. "I see that, like myself, you're a keen badger enthusiast." He waved a camera in the air. "It's not easy, but seeing them at night in their natural habitat, ah sure, 'tis a sight to behold, isn't it? I've taken lots of pictures, loads of pictures."

"Who... who are you? What are you doing in my car?"

The big guy smacked the palm of his hand into his forehead in mock frustration. "Sorry, Your Worship – where are me manners? Detective Bunny McGarry, at your service." He extended his hand for a handshake, but it was left hanging there.

JC wanted to run, but it didn't seem like he'd get far. This also didn't feel like an arrest. He'd been through them a few times, they weren't normally this chatty.

"I..." said the Whale, "There's clearly been a mistake. I don't know what you think is happening here. I was just giving my nephew a lift home and..."

The rest of the car looked at the Whale in disapproval. He now noticed that, in his shock, his hand was still on the back of JC's neck. He pulled it away. The man in the back leaned forward and whispered. "Do you want to take another run at that, Councillor?"

"I... I mean... I was giving this young man a lift home."

The man in the back seat leaned back and clapped his hands together. "Course you were. That makes more sense, doesn't it? Just a coincidence I was here, taking lots and lots of pictures of badgers."

He held the camera up again, to re-emphasise his point.

"Anyway, I'll probably bump into you again on Monday night, Councillor, I'll be at the vote about St Jude's. I'm really hoping we can save our little hurling club."

The Whale nodded emphatically. "Yes... no, absolutely. I'm... sure we can."

"Your support of our boys is most gratifying. I'll be happy to give your friend a lift home, if you'd like. I'm done badger watching for the night."

"Right, yes, absolutely."

With that, the large man leaned forward and grabbed the wad of money off the dashboard. "For the badgers."

He opened the door and stepped out again.

The Whale all but pushed JC out of the door. He drove off, the passenger door still open and flapping about as he sped around the corner.

The light pollution bouncing off the clouds meant that it was never really dark in Dublin, even in the park. Not like it was in the country, where JC was from. In another life. He looked across at the big man – Bunny? Was that what he'd called himself?

"Am I under arrest?"

The big man looked across at him. "No, son, you're not." Then he looked down at the wad of money.

JC felt the cold down his spine again. "Don't suppose you'll let me have that?"

"No."

"If you like, I can—"

"Don't," said the other man, looking down at his feet. "Just, don't." He put his hand in his inside pocket and started rummaging around. "I'll give it to you, when you really need it."

"I do, I—"

The man held his hand up. "Save me the junkie ballads, there, Bosco." He pulled a card from his pocket and held it out. "You ever really want to get off that shit, then you ring me – any time, day or night. You ring that number, and I'll come get you. Friend of mine runs a place, he'll help you get clean."

Johnny glowered at him. "Oh thanks a fucking bunch, ye fucking hypocrite. Stealing my fucking money."

"I can still arrest you if you like?"

"Yeah, and I can tell everybody how you're blackmailing that fella."

"Sure you could, who wouldn't believe a junkie?" He extended the card again.

"Fuck you," said JC.

"Don't take it and I'll leave you here. Take it, and I'll drop you anywhere you want to go. No questions asked."

JC reached up and scratched his right shoulder. It was cold and he did hate the dark. He reached across and took the card.

"Right then. I'm parked just around the corner."

The big man started trudging off back down the road. JC hesitated for a minute and then followed.

"By the way," said the big man, "What's your name?"

"JC."

"As in Jesus Christ? Charmed to make your acquaintance. I wondered where you ended up."

"You're a scream," said JC.

The big man stopped.

"What's your real name?"

"Does it matter?"

"Yes, it matters. What does your ma call you?"

JC looked into the man's eyes, noticing for the first time that the left one was all wonky. "Do you think my ma still talks to me?"

The big man said nothing, just continued to look at him.

JC shrugged.

"Johnny," he said. "Johnny Canning."

CHAPTER THIRTY-EIGHT

*Gerry: We're getting reports in folks and... I'll be honest here, I am
frustrated. There are unconfirmed reports that are all over social media, but
our station manager has told me that we can't report them due to broadcast
restrictions. This isn't on the playlist, but I brought in the CD last week
and... why the hell not? Here is T. Rex and 'Children of the Revolution'.*

Inder O'Riordan was fully aware of his reputation as an odd fish. In
fact, he kind of enjoyed it a little bit. It wasn't like he had ever fit in
before in his life, but at least now it felt like he wasn't fitting in on his
own terms. The son of a Pakistani mother and Irish father, he had
managed to not fit in on two continents. On the family visits to
Lahore he had felt very Irish, and in Belfast he had felt very Pakistani.
Life at home had been exhausting too. His parents may well have
loved each other, but they had never seemed to like each other much.

Books had been his escape from this. Science, mathematics; he'd
had a love of numbers from an early age. Even that release had come
at a price. The word 'genius' had been attached to him since the age

of four, and he'd grown to hate it. He had felt pressure from all sides. To perform, to be the best he could be, to make his parents proud. At some point in his child's mind perhaps he had believed that, if he did well enough, the wounds in his parents' marriage would heal. He knew better now.

Still, at sixteen, when he'd gone to Queen's University on a full mathematics scholarship, big things had been expected of him. It had been something of a culture shock, although not in the way many might have expected. He had read extensively on what he could expect from the university experience. He had watched the National Lampoon films. He was fully prepared to engage in high-jinks, should the need arise. No, what he had not expected was the feeling of being ordinary. Being a genius meant being in the top 1% of the population. However, once they'd separated that 1% from the rest, for the first time in his life Inder had felt the sensation of being the dumbest person in the room. He had gone off the rails, but not in the National Lampoon way he had hoped for. The feeling had made him angry and bitter at the world, but he had become so at a very low volume. Over the space of a couple of years, he had very quietly fallen apart.

Fionnuala Beckering had been the breaking point. It had happened two days before his eighteenth birthday. She had been fifteen, three years his junior. Not a significant gap now, but a vast desert to a teenager. When she had stood up in that tutorial, in that small wood-panelled room that never had enough light and always smelt oddly of lemons, and tackled the equation he had been working on for two weeks – barely eating, sleeping or bathing in that time – and she had solved it in what appeared to be five minutes, he had very quietly walked out. He hadn't even picked up his coat. The tutors had assumed he was just going to the bathroom.

What followed were Inder's 'lost years', although he never understood that expression; he had always known where he had been. Amongst other things, he had attempted to count cards at a casino in France. It was there that he had experienced physical violence for the first time. He had always assumed he would have no flair for it, correctly as it turned out. He'd attempted bar work, which he had enjoyed for a time. He had taken a run at drinking and drugs, but he had not seen what the fuss was about on either front. He'd moved in with an older woman in Portugal called Isabella, who had taught him more in six months than he would have learned in ten years if he'd remained at Queen's. Her last lesson to him had been heartbreak, and she had taught it well. She had ran off with a rat-faced Italian hacker who called himself Nero. Inder had crawled back to Ireland, having discovered on the ferry home that he wasn't capable of throwing himself overboard in a futile gesture of romance.

His parents had since relocated to Dublin, his father working in his brother-in-law's booming recycling business as financial controller. Inder had stayed more or less in his room for six months, while his parents had fretted and panicked. Then, over a dinner one night, his father had laughingly explained to his mother how the company's accountancy software had developed a peculiar fault, randomly rounding up certain numbers. The next day, Inder had unexpectedly shown up at his office. He had never shown much interest in computers up until this point. Still, it had taken him all of ten minutes to confirm a theory. His father's assistant had hacked the software and was siphoning money off. When the Gardaí had been brought in, Inder had been introduced to a pleasant man called Mick Cusack, who was a civilian Garda employee tasked with computer crime. He had been impressed by Inder's abilities, and they'd stayed in contact. Eventually, Mick had got Inder a six-month placement in his team, and that had been that. Four years later, the great mystery was why someone with Inder's skills was still working for the police. His skills as an expert in computer security could have made him a very rich man. Occasionally the Gardaí lent him to other countries as a favour. He and Mick had been to Sweden, Ghana and Romania. Inder stayed because Mick never asked him to fill out a report, turn up at a very specific time or sit through an assessment. Mick got Inder, and Inder didn't like the idea of working for anyone else. A part of him also liked the idea of one day seeing police slap cuffs on Nero. He didn't like people who stole.

Inder still enjoyed mathematics. He also read about human psychology a great deal, now seeing humans as fascinating systems, worthy of study. He had been called to the building known as 'the Ark' due to what they'd found in the basement. Within twenty minutes, Inder had diagnosed what the four individuals in question had been attempting, and why it wouldn't have worked. Honestly, trying to tap directly into a bank's fibreoptic cabling was so 2015. He'd then spent another twenty minutes explaining it to Mick, who explained it to everyone else. Inder didn't like basements and confined spaces, so he had come up to the fifth floor to get some space. He enjoyed height. He liked the clean perspective it gave to life.

Standing at the window, with his head pressed pleasingly against the cold glass, it afforded him a fine view of the crowd below. It was intoxicating, watching it grow and swell. He had quickly diagnosed what was going to happen, but the sequence of events was still fascinating. Seven-eighths of the building was surrounded by linked metal fencing, and behind that, Gardaí in high-vis jackets had been placed at six-foot intervals to prevent anyone from jumping over. The one-eighth of the octagon that was unfenced was covered by a line of Gardaí in riot gear. It had been left open to allow for police vehicles to enter and exit the cordon. Around that was where the majority of the protesters had gathered. This was also where the TV cameras were situated, hence drawing more people.

Individually, people can be infuriatingly unpredictable, but collectively they obeyed certain rules. Inder had studied this. As the crowds grew steadily in size, now six or seven deep in places around the barriers and more at the entrance, the Gardaí became understandably more nervous. It was basic economics. As the opportunity cost of rule-breaking decreased – inherent human logic dictating that they can't arrest everybody – the confidence of the crowd increased. Many of them would have been there to voice concerns at what they saw as an injustice; many more would have been there out of concern arising from the initial, unconfirmed reports of the death of a significant man; yet more would have been there just to say they were there – their prime motivation being voyeuristic. Then, there would always be the fourth group. Those that cared little for the cause, and who were enticed by the prospect of trouble. Those who longed for a chance to kick out at a world that they felt had wronged them.

It would be Inder's guess that the three men in their early twenties, who had approached from the south side, had probably been in the third group. Certainly, as they stood at the back surveying the crowd, they appeared to be in good spirits. They seemed to be looking for somebody. It was only a hypothesis, but perhaps a friend had texted/tweeted/WhatsApp-ed them, and they had left the pub to meet that individual. Certainly, they had initially appeared to be in a boisterous mood. Inder had noticed them wave to someone, and then proceed to try and push through the crowd.

This insertion of three robust individuals had resulted in the crowd becoming more tightly packed.

The pressure at the front had thus increased.

The line of Gardaí in riot gear had initially taken a step back, then, as per their training, they had pushed forward in an effort to re-establish their line.

The movement had caused a surge of interest, as many people moved forward to see what had happened. As well as this, the members of group four – those individuals there waiting for the something that was going to happen to actually happen – had also surged towards the potential flashpoint, moving it further towards being the flashpoint.

This secondary surge elicited a counter-surge from the Gardaí to again maintain their line.

During this, a seventeen-year-old girl who was in the second line of protesters lost her balance and went down.

A member of the Gardaí, reacting as a human as opposed to a riot control officer, broke from the line to push forward and check if she was all right.

The throng then surged from the left, and that guard lost his balance and disappeared under the feet of the crowd.

Some protesters tried to assist him, but at least two attempted to put the boot in.

The other Gardaí, having seen their colleague fall, surged forward in an effort to protect him.

And thus, Inder observed, what would later be referred to as 'the Ark Riot' had begun.

CHAPTER THIRTY-NINE

"Christ, I need a drink."

Those had been the first words Brigit had spoken since they had made a hasty retreat from the confrontation with Duncan. There'd been some nervous moments when a Garda car with its siren screaming had zoomed by, but it had gone right on past the park towards the city centre.

"The nearest drink would be Meehan's," Paul said, pointing back up the road.

"Fair enough." Brigit nodded, and they'd headed off in that direction once Maggie had finished relieving herself against a lamp post.

Brigit looked down at her. "Is she... safe?"

"Define 'safe'? Let me put it this way," said Paul. "She's not all there, but the most of her that is, appears to be mostly on our side."

"That's reassuring... and what kind of bitch cocks her leg when she pees?"

"Phil actually Googled that a couple of days ago. Apparently it is a behaviour exhibited in highly dominant bitches."

"Really? I must give it a go. What's it got to do with Phil, anyway?"

Paul was glad of the distraction of two further Garda cars passing, sirens howling, slicing their way through the evening traffic. He'd not managed to find a way to bring up the whole Hartigan situation. He knew he needed to, but having just got out of Brigit's doghouse, he couldn't quite bring himself to do it. There was a sneaking suspicion he'd been a spectacular idiot to get himself involved, but he didn't want to get it confirmed just yet. He was definitely going to have to tell her, but it was a question of finding the right moment.

"Phil's been helping me out with some stuff," said Paul. "So, what do you reckon about Duncan?"

Brigit sighed. "I don't know, but I can't see that worm having had the bottle to go toe-to-toe with Bunny McGarry, can you?"

"Nah, he'd be too worried about his hair becoming permanently unplugged."

"Yeah," said Brigit. "Christ, I have awful taste in men."

There was almost a thunking noise as those words dropped between them. She hadn't meant it as a dig at him, he knew that. Her face immediately reddening only emphasised the point. At a different time they'd have perhaps laughed it off, but now was not that time. They needed one hell of a clear the air chat, but it didn't seem right to focus on their own crap. Bunny, after all, was still missing. That was priority number one. Their personal baggage could be added to the list of things in need of a right moment.

Thankfully, the awkward silence didn't have too much space to fill, as they had reached the doors of Meehan's. It was a large pub, on the more soulless end of the spectrum. Twos and threes of after-work drinkers sat scattered around the tables, with a couple more at the bar. It would normally have been busier, but Paul guessed that the crowds had gone in search of anywhere with a beer garden. Those that were there, were all gawping at the plasma TVs that were conveniently positioned on every other wall.

The screens were showing footage of a line of riot police, shields raised as youths hurled glass bottles and bricks at them.

"Christ," said Paul, "is there football on again?"

The barmaid turned and pointed over her shoulder at the screen. "That is O'Connell Street. What you want?"

The camera angle changed, and they could see the Spire of Dublin monument outside the GPO, aka the needless needle, pointlessly pointing off into space behind the line of cops. It was O'Connell Street all right. In the foreground, a car was on fire and somebody was trying to throw a crowd control barrier through the window of one of those shops that only tourists go into.

"Why do that?" said the barmaid. Her accent was from somewhere Eastern European, but Paul had no ear for those things.

"Mindless violence," said Brigit.

"No," said the barmaid, "Is a Sports Exchange store three doors away, much better stuff. Who wants shitty leprechaun T-shirt?" she pulled a face of disgust. "You want drink?"

"When did this start?" asked Paul.

"Earlier," said the barmaid turning back to the TV, having decided that Paul and Brigit were more lookers than drinkers. "Priest dead."

"What?" asked Brigit. Something in her tone made Paul turn to look at her. Her face was pale. "What priest?"

"Famous one," she shrugged. "Always on TV."

"Do you... do you mean Father Franks?"

"Yes, dead. Police shoot him."

"Actually..." they all turned to look at the source of the voice. It was a larger lady, sitting at a nearby table, "...the Gardaí have said he died of natural causes."

The woman's expression changed to one of shock as the barmaid blew a raspberry. "Yes, when men with machine guns kick door down, lots of 'natural causes.'"

"I met him two days ago," said Brigit.

Both of the other women turned to look at her. The customer threw on a patronising smile that didn't do her face any favours. "I don't think so. He's been locked inside that Ark building for weeks."

Paul touched Brigit on the arm and pointed at the empty booth in the corner. "Usual?"

She nodded and walked towards it as Paul turned to the barmaid.

"A large white wine and a pint of Guinness please—"

A soft growl rose from beneath the bar.

"Two pints of Guinness please."

The barmaid leaned over and looked down at Maggie.

"She's a trainee guide dog."

The barmaid shrugged. "I don't care. Dog wants pork scratchings too?"

On the screen behind her, Paul could see a half-dozen mostly shirtless young fellas, their faces half-covered with improvised bandanas, pushing a flaming wheelie bin towards the line of Gardaí.

They sat in that corner booth for the next half an hour, listening to Maggie demolish three packets of pork scratchings, while watching the world unravel on the muted TV above the bar. Brigit brought Paul up to speed on her investigation into the whereabouts of Bunny McGarry. He'd known about the final bit – the revelation of exactly why Bunny had been visiting escorts – but she filled in all the gaps up until that point. Bunny's phone bill, meeting Johnny Canning, the trip to the Ark with Dr Sinha and the rest of it. If nothing else, it proved that Paul had been right about one thing. It would have taken him months to get as far as she had in under a week. She had a flair for this kind of thing.

"You've done really well," said Paul.

"Have I?" said Brigit, "doesn't feel like it. Bunny is still missing, and I've no idea what the hell happened to him. I've not got the foggiest who this Simone woman is, either. Last time Bunny was seen was in O'Hagan's a week ago last Friday, and..."

Brigit stopped, and started irritably flicking at the beer mat in front of her with her fingers.

"Should we go back to the Gardaí?" asked Paul.

"With what? We've no evidence of anything. And besides," said Brigit, pointing up at the screen, "I don't know if you've noticed, but they're a tad busy at the minute."

Paul exhaled loudly.

"And there's something else," said Brigit. "Franks swore blind that he'd not spoken to Bunny in years, but his phone bill showed calls and texts between the two of them."

"Do you think they were up to something?"

"I don't know. The only lead we've really got is that Bunny had some kind of tracker, and..."

Brigit rubbed her knuckles lightly along the front of her teeth and looked down at the table. The memory of this little tic that showed she was deep in thought filled Paul with a wave of emotion. "I'll get some more drinks."

"Diet Coke for me," she said, without looking up. "Driving."

"Right."

Paul looped the top of the snoring Maggie's lead under his chair leg, and went to the bar.

By the time he returned, Brigit was excitedly tapping away on her iPhone.

"They only have Diet Pepsi, so..."

"Whatever," said Brigit, her face now bright with excitement. "Remember what Duncan said? That Bunny's 'doo-dah' had a little green man on the side?"

"Yeah."

"Well, I started looking at one of them spy shops for trackers. Figuring, y'know, Bunny must have got it from somewhere. Maybe there was a shop in Dublin we could go to—"

"Good idea."

"I've had a way better one."

Brigit held up her phone to show him a picture of a black box the size of a cigarette packet, with a cartoon picture of a little green man on the side of it. "The Sniffer 408 GPS tracker – easy to use, magnetically fixes to any vehicle. I'd bet you this is what Bunny had..."

"OK," said Paul, "what does that tell us?"

"Nothing," said Brigit, excitedly clicking through screens on her phone, "but it might be something."

"Right, so..."

Brigit was talking, but not really to him. He just happened to be there while she talked to herself. "It uses a SIM card... so, a mobile phone number and... NO! It can't be that..."

"What?"

Brigit didn't answer, instead she scrolled down the page she was on. "Features... attaching it to... battery life..."

He watched her eyes widen with excitement as she read. It took all of Paul's self-control not to snatch the phone away from her to see for himself.

"Are you—"

"Shut up," snapped Brigit, then she glanced up quickly. "I mean, just give me a sec..."

She read for about a minute longer and then picked the phone up and started doing something else.

"Have you—"

Brigit held up one finger for silence as she tapped something into her phone. With a final flourish she stabbed at the phone with her thumb, and then placed it carefully on the table in front of her. Then she looked up at Paul with a smile.

"What? For Christ's sake, woman!"

"All right, don't get your hopes up, but..." she left a pause.

"You really need to stop playing for drama here, or I swear to God—"

"Simone," said Brigit, "isn't a woman, or at least not just a... I mean—"

"What?!"

"'Simone' is a password. How you activate the tracker is: you text the password you set up to the mobile phone number of the SIM card—"

"Wait, d'you mean?"

"We've been trying to ring Simone. What we should have done is texted the word 'Simone' to that number. Fingers crossed, it takes it a while to sync the first time apparently, but then 'Simone', aka the tracker – if that's what it actually is – will text us back a link to its exact location."

"You're kidding!"

"Like I said, don't get your hopes up." Even as she said it, her face beamed hope back at him. "If only we'd known sooner. Hopefully the thing still has charge and... shit!" Brigit snatched her phone back up, "I need to download the app. It said it normally takes 30 minutes or so to get an initial response, and—"

"What'll we do if we get a location?" asked Paul.

Brigit didn't look up. "I dunno. We could try and get the guards interested, although they frankly don't seem to have given two shits where he is so far."

"Ah here, I was watching that!" Paul looked up to see the plaintive cry had come from a man in a crumpled suit who was propping up the bar.

The picture on the TV screens had changed. It was a place Paul recognised.

"I didn't change channel," responded the barmaid, "is news people."

"What's more important than the riot?" asked Crumpled, in a drunken slur of outrage.

Paul stood up and moved over to the bar. "Turn it up, please."

"We don't put sound on," said the barmaid. "Boss says is bad for ambience."

"Please!" said Paul.

With a shrug, she pointed a remote at the screen.

The volume came up just in time to capture the clamour of camera flashes and shouted questions as Jerome Hartigan and Paschal Maloney, the surviving members of the Skylark Three, emerged from Hartigan's front door. They were holding a news conference. The lawyer that Paul had seen Hartigan with previously followed them out.

"Ah, not these two pricks," said Crumpled.

The lawyer stepped forward and raised his hands for silence. "Please." Eventually the noise settled to a low hum. "Thank you. My clients would now like to make a brief statement."

With that, he stepped aside and Jerome Hartigan stepped

forward, giving his best "politician's sombre nod" towards the camera.

"Thank you all for coming. As you know, we suffered the tragic loss of our friend and colleague Craig Blake last week, in the most brutal of circumstances. This was followed by the equally senseless death of Councillor John Baylor, a public servant who has worked tirelessly in the service of the everyday people of Dublin. Through all of this, we received assurances from the Gardaí that the so-called Púca, whoever they are, would be swiftly brought to justice. Despite those assurances, no progress appears to have been made."

As he left a gap, a voice tried to pipe up with a question but a combination of Hartigan's raised palm and the shushes from an unseen assembly silenced it.

Brigit had now moved to stand beside Paul. "What's going on?"

Paul didn't respond. Paschal Maloney had moved forward to take over speaking, squinting under the renewed barrage of flash bulbs. He reminded Paul of a lost child waiting for his mummy. When he spoke, there was a tearful edge to his voice.

"As can be seen from the horrific events unfolding throughout Dublin tonight, the rule of law appears to be breaking down in this city. There are riots in the streets, vigilantes are running amok, and the Gardaí and the government seem powerless to stop it. Myself and my colleague feel we have to speak out, as we no longer have any faith in the Garda Síochána. It has come to our attention that they have had a suspect in the deaths of Craig Blake and Councillor Baylor for over a day now, and yet they are doing nothing to apprehend him. The reason for this is that the man in question is formerly one of their own."

"Oh Christ," said Brigit, grabbing Paul's hand.

Hartigan took over speaking, looking directly into the camera. "Our question for the Gardaí is a simple one. Where is the man known as Bunny McGarry, and why has he not been apprehended?"

"Well," said Paul, "at least it won't be hard to get them interested now."

CHAPTER FORTY

Gerry: I can now tell you that those reports of rioting up at the IFSC have been confirmed, and it has spread around the city. Our studio is just off O'Connell Bridge and as I look out the window I can see large crowds, and they're getting bigger all the time. There have been repeated clashes with Gardaí and... from where we are, it seems as if the Gardaí are being forced to retreat by sheer weight of numbers.

Also... I can... it is with great sadness that I can announce that, within the last few minutes, sources have confirmed that Father Daniel Franks is dead. We don't know any further details. There are unconfirmed reports of some form of raid on the Ark. We'll let you know more as soon as we have it.

Paul was running.

His chat with Brigit had not gone well. He'd been afraid she'd get angry, now he wished she had. Instead, she'd had an air of frustrated resignation, like how he remembered the teachers in school sounding when talking to the weird kid. A low point had undoubtedly been 'you took a job from someone, and you don't even know their name?' It had sounded a lot worse when she'd said it. Not going to the Gardaí with his suspicions about Hartigan had sounded even dumber. By the end of the brief chat they'd had while speed-walking down Dawson Street, he'd felt about as useful as a chocolate teapot.

Before they had parted company, Brigit had laid out a plan.

Whoever the Devil in the Red Dress was – and thankfully, he'd not referred to her as such to Brigit – she knew a lot about what was going on. His plan that morning, as much as he'd had one, was to be in the office this evening for the meeting and give her a report on what he'd witnessed Hartigan doing. Maybe that would have got him paid, even if it wasn't exactly what she had asked to know. Now, though – if Hartigan was trying to frame Bunny, then getting Paul to follow him must have been an attempt to derail that plan, mustn't it? Why else would she come to him? Whatever her intentions, the idea that he'd been hired by coincidence to follow a man who one week later would accuse Bunny of being a violent psychopath on national television seemed pretty damned unlikely. Whatever this was they needed answers, and Paul had one and only one way to get hold of his employer. They had a meeting scheduled at 8 pm and, come hell or high water, he now *had* to make it. The only problem being, there was a riot between where he was, and where he needed to be. According to the news, it already stretched from the International Financial Services Centre down to O'Connell Street, and it was spreading.

Brigit, for her part, had headed off running in a different direction, towards her car. Assuming Bunny's tracker was still up and running, it would start sending her its location within minutes.

Paul's lungs were hurting. He wasn't used to physical exercise, and running through the city centre was proving problematic. There seemed to be groups of what the press would no doubt call 'youths' heading to join the riot, others heading away from the riot, and a general mass of people just standing about gawping. The traffic around College Green was jammed up, and the air was a cacophony of car horns and frayed tempers. It was always a busy area, but the work to extend the Luas light rail system combined with people trying to get out of the path of trouble, meant gridlock. What taxis there were already had passengers, and after his first few attempts, Paul had given up trying to get one. Dublin taxi drivers knew deep down that they were the ones most in danger. Every last one of them had cruised by with their light on while some drenched and irate punter had screamed at them from a puddle. It was a perk of the job. There was a flipside to that coin too. Those self-same punters were currently running wild. It was rule one of any large-scale civil disturbance – taxis are always the first cars to be torched. It was time to get the hell out of Dodge.

So Paul had run. He had got off the pavement for the sake of expediency, weaving around the stopped traffic instead. After they'd wrapped themselves around a slow moving tourist and nearly taken out a cyclist, he had let Maggie off the lead. She was running beside him, in front of him; always somewhere around. She seemed disinclined to wander away, and nothing got people to move out of your way faster than a big dog off a lead. It kicked directly at some primordial instinct in the human brain. Avoid the wolf.

As Paul ran down Westmoreland Street, he could see a crowd gathered on the south side of O'Connell Bridge. Gardaí were trying to close the bridge off with orange crowd-control barriers. It was unclear if they were trying to keep the riot contained on the north side, or to stop people joining it from the south side. The Gardaí didn't seem clear either. On a closer look, many of those in uniform looked barely old enough to shave. Trainees, most likely, pressed into action and trying to look like they had the first idea what they were doing. As Paul stood there panting heavily, a group of about twenty kids ran for the right side of the bridge, sparking an improvised game of British Bulldog. The Gardaí grabbed a couple, but most got through and then stopped to cheer and taunt the flailing police. Paul picked a spot on the left side of the bridge and ran towards it. He was slower than the kids, and one of the guards moved across to grab his right arm as he tried to jog by.

"Where do you think—"

The guard looked down at the warning growl from Maggie and

then let Paul go, showing impeccable survival instincts. He'd stop somebody else, it didn't look like there'd be a shortage of opportunities any time soon.

One of the kids tried to high-five Paul as he trotted by, he left him hanging. His watch said 7:28 pm. He was going to be hard pressed to make the office. That was assuming he could get through this mess at all, and what a mess it was.

The crowds seemed to get more dense as Paul looked up the street. The main action appeared to now be at the north end of O'Connell Street. A van lay on its side in front of Easons, kids jumping up and down on top of it. Litter swirled about beneath people's feet as the alarms of various shops warbled plaintively around them.

The work to extend the trams meant that the centre of the wide thoroughfare that was O'Connell Street was one long building site – or arsenal as it now appeared to be, complete with rubble aplenty, oh so convenient for the busy rioter on the go. In the distance, Paul could see a steady stream of missiles flying through the air. He guessed that the police line – what was left of it – was at the far end of the street, certainly there were no Gardaí on O'Connell Street itself. It reminded Paul of the throng of supporters heading to Croke Park that he occasionally had to pass through if he timed it wrong. Only here, they were more milling than "proceeding in an orderly fashion". To his left, three blokes were hurling large paving stones at the front window of Easons. The spiderwebbing cracks in the reinforced glass were growing more pronounced all the time. On the other side, a security guard looked on, appalled. Each time a paving stone hit, the crowd cheered.

Go on, thought Paul, steal a few books, ye morons, see if you can't learn something.

A middle-aged woman passed by him with arms full of clothes, still on their hangers. Her roar of 'We're taking our country back!' was greeted by a smattering of cheers. If she is, thought Paul, she'll not have the receipt for it.

The most logical way to head back to the office would normally have been to head up Abbey Street, but as he looked down there he could see a higher density of people, and what appeared to be another line of Gardaí. Both sides were currently just looking at each other, but that would probably not last long.

From what he knew, he reckoned his best chance was to head up O'Connell Street and find a way out further along.

He passed the statue of O'Connell himself – his head, as always, covered in birdshit. Kids were boosting each other up onto his plinth to get a better view. Spray painted onto the bottom of it in raggedy letters was the phrase, 'We are the Púca'.

And, thought Paul, this is the day that never comes.

CHAPTER FORTY-ONE

If Assistant Commissioner Michael Sharpe's voice got half an octave higher, Burns reckoned only dogs would be able to hear him. Personally, she was longing for that moment, as he was really getting on her tits. You'd swear he'd never been trapped in a building by a howling mob baying for his blood before. He was pacing up and down screaming into his phone at whatever poor sap at HQ had been unlucky enough to pick up. Sharpe seemed to be of the strong opinion that rescuing him from this building should be the Irish police force's number one priority. He was having difficulty getting others to see it that way.

"For the love of God, Cormac, we have women trapped in here."

He shot a look in Burns's direction; she made no attempt to hide her disgust. Oh, Michael, she thought, you fuck off and die right now. Wrapping your own cowardice up and trying to present it to the world as chivalry, you pathetic little man. Whatever happens from now on, know that this was the moment that I decided to kill your career if it's the last thing I do.

Her moment of self-doubt of a few hours ago had dissipated. Now she felt in control again. Not of the situation, that was spiralling out of control faster than an AA meeting in a brewery. No, she felt in control of herself again.

Burns turned to look out the window. The riot had happened fast, and had turned ugly even faster. The Gardaí simply weren't used to dealing with large-scale civil disturbances, and no training day in the world was going to prepare you for it. She'd watched it unfold from up here. Most of her colleagues had behaved with restraint, trying to maintain order. A few had lashed out in panic and had only inflamed the situation further. Guards and protesters alike had been dragged out, bleeding from head wounds. Eventually the sheer weight of numbers on the protesters' side had told, and the Gardaí had gone into full retreat. The entire square outside the building was now filled with people. Gathered around the doors below her was a large group who kept chanting over and over again, 'we want Franks! We want Franks!'

Generally it was younger people, but there were some older ones in there too. Of course, around them were a ring of people with their cameras out, filming. It was the twenty-first century disease: nothing has really happened unless it's been recorded. Burns didn't doubt that the majority of those gathered below were probably sincerely and justifiably angry. They'd seen hope in what Father Franks represented, and it had been taken away. Maybe the Gardaí's idiotic raid had only hastened his passing by a few days, but still, it was a monumental screw up. It wasn't those people that worried Burns, it was the others. She'd been a copper long enough to know that it was the conflict junkies, those filled with anger and looking for something, anything to aim it at – those were the ones you had to worry about. Football hooliganism, terrorism, peaceful protests that descend into violence; it was always those men – and 99% of them were men – who turned up, tapped into the fear or anger of those around them, and proceeded to try and set the world on fire.

And the fire was spreading. From what scattered information they'd been able to glean, what had started here as an essentially political protest had spread fast. There were reports of wide-scale looting in O'Connell Street and down into the shops on Henry Street.

It was always the same. The only thing stopping a certain group of people from trying to take whatever they could was the fear of getting caught. The Gardaí were now trapped in the perfect storm. A riot coming out of nowhere, in the middle of the summer holiday season, on the hottest day of the year. If only it had rained. Nothing stops a riot faster than rain.

Her phone rang.

"Burns."

"Sir, ahem, sorry – ma'am."

"What is it, Wilson?"

"How're things?"

"Super. Lovely view of the riot. Is this a social call?"

"No, ma'am. It's McGarry, ma'am."

"We've found him?"

"No. Mhm ... Hartigan and Maloney, they just announced him on national television as our prime suspect and—"

"Oh, Christ Almighty."

"Yes, ma'am."

"Get to them – now. Find out where the hell they got that from."

"What if they—"

"I don't care, do it."

"Right."

CHAPTER FORTY-TWO

Paul and Maggie crossed the road to skirt around Clerys. The landmark store had been closed for a couple of years now, but the shops around it were garnering a lot of attention. On one side was a jewellery store, whose reinforced glass fronting was not designed to stand up to the attentions of the mini JCB digger that had been hijacked from the building site. On the other side of that lay an Ann Summers shop. It was an interesting phenomenon that some lads who probably wouldn't have been seen dead in there normally, were more than happy to loot the place.

Paul felt the mobile in his back pocket vibrate. As he pulled it out, he realised that he had twelve missed calls from Phil. He answered unlucky thirteen.

"Howerya, Phil?"

"Where the bleedin' hell have you been?"

"Sorry," said Paul, "I've been kinda busy."

As he spoke, Paul weaved his way around the mix of gawpers watching the show, and looters surveying their hauls. Two women seemed to be fighting over a large, pink box whose contents Paul couldn't see, but he could guess at.

"Yeah well that psychonaut Hartigan is trying to frame Bunny for all them murders."

"I know Phil, I saw it on telly too."

"Screw telly. I'm here."

"Wait, you're outside Hartigan's now?"

"Yeah!," said Phil, sounding exasperated. "Aren't we supposed to be finding out who the arsehole is knobbing?"

That was Phil, he was a lot of things, but a quitter wasn't one of them.

Two young fellas of no more than thirteen years of age ran by Paul, carrying a naked female mannequin between them. He didn't want to think about it.

"To be honest Phil, I've no idea what the hell is going on, but I'm heading back to the office now for that meeting with our client."

"But ye've no proof?"

"I don't care about that. Brigit reckons the client might know something about where Bunny is. It has got to be worth a shot."

"Does this mean Brigit is back in charge now?"

On some level, Paul resented the question. He didn't mind realising himself that he had no idea what he was doing, but he resented Phil recognising it. He was considering an appropriate answer when Maggie yelped behind him. He turned to see a scrawny bloke with a regrettable mullet and arms full of pint-sized brown cardboard boxes who, it appeared, had just trodden on her paw.

"What the—"

On Maggie's growl, the mullet showed admirable survival instincts by jumping backwards, dropping half of his merchandise in the process.

"Watch where you're going!" said Paul.

"Me?! The fuckin' cheek, your dog shouldn't be here."

Maggie bared her teeth at him.

"Want to tell her that?"

The mullet mumbled something under his breath and bent to pick up his boxes. Maggie growled. He froze, except for the slow movement of his head as he looked from Maggie to Paul.

"She's not a big fan of thieves," said Paul.

"Who are you calling a thief?"

Maggie's bark sent him staggering backwards, where he tripped over one of the discarded barriers and landed on his bony arse.

"Aw for— me back! That's assault, I'm going to have you."

"Yeah?" said Paul. "Good luck finding a policeman."

They moved on, those that had stopped to watch taking a step back to give Maggie room.

Paul put the phone back to his ear. "Sorry Phil."

"What the hell was that?"

"Bit of a discussion on riot etiquette."

"Riot? What riot?"

"Have a Google Phil, there's been some developments. It's the end of the world as we know it."

Paul's phone beeped in his ear. "Hang on." He pulled it back to see that Brigit was trying to get through to him. "I'll call you back."

He tapped to disconnect Phil.

"Brigit."

Paul had to pull the phone away from his ear as— "Cop yourself on, ye useless div! Pull your head out of your arse!"

"Christ."

Brigit's voice returned, unnervingly calm. "Sorry, that wasn't meant for you. It's like Mad Max trying to get off Capel Street."

"I can imagine," said Paul, and he could. Brigit's driving was erratic at best in normal circumstances, he imagined it really came into its own in a situation like this.

"That Hartigan fella you were following; where did you say he lived?"

"Out in Seapoint."

"Right. A road called Sandy Way, by any chance?"

"Yeah, how did—"

"Bunny's tracker just came back. It's showing he's on that road."

"What? But..."

Paul couldn't think. None of this was making any sense. If Bunny had been standing there at the press conference where he'd been announced as being the Púca, somebody would have surely mentioned it.

"I'm heading there now," said Brigit, "assuming I can ever get out of this bloody traffic jam."

"Phil is already there."

"Why is—"

"I'll ring him now."

Paul hung up, hit "recent numbers" and pressed on Phil's. The phone rang three times before answering.

"Did you hang up on me?"

"Look – is Bunny there?"

"What? are ye mad?"

"Just, have a look around. Are there any parked cars? Maybe he is in disguise or... I dunno."

"But why would he be—"

"Just do it, ye fucking idiot."

"All right" said Phil, sounding hurt. "There's no need to be all—"

Paul lost the rest in a clamour of sudden noise on the line.

"Phil?"

Phil was shouting to be heard over a babble of indistinct voices. "Sorry. Yer man Maloney, the little fella, he has just come out and they're all trying to ask him questions and that, and—"

Paul pulled the phone away from his ear, as what sounded like a large explosion issued from it.

"Phil?! Phil?!"

Paul could hear screaming, another explosion and then the line went dead.

"Phil?"

"PHIL!"

CHAPTER FORTY-THREE

"Explosion?" said Burns, "What kind of explosion?"

She was sat leaning against the window, the glorious evening sun throwing her long shadow across the carpet.

"I don't know," said Wilson, "I just got here and it's... pandemonium. Hartigan's house just... it just blew up, it ..."

Wilson's voice faded out, and raised voices and alarms could be heard in the background.

"Wilson... Wilson!"

"Sorry, sir... it's just..." Wilson's voice dissipated into a coughing fit.

"Wilson, are you all right?"

Assistant Commissioner Michael Sharpe, having caught enough of her call to temporarily pause from berating someone else at HQ, leaned into her eyeline. Burns turned to block him out and moved a few steps away.

"Wilson. Talk to me."

"It's... there's people wandering about. I don't know how many injured or..."

She could hear movement, and then Wilson speaking to someone with a foreign accent. Only snatches of their conversation filtered through.

"Are you OK... I don't know... I don't know... over there... wrap something around... I don't know."

Burns could feel her own panic rising. "Wilson?"

Movement and Wilson's voice again, closer now, if not exactly present. "Sorry chief it's... still on fire, so much smoke and..."

"Are there other officers there, Wilson?"

All Burns could hear was the background noise, and Wilson's ragged breathing.

"Susan."

Burns glanced around to see Sharpe standing behind her.

"Not now," before adding into the phone. "Wilson, you need to talk to me, OK?"

"I demand to know—"

"Shut up, Michael."

Sharpe reared back like he'd just been slapped in the face. "How dare you—"

"Wilson?" Burns racked her brain. She normally had a great memory for detail but Sharpe yapping was distracting her. "Donnacha?" Saying it once gave her the confidence she'd recalled it correctly. "Donnacha?"

"I am your superior officer—"

Burns wheeled around. "And for how much longer exactly do you think that'll be?" She waved her free hand at the window. "I don't know if you noticed, but you started a fucking riot Michael, and I've sat here for two hours listening while your political friends have avoided your calls. One of my officers needs assistance, so shut up and let me do my job, you sanctimonious prick."

Sharpe's mouth flapped open like a landed fish. While she had the advantage, Burns moved past him and strode towards the other side of the office.

"Detective Wilson, answer me!"

Brief pause. "Yes, ma'am."

"Good. You are in the middle of a situation. Make sure everyone is safely back from any burning buildings or possible secondary explosions."

"Yes, ma'am."

"Then Wilson – and this is important. That is also an active crime scene. Nobody leaves unless they're doing it in an ambulance."

"Right, ma'am."

"Anybody gives you any shit – just keep quoting the Terrorism Act 2005."

"Is that for—"

"Anything. They don't know what's in it. Do whatever the hell is needed, and I'll cover your ass."

Burns could hear sirens in the distance. "Also… Wilson?"

"Yes, ma'am?"

"Tell the fire brigade it's an active crime scene – foul play. Preserve where possible. They know what to do, then."

"Yes, ma'am."

"Good man."

"Sorry about—"

"You're fine, Wilson. I'd be freaking out too, but it's 'go to work' time now, all right?"

"Right."

"Call me back in fifteen minutes with an update. I'll inform the team and get others out there with you."

"Yes, ma'am."

"And look at it this way. At least you didn't throw up this time."

CHAPTER FORTY-FOUR

"Come on, come on, come on, come on..."

Paul held the phone to his ear and paced back and forth in the doorway of the Savoy cinema, as Maggie sat placidly watching him.

Click. A pause. "You have reached the—"

"Fuuuck."

Paul hung up the phone. It took every ounce of his self-restraint not to hurl it off into the great beyond.

Calling him a fucking idiot; that had been his last words to Phil. Paul looked down at Maggie.

"He's fine, he's always fine. He's Phil Nellis, for God sake. When they drop the big bombs, the only thing left alive will be cockroaches and Phil Nellis."

Paul felt the phone vibrate in his hand. Brigit.

"Brigit, there's been some kind of—"

"I heard something on the radio. What is—"

"Phil was, Phil was—"

...and then the phone went dead.

Paul looked down at it in disbelief. No signal. He'd had four bars a second ago.

Then he looked up to see that, amongst the crowd, there were other people looking at their phones and holding them up in the air.

CHAPTER FORTY-FIVE

Gerry: Ah for— I can't believe this! I'm looking out the window, folks, and my car is on fire! What the hell? That's just mindless violence, that is. That was a new Audi! You shower of fucking fucker fucks – no, Tina, I won't shut up, I won't! I'm sick of this crap! Some prick set my beautiful car on fire, you animals! You—

"Phillips, Mills and Naylor have all gone out to assist Wilson. We need—"

Burns looked down at her phone. No service.

She sighed. "Damn it."

Burns put her phone away, and walked into the large open-plan area where most of the building's current occupants had assembled. These were the people unlucky enough to have been inside when it really kicked off. Burns needed a glass of water, as she was developing one hell of a headache and she'd managed to locate two paracetemol at the bottom of her handbag. The space looked like it had been a family area back when the building had been the 'Ark', at least judging from the display of crayon drawings stuck up on the wall. That had been about six hours ago, but it felt like a whole other life.

Somebody had made tea. It was the Irish solution to any problem.

There were about twelve people in total. Clustered around the room were a few civilian staff from the Technical Bureau, two doctors, the ambulance crew who had first attended to Franks, the Garda ombudsman and a couple of his staff. All of the Ark's previous tenants had been shipped out to Cathal Brugha Street Garda station for processing. The ombudsman was a man called Charles Delacourt, and something about him reminded Burns of the tortoise she'd had when she'd been a kid. It wasn't that he moved slowly, it was something about his neck. From the brief moments she'd not been on the phone in the last couple of hours, she'd also noticed how much his attitude towards excessive use of force by the Gardaí had changed since he'd been barricaded into a building with a howling mob outside.

Several people were waving their phones about and looking slightly bereft.

"I wouldn't bother," said Burns. A woman gave her a confused look. "They've shut down the mobile networks. Standard practice now in a riot. Stops them communicating."

"Us too," said someone at the far end of the room.

"Well, yes," agreed Burns, "there is that."

"Isn't there a landline we can use?" asked Delacourt.

Burns shook her head. "This building hasn't got any. We cut them. I'm sure they'll be coming to get us out of here soon."

Burns had said it because she knew it was expected. She felt considerably less optimistic than she was trying to sound. Last she'd heard, there was extensive rioting from here down into O'Connell Street and Henry Street, and it had now crossed over the Liffey. Somebody had noticed two crucial facts: there didn't seem to be anywhere near enough Gardaí to stop a mob, and Grafton Street has much nicer shops. The crowd outside their windows right now were the people who either didn't know or care about the bargains on offer. They wanted answers about Franks, and nobody inside the building had an answer that was going to make them happy.

"So we're totally cut off?" someone asked.

"No," said Burns, "the armed response guys will have radios. There were a couple of them here still waiting to give statements, weren't there?"

Delacourt nodded.

Just then a ragged cheer rose up from outside.

"Christ," said Burns, "what now?"

She moved to the window. A group of men were proceeding through the crowd carrying a telegraph pole.

"Oh for—"

She stopped herself as she realised Delacourt was standing beside her, licking his lips nervously.

"They've—" he started.

"Yes," she finished, "they've found a ram."

A thought suddenly struck her. She really hoped she was wrong.

"Where are the armed response guys?"

"I believe Assistant Commissioner Sharpe deployed them somewhere."

"Shit."

She was starting to hate being right.

"Everybody come with me."

CHAPTER FORTY-SIX

Paul was running again.

He was still heading in the general direction of the office, but that was no longer his primary motivation.

'Don't be a fucking idiot!' Those had been his last words to Phil. The fella who was his best friend, who'd been trying to help him out, whom he'd put in harm's way. 'A fucking idiot.'

They were on Cathal Brugha Street now. The crowds had thinned out as there were considerably less desirable 'shopping' options up this end. Maggie still trotted beside him.

The only other time he'd gone looking for a phone box was a couple of months ago, when he'd been supposed to meet Brigit to go to the cinema and he'd forgotten to charge his phone. It'd been a nightmare to find a working one then, and – unsurprisingly – the riot had done nothing to improve the situation.

He just needed to ring him, find out he was all right. Of course he'd be all right. He had to be all right.

It was then he noticed the three blokes in the midst of booting in the door of the bookies on the corner. Paul guessed a bookies would have had a strong door to begin with, but it wouldn't have been designed to withstand a sustained assault from people fearing no consequences. These lads had obviously been putting the work in, as it was all but off its hinges. They were figuring that, being a bookies, it'd have cash. Paul was betting that it'd have a phone.

He moved over and stood behind the group. A muscular bloke in a United strip was door-booter-in-chief. Things would have been going quicker if he hadn't insisted on throwing in the odd roundhouse kick, clearly keen to show his range. His two shirtless mates were cheering him on; one of them had the body to pull the look off, the other definitely didn't. A woman in her forties stood back and smoked a cigarette. As Paul walked towards them, she turned and sneered at him. "Fuck off, this is ours."

"I just need to use the phone."

"Tough. Get out of it."

She pointed Paul in the direction he'd come. He stood his ground.

"I'm using the phone."

"Oh are ye?" She turned and raised her voice. "Here, Deano, this prick wants in."

The one who wasn't beach body ready turned and looked at him. He had a large tattoo of Bob Marley on his left man boob that was probably not how the man wanted to be remembered.

"Get out of it, ye bleedin' vulture."

"I don't want any trouble," said Paul, "I'm just—"

"Doesn't want trouble, Deano," the woman chimed in. "Sounds like he's got no respect for you neither."

"This street is mine, ye fuckin' reading me, pal? I own it."

"Yeah, course you do."

Paul was surprised when those words came out of his mouth. The only explanation was that he was stressed, emotional and tired. Normally he wasn't the type to speak truth to power, never mind sarcasm to violence. Paul registered two things simultaneously; the rage on the fat man's face, and the delight of the woman standing behind him as she beamed a sour grin.

"Ah man, he's straight up fucking dissing you, Deano. He ain't showing a brother no respect."

In normal circumstances, Paul would have found this Dublinised bastardisation of American street slang humorous. Those circumstances, however, would have included him not being at the centre of this little play.

"Look, I—"

The big bloke moved with surprising speed, lunging forward and grabbing Paul's shirt with his left hand, while slamming his right fist into his face. There was a bright flash of impact, and then Paul ricocheted off a nearby lamp post before stumbling to the ground, landing hard on his knees. Behind him he heard Maggie's bark and some swearing, then an avalanche of humanity drove him into the ground face-first and forced all the air from his lungs. The fat man lay on top of him, trying to fend off an irate German Shepherd as Paul squirmed to free himself from under his immense bulk. His vision was blurred, and there was a metallic tang of blood in his mouth. Paul turned his head to see Maggie sink her teeth into Fattie's lower leg, who instantly howled in agony. Then Maggie let out a sickening yelp, as the bloke in the United jersey connected with a vicious kick that sent her hurtling out of Paul's field of vision.

The fat man started raining punches into the back of Paul's skull. They had not got much force behind them, but the cumulative effect was making his head swim. Paul twisted his body as vigorously as he could with his arms still pinned. The fat man shifted his body to counter. Paul's panic grew and grew. He could not breathe. He bucked and twisted with a desperate ferocity. He managed to partially turn his body. Bob Marley appeared before him, and he sunk his teeth into the tattooed flesh. He tasted suntan lotion and salt, and then other things he would rather not think about. The fat man screamed and pulled away. Paul heaved in a gasping breath and then coughed out a lump of flesh that was not his.

As he hauled himself up onto his knees, all around him was chaos. Maggie snarled. Several voices shouted over each other. Flashes of sky, legs, pavement. Someone kicked him in the head but mostly missed, only delivering a glancing blow. The fat man was screaming a lot now.

Paul retched but nothing came. Then somebody kicked him

again. This time he took the blow in the stomach. He felt something crack, but he hung onto his attacker's leg, tumbling its owner messily to the ground with him.

Something hit him in the back.

More growling.

Someone kicked at his legs, then there was motion as that person stumbled across Paul.

He saw a flash of fur, and heard more screamed invectives.

Then the fat man staggered to his feet, and started limping away.

"I'm out of here."

Paul managed to turn himself around again. The trio of men and the woman were now moving off. Two staggered, and all of them were bleeding from somewhere.

Maggie limped after them, snarling.

"Maggie," said Paul.

She kept going.

"Maggie!"

She stopped and looked back at him. Then she turned. The fight gone out of her, she limped slowly back towards him, holding her front left paw off the ground.

Paul sat on the pavement, holding his aching ribs as Maggie hopped over to him. She licked his face.

He rubbed her on the back of the neck.

"Your breath really stinks."

He felt dizzy, and as adrenalin flooded out of his body, pain seeped in. He closed his eyes and wiped the blood from his face, trying not to think about it. He did not deal well with blood; his own or other people's.

He sat there in silence with his eyes closed, with nothing but Maggie's panting breath for company. He felt his head droop forward. Maggie barked beside him.

"Right, yeah. Right."

With difficulty, Paul pushed himself up the wall and limped gingerly over to the door of the bookies. It had been all but kicked in.

He was able to squeeze himself through without having to do any further damage to it.

His feet crunched on broken glass as he stepped inside. The walls were lined with half-tables with pens chained to them, and gaming machines that flashed in garish colours. What space that left was filled with wide-screen TVs. At the end of the room a half-wall of thick glass protected a counter. Behind it stood a woman in her fifties. She held a large kitchen knife out in front of her in both hands.

"I'm not going to hurt you," said Paul.

"Yeah? Well... I... I'm going to hurt you. Get out now or I'll cut ye knackers off."

Paul raised his hands, and winced at the pain in his midsection as he did it.

"Look, I..." Paul indicated Maggie, "We, just fought off the guys who were trying to break in here."

"I know," she said, nodding towards a screen beside her. "I saw on the CCTV. Doesn't mean you get to rob the place instead."

"I just need to use your phone. Check my friend is OK."

She shook her head emphatically. "Nobody is allowed behind the counter."

"Look I just—"

"I'm not even supposed to be here. The boss asked me to stay late to do the books. I'm not paid enough to fend off a bleeding horde and their rabid dogs."

Paul looked down at Maggie. She was calmly sitting on her back haunches, licking at her paw.

"Honestly, I just need to—"

Paul stopped talking. His eye had wandered to one of the big screens on the wall, which was showing news coverage of the riots. Only it wasn't any more. Now it had switched to a shot of the road Paul barely recognised as Sandy Way. There was Hartigan's house in the background, or at least what was left of it. The fire brigade had two hoses on the rubble.

An ashen-faced correspondent was delivering a report to camera. Paul had no idea what he was saying as the sound was down, but it didn't matter. As he spoke, a great big lanky idiot wandered by in the background, chatting to an EMT. He looked confused even by his usual standards, but judging by the wildly gesticulating arm movements, Paul guessed he was describing what had happened. The paramedic kept nodding her understanding while endeavouring to guide Phil towards one of the ambulances.

Paul looked down at Maggie.

"Let's go home."

CHAPTER FORTY-SEVEN

The fact that DSI Burns had managed to make it down the five flights of stairs to the lobby without at least twisting an ankle was a minor miracle. The lighting was minimal, and she had been taking steps two at a time in places. She crashed through the door to be greeted by one of the armed response units with his gun pointed towards her.

"What the hell?" she said.

He lowered his weapon with an apologetic wave and turned his gaze back towards the main doors, not that the doors were actually visible behind the hastily re-erected barricades of furniture in front of them. The irony wasn't lost on Burns – the barricades that one group of protesters had used for weeks to keep the Gardaí out – were now being used by the Gardaí to keep a different group of protesters out. The filing cabinets and sofas vibrated each time the improvised ram boomed against the doors behind them. Each blow was greeted with a cheer from outside.

Aside from DSI Burns, the lobby contained the two armed response guys, Livingstone the head Casper, Sergeant Paice and Assistant Commissioner Sharpe. It was the first time Burns had been in the same room as that group since the meeting in the Portakabin when they'd started this debacle. She'd watched it go up in flames about an hour ago. Sharpe was holding a megaphone in his hands.

"DSI Burns, please return upstairs."

Burns heard the door open behind her, and the building's other occupants filing in.

"None of you should be down here."

"What's the plan here, sir?" said Burns.

Boom.

Sharpe turned away from her and put the megaphone to his lips.

"This is the Gardaí. The actions you are taking are illegal. Disperse immediately."

Boom.

Burns threw her hands up in the air. "Oh, for God's sake."

"The situation is under control."

Boom.

"Is it fuck."

"I am in command here."

Boom.

"Fine. I resign."

"What do you suggest, Burns? We all find a cupboard to hide in?"

Boom. A cracking noise as metal started to give way.

"It can't be a worse idea than this."

Burns moved forward and started dragging one of the sofas away.

"What the hell are you doing?"

Boom.

"Stop that!"

Sharpe put his hand on her arm and tried to pull her away. She shrugged him off.

"Lay a hand on me again, Michael and you'll be glad there are doctors here."

Boom.

She pushed the sofa out of the way with her arse while trying to reach around and gain some purchase on the large filing cabinet.

"Officers, restrain this woman."

Boom. Burns could feel it vibrate through her, now.

She turned to the two armed response officers moving tentatively towards her. "What's the end game here, lads?" Burns pointed towards the door. "They're getting in here soon, and then what? You're not going to be the men who open fire on unarmed civilians, I know you're not. That's not what you signed up for, is it?"

Boom.

The two men glanced nervously at each other.

"Let's see if a bit of talking might do the trick, what do you reckon?"

A cry of 'let her try!' came from the group by the stairs.

Boom.

The barricade behind her rattled.

"It's 'shit or get off the pot' time, lads."

The younger man looked at the older, who paused and then nodded.

Boom.

"Good," said Burns. "Now give me a hand here."

"This is all going in my report," said Sharpe.

They moved the sofa and the filing cabinet to one side.

As the filing cabinet moved, there was a cheer from outside.

The late evening light spilled in across the floor and the red sunset, peeking over the heads of the crowd, momentarily dazzled Burns. She shielded her eyes and looked into the faces – dozens upon dozens of faces. It oddly reminded her of the day early in her career when she'd done crowd control duty at Páirc Uí Chaoimh for the Munster hurling final. The shattered glass in the large windows warped their faces.

Burns raised her hands.

"Wait! Please!"

Boom!

The desk in front of her bucked as the door behind it buckled yet further.

"Ah for—"

Unsteadily Burns climbed up onto the desk, leaning on the cabinet for support.

"Wait, please, hang on!"

Boom!

The desk bucked violently.

Burns looked down to see Delacourt shoving the megaphone into her hand.

She held it up and pushed the button.

"Wait, hang on, please – we're going to let you in!"

The ram clattered against the door at half its previous ferocity and then ceased. A clamour of voices rose up. Burns put her hands out again.

"Please, just give me a second."

From up here, she could see the faces of the whole crowd spread out before her, some straining to see who was talking.

"My name is Susan Burns, and I'm a civil servant—"

"Fucking cop," came a voice.

"Yes, one of them too. My ma was a teacher and my dad ran the local shop down in Balmullet, Waterford, where I'm from. I cut my teeth catching heroin-dealing scumbags, down in Limerick."

"They're all scumbags down there", said another voice.

"Feck off, ye jackeen prick!" said Burns.

This got a few laughs and a small cheer.

Burns moved on quickly. She pointed at the older of the two armed response officers. "This is Pete; he's married, big fan of Formula One and DIY. His eldest made her confirmation this year."

She pointed at the younger. "This is Keith; he just became a dad and he's getting married at Christmas."

"Dirty bastard," came an older voice with a strong Dublin accent. A few laughs.

Burns smiled. "He's also a big fan of Spurs."

"Dirty bastard," repeated the same voice, to a louder peal of laughter.

"We're ordinary people, just like you, and—"

"Where's Father Franks?", from a female voice located somewhere near the front.

Burns took a deep breath. "Father Franks is dead."

A chorus of boos and shouts erupted from the crowd. The table wobbled under her as the crowd at the front pushed against the doors. A bottle flew from the back and smashed against the top of the window, raising indignant hollers from those at the front as glass rained down upon them.

"Please, please" shouted Burns, "just—"

"You shot him... fucking pigs... fascists!"

The armed response guys shifted their feet nervously behind her.

"Please!" screamed Burns, holding a finger up. "Give me one minute, just one and then we'll let you in – I promise."

Shouts and shushes competed with each other until the din had died down enough.

"These guys" said Burns, pointing at the two men behind her, "got ordered to come in here but they never fired a shot."

The older of the two removed the ammunition clip from his MP7 sub-machine gun and held it aloft, his younger colleague followed suit.

"Father Franks was ill," – some boos rose up again – "he was ill, and the shock of all this killed him. It's fucked up, but that's what happened."

Boos were growing, Burns decided to plough on. "Look, you're right to be angry. This raid should never have happened. It was political bullshit. Somebody should answer for that. Keith and Pete didn't decide to do it – they were ordered to. Remember who they are. When a drug dealer is off his face on his own supply and waving guns about, these are the boys we send for. Do you want that job? I don't."

There were a few shouts and some murmuring from around them.

"You're angry, I get it. I'm angry. And not just at this. For a decade we've been told we've to all suck it up, tighten our belts. We all know what Franks said was true. Certain people played fast and loose with our futures and screwed us all, screwed whole generations. It just isn't right. Those to blame need to face justice. That's what Franks wanted. But murder isn't justice. Whoever is behind this Púca nonsense, I guarantee you, it's just some psychopath. You're not his cause, you're his excuse. That's not justice, and this," she said, casting her hands wide, "this – isn't justice. I promise you, nobody in this building is the problem, and what you're doing now isn't the solution. You do this, and it is easy for them to label you as mindless thugs. This city is tearing itself apart, and it hurts all of us. Now... we're going to open these doors and half a dozen of you can come up and see Father Franks's body, God rest his soul. The doctors are here, you'll see the evidence, all right? The rest of you – please – go home. There's been a lot of damage done tonight, let's say enough is enough."

She stopped and looked out at the crowd. There were small discussions breaking out. A few people at the back appeared to be wandering off into the night.

Burns turned and took Delacourt's proffered hand to help her down.

"Very well done, DSI Burns."

"We'll see," she said. "Now if you'll excuse me, I've a murder investigation to run."

Burns turned to the armed response officers and indicated the barricades. "Can you move all this?"

They nodded.

"And if someone could give them a hand?"

The ambulance team and a couple of others moved forward. One of the ombudsman's assistants grabbed the other side of one of the sofas from the younger of the armed response officers.

"Jesus, Keith, that was close."

"Who the fuck is Keith? My name is Padraig and I bleedin' hate Spurs."

CHAPTER FORTY-EIGHT

"For your penance I give you six Our Fathers and three Hail Marys. May the grace of God go with you."

"And also with you. God bless you, Father."

"And you, Mary. Tell James I was asking for him."

"I will."

Father Daniel Franks slid the panel closed on the confessional booth to his right and took a deep breath. He could feel a migraine building, and it was going to be a bad one. He tried to relax the muscles in his jaw, as the GP had said that might help. He rolled his head around his shoulders and listened to the static of tension crackling through his neck. He must be nearly done, Monday afternoon confession was never that busy, then he could go and have a lie down. He took a sip from the bottle of water that he'd remembered to bring with him, as he heard the shuffle of movement in the booth to his left.

He momentarily shifted the rosary beads from his right to his left hand and wiped his sweaty palm on his vestments. He should maybe go back and see the GP after all, see about those tablets. Another deep breath, and then he sat back and slid open the small door to his left.

"Hello, my child, you're very welcome to confession today. May God be with you."

A familiar voice he thought he'd never hear again rang out. "Bless me, Father, for I have sinned like a mad whore in a barrel full of mickeys."

"Christ, Bunny."

"Ah, Jesus, Padre, how'd you know it was me?"

Franks shifted nervously in his seat. "Your disrespectful attitude is rather distinctive."

"Sure, isn't that one of the sins I've come to confess."

"Well. It's good to... I'm glad you've come back. I've not seen you at Mass since..." he left it hang there, he couldn't think of anything else to say.

"Yeah," said Bunny, "I sort of knocked the whole Mass thing on the head."

"I'm sorry to hear that. Would you... would you like me to hear your confession?"

A pause grew between them.

"Is riding still a sin, Padre?" asked Bunny.

"If by that you mean sex outside the sanctity of wedlock," said Father Franks, "then yes, it is."

"I thought they'd changed it?"

"No."

"Are you sure? I'm sure I read something."

"Ara, stop pissing about, Bunny." Father Franks knew this dance all too well; the deflection, using humour as a defence mechanism. Classic Bunny.

"I'm serious. Didn't the Pope say something? You should check. They might not be keeping you up-to-date."

"The Ten Commandments are written in stone, Bunny, not crayon. Now, can I help ye with something?"

"I've got plenty to confess, Father. In the last few days alone I've stolen, threatened and blackmailed. I've helped to break a good man, and I've allowed a bad one to walk away from his sins for my own purposes."

"I see."

"How long has it been now – three years?"

Franks did the sums in his mind, had it really been that long? "Aye, I guess it must be about that all right."

"After what happened... I couldn't find God here anymore. It just wasn't... I'd real, serious penance to do, so I set up a hurling team. Something to grab hold of some young fellas early, get 'em off the streets. We've enough bad men in the world."

"That we do," conceded Franks, "it's a noble cause."

Franks had heard about it. He'd been so glad. Knowing Bunny was out there doing something positive with himself had assuaged his own feelings of guilt, if only slightly.

"Works, too," said Bunny. "Makes a difference, a real difference mind, in the lives of these young fellas."

"I'm sure it does."

"And now they're taking it all away."

"I'm... I'm sorry to hear that."

"Some moneyed-up pricks have gone out and bought themselves a council and hard fucks to the working man. "

"That's a great shame."

"I've pulled every trick in the book, Danny, every fecking one, and it isn't going to be enough. In two hours, it'll be over. That club..."

Bunny's voice cracked slightly in the darkness. Franks could hear the soft rustle of movement.

"It's the one truly good thing I've done. After, after what we did..."

The silence reached out between them. Franks ran the beads through his fingers. Wrapping them around the knuckle until it turned white.

"D'ye know something?" said Bunny.

"What?"

"No disrespect to the lad, but Jesus had it easy."

"I don't think you've read your Bible in a while, Bunny."

"I mean, everyone did, back in those days. Himself – he made thirty-three, that was a pretty good innings in those days. Life was tough, sure, but it wasn't long."

"True enough."

"They'd hardly enough time to really make a mess of things. Whereas today, neither of us is a picture of health yet we'll probably make eighty. People say life is short, but it's not. It's long, so damn long – ye can't help but make a mess of it. 'Tis like roulette. You sit at that table for an hour, you might just come away a winner. You sit there long enough, and the house always wins."

"That's a very grim outlook you've got there, Bunny."

"When you've seen what I've seen, Padre..."

In the silence, Franks could hear a hoover in the distance. Mrs Byrne must be doing the altar. You couldn't stop that woman from hoovering.

"Do you still think about it?" asked Bunny, his voice soft and low.

"Think about what?" The silence bloomed like a bloodstain between them. It had been a stupid question that didn't warrant an answer. Images came back unbidden to his mind. When he spoke next, his voice came back in a whisper. "Every day."

"So do I. I mean..." Bunny's voice faltered. "It's the kind of thing that... not so much thinking, y'know. It's more... I suppose what I'm saying is that 'tis worst at night. I get dreams."

Franks said nothing.

"We did the right thing," added Bunny.

Those words hung in the air. Franks could neither agree nor refute them.

"He'd have done it again, you know he would."

Franks finally found his voice again. "The right to judgement belongs to our Lord alone."

"God wasn't available at the time. We had to make do with me."

"Why're you here Bunny? Is it to discuss our past sins?"

"Sin is a funny thing, isn't it, Danny? Some people, they see a man – a councillor no less – who goes to Mass every day, gets himself confessed once a week, they think 'sure, isn't he a right holy roller, a pure soul.' Me, I see that fella and I think, 'there's a man with a great big black sin that he just can't shift.'"

"I've a queue of people outside, Bunny. Maybe you could come back tonight."

"There's no time, Father. In exactly..." a faint light offered a brief splutter of illumination in the other side of the booth, "one hour and fifty-two minutes, that holy roller is going to walk into a council chamber and wipe away my one good deed. I'm not prepared to let that happen. For what its worth, I'm sorry. I'm sorry that last year yer man was put under surveillance. I'm sorry they reported that he comes here every week. Of all the churches... Christ, what are the odds? I'm sorry. I'm sorry that I know that, but I do."

Franks could feel a cold sweat run down his back.

"Stop, Bunny. I can't and I won't discuss anything with you. It is against the rules."

"Whose rules?" asked Bunny. "God's, is it? Sure, doesn't He have all manner of rules, Danny."

"I never asked you to—"

"Don't. Don't you dare. You know what you did and I don't blame you for it, I honestly don't. Something had to be done. But you could've told anyone, and you chose me. That monster chose to lay it on you, and you chose to lay it on me. I'm... I'm not a good man, Father. Sure, I try and I've... I'd like to think I've done some good, but that doesn't make me good. But you – you made me what I am now. So don't talk to me about sin, Father, because you put that one on me."

Franks felt hot tears roll down his cheeks. "What you're asking, Bunny... the seal of confession is the most sacred thing. What... what we did was wrong, but it was... he was going to do it again – sweet God in heaven, forgive me – but he was. But this man, the man you're talking about, it isn't the same..."

"I've got no choice," said Bunny.

"You can't ask me to do this," said Franks.

"I am. You put that sin on me and now I'm calling it in."

"It's not—"

"I don't care, Danny. I don't. All your rules and reasons mean nothing to me. I'm lost, but this isn't. This is here and now, and it is worth fighting for. Let your God sort it out in the next life if He wants, but in this one, I'm doing everything I can to save my one good deed."

"You can't."

"I am."

"I won't."

"You will."

CHAPTER FORTY-NINE

Gerry: OK, I'd like to formally apologise on behalf of myself and the station for my earlier outburst. It was, – well, we're all under a lot of stress and... I loved that car. I'm now being told that we have a Sergeant O'Brien from Clondalkin Garda Station on the line.

Sergeant O'Brien: Yes, Gerry, hello. Long time listener, first time caller. Me and the lads are big fans, we have you on all the time.

Gerry: Well, thank you, sergeant.

Sergeant O'Brien: We know you're up on the Quays there, right in the middle of it all, you're understandably worried.

Gerry: Well, yes, yes we are.

Sergeant O'Brien: Don't worry about anything, and never mind all those things you said about the force over the years.

Gerry: Well thanks, but—

Sergeant O'Brien: We've broken out the riot gear, we've got the van outside – we're coming to rescue you.

Gerry: Wow, that is... I'm speechless...

Sergeant O'Brien: No problem. But first, would you mind playing the new one from Adele? (Laughter – line goes dead)

Gerry: You absolute shower of p—

"Mr Maloney?" said Detective Wilson.

The man at the other side of the desk in the interview room looked back at him as if suddenly waking from a dream. He'd been interviewing Maloney for nearly an hour now, and beyond asserting that Hartigan and their lawyer Marcus Penrose had been alive and well when he'd left them, and that he hadn't seen any suspicious packages lying about the place, he'd got nothing of use out of him. It was early days, but Janice from the Tech Bureau had said that the explosion appeared to have originated within the house, and they had taken some debris away for testing in an effort to determine the source. Wilson repeated the question. "I said, have you ever met Bunny McGarry?"

"Well clearly not, I'm still alive, aren't I?"

"Can I ask you what information you are in possession of that leads you to believe that Mr McGarry is a suspect in this case?"

"Are you saying he's not?"

"No, I—"

"This is absolutely typical. Craig Blake is dead. John Baylor is dead. Marcus Penrose and my good friend Jerome Hartigan just died while the world watched on in horror and, but for a miracle, I would be dead too... and, after all that, all you care about is how I know the name of the man who is trying to kill me? Have I got that right?"

Wilson glanced down at his notes for a moment to compose himself. Mr Maloney was not exactly the easiest interviewee. They'd almost had to arrest him to get him to give a statement and even then, he was only willing to do so if his chauffeur was present, citing the possibility of the entire Garda Síochána being involved in a conspiracy against him. Wilson would have been tempted to write him off as a paranoid lunatic if someone hadn't just attempted to kill him.

Wilson glanced again at the driver sitting behind his boss and was struck, not for the first time, that he seemed to be finding the whole affair quietly amusing. He sat with a casual slouch, as if he was merely sitting around in a doctor's waiting room rather than in a Garda interview room. Maloney had declined to ring a lawyer, citing that the only one he trusted had just been blown to kingdom come.

"Do you know what the problem is with this country?" asked Maloney.

Wilson was tempted to try and get him back on track but then he remembered something DI Jimmy Stewart, his old mentor, had said to him in one of their now regular chats: 'Always let them talk, because they often say more than they mean to.'

"No," said Wilson, "what's wrong with this country?"

Maloney jabbed his pudgy finger across the desk at him. "A hatred of ambition, that's what. You show a bit of 'get up and go' and the chattering classes despise you for it. Nothing annoys them more than ambition. This world was built by the risk-takers."

"Was that what Skylark was – a risk?"

Wilson couldn't justify the question from an investigative standpoint. He had to admit to himself, he'd only asked it because Maloney – despite the situation he found himself in – was a very hard man to like. It had been a bad day on the back of several, and on top of seeing his home town ripping itself to pieces and a house blowing up before his eyes, Maloney's repeated assertions as to the ineptitude of the force were really getting on Wilson's nerves.

Maloney quickly cycled through a range of facial expressions, like he was trying to find the definition of ugly. He started to say something and then stopped, standing up instead, petulantly allowing his chair to topple to the floor behind him.

"I can see we're done here. Rest assured, Detective Wilson, I shall be making my displeasure with your performance known to your superiors."

"I'm sorry to hear that. Can I state again for the record that I strongly recommend that you allow us to provide you with protection, as—"

"Oh please! Like I would trust the Irish police to protect my hamster! I intend to depart this godforsaken country tonight.

Nowhere is safe for me here while vigilantes are allowed to roam the streets willy nilly."

"I must advise—"

"Don't bother."

Maloney turned to leave. Wilson watched as the driver slipped his phone from his inside jacket pocket and nodded towards it.

"Oh yes," said Maloney, "one of the final things poor Jerome said to me was that he was worried that, over the last few days, someone had been following him. My chauffeur, Mr Coetzee, noticed someone acting suspiciously when I visited Jerome earlier in the week. He took a picture..."

The bodyguard tapped a couple of buttons and scrolled through a few screens before standing, leaning across the desk and showing the picture to Wilson.

He tried hard not to react when he saw it. He recognised the face – it was Paul Mulchrone.

CHAPTER FIFTY

"God damn it, don't you die on me."

Brigit looked down at her phone. 4%.

She went to ring the doorbell again when a blurred silhouette appeared in the opaque glass.

"Who is it?" came an older male voice from the other side of the door. Brigit sagged slightly. This was the sixth door she'd tried and so far she'd had nobody under seventy, other than the inexplicably angry woman who'd shooed her off with a barrage of profanity that seemed to imply that Brigit was having sex with somebody called Barry.

"Hi," said Brigit, in her least-threatening voice. "I know how odd this sounds, and believe me I wouldn't ask if it wasn't really important but, by any chance do you have an iPhone charger I could borrow?"

There was a long tranche of silence followed by, "What?"

"My phone is nearly dead, and honestly, it's life and death. I have to charge it because, well... it is a long story."

Silence.

More silence.

"What?"

"Could you just open the door for a second, honestly, I promise this is really important."

"How do I know you're not one of those looters?"

Brigit sighed and looked around her. She was standing on a road called Sweetman's Avenue in Blackrock, although so far nobody had reached civil, never mind sweet. It seemed like an unlikely place for the solo looter to go on the rampage, not least because it sat almost directly opposite Blackrock District Garda Station. She glanced at her phone again. 3%. Ah, holy fuck.

Initially she had been elated when the Sniffer app had installed on her phone and minutes later the tracker, or Bunny's 'doo-dah' as Duncan had referred to it, had sent back its location. This had been followed by confusion when the location turned out to be the house of Jerome Hartigan, who, as she had only just found out, Paul had been following for a week. How the hell he had taken on a case at all – never mind one for a client whose name he didn't know – was something she hadn't even begun to process. Before she'd had a chance, Hartigan had literally gone up in smoke. The flashing red dot on her screen had then started moving a few minutes later, she had tried to not think of it as fleeing the scene of the crime.

Brigit didn't know who, or what, she was tracking. Bunny's name was now all over the news as being the man behind 'the Púca'. She didn't believe it. Bunny didn't seem the killing spree type. It wasn't the murdering part that seemed far-fetched, but the sneaking around bit certainly did. Regardless, her only shot at an answer was the tracker. It appeared to be on a vehicle, and the vehicle in question appeared to now be sitting in the car park behind the station. Her attempt to ascertain exactly what vehicle it might be, had been thwarted by a female guard wielding a clipboard with serious intent. Turns out riots make police fierce jumpy. Brigit had backed off, as she had no reason she was willing to share for her interest in being in a Garda car park. That'd been half an hour ago. While she waited for the tracker to move again she'd decided to deal with the dying phone issue, which was turning out to be surprisingly difficult. None of the shops on the nearby high street sold chargers. This was why she'd resorted to the desperate measure of going door-to-door.

"I promise I'm not a looter."

"That's exactly what a looter would say."

"OK, sure but... looters wouldn't ring the doorbell would they?"

"I dunno, I've never been looted before."

"Just, open the door."

"Don't you take that tone with me, young lady."

Brigit took a deep breath. "I'm very sorry, it has been a nightmare of a day. To be honest, it has been an awful week. I got suspended from work for, well, that doesn't matter. I found out my ex-boyfriend who cheated on me, didn't; but he was set-up by my ex-fiancé – who did, repeatedly – and..." Brigit was aware she was babbling. "None of that's important, but what is important is that my friend is missing and the only clue we've got is a tracker that might lead to him, or at least... I also keep trying to ring Paul – he's the ex, the non-cheating one – and he's in the riot and I can't get him on the phone. They said on the radio they'd shut the mobile network down in the city centre and... the thing is – I just really need to charge my phone. I'm sorry if I came across as rude, and I know this must sound mental, but I swear I'm a good person having a bad day. Just do me this one service, I'm begging you. Have you got an iPhone charger?"

Brigit stopped talking and let the silence stretch out.

She watched the door in anticipation. There was a complete lack of movement.

After about thirty long seconds she could hear a toilet flush at the back of the house.

It was all she could manage not to kick the door in.

She looked up and down the street and then over at the Garda station. Not for the first time she wondered if the most sensible course of action might not be to just walk in and tell them everything she knew. Thing is, seeing as Bunny's tracker was currently on what she assumed was a vehicle that was sitting in their car park, could she rule out the Gardaí being involved? It was only eight months ago that Bunny had uncovered corruption at the highest level of the force, and

THE DAY THAT NEVER COMES

thrown one of the main culprits out a window. It was very possible somebody still held a grudge and she couldn't bring herself to help anyone who might want to do him harm.

That's what it came back to. Whatever Bunny McGarry had done or was doing, the last thing she definitely knew he'd been up to was proving that Paul was not yet another philandering scumbag. That didn't mesh with the psychopathic monster that the radio was proclaiming.

Brigit sat down on the front step of the terraced house and looked at her phone. Another low battery warning flashed up.

Then, the red dot started moving again.

2%...

CHAPTER FIFTY-ONE

Was this Hell?

There was no fire, only darkness. But the darkness burned. It ate him whole. The darkness and the silence.

He didn't know how long he had been there, how he had got there or where 'there' was. This body was not his. This one was broken. None of it felt familiar.

He had woken to darkness, chained to a wall, water running down the stone behind him.

Nothing but darkness and silence for near eternity, then the blinding light would crash in and the pain would come. The first couple of times he'd watched the figure approach through slatted fingers, as the light burned his eyes. The darkness had formed into a man with the sole purpose of raining punishment down upon him. Blow after blow. The first couple of times he'd not seen them coming, as the light blinded. After that, his eyes had swollen near shut so all he could see was a dash of confused colour from the left and nothing from the right. Just enough to know there was light, which would mean pain. The darkness hurt you with the light.

At first, he'd stood and tried to defend himself, held back by the heavy, impregnable chains tethering him to the wall. He had even got a shot or two in himself, those had been sweet moments. But it wasn't a fight. It was a beating followed by another and another and another.

At first, he'd asked questions of the darkness.

Then he'd hurled insults at it.

The last couple of times he'd silently huddled down and waited for the rain to stop. For the darkness to have spent its anger. Then it would leave food and water. The darkness cared.

In between the flurries of violence, in the crushing silence, the ghosts had come to him. An elegantly-attired man standing on a stool. A grinning corpse. A pale woman, her faint pulse dying in his arms even as he tried to shake her back to life. An old friend. And her. Simone. His angel. She had come to him too, and held him in her arms, and whispered her song into the darkness.

That was how he knew. This could not be Hell. The darkness would not have allowed him her, if it was.

That meant there was hope.

This could end.

He could die.

CHAPTER FIFTY-TWO

Paul cracked open a can of the unpronounceable and ill-advisable East European beer, and held it up in toast. At the far side of the bank of tables sat Maggie, lapping her beer up from the bowl he'd already given her. Paul looked around the office.

"Well, this was worthwhile, wasn't it? Fought our way through a riot, and for what?"

Maggie didn't answer. Paul took a slug of his drink and instantly regretted it. They'd picked themselves up and limped back, making it to the office for 7:58 pm. It was now nearly 9 pm. The Devil in the Red Dress had not shown up. Paul had tried to ring Brigit, but it appeared that the mobile phone network was still down. He had no idea how she was getting on; he hoped it was better than he was.

He'd cleaned himself up as best he could in the small toilet down the hall. He was more or less in one piece, although his ribs were tender to the touch, his ankle hurt to walk on and there was an unpleasant buzzing, like feedback, in his ear. Outside of that, a few cuts and bruises, plus he had a lovely shiner coming up. Maggie on the other hand; well, who knew? He'd tried to check out her injuries but a quick growl had indicated that – violent bonding experiences or not – her position on being touched had not changed. Paul would find an unlucky vet and get her checked out in the morning, assuming the world hadn't burned down by then.

He looked out the window. A couple of plumes of smoke could be seen in the distance, rising into the blood-red sunset. The riot was still going on. His phone could still access the Internet via next door's wi-fi. Last he'd seen, the Irish Army had marched down the quays to retake O'Connell Street. It turned out they had a stash of riot gear for just such an eventuality.

Paul had the window open, and along with the mouthwatering smell of cooking, he could hear the babble from a TV in the Oriental Palace's kitchen. Judging by the sound of scooters flying in and out, business was brisk for a Monday night. He guessed people were staying in to watch the riot on the telly.

He looked at his phone again. No signal.

He'd gone downstairs fifteen minutes ago to use the Palace's landline to ring Brigit, but it'd gone straight to voicemail. Same with Phil's. He'd left both of them the number, and Mickey had assured him they'd shout if he got any calls.

"What do you think we should do?"

Maggie gave him a nonplussed expression.

"We could go to the Guards? Only, what are we going to tell 'em? You know that bloke who got blown up? Well we reckoned he was actually the killer. That'll go down well."

Maggie seemed unenthusiastic.

"We could go to the hospital and try and find Phil, only..." Paul didn't want to say it, but Phil's Auntie Lynn would no doubt be there, and looking for someone to blame for her darling nephew nearly getting blown up. With all his heart, Paul did not want to be that person. Lynn on the warpath was not something you wanted to be trapped in front of.

"We can't help Brigit," said Paul, "because we haven't the first clue where the hell she is."

Maggie continued to stare at him.

"Don't look at me like that, you've not come up with any ideas have ye?"

Maggie turned her head slightly.

"Neither of us are any good for this. What we need to ask ourselves is, 'What would Brigit do?' She's the clever one. Figuring out that tracker thing, downloading the app, sending the... ah, shite."

Paul opened his desk drawer and grabbed the keys to Bunny's car.

"Would it have killed ye to say something before now? C'mon."

CHAPTER FIFTY-THREE

To be fair, Brigit had known it was a bad idea as soon as she'd had it. The problem was, she didn't have any other ideas to replace it with. Her phone had managed to hang on just long enough to show her the flashing red dot in the tracker app turning onto the coast road. She'd then put her foot down and got there just in time to see a blue BMW turning off in the distance, through the gates of a compound containing three apparently derelict buildings. The car had disappeared entirely from view by the time the winding road had let her reach the gates. Brigit parked up.

Judging by the dust-covered sign that lay strewn on the ground inside the fence, the place had once been a cement factory. One building the size of a large warehouse was flanked either side by two, more conventional, two-storey structures. Each was now reduced to a boarded-up, graffiti-covered husk; they looked as if they would benefit from being put out of their collective miseries. A large sign proclaimed this to be the proposed site of the Seaview two-bed luxury apartments, and promised a brighter tomorrow. Brigit guessed that interest had not been strong. The only thing that looked new or well-maintained was the fence. It was nine-foot high, with barbed wire atop it. Clearly some people had thought the location would make an excellent dump. The grass verge in front of the fence was strewn with rubbish of all descriptions, from bin bags to household appliances, clothing and more. It looked like half an unhappy car boot sale had been discarded there.

Brigit had considered her options, what little there were. She could drive back to Howth, find a phone and ring the police. She had not got a clue what she would say to them, though. She wasn't even sure that the car she'd seen was the one with the tracker.

She could wait for the car to re-emerge and try to follow it without the assistance of the tracker. She wasn't wildly optimistic about her chances of doing that successfully. Even if she did, this did rather look like the spot where something nefarious could be going on.

When in doubt, do something; that was her unofficial motto. Admittedly, that something had almost certainly been a terrible idea, but still, she was getting tired of searching and finding nothing but yet more questions. She had a hunch that whatever lay inside those buildings might finally hold an answer.

This was how she had justified doing a fly-tipping-assisted assault course. An old washing machine had proven just about sturdy enough to stand on, allowing Brigit to hurl a roll of mouldy carpet onto the top of the barbed wire fence. She'd then spent five minutes she'd rather forget, attempting to climb over while blanking the foul stench of the carpet out of her mind, along with any thoughts of what might have caused it. A ripped pair of jeans, a bruised arse and an unpleasant stickiness in her hair later, and she was over.

It was only when she got over that she noticed the sign that warned of guard dogs. Seriously, who put that kind of sign facing inwards on a fence? Some sick and twisted individual, that was who.

Brigit moved as quickly and quietly as she could around the buildings. First sign of trouble she'd leg it and call the Guards; it seemed like a sound plan.

She skirted one of the smaller structures but couldn't hear anything, and the windows were firmly boarded up. As she approached the main doors of the hangar, she could see tyre tracks leading in past the large wooden doors. She pressed her ear against them and could hear the faint, indistinct murmur of voices.

Then, from behind her, someone cleared their throat.

She looked over her shoulder to see a man standing there. He was tall, with a stocky build and a tightly-cropped head of hair. His lips were smiling, but his eyes were definitely not. It took Brigit a couple of seconds to notice that though, as the foreground of her vision was dominated by the large handgun he was holding inches from her head.

"Hi, ehm... I know this is going to sound mad, but... you don't happen to have a charger for an iPhone do you?"

CHAPTER FIFTY-FOUR

"Are you sure about this?" asked Mavis Chambers. She clutched at her handbag nervously as she looked around them. City Hall made her nervous, it was all marble and southsiders, neither of which she was used to.

In the absence of an answer, she looked up at Bunny McGarry, who stood beside her staring at the floor.

"Are you listening to me?"

"No, Mavis, I'm not."

"Well you feckin' should be. Are you sure we're going to be all right?"

Bunny pointed at the intricate design on the floor. "Do you know what this is?"

Mavis looked down at it irritably. "A nightmare to clean I'd imagine. What's your point?"

"It's the official Dublin city crest. See that Latin there, *Obedientia Civium Urbis Felictas*', that means, 'The obedience of the citizens produces a happy city'. What gobshite do you think came up with that?"

"You speak Latin now, do you?"

"I do, actually. That's the Christian Brothers for you. They'll educate you, or kill you in the attempt."

"Well now you won't have a hurling team to coach any more, maybe you can start giving classes in it."

"Relax," Bunny repeated, "I told you, we'll be fine."

Mavis looked up as the familiar figure of Councillor Jarleth Court walked by. He looked like he'd been dragged arse-ways through a hedge.

"Good evening, Councillor" said Mavis.

"Jarleth," said Bunny with a nod.

Court didn't even look up as he continued to trudge past. "Fuck you, Bunny."

Mavis grabbed Bunny's arm. "I thought you said he was on our side now?"

"He is," said Bunny.

"Christ Almighty, in that case, I'd hate to meet the undecideds."

Bunny carefully removed Mavis's hand from his arm, where she belatedly realised she had been gripping a tad too tightly.

She looked around the chamber. With five minutes to go, there were plenty of people milling about. Councillors, interested parties and what have you. She looked behind them. Her eight-year-old granddaughter Tamara was sitting in a chair, swinging her legs back and forth. Bored as only a child could be when forced to come to some really dull adult stuff and then being told not to touch anything.

Mavis's attention was drawn away by a loud bellow of laughter from a group of men standing in the corner. She glared across at them. She knew all too well who they were.

"If we're going to be fine," she said, "then how come the enemy over there look so happy with their lot in life?"

"I dunno," said Bunny, "perhaps they're taking the news really well."

As if on cue, one of the men looked across and made eye contact with them. He whispered a quick remark to his colleagues and then started moving across the lobby towards where Mavis and Bunny stood. The surreptitious glances and badly-hidden smirks from his group gave the game away. Little boys who had dared one of their number to torture the new kid.

The man himself wasn't much to look at; small, glasses, with a head of hair that was fading fast and a shit-eating grin that was only growing. He extended his hand out to Bunny as he reached them.

"Paschal Maloney. I believe you are Mr Bunny McGarry."

Bunny took his hand and shook it. "Detective, actually."

"Yes, of course. How forgetful of me." Maloney grinned up at the bigger man. "Can I just say how much I have enjoyed your ha... efforts, over the last few days. They have been most entertaining to watch."

"Well, thanks very much. That means a lot coming from a whimpering little shite like yourself."

Maloney pulled a disappointed face. "Now, now, Detective, nobody likes a sore loser."

"I've not lost."

"That's the spirit. I hope you'll come to see that the regeneration of the area—"

Bunny laughed. "You love that word don't you? Regeneration. Reminds me of that old show on the telly, Doctor Who. D'ye know the one? Where every couple of years, the Doctor would 'regenerate'."

Maloney nodded. "Yes, yes. I was always a fan."

"Thing is, while they called it 'regeneration', it wasn't really, was it? It was somebody entirely different. The old Doctor was just replaced, moved on, wiped from the face of the Earth. Like you're trying to do with the people who already live there."

"You're more moralistic than I would have suspected from your recent actions, Detective."

Bunny laughed. "Oh no, I'm actually worse than you, ye little rat-faced rim-rubber. That's why I've won."

Maloney tipped his head to the side and gave his best face of faked sincerity. "Oh dear, I'm afraid I know a few things that you don't."

"Yeah," said Bunny, "I could say the same."

Mavis turned at the sound of the doors opening. Councillor Baylor had entered, with his entourage in tow. "Here comes that 'Snow White' bastard."

She looked back at Bunny, who was reaching his hand into his coat as he looked down at Maloney. "Let's pull our mickeys out and see who wins?"

Bunny took something from his coat and turned around, swinging his arm just enough as he did so that Maloney flinched back reflexively.

"Tamara," said Bunny, "come here, sweetheart."

Tamara, always the well-behaved girl, looked at her granny for a nod of confirmation before scampering across. Bunny bent down and spoke softly to her.

"Now love, you see that white-haired man who just walked in?" She nodded. "Good. Go and give him this note and tell him he has to read it straight away. No peeking now."

She took the note he extended to her, and immediately set about her task. Mavis glanced back at Maloney, whose face was more curious than concerned. Tamara skipped across to Councillor Baylor and said her line with a look of intense concentration. Baylor stopped and bent down to talk to her. No politician, no matter how much of a rush they're in, walks by a little girl who wants to say something. Somebody might have a camera. She handed him the note and then skipped off. Baylor shared a quick smile with the man and woman who had walked in with him, then opened the note.

He read it.

Then he re-read it.

Then the colour drained from his face.

For a moment, it looked like he might collapse. The younger man with him extended a hand to support his boss. He and his female colleague shared a look of uncomprehending shock. The woman reached down to take the note from Baylor's hand. At the last second, her boss realised what she was doing and quickly shoved it into the pocket of his overcoat. The rest of the large reception area had grown silent, as one by one they noticed the stares of others being directed towards the doors.

Mavis looked back at Maloney's face. His smug grin was now gone, replaced by a look of confusion. Tamara skipped back to her grandmother's side.

"Did I do it right, Granny?"

"You were perfect, my angel, perfect."

Maloney pushed by them, exchanging looks with his group of associates, their confused expressions mirroring his own. He strode towards Baylor. The Councillor still looked ill, running his hand across his forehead. Mavis had seen similar reactions from people who'd just been informed of a shocking death in the family. She looked up at Bunny. His face betrayed no emotion as he watched. Maloney was now in whispered conversation with Baylor and his two confederates.

Bunny leaned down and whispered something in Tamara's ear, only looking up when Maloney raised his voice in disbelief. "What?" It echoed around the large reception chamber.

There was more hushed conversation as Baylor's two assistants tried to placate a now highly irritated Maloney. Baylor, for his part, had taken a step back and was looking off into the distance, an unreadable expression on his face. Then Baylor looked at Tamara, and looked up to see Bunny standing above her. They locked eyes for a long moment before Baylor looked away.

Maloney tried to move forward to talk to Baylor, but the male assistant put his hand on the smaller man's arm to stop him. Maloney shook it off angrily and hissed something in Baylor's direction. Baylor spoke a few final words and then pushed by him, heading towards the council chamber. His associates followed, leaving a shell-shocked Maloney in their wake.

Mavis looked at Bunny. "What is going on, Bunny?"

"We might be done with the past," said Bunny, "but the past ain't done with us."

Maloney strode towards them, his face beetroot red with fury, his lips convulsing in and out of a puckering pout. Gone was the smarmy politeness, replaced by a barely contained fury.

"You can't..." stammered Maloney, "what the hell have you done?"

Bunny picked up his sheepskin coat from the chair beside where Tamara had sat. "What I needed to."

"You can't just... blackmail people."

"Oh please," said Bunny. "Pull the other one, it's got my bollocks attached."

"Bunny!" exclaimed Mavis, looking down pointedly at Tamara.

"Sorry. Excuse my French."

Maloney's face was bright red now.

"I'll get you for this, you buffoon. You see if I don't. Nobody humiliates me."

Bunny sighed. "I didn't do this to humiliate you, ye egotistical little arse muncher. I did it because it was what was right. It was what was necessary. Because sometimes, the only way to beat the dirty dogs is to get dirtier. I didn't do it to humiliate you," repeated Bunny.

Bunny glanced down at Tamara who was looking up at him patiently.

"Now, sweetheart."

She nodded and punched Maloney as hard as she could in the testicles.

He folded over like a deflating parade balloon and crumpled to the floor.

Bunny calmly stepped over him and started walking towards the exit.

"Now that... I did to humiliate you."

CHAPTER FIFTY-FIVE

The hand at her back pushed Brigit roughly through the door, causing her to stumble into the wall.

"All right! Go easy. This is all a big misunderstanding."

The same unnervingly blank smile greeted her.

She turned and looked around her. The room had probably once been an office, but judging by the graffiti, beer cans and broken glass amongst the other rubbish on the floor, it had been a while. An overwhelming stench of decay and urine permeated the area. This place must have been manna from heaven for the local unsavoury youths until the new fencing had been installed. Brigit looked up to see a face she recognised, in a context she didn't. Paschal Maloney, the little rodent-faced one from the Skylark Three, stood in the centre of the room looking at her. Her captor slammed the door closed behind them and stood with his gun trained on her. With his muscular build, and salt and pepper hair cut tight, he looked like George Clooney halfway through a difficult bowel movement. Not that George ever sneered like that.

"Who are you?" asked Maloney. "What are you doing here?"

"I'm really sorry," said Brigit, "I... I just wanted to come in and look at the place, is all."

"Don't lie to me."

"Honestly, I'm just... I'm a big fan of old buildings."

Maloney pointed at the other man. "This is Mr Coetzee, he has a tremendous capacity for pain. Other people's."

Coetzee moved towards her, Brigit tried to back away towards the corner. Coetzee smiled at her as he advanced. Broken glass crunched under Brigit's feet as she tried to back away.

"OK, just calm down—"

"I'll ask you again, what are you doing here?"

"Seriously, I'm a big fan of old buildings—"

The backhanded slap hit her like an unexpected wave in the sea, knocking her to the ground and scrambling her senses. The left side of her face stung and her jaw ached. She spun off the wall and landed hard on the ground, glass cutting into her hand as she put it out to break her fall. She tried to kick her left leg out behind her only to have her foot grabbed, while a heavy boot pinned her right leg. She screamed, partly through pain and partly through fear of what was going to happen next.

"Stop!"

Brigit turned towards the female voice. A blonde woman stood in the doorway behind Maloney. She looked utterly incongruous amidst the grime and graffiti, looking like she'd just stepped off the cover of a magazine. She took a couple of steps into the room.

"Her name is Brigit Conroy. She is the other partner in their little detective agency."

Maloney turned to her. "You told me she was out of the picture."

The blonde woman shrugged, "Mulchrone said she was."

"Clearly you got it wrong, didn't you?"

"Don't blame me for this. You were the one who wanted to involve them in the first place. I said we should—"

"Are you questioning me, Megan?" Maloney's voice went up an octave and his face reddened. "I am in charge here. You will not question me!"

"No, baby, no." She walked over and placed her hand upon Maloney's chest. She was a good six inches taller than him and a good six divisions ahead of him in the attractiveness stakes. "I'm sorry, it's just, we're so close now. You have just announced that McGarry is the Púca." She looked across at the man Maloney had referred to as Coetzee, and her eyes hardened once again. "Someone must have allowed an amateur to follow you here."

"You bloody idiot," said Maloney to Coetzee. The larger man said nothing, and just looked back at him through those dead eyes. Maloney shifted nervously, wilting under the other man's gaze. When he next spoke, his tone was much lighter. "This riot is a gift from God though, better than anything we dared hope for. The police killing Franks, that is just too delicious!"

"Let's just get this over with and get to the boat, baby," purred Megan.

Maloney glanced down at Brigit. "Lock her up for now, then go and check outside. Make sure there's nobody else here."

Coetzee released his hold on Brigit's leg and took his foot off her. Now that the most immediate threat was gone, Brigit could feel the ache in her jaw start to build.

Megan moved across and offered her a hand up, which Brigit gingerly took.

"Against the wall," she said softly.

Brigit turned around and Megan frisked her, finding her phone in her back pocket.

"Dead."

She tossed it onto the floor.

"Ah for... that's only new." Brigit felt a click in her jaw as she spoke.

Megan didn't answer, instead looking over at Coetzee. "Take her."

He grabbed Brigit's arm and dragged her from the room, the gun still held in the other hand.

"And just lock her up," said Megan. "We don't have time for any of your other... interests."

As she was dragged from the room Brigit was fairly sure she'd heard the other woman adding 'animal' under her breath.

They moved fast down a litter-strewn corridor. Brigit had neither opportunity nor inclination to try and make a break for it. Coetzee didn't seem the type to allow her to go for a well-placed kick in the shins. They turned left, and then right, before stopping at a heavy iron door. Coetzee threw her roughly to the ground, causing her head to wallop against the wall.

He trained his gun on her as he pulled a large key from his pocket and placed it in the lock. With a groan of protest the door opened, and Coetzee shouldered it wider. A foul stench of excrement escaped the room. He reached down and grabbed Brigit's hair. As she tried to stand to follow his grip, he hurled her forward into the darkness behind the door. She fell. Disorientated, her hands couldn't prevent her face slamming into the wall again. Amidst the pain, she could feel blood starting to trickle from her nose.

The door closed with a pained squeal of metal, and Brigit found herself sitting in pitch darkness. She screamed out, as loud as she could. "Fuck you, ye limp-dicked bag of balls."

She jumped as the voice came from the darkness.

"Jesus, Conroy," said Bunny, "where did a good Leitrim girl learn that kind of language?"

CHAPTER FIFTY-SIX

The only light in the room was the memory of it fading in Brigit's vision.

"Bunny?"

"Over here."

It was him, only... not him. His voice had a slur to it, like how stroke victims got after they'd lost control of the muscles on one side of their face.

Brigit reached out tentatively, and found a cold stone wall. She pulled herself up off her bloodied knees and started following it around slowly. "Are you all right?" she said.

"Grand. How's yourself?"

Brigit found a corner. Bunny's voice was closer now.

"To be honest, I've had better days," said Brigit.

She could hear laboured breathing near her feet, and she reached a hand down towards it.

"Bunny?"

Her fingers brushed against skin and she felt him flinch away with a gasp.

"It's OK, it's me. It's Brigit."

"You're..." his voice dropped to a barely audible whisper, "you're here."

There was a jangle of chains. A hand touched her leg then reached up and found her hand. It was callused and crusted.

"Course I am," she said.

"I thought you were... there's been... I... I... you're real."

"Yes," said Brigit, and she put her other hand on top of his. She felt swelling over the knuckles, and one of the fingers seemed to be pointing in the wrong direction.

"Christ, are you..."

She reached down and found the top of his head. He pulled away slightly but she persisted, moving her hands around his face.

"Good God."

The flesh felt hideously swollen and bulbous everywhere she touched, his nose at a sickeningly unnatural angle. Every breath sounded like a gurgling struggle.

"I'm not looking me best. I wasn't expecting company."

Brigit put a hand on the wall and then carefully lowered herself down onto the floor beside Bunny. She rubbed her sleeve across her nose to staunch the flow of blood, at least temporarily.

"Why have..." she didn't know what to ask him.

The silence stretched out between them.

"The big fella comes in, every couple of days I'd guess, we have one of our little chats."

"What does he ask you?"

"I was being euphemistic, Conroy, there's no talking. He just beats the shite out of me."

Brigit could feel tears start to well in her eyes, but she tried her best to keep them out of her voice. "How bad is it?"

"Lemme put it this way. I'd die happy if I could have a couple of minutes where he is the one chained to the wall. If he..." Bunny hesitated. "Before you – this is important Conroy – if he comes back, let me. I'll talk. I'll take most of it that way. It'll be better. You stay back, let me—"

Brigit didn't know what to say so she leaned across and softly kissed him on the forehead. "You're a good man."

"Don't go hitting on me Conroy, I'm out of your league."

Brigit smiled and rubbed her eyes.

"How did you find me?" said Bunny.

"Your doo-dah."

"Ah, right. I don't know what the hell happened, I got blindsided. I'm not even sure where I was."

"Had you just left O'Hagans by any chance?"

"Oh yeah." He actually sounded embarrassed. "I came to in the boot of a car. No phone, but I still had the tracker. Does this mean you're up to speed about Paulie?"

Brigit leaned back, bumping her head softly against the wall. "That he's not a cheating scumbag and that I was an idiot for thinking he was?"

"Don't beat yourself up, you couldn't have known."

"You did," said Brigit.

"Ah, lucky guess. Easier for me to see the wood for the trees than it was for you... or him."

"Thank you," she said softly.

"Ah sure, least I could do. He's a good lad."

"He is."

Brigit put her hand out and found his. She rubbed it gently. His fingers felt hard, the skin cracked and worn.

"I'm sorry," said Brigit.

"What are you sorry for?"

"Sorry I didn't... I'm sorry it took me so long to find you. I could've—"

"Ara don't be daft, Conroy. By the way, what are the prospects of the cavalry showing up?"

"Not great. I don't think anyone knows where I am. On the upside; a lot of the country are looking for you."

"And you found me. You've done Leitrim proud. Seeing as you did, would you mind telling me what in the name of all things holy I'm doing here?"

"Don't you know? I thought... Paschal Maloney seems to be in charge."

There was a moment of silence save for Bunny's laboured breathing.

"Paschal feckin' Maloney?!" Bunny started laughing. There was an unhinged edge to it.

"What?"

"I'd... I've been sitting here, trying to figure out what in the hell this is all about and you're telling me it's him? Him! That little scrote. I've not given him a moment's thought in what... sixteen years? I'd never even thought of him. I thought—"

"So I take it you know Maloney?"

"We had a bit of a run-in back in... what? 2000 it would've been. He saw St Jude's as an exciting development opportunity. I disagreed."

"And now... now he's gone to all this trouble to get revenge on you? He's had you framed as a killer? A bloody terrorist basically, over a planning dispute? Are you kidding me?"

There was a moment of silence.

"Conroy, what the feck are you talking about?"

"Oh you... you don't know?"

"Yeah, I've been a bit out of the loop, what with the whole Terry Waite tribute act."

"Sorry."

Brigit then brought Bunny up to speed as best she could. He mostly listened in silence, until she got to the part about the calls to Father Franks.

"I've not spoken to the Padre in sixteen years. He was involved in the... y'know, the planning thing."

"He said the same thing, about not talking to you I mean. How was he involved in the planning thing?"

"Let's not get into that. I'd guess Maloney must've found a way of getting stuff onto our phone bills. Leading the Gardaí on a merry dance, adding to this Púca bollocks. He's... I guess he's, what – trying to kill off his enemies or some shit? I'm supposed to have killed Craig Blake, Jerome Hartigan—"

"And his lawyer, I think."

"Shit, a dead lawyer," said Bunny, "now it really is a tragedy."

"And John Baylor."

"Old Snow White? He's dead too?"

"Yes."

"That'd explain Maloney trying to link in Franks. He can tell the Gardaí these phone calls are rubbish though, so—"

"Oh," said Brigit. "I... I didn't get around to telling you yet. The Guards raided the Ark today. Franks is... I'm sorry – he's dead."

"They killed him?"

"I don't... last I heard on the radio, they were saying it was an accident. It's all a bit confused, what with the riot and all."

"There's a fucking riot?" Bunny's voice echoed off the walls.

"Yes, ehm... when news of Franks broke I guess... people got... y'know."

"Christ," said Bunny. "I can't leave you people alone for five minutes without the whole country going to shite."

There was a pause and then Bunny spoke so softly as to be barely above a whisper. "Danny and I, we... we'd a lot of history. I thought we'd one day, ye know... straighten it all out."

"I'm sorry," said Brigit.

"Speaking of which, are you and Paulie back on the tracks then?"

"Well it's... I mean, I only found out yesterday and we've been looking for you—"

"Christ on a pogo stick, you pair. It's like watching two lepers trying to arm-wrestle."

"Now isn't the time, Bunny."

"Take it from one who knows, Conroy, now should always be the time."

"Can I—" Brigit stopped, asking felt like a violation. As always though, her curiosity overrode all. "Who is Simone?"

There was another silence as even Bunny's breathing quietened.

"She's the last thing I'll see. She's..."

The silence again stretched out between them.

"Hang on," said Brigit, "If you didn't know about Maloney, what did you think this was about?"

Before Bunny could answer, they were disturbed by a key in the lock. He let go of Brigit's hand and stretched a manacled arm over her. His breathing became gasping pants. "Say nothing and stay back. Close your eyes, don't try to stop—"

The door opened and bright light flooded in. Brigit shielded her eyes as best she could. Through her fingers she caught a brief glimpse of Bunny's face. A ragged beard grew on a visage so distended in painful shades of black and purple as to be unrecognisable; unrecognisable not just as Bunny, but as a human face. Crusted blood was smeared on Bunny's chin. Brigit felt her stomach heave even as her heart broke. His swollen eyes clamped shut. His chin pushed forward and upwards towards the light as he screamed his defiance. "C'mon, you prick. Come get me, ye dinky-dicked donkey gobbler."

Brigit, her eyes now adjusted enough to the light, pulled her hand slowly away.

The blonde and Coetzee stood before them, each of them holding a gun. Coetzee was once again wearing that vacant smile of amusement. The blonde – Megan, wasn't it? She at least looked horrified.

Coetzee tossed a set of keys to Brigit.

"Unlock him," said the blonde. "It's time."

CHAPTER FIFTY-SEVEN

The corridor seemed a lot longer the second time Brigit had to go down it.

This time, she had Bunny's right arm around her shoulder and was doing her best to hold him up. He was having a lot of difficulty walking under his own steam. His face looked even worse in the full light; the swelling around his eyes and lips making him a sickeningly distorted version of himself. His jumper was a ragged mixture of blood and other stains. He could put hardly any weight on his right leg, so the going was slow. He also held his left arm gingerly in front of him; Brigit suspected it was broken. As he'd first gained his feet, with the help of the wall and Brigit for support, he'd leaned into her. "Conroy," he'd whispered, "I'm not seeing too good here. Yer gonna have to help me."

For all her medical experience, seeing such a big strong man laid so low was shocking. She put herself under his right armpit. "C'mon, old fella, let's get you out of here."

Coetzee shoved her in the back again.

"And you can piss off and all, you psycho son of a bitch. Beating on a man chained to a wall. Why don't you—"

She stopped as she felt the barrel of a gun being pushed into the back of her head.

"Coetzee," came Megan's voice, unseen behind them, "that is enough."

They'd been shoved into the large, hangar-like area that took up most of the building. The big wooden doors that Brigit had stood outside maybe an hour ago were at one end. Inside them sat Maloney's BMW and Brigit's own car. They both had their lights on to help illuminate the large space. At the other end of the room, mobile floodlights threw light upon an area containing a table and some chairs. From what else she could see in the semi-darkness around them, the room was littered with rusted hulks of machinery and random chunks of debris.

As they finally reached the circle of light, Megan gave Brigit a hand to lower Bunny down into one of the plastic chairs. Then Coetzee pushed her into the other one.

"Put your hands behind your back," said Megan.

Brigit complied, and winced as Megan bound them together, the cable ties cutting into her skin. She then stood in front of Bunny. "And you – hands behind your back."

"Normally," said Bunny, squinting in the direction of her voice, "I'd be mad for a bit of light bondage with a lovely lady but alas, your gorilla has broken my collarbone, so I can't."

Megan looked down at him for a second and then looked at Coetzee, who actually smiled and shrugged. Megan mumbled something under her breath and stepped back.

Brigit could hear footsteps approaching from behind them. "Ah, Mr McGarry, so good of you to join us." Maloney swaggered into the circle of light and then stopped when he saw the state of Bunny's face. He glanced at Megan who looked pointedly at Coetzee.

Maloney looked at him briefly, then averted his gaze and spoke quietly. "I never said to... the body was supposed to be identifiable. How do we explain..."

Maloney left it hanging. Like most people, faced with the evidence of such sheer brutality, he seemed unable to fully comprehend it. Coetzee just shrugged again, like a teenager who was being told off by someone who they knew had no real authority over them.

"Who's that?" interrupted Bunny.

The smile returned to Maloney's face, as if a switch had been flipped. He tapped the gun he held against his leg as he spoke. "Oh, I know it has been a while, but don't tell me you've forgotten me? I've not aged that badly. Certainly better than you've done." Maloney grinned at Megan, who forced a half-hearted smile back in his direction.

"Sorry, champ," said Bunny, "I'm afraid I can't see a bloody thing here. Who are ye?"

"Paschal Maloney."

"Never heard of you."

"Most amusing."

"Were you the lad I arrested for fucking that goat?"

Terrified as she was, Brigit smiled to herself. Bunny, despite everything, was still Bunny.

"My name is Paschal Maloney."

"Did you used to be a woman?"

"No, I... no. Take this seriously."

"I am. I support your choices and that. I was trapped in a woman's body once meself."

"Yes, ha ha," said Maloney in a humourless whine, "Do try and enjoy these last moments, Mr McGarry, for all the good they'll do you. You know very well who I am. Sixteen years ago you humiliated me and tried to ruin my life."

"Christ, we were courting? You should've said. Be fair, I bet I bought you a bag of chips at least."

"I'll tell you who I am," said Maloney, irritation etched across his pudgy little face. "I'm the man who had you kidnapped and who has been systematically destroying your life. I'm the man who has made you public enemy number one. I'm the man who has made you into the big bad Púca." Maloney giggled hysterically, nobody else did.

Bunny tilted his head in the general direction of Megan. "Seriously, who the fecking hell is this guy?"

"Ignore the idiot, Paschal," interjected Megan, "Let's just—"

"No, no," said Maloney, "let him enjoy himself, this is good. Laugh it up McGarry. Laugh. It. Up."

Megan stepped forward and placed her hand on Maloney's arm, "Paschal, maybe we should—"

He shook her off roughly. "Shut up, Megan."

"Now, now," said Bunny, "there's no need to be ungentlemanly. I do know who you are. You're her boyfriend. She talks about you all the time. And she's right; it isn't that big a deal and it does happen to a lot of men."

Maloney stepped forward and shoved his gun into Bunny's forehead, pushing his head back. "You think you're clever, don't you? Let me tell you what clever is. I think you deserve to know your place in the grand scheme of things."

"Couldn't give a monkey's, to be honest with ye."

Maloney ignored him. He pulled what appeared to be a silver cigarette case from his pocket and flipped it open. In it sat four ordinary looking black data sticks. "Do you see these?"

"You're not getting the whole 'blind' thing, are you?"

"You wouldn't understand it anyway. All you need to know is that these are the four keys to a buried treasure. Seventy-eight million untraceable dollars, to be exact."

"Is this the money belonging to the poor saps who invested in Skylark, by any chance?" asked Brigit.

"Shut up, Miss Conroy, or I'll allow Mr Coetzee to play with you."

Megan stepped forward and indicated the silver case. "Can I?"

Maloney handed it to her. She moved over to the laptop on the table and began working.

"Mr Coetzee has proven to be quite a find," continued Maloney. "His skill set and – let's call it... moral flexibility – are really very rare."

"Also, he's a great kisser," said Bunny.

Maloney pressed the barrel of his gun to Bunny's forehead.

"Shush now," said Maloney, "So tell me, what big bad secret did you have on Baylor?"

Bunny leaned forward, pushing into the gun. "He once had red wine with fish, the scuttering gobshite."

Annoyance flared again across Maloney's face. He shoved his gun into Bunny's mouth. "You really are quite tedious. By the way, I decided to drag your little protégé Mulchrone into this too. I wanted you to know, with certainty, that his life has been destroyed just by being associated with yours. Megan, are we ready yet?"

Megan didn't look up. "Almost."

Bunny tried to say something but it came out as a garbled mumble around the gun.

Maloney withdrew it. Bunny spat the taste of it out and then tried to stretch his neck. "I remember you now," said Bunny in a hoarse whisper.

"I thought you might."

"Yeah." Bunny drew a deep breath, "You're that fella we arrested for fondling himself in that kiddie's ball pit at Funderland."

"Shut up!"

"To be fair," continued Bunny, "You were only touching yourself. I said at the time, 'I think it's the balls that are doing it for him lads, not the kids,' but—"

"STOP MOCKING ME!" Maloney's face was a mask of pure rage as he screamed into Bunny's face.

"Paschal," Megan started looking up from the laptop, "just—"

Maloney stepped away, took aim and shot Bunny in the foot. Bunny screamed in agony.

Maloney dropped the gun, as if shocked by the reality of his own actions.

"You..." Brigit started, but she couldn't find words as Bunny howled beside her.

"For God's sake, Paschal—"

He turned to Megan and pointed at her. "Just do your job! Why does nobody take me seriously?"

Brigit looked across at Bunny, who was swaying back and forth, almost falling off his chair. His right shoe was now soaked through with blood. His howls descended into high-pitched, gasping breaths.

Maloney took a step back, banging into Coetzee standing behind him. He glanced backwards and then, seemingly reassured by Coetzee's presence, took a step forward and snatched his gun up from the ground.

"The reason you're still alive, McGarry, is because I wanted you here for this moment. To see my victory. So you would know, you would know, that you didn't beat me. You didn't beat me. You did not BEAT ME!"

Maloney turned and paced back and forth.

Bunny's yowls of pain decreased and then transformed into high-pitched, breathy laughter. "Oh Paschal, Paschal, Paschal, Paschal." Bunny's voice moved to a mocking sing-song, "I know something you don't know."

Maloney turned back to him, slowly regaining control of himself. "I doubt that."

Bunny, drawing panting breaths, looked unseeing in Brigit's direction, his head sagging down slightly, even as a peculiar smile played across his lips. "Everybody, Paschal, is the hero of their own story."

"Oh, how deep," said Maloney, waving his hands in a mocking curtsey.

Bunny nodded in Megan's approximate direction. "When she's done doing whatever she is doing, you'll have seventy-eight million untraceable dollars, is that right?"

"Yes."

Bunny started laughing again.

"I'm glad that amuses you," said Maloney.

"Oh it does," said Bunny. "It's a regular fecking laugh riot. Would you like to know a secret, Paschal?"

"I'm bored of your pointless games, McGarry."

"But this is a doozy, I promise ye. You see; there's a thing about people who'll kill for money..."

Maloney folded his arms. "And what's that?"

"They. Will. Kill. For. Money."

Brigit watched Maloney's face. She saw the exact moment he got Bunny's point. "Mr C—"

His head exploded. Brigit squeezed her eyes shut and felt blood and brain matter splatter onto her face. She opened them again, to see Maloney's body crumpled on the floor in front of her. His glasses, inexplicably still in one piece, sat on her lap.

Above the fallen body of his extremely-former employer, Coetzee stood with his gun held aloft, looking very calm.

Megan screamed but it died in her throat as Coetzee turned the gun to point at her.

"You people talk too much."

CHAPTER FIFTY-EIGHT

At the first gunshot, Paul called the police. He and Maggie had been standing outside the metal gates of the compound, looking at the flashing red dot on his phone.

"My name is Paul Mulchrone. Bunny McGarry is at the old cement factory on the Coast Road near Howth. Send everything, shots have been fired."

He'd hung up before they could ask further questions.

As soon as the car had reached Glasnevin, they'd managed to escape the area around the city centre where the phone network had been turned off and Paul had got a signal on his phone. He'd downloaded the Sniffer app, texted the word "Simone" to the number, and waited. Within fifteen minutes it had shown him the location in Howth. He put his foot down and drove Bunny's car like a man possessed. Weaving in and out of honking traffic, running red lights, and at one point mounting a pavement to get around a line of traffic. He didn't care. Brigit was still not picking up and he was starting to fear the worst. Besides, it was pretty clear that every available Garda within fifty miles was in the city centre dealing with the riot.

Paul looked down at Maggie.

"The police will be here soon. They've armed response units and everything. We'll wait for them. That makes the most sense, right? Charging in there... I might get someone killed."

Maggie looked silently back up at him.

Then they heard the second shot.

CHAPTER FIFTY-NINE

Megan was working away at the laptop. Coetzee stood behind her, rubbing the barrel of his gun through her hair. Her gun was stuck into the belt of his trousers.

"I can't work with you distracting me."

"Yes, you can," he replied. His accent was entirely unplaceable to Brigit's ear. He pulled a piece of paper out of his trouser pocket and put it on the table.

"Split the money between these six accounts."

"You... had this planned?"

He leaned in close and smelt her hair. "Yes, the monkey had a plan of his own."

"OK I'll do this, and... then, you'll let me go?"

He moved in close behind her and whispered. "We'll see."

Tears rolled down her face. "I'm... look, I... I'm not going to do this if you're going to kill me."

He started running his hand up and down Megan's body. "There are a lot of worse things that could happen."

"You're scum," said Brigit.

Coetzee looked at her as he stroked Megan's hair. "You can be next, if you like?"

"Anything you put near me, don't expect to get it back."

Coetzee just smiled at her. Brigit looked away, trying not to notice the slickness beneath her feet that was Maloney's blood spreading out across the floor.

"You're not touching anybody," said Bunny, his unseeing eyes turned towards the noise, "Not until you go through me!"

He tried to stand and stumbled backwards, nearly missing his chair on the way back down.

Coetzee grinned at him. "I guess you won't be able to watch, but I'll let you listen."

"You arsehole. Why don't you—"

Brigit stopped talking as Bunny put his hand out for silence.

"Can you hear it?"

Brigit listened. She heard nothing at first but then... an engine. Revving.

A smile spread across Bunny's bruised and battered face. "She purrs like a kitty cat."

There was a clang of metal from outside and then the engine grew louder and louder until...

The wooden front doors exploded in a shower of splintered debris as Bunny's car came hurtling through, travelling at high speed. There was a screech of tortured brakes, and then it smashed into the back of Brigit's car with a loud, unpleasant crunch.

"Christ!" said Brigit.

"What's happening?" asked Bunny.

Megan used the opportunity to attempt to escape. She got four feet before Coetzee grabbed her hair with one hand and slammed the butt of his gun into the back of her head with the other. Her unconscious body flopped to the ground.

With a screech of outraged metal, the door of Bunny's car opened and Paul stumbled out. Blood was pumping from a wound in his forehead.

"Nobody... nobody move," said Paul, and Brigit saw the gun in his hand. While he held it out, it wasn't pointing in the right direction and his hand was weaving about. "No airbags. Stupid car."

Coetzee shot, and Paul ducked before shooting back. Or at least he tried to. The gun dry clicked in his hands and again and again.

Coetzee laughed, a brief giggle at first that grew and grew until he was roaring, bent double, hands on his knees. He looked between Paul and Brigit with tears in his eyes. "Honestly, you people are hilarious!" He moved towards Paul, his steps a mocking dance as he closed the twenty or so feet that lay between them. Paul's gun continued to click out a useless staccato rhythm. With his free hand Coetzee mimed a gun shooting back at him. "You forgot the fucking bullets, didn't you? You absolute moron. What kind of a fucking idiot doesn't know if he has bullets?"

"Actually" said Paul, "I knew there were no bullets. I just wanted to give her time."

Coetzee looked back towards Brigit. "Time," he said, "is something none of you have."

"Not her," said Paul.

As Coetzee raised his gun, Maggie jumped up and sunk her teeth into his arm. He screamed in rage.

Paul rushed towards him, getting there just as Coetzee managed to fire a powerful kick into Maggie. She gave out a sickening yelp as she flew through the air before landing with a thud against a rusted husk of machinery. She remained absolutely still.

"That's my dog!" screamed Paul.

He crashed into Coetzee, and they stumbled messily to the ground. They were a mass of flailing limbs – Paul countering the other man's superior strength and size with a sheer desperate fury. He latched onto his gun arm and didn't let go, despite a flurry of blows from Coetzee's other hand.

Brigit sensed Bunny dropping to the ground beside her.

She turned to see him scrabbling around Maloney's body with his one good hand.

Brigit looked back at Paul and Coetzee, just in time to see Coetzee send a knee into Paul's face with a sickening crunch.

"Where?" said Bunny.

He was holding Maloney's gun out; it rotated back and forth in a semicircle, pointing nowhere near the two men.

They were locked in a clench. Coetzee rammed an elbow down repeatedly into Paul's arm.

"Right, right, right," shouted Brigit.

Bunny turned left.

"No, other way."

Paul was on his feet again now, his face covered in blood, swinging wildly-inaccurate haymakers at the air. "C'mon ye... fight me!"

Coetzee danced around him, like a cat toying with a mouse.

Brigit looked again at Bunny, his gun now pointing directly at her.

"Left, forty-five degrees from the sound of my voice."

The gun veered in the approximate direction, but—

"Wait! You'll hit Paul."

"MULCHRONE!" bellowed Bunny, "GIVE ME TWENTY!"

It hung in the air for a moment, while the whole world seemed to slow.

Bunny, bruised and broken, kneeling in a pool of his own and Maloney's blood, swollen eyes blindly searching behind the barrel of a gun.

Coetzee, the sneer having dropped from his face, to be replaced by a look of curiosity, if not concern.

Paul, bloodied face, mouth open; a picture of concussed confusion.

Then – she would argue with her own memory of this for the rest of her days – but Brigit swore she saw a tiny smile spread across his face, as a long-forgotten memory of a training pitch years ago returned to him.

He dived for the ground.

Bunny fired six shots in an arc before collapsing backwards onto the ground.

"Did I get him? Did I get him?"

EPILOGUE 1

TWO DAYS LATER

DSI Susan Burns placed her feet up on her desk, and began reading through the transcript of the interview with suspect Megan Wilde for the third time. It was copious in length and fulsome in detail. What made her nervous was quite how much of it was clearly bullshit. Miss Wilde, the statuesque blonde mistress of Paschal Maloney, was in many ways a great witness. She had laid out in detail the intricate deception that Maloney had engineered. It had set in motion a chain of events that had led to several deaths and a riot with – admittedly – an assist from some over-eager policing on that score. All of that meant there would be a lot of questions being asked, most probably for years to come, and Burns was conscious that the document she held in her hands would be the first port of call for most of the answers.

Miss Wilde was no dummy. As soon as anyone would listen, she'd started building her case for the Patty Hearst defence. She was a poor, innocent ingénue, fallen under the spell of the charismatic Maloney, who had dragged her into his web of deceit. Once trapped inside it she couldn't get out, as she lived in fear for her very life, Your Honour. It was crap, of course, but that didn't mean it wouldn't work. The press were going to eat Wilde up. She was easy on the eye, good with a lie and Burns would bet the farm she could cry on demand. It also helped that Maloney was dead, and that the man they were calling Coetzee wasn't. He was a barrister's manna from heaven when it came to proving anyone being in fear for their life. He'd taken three bullets, apparently fired by the temporarily-blind Bunny McGarry, but the doctors said he was going to pull through. It was early days, and already he'd been identified as an individual known as Marcus Barkley who was wanted for war crimes in the Democratic Republic of the Congo, and also as Draco Mistaran who was of great interest to the Ukranian authorities. They'd already doubled the armed guards on his hospital room twice; once when they'd realised quite what an international man of butchery he was, and secondly when Interpol had tipped them off that a Russian oligarch, who was minus a brother and two fingers, was very keen to get reacquainted with the man who had cost him both.

While Wilde had done a frankly masterful job laying the groundwork beneath them for a possible legal defence, these were the facts from her statement that Burns did believe.

Paschal Maloney, along with Jerome Hartigan and Craig Blake, aka the Skylark Three, had embezzled seventy-eight million dollars that by all rights belonged in the Skylark Project. It would appear that Councillor John Baylor had been their silent partner in all this, greasing the wheels of government wherever needed. It was currently unclear when their plans for the project had tipped into being an out-and-out scam. Had they always planned to siphon off a large wad of cash, or had they only hit on the idea after it looked like things were about to get tricky? Regardless, the method they'd found for squirreling away these fraudulently acquired funds was certainly innovative. It was something called a digital chest. A rather peculiar Asian guy from the Technical Bureau had explained it to Burns. As far as she could understand it, it worked on a similar principle to Bitcoins. Four digital keys were required to access the funds. As long as each man held one, nobody could screw over anybody else. That assumed, of course, that you weren't Paschal Maloney.

Burns stopped and added a note to the list on the pad in front of her. Given all the recently acquired new evidence, she might well have to request the reopening of the inquest into the apparent suicide of the financial controller for the Skylark project. It seemed odds-on that his death may well have been Coetzee's first intervention into proceedings.

Certainly, Wilde's testimony made it clear that Craig Blake had been Coetzee's work. He'd been tortured until he had given up the code for his personal safe, and so Maloney then had two of the four keys he needed. Baylor had apparently been easier, meeting with Maloney's representative to hand over his key in exchange for a supposed 8.6 million euros in cash and bonds. His own greed had walked the venerable councillor to his death, and the third key into Maloney's possession. That had left Hartigan, who by now had seventy eight million reasons to not trust his one remaining partner. Maloney supposedly convinced Hartigan that he'd found a way to access the funds with only two keys, Baylor and Blake's having been 'lost' as far as Hartigan knew. Burns had no idea if, by this point, Hartigan had begun to suspect that the Púca wasn't what it seemed, but regardless, he had been smart enough to seek an assurance before handing over his key. He'd only agreed to do so when Maloney had signed a confession owning up to, and taking sole responsibility for, the embezzlement of the Skylark money. If Maloney did a bunk, Hartigan could burn him to the ground. Maloney had signed the paperwork in front of Hartigan and his lawyer, then the trio had stepped outside to announce to the world that Bunny McGarry was the big bad wolf behind the Púca. Once Maloney had departed Hartigan's house with the fourth and final key, Coetzee had activated a bomb he'd hidden there several days before. Kaboom. Four keys and no witnesses.

Burns had to admit there was a certain kind of twisted genius to it; inventing a terrorist organisation that tapped into a nation's anger at you and your ilk to act as a cover for your actions. It reminded her of the two words her Criminology lecturer in Templemore had engraved on a plaque on his wall: '*Cui Bono?*' a Latin phrase meaning 'to whose benefit?'. When you stripped it all away, it was about cash. A big pile of grubby money.

The final stage of the plan was supposed to proceed like this; Maloney was set to 'flee the country in fear of his life' aboard his boat *The Little General*. The vessel would be blown up dramatically half way across the Irish Sea, the last act of Bunny McGarry in his one-man demented killing spree which the Púca was supposed to be. McGarry's body would be found in the wreckage, but Maloney's or Wilde's never would. That was because they would be in a South American country living under new identities with a great big pile of untraceable cash, having been picked up in a pre-arranged rendezvous with another vessel.

Only it hadn't worked out that way. *The Little General* was currently still moored out at Howth Harbour, the marina having been evacuated for a day as the bomb squad dealt with the bomb hidden away in it.

Where the whole enterprise had seemingly come unstuck was with Maloney's desire to use his grand scheme to exact revenge on Bunny McGarry. Apparently, McGarry had slighted him in some past life. Burns could well believe it. Everything she'd heard did indicate that McGarry had a unique ability to leave an impression. Maloney had wanted it all, the greedy little shit. It seemed Conroy and Mulchrone had some how tracked McGarry down. Burns was still unsure exactly how, but they were scheduled to come in to give statements tomorrow. For the second time in a year, this unlikely trio had cracked a massive case and made the Garda Síochána look bad while doing it. Not that the Gardaí had needed much help on that score; the inquest on the death of Father Daniel Franks had already been opened. Assistant Commissioner Michael Sharpe was about to suddenly retire due to an unspecified but pressing medical condition, quite possibly a terminal case of having his head rammed up his own arse.

There was a knock on her office door.

"Come in."

The door opened and Desk Sergeant Clarke, poked her head in.

"Need you now chief, suspicious package."

"What the...? Why am I...?"

Burns realised she was talking to herself, Clarke's head having disappeared from view.

Burns stood up, muttering to herself. "I've to do everything around here apparently. Nobody can even—"

She exited her office and shut up as she was greeted by a sea of beaming faces. They had a welcome banner up over the boards that were normally used for evidence. Clarke stood in the middle.

"We didn't get a chance to welcome you properly, what with the—"

"Monumental shit-storm of biblical proportions?" finished Burns.

"Yeah," beamed Clarke, "that. We even got you a cake."

Clarke moved to the side to reveal Wilson standing behind her, holding a custom-made cake. On the top of it was a very realistic three-dimensional rendering of a Louboutin shoe that had seen better days. Wilson wore a nervous smile above it, clearly less confident than others about the appropriateness of the joke.

The crowd broke into a smattering of applause which Burns acknowledged with a gracious wave.

"Yes, very good. Thank you all very much."

She watched the relief wash over Wilson's face.

"By the way Wilson, your flies are undone again."

"Ah for—"

"Made ye look."

EPILOGUE 2

Paul stood at the front of the church and fiddled with his dickie bow. He felt frankly ridiculous wearing the thing, but it hadn't been his choice. He looked down at the groom's side of the church. Bunny was supposed to be wearing a dickie bow too, but in typical Bunny style, he wasn't. Instead, he'd rocked up in one of his own suits, which looked remarkably like every other suit Paul had seen him wear. There were still some signs of the ordeal he'd gone through at the cement factory, but you had to look now to really see them. His face had healed remarkably quickly. There was still a slight limp to his walk, but the doctors had been able to save his foot.

Beside him sat Maggie. She'd been a lot more touch and go than Bunny. Luckily, Bunny had known a good vet who'd operated to repair the broken ribs and leg Maggie had suffered. She'd even been very understanding when Maggie had reacted unusually to the painkillers.

Paul ran his finger along the inside of his collar again. There was a stir of movement at the back of the church, and then the great doors at the other end opened.

Bright sunlight washed in, reflecting off the marble floors and casting a warming glow amongst the church's sombre twilight.

Paul held his breath as Brigit walked in. Dressed all in white, the sun dancing in her hair as a wide smile played across her lips. She was a vision.

His heart pounded in his chest.

He watched as she stepped to the side.

"Paul... Paul!"

Paul snapped out of his reverie as Auntie Lynn appeared in his eye-line.

"What?"

"What do you mean 'what'?"

Paul glanced behind him. "Oh, shit!" He made brief eye contact with the priest, "Sorry, Father," before darting across to the Sacristy door and knocking on it. "Phil! Phil!"

The door opened and Phil was standing there. "Sorry, Paulie, nervous wee. How do I look?"

"Fantastic. I mean, I'd probably close your flies, but other than that..."

"Oh, right." Phil turned around and then back again, this time with the cage well and truly closed.

"Right, then," said Paul, "let's go get you married."

To the surprise of everyone bar Phil, after he'd sent the money off as requested – to a man, who knew another man, who knew whom to bribe, and another person with a truck and... long story short, the very much real Da Xin and her family – parents, two sisters and grandma – had indeed made it out of China and moved to Ireland. They were in the process of being granted political asylum, Da Xin's father being quite the celebrity. Paul didn't think poets could be celebrities, but apparently, if they stand up to corrupt government officials and then have to get their whole family snuck out of a country in a turnip truck, they can be. The wedding had been organised in quite a rush, to fit around the family's campaigning commitments. They'd been in Paris last week meeting the Dalai

Lama. Apparently Phil had spent quite a lot of time explaining to him what a chicken ball was.

NEXT BOOK AND FREE STUFF

Hi there reader-person,

I hope you enjoyed the book, thanks for taking the time to read it. Like one of those choose your own adventure books I loved as a kid, you now have two options on what to read next. If you've not done so already, I'd definitely recommend reading the prequel to The Dublin Trilogy, *Angels in the Moonlight*. If you already have, then it's off to *Last Orders*, or the sequel to *Angels in the Moonlight, Dead Man's Sins*. You might want also want to check out the McGarry Stateside series for more fun and games.

And if you'd like to find out more about the mysterious Maggie and how she ended up in the possession of Bunny McGarry, the answers are contained in my short fiction collection *How to Send a Message*. The paperback is $10.99/£7.99 in the shops but you can get the e-book FOR FREE by signing up to my monthly newsletter. All you have to do is go to WhiteHairedIrishman.com.

Slainte,

Caimh

ALSO BY CAIMH MCDONNELL

Visit www.WhiteHairedIrishman.com to find out more.

THE STRANGER TIMES: C.K. MCDONNELL

There are dark forces at work in our world so thank God *The Stranger Times* is on hand to report them. A weekly newspaper dedicated to the weird and the wonderful (but mostly the weird), it is the go-to publication for the unexplained and inexplicable . . .

At least that's their pitch. The reality is rather less auspicious. Their editor is a drunken, foul-tempered and foul-mouthed husk of a man who thinks little of the publication he edits. His staff are a ragtag group of misfits. And as for the assistant editor . . . well, that job is a revolving door – and it has just revolved to reveal Hannah Willis, who's got problems of her own.

When tragedy strikes in her first week on the job *The Stranger Times* is forced to do some serious investigating. What they discover leads to a shocking realisation: some of the stories they'd previously dismissed as nonsense are in fact terrifyingly real. Soon they come face-to-face with darker forces than they could ever have imagined.

The Stranger Times is the first book from C.K. McDonnell, the pen name of Caimh McDonnell. It combines his distinctive dark wit with his love of the weird and wonderful to deliver a joyous celebration of how truth really can be stranger than fiction.

Made in United States
North Haven, CT
05 August 2022

22321408R00221